GUARANTEED
HEROES

OTHER TITLES BY WILLIAM LASHNER

The Barkeep
The Accounting
Blood and Bone

THE VICTOR CARL NOVELS

Bagmen
A Killer's Kiss
Marked Man
Falls the Shadow
Past Due
Fatal Flaw
Bitter Truth
Hostile Witness

WRITING AS TYLER KNOX

Kockroach

WILLIAM LASHNER

GUARANTEED HEROES

 THOMAS & MERCER

Published by Thomas & Mercer, Seattle

www.apub.com

Amazon, the Amazon logo, and Thomas & Mercer are trademarks of Amazon.com, Inc., or its affiliates.

ISBN-13: 9781477827635

ISBN-10: 1477827633

Cover design by M.S. Corley

Printed in the United States of America

*To my sister Jane, who introduced me to rock 'n' roll
with her magic stack of 45s.*

I have always thought that in revolutions, especially democratic revolutions, madmen, not those so called by courtesy, but genuine madmen, have played a very considerable political part.

Alexis de Tocqueville

PROLOGUE
OLD BOTTLE, NEW WINE

In the wake of the unprecedented financial, martial, and nuclear disasters that struck the United States in the early 1960s, and during a time of violent unrest all across the land, with great pomp and difficult circumstance, a second constitutional convention was convened in 1964 within the riot-ravaged heart of Philadelphia.

There were bands and gaudy public ceremonies, mass prayers, and far too many flags, as from every state still remaining in the union the preeminent politicians, business leaders, and thinkers of three generations traveled to Philadelphia. The task facing these intrepid men, and the single woman who was allowed in their ranks, was to envision a different kind of nation, no longer conceived in false notions of liberty, nor premised upon rights to be exercised only by the brave or the criminal. Something new was required, something sturdy and bold: a fair deal to embolden a reborn American patriotism.

As the forward course of the country was debated in closed sessions in New Independence Hall, an entire nation huddled around its televisions and radios for any hint of what was happening inside the locked room. Reports of varying accuracy were leaked from the convention site and the various options were debated by solemn newsmen, discussing possibilities from fascism to communism and every type of political scheme in between. Finally, after months of rumor and speculation, the presiding officer of the convention, the distinguished CEO of General Motors, Robert Krist, announced over the airwaves the premise of the revised Constitution to an expectant nation. In high tower and isolated farmhouse, the citizenry held its breath as the future of its nation was revealed.

The new Constitution, Krist declared, would offer something radically different to rebuild the nation's confidence and solidarity, premised upon the singular idea that the people's government would not just provide, but guarantee the building blocks of the American dream. Every citizen of the new nation would be guaranteed education, health care, housing, and, most significantly, employment at a living wage. In short, all citizens would be guaranteed dignity and economic security for the whole of their lives.

The reaction was overwhelming and overwhelmingly positive, but even as cheers and hurrahs rose from the four corners of the land, Krist warned in his crisp southern accent that this would not be a government of handouts or tender mercies. There was a nation to renew, a pride in the fruits of one's labor to be restored. Every citizen would be required to do his part; every person had a role to fill in rebuilding this great and good nation. There would be no slackers. In the New America, work would not only be guaranteed but required.

"Let us bind our wounds," Krist famously said, nine months before he would ascend to the presidency, which he would hold for nearly two decades, "and march arm in arm into our future. Let us support one another as we retrench and rebuild. Let us create a bounty to be delivered to our children and our children's children. And most importantly, let us get to work. God bless you all, God bless the Grand

Constitution of the New American Government, and God bless the United States."

True to the promise of that announcement, the nation in time entered an era of broad and sustained prosperity buttressed by a soaring stock market. The guaranteed jobs program became a rousing success, even as the government, to continue to shoulder the costs of its guarantees, was forced to drastically cut back its spending and eliminate services in the sectors of the country blighted by nuclear disaster. Through the process of disincorporation and relocation, stripping the radiated lands south of the Dakotas and west of the Mississippi of their populations and their federal protections, hundreds of billions were saved in government expenditures, allowing the guarantees to continue without ruinous rates of taxation.

Protests over the relocations raged briefly, but a firm military response, along with the announcement from President Krist that the nation had finally reached full employment, subdued the dissent. Employment thereafter remained officially full month after month, year after year. Anyone who couldn't find a job was legally determined not to be trying hard enough.

Even as the last of the relocation riots were quelled, the first Labor Camp for the Malcontented was built alongside a mountaintop mine in Martin County, Kentucky.

I

Orphans

1

RADEN'S GIRL

The men knew better than to mess with Raden's girl.

They were a pack of thieving rapists, a plague of locusts ravaging the D-Lands, descending with a murderous roar and leaving nothing unviolated in their wake, but they held their natures in check when it came to her. She was a statuesque siren in three-inch heels, a dusky dream girl with breasts like ripe mangoes and the pallor of illness about her eyes that was well-nigh irresistible. To watch her walking through the yard to the shower house in the morning sun was to taste the sweet meat of mutiny. But whatever stark desire they felt for her was trumped by raw fear.

They had followed Raden into battle, seen Raden berserk with anger, walked through the blood-soaked desolation he had left behind. If they had their way with her, there would be little left to bury, but they remained quiet and cowed because she was Raden's girl.

***

"Is there anything else we can get for you?" said Garth. Fussy and pear-shaped, always neatly dressed, a penguin among the Visigoths, Garth had been entrusted by Raden to keep her happy, keep her safe, and keep her in the camp. Each night, Garth entered her cabin to see if there were any needs unfulfilled. "Whatever you want is yours."

"My freedom," she said.

"Paulo says you haven't been eating."

"It's hard to eat inside a cage."

"This is not a cage. You are our guest."

"It feels like a cage."

"Are there bars on the window?"

"The shutters are nailed shut."

"To keep out bees. Are you not free to walk outside whenever you choose?"

"Always watched, always guarded."

"You should be grateful for the guards. Things are not so civilized on this side of the river. Would you like something special for dinner? Fish, maybe?"

"I don't want fish."

"I'm not talking about the glowers from the Mississippi. We can get flash-frozen flown in from the coast. A delicacy just for you."

"No fish."

"How about more books? Any book you want."

"*The Man in the Iron Mask*? *Papillon*? *On the Yard*?"

"I'm seeing a pattern."

"*Darkness at Noon*?"

"I think your attitude is not helping things," said Garth.

***

Every morning Kyrk escorted her from her cabin to the shower house built in the yard of the old tourist motel where they had set up camp.

Kyrk, Raden's most trusted captain, walked behind her with a gun strapped to his leg, staring through his mirrored sunglasses at the way her rear shifted within the terry-cloth robe. His hands jiggled with all the sweet pain he wanted to inflict upon her.

The collection of cabins and the dining hall were on the wrong side of the Mississippi, deserted after the disincorporation. Under Garth's direction they had fixed what needed fixing in the camp, put a generator behind the old dining hall, raised the wooden shower house and supplied it with a propane burner to heat the water. As Raden's girl made her way across the yard to the shower, the men peered out windows or leaned on their bikes. They scratched, they spat red spit, they bared red teeth and thought vile thoughts.

Raden's girl moved with her head bowed, along the flat dirt, past the motorbikes and trucks, past the great silver tankers, one filled with water from the other side, the second with gasoline. She carried her sweet soaps and shampoos in a bucket; with every step her nude feet raised soft gulps of dust.

While she showered, Kyrk leaned against the brick wall outside the open entrance and imagined her lathering the soap in her long black hair, upon her full breasts, across the skin of her sides striated with ribs, those smooth legs, the arches of her narrow feet. He fingered the ivory handle of his gun and gritted teeth stained crimson from the cud and tasted the bitter tang of soap, as if his tongue were the washcloth roughly cleaning every crevice.

***

"Don't think of this as a prison," said Garth. "Think of this as a sanitarium for your health. Imagine you're on vacation."

"Vacations are voluntary," said Raden's girl. "And on a beach. With a mai tai."

"We could get you a mai tai."

"I didn't choose to be here. I was kidnapped."

"Such a harsh word, kidnapped." Garth sat calmly on the room's rickety wooden chair, one of his chubby legs crossed over the other. He picked at an imaginary piece of lint on his spotless gray pants. His teeth gleamed white. "What we have done, we have done for your own benefit."

"I was fine in Moline."

"You were dying in Moline. Look in the mirror. Your eyes are much brighter. Your skin is losing its unhealthy sheen. The tea is working wonderfully."

"What about the beach?"

"We'll dig a pool for you."

"Vacations don't include guards at the door."

"For your protection, I promise you."

"And they don't usually end in rape."

"Who said anything about rape?"

"You've kidnapped me, you've locked me in this room, you're saving me for Raden. What would you call the inevitable result?"

"We're hoping, with all he's done for you, the boss's desire will be reciprocated."

"And if not?"

"He is surprisingly patient when it comes to love."

"Tell Raden to go to hell."

"Very patient," said Garth, "which is fortunate for you."

***

Paulo brought food to her cabin three times a day. He was short and swarthy, stoop-backed, unshaven, gap-toothed. Paulo made a fuss of setting the tray gently on the rough-hewn table and snapping open the cloth napkin. He bowed low as he poured the first cup of bitter red tea in the morning. He smiled at her like she was a sunny day, but when she looked away he stared at her body with a slack face.

Culbert guarded her cabin at night. Large and lumpish, he sat on a chair outside her closed door, quiet through the late hours, drinking beer and smoking. Intermittently, the sweet, sharp scent of reefer floated into her room from the crack beneath the door. Whenever he saw her, he lowered his gaze, his innocence palpable, but sometimes, when she woke suddenly in the dark of the night, she could hear his chair bang up against the wall—bang up, bang up—as if some great dog were sitting on the chair, ferociously scratching its neck with its hind paw.

Garth came to her cabin every evening to chat. He sat, legs crossed, and barely looked at her as he talked about this and that and Raden. Garth was apparently the only one of Raden's men who wasn't impaled by her beauty. Neatly dressed and scrubbed clean, he could have fit into any office in the incorporated territory.

"So why doesn't he come?" she said. "Why does he avoid me? Is it the disease?"

"Raden apologizes for not visiting," said Garth, "but he is quite busy."

"Busy kidnapping women?"

"This side of the river is a vacuum in which the worst impulses of humanity have been left to fester and grow. It needs to have the basic rules of civilization enforced and it has been left to Raden to be the enforcer. You could not imagine the burdens. Raden spends his days and nights fighting to keep whatever exists on this side of the line from burning itself into an ash heap."

"Maybe he should find another line of work."

Garth smiled wryly. "What would you suggest?"

"Librarian?"

"That wouldn't quite fit his talents."

"Because it would mean he would have to be able to read?"

"Some men play with history books, the bold make history. You should be grateful that one of the bold has fallen for you."

***

It didn't take Raden's girl long to learn the rhythms of the camp—the clang and roar of work during the day, the sound of drinking over the fires at night, the fights and arguments and laughter followed by drunken snoring in the wee hours. And it didn't take long to catch on to Culbert's rhythms as he sat at her doorstep—his drinking, his drug use, his flogging, his sleeping.

One night, during the riotous noise by the fires, she pressed the heel of her palm against the nailed-up shutters at the rear of the cabin. She pressed harder and harder still, the wood braces digging into her flesh, until, with a loud crack, a shutter swung open.

Her breath caught in her throat as she closed the shutter and waited for the door to crash open.

It didn't.

***

In the dead hour of the night, surrounded by a quiet interrupted only by snores, she dressed in what clothes she had—a camisole top, black pants, a pair of shoes with the heels snapped off to quicken her flight—pushed open the shutters, and slipped her slim body through the now-open window.

Her hands hit the ground first, her knees following. When she was entirely outside, she crouched low and waited, waited. She smelled the loam, the smoke, her own fear. There were no calls from the fires in the yard, not a sound from Culbert, just the quiet of stunted nature. She stayed low as she moved forward, her frame washed dimly by the moonlight. The cabin backed onto a wooded rise blanketed in shadow.

She began to climb through absolute darkness as slowly and silently as she could manage.

The camp was lit unevenly behind her, the woods through which she moved ever higher were so dark she had to feel her way forward, tentatively reaching her fingers toward the branches and trunks she knew were there. Her progress was painfully slow, her shoes slipped on the moist ground, and her weakened lungs struggled to grab enough air to maintain her exertions without a noisy wheeze, but her movement forward was steady and quiet, and soon enough she began to see ahead of her, through the thicket of trees, the starry freedom of the sky. Beyond the rise was a path down to the river. She would climb silently down and then clamber along the banks, the sound of her struggles muffled by the music of the water, clamber to someplace away from the camp and the men and the monster Raden, someplace where she could catch her breath and figure out how to get back to her life on the other side of the river.

She was reaching her hand toward the crest of the rise when a light hit her face like a fist.

"Looky, looky," said a voice behind the light. "Someone's come to party with Jake."

In that instant of light-blindness, the beam jabbing sharp as a shiv into her brain, she was enveloped in a despair so strong it choked the breath of hope right out of her. She could see it happening, all of the violent violation. Grabbed up, thrown to the ground, her pants pulled down, her legs spread, the sound of his belt unbuckling, the vile smell of him, the pain, the taste of his flesh as she fought back with fist and knee and tooth.

And that's when the emotion rose within her, something soft and precious as a newborn dove, a prayer from someplace buried deep but not yet lost, a place that remembered her first days, her first years, the way she used to stare at the great hero of her girlhood. In the deepest trouble of her troubled life, she had nothing left but this prayer, offered to the one person she always believed in, would always believe in, despite all his manifest failures.

Oh, Moonis, my Moonis, it whispered, this primal prayer of hope from Raden's girl. *I know, I know, it's impossible, yes, but who other than you, my darling brother, could ever save me?*

2
SLACKERS

Moonis Fell, in orange pants and a ribbed T-shirt, his wiry black hair greased tight to his skull, leaned his tall frame over the chessboard and let the possibilities unspool like film through his mind.

If he backed away, his position would be nigh impregnable and Gaston, with his unchecked ferocity, would wreck his army on the shoals of Moonis's defense. Yet there was something unsatisfying about hunkering down and waiting. His life heretofore had been nothing but retreats; he played chess to transcend his limitations, not enforce them. Staring at the position so hard the pieces shimmered on their squares, he began to see the possibility of an unexpected attack. Everything depended on an aggressive response by Gaston, but if there was anything he could count on from Gaston it was aggression. Moonis let the moves play through his mind one after another—bam, bam, check, bam, bam, bam, mate—saw clearly the whole of the sequence, bright and strong as polished steel.

Chess was not the most popular game in the gray wooden barracks. Most of the men played poker on the round table in the middle of the long room or huddled by the far wall, outside the view of the cameras, and threw the red dice with their corners rounded by the rough cement floor. But the misfits of the crew—the unhinged, the psychopathic, the blithely violent—gravitated to chess. Moonis was a regular.

The others liked playing against Moonis; he kept his mouth shut and was prone to the crushing mistake. It was common knowledge among the chess players that if you stayed alive long enough with Moonis Fell, you'd end up with his cigarettes in your pocket. But the truth was, Moonis never lost a game in his head. Once he saw the victory play out in his consciousness, he no longer cared much about the board, and it didn't pay to win too many games against these mutants. Especially someone like Gaston, thick as a hydrant, with a bull neck beneath his wide, ugly face and a shiv in his shoe. The only challenge then was making defeat seem wholly legitimate, a challenge Moonis cheerfully met more often than not. Each time he lost, it was designed to bespeak a failure of character, not strategy. In chess as in life he had raised losing to an art form.

But he and Gaston tonight weren't playing for a few dried-out Marlboros. Gaston had goaded him into playing for a full unopened pack of cigarettes, and though Moonis had placed his usual box of Marlboros beside the board, Gaston had somehow gotten his hands on a pack of Gauloises. Filterless? *Mais bien sûr.* Moonis considered the danger and weighed it against a perfectly harsh French smoke, something Camus might have slipped between his teeth before working on his scorn. Moonis rubbed his jaw, pushed his bishop, punched his clock.

Two spectators, leaning on a post as they waited to play, chewed their cud and shook their heads as if the mistake were as plain as that tattooed number on Moonis's shoulder. "Cud" was what the farmhands called the betel nuts supplied by the company to prisoner and guard alike, along with uncured tobacco leaf and lime powder, a concoction designed to enhance the work product of the farm.

"A desperate attack to delay the inevitable, my friend," said Gaston in his rough French Canadian accent. Gaston was also chewing the cud, his smile a crimson smear of malice. "So out of character. It is a pity, but I will have to punish your disrespect."

Moonis didn't respond, didn't look up from the board. His eyes behind his thick round glasses remained as impassive as the bishop he had advanced.

"Let us see how my queen sticks like a fork in your throat." Gaston slid his queen forward, simultaneously attacking Moonis's knight and rook, exactly the overly aggressive move Moonis had anticipated.

As Gaston punched the clock, and the spectators chortled, Moonis again saw all the moves, including now the violent moves that would come after the mate, and understood the consequences of continuing that route. This was his last chance to turn away from victory. Moonis was always more comfortable in defeat and, after losing, he was sure that he could bum one of the French cigarettes off Gaston. Moving his rook out of danger would tilt the board in Gaston's favor. But as he stared down at the table, the cellophane on the pack of Gauloises glinted like a Frenchwoman's pale-blue high heel, and Moonis realized he wanted it, not just a single cigarette but the whole damn pack. There was so little to want in this craphole, other than escape or death, but he wanted this.

So it would be weakness, not strength that drove him once again, consequences be damned. Fine. Better to embrace weakness than nothing. He made his move.

Bam.

Gaston placed his hand on his queen, stared up at Moonis, and spit a red blob of betel into a steel pail on the floor before making a slashing move. The rook died a quick painless death.

"Check," said Moonis as he made his move and punched the clock.

"Wait a minute," said Gaston, examining the board anew as if it were a live, mutating thing that had just bared fangs it hadn't possessed a moment before. "Wait. What?"

"What I said was clear enough."

"I heard you, yes, but wait."

"Don't worry, I'm not going anywhere," said Moonis, raising his gaze now to stare straight at Gaston. "Except maybe outside under a ribbon of stars to smoke your Frog cigarettes."

The laughter of the spectators stiffened Gaston's jaw. Peering into his opponent's eyes, it was as if Moonis saw a spark of his own disrespect igniting a vapor cloud of gasoline. There wasn't going to be another move; Gaston wasn't going to allow Moonis the satisfaction of playing out the mate.

Gaston, proceeding directly into his after-mate rage, pushed himself to standing and narrowed his eyes. As the spectators whooped and backed away, Moonis jumped to his feet and grabbed the two packs of cigarettes off the table just before Gaston, with a mighty heave, sent the table flying toward the wall, where table, board, clock, and pieces landed on the huddle of craps players.

Amidst the twisting sounds of crash and shout, Moonis and Gaston faced off. Gaston bared his stained teeth, and then bowed as if making a courtly Old World gesture of respect to his opponent before rising with a blade in his hand.

"You cheated me, you black bastard," said Gaston.

"Life is loss, Gaston," said Moonis. "Accept that and your time here will be less troubled."

"I accept only that you are a lying thief."

By now the whole of the barracks was in an uproar. A crowd of men in orange pants, swarthy men either shirtless or with ribbed T-shirts, encircled the combatants, the metal of their shackles—their Oregon boots—scraping the cement, the men anxious for a show of raw violence. Crimson teeth were bared, fists were balled. Blood dripped across the smile of one of the dice shooters who had been crowned by the sharp corner of the chessboard. The smell of body odor and tobacco, of men confined together in hatred and despair, was well-nigh overwhelming as it mixed with the men's cheers and curses.

"Knife the bastard."

"Rip him in the gut."

"Kick him in the nuts."

"If Moonis falls, I get his shoes."

The two men circled each other, their left legs sliding across the floor due to the shackles on their ankles.

"Six to five on the Canadian."

"Done."

"Burst his spleen, Gaston, but don't get blood on my new shoes."

Moonis was taller than Gaston—he was one of the tallest men in the camp—but Gaston was twice as strong. If it came to a wrestling match, Gaston would snap Moonis's back like a twig. Moonis needed to dodge Gaston's attacks like a matador in a ring. He might have a chance to survive if he could—

Gaston lunged.

Moonis faked left, slipped right, and pushed Gaston past him with the hand not holding the two packs so that Gaston fell into the crowd, jabbing the knife into some poor sap's leg. Moonis backed away with satisfaction. Goal number two was to avoid death; goal number one was not to crush the cigarettes. He spotted a young detainee in the crowd.

"Hold these for me, kid, will you?" he said as he handed over the two packs of cigs.

"For three Ros."

"Two."

"Four," said the kid.

Gaston now was back upright, tossing the knife from hand to hand, sliding his left foot so the metal bar beneath his shoe scraped the floor like an iron fingernail.

"Five," said the kid.

"You learn fast. It will be your undoing. Done," said Moonis before calling out to Gaston. "Can't we work this out?"

"That is what we are doing, my friend," said Gaston. "Working it out."

"I mean without the rumble and the blood."

"No."

"The problem with violence, Gaston, is that it's boring. Violence has been done to death. Let's try to be a little more inspired. What about a game of chess to decide?"

"So you can cheat me again."

"Chess isn't like love; you can't cheat chess."

Gaston—leaning low at the waist, his knife held out in front, his eyes now as red as his teeth—bellowed like a wild beast and charged madly, knifepoint diving at Moonis's gut.

Moonis faked left, faked right, stood frozen for a moment as the Canadian rushed forward, and then slammed his hands on top of Gaston's head as he leaped over the charging mass of muscle and steel. Gaston flew into the crowd once again as Moonis landed awkwardly and pain slashed through his weighted ankle. He fell forward, slamming his forehead on the cement floor.

By the time Moonis shook his head clear and spun around, still on the ground, a leering Gaston, blood streaming from his nose and running across his mouth, was staggering toward him.

Moonis backed away like a crab as Gaston advanced. Moonis looked around for a weapon—nothing. He looked for a route of escape—nowhere to run. He thought of something, anything to say that would save his life.

"*Vive la France?*"

"Fuck France," said Gaston.

"Yes," said Moonis. "I'm with you there."

That's when the doors burst open with whistles and shouts. The crowd blew apart as six guards in their brown uniforms, billy sticks high, charged into the barracks, slamming their cudgels down on any head they could find until they reached Gaston, still standing in the middle of the circle, the knife suddenly gone. It took four of the guards to subdue the bellowing Canadian, cuff him, and throw him up against the wall.

Just another stinking night in Archer Daniels Midland LCM 204. And Moonis Fell, still on the floor, his ankle screaming in pain, shook his head and laughed that he was still here, in this camp, still alive. Would the tangle of brutal disappointments in this life know no end?

3
UNDERGROUND MAN

Moonis stood outside the barracks with a book, smoking a Gauloises and looking up at the bright swath of the Milky Way. The LCM was surrounded by a tall chain-link fence topped by barbed wire, but that couldn't keep out the stars. Sometimes looking up at the distant heavens was the only way to feel free in this world.

They had thrown Gaston in the brig, and Moonis felt a little bad about that. Gaston had tried to stick a knife in his heart, there was that, yes, but Gaston also was right that Moonis had cheated him. Moonis hadn't slipped a spare bishop out of his sleeve, no, but by losing on purpose so frequently, he had set up Gaston to be flat-out hustled once the stakes were high enough. That a fresh pack of Gauloises constituted a high enough stake was a pathetic comment on Moonis's character, true, but once Moonis decided to win, it was inevitable that the game would end with Gaston in the brig. If Moonis had learned anything in his life, it was the inexorable workings of fate.

Moonis waited for a clot of laborers, spitting out red wads, to cross the yard. The men walked with limps because of the thick circular weights bolted around their left calves. The weights were lifted off the bump of their anklebones by a metal brace slipped over their boots. Without the brace, the weight would destroy the ankle; even with the brace, it was painful enough that it forced the laborers to slide their left legs across the ground to keep the lead from banging bone. The Oregon boot was enough to prevent even the most hardened malcontent from contemplating escape. When the men had passed, Moonis, with the same constricted gait, stepped toward the small brick-walled brig, illuminated by a single light burning overhead. He leaned against the wall by the barred window.

"Cigarette?" he said.

"Go to hell, you cheating bastard," rose the accented voice from inside the brig. "But okay, yes. I'll have one of my cigarettes."

Moonis pulled a Gauloises out of the pack, lit it off his, and poked it through the bars. It was plucked like a fruit from between his fingers.

"I wasn't going to kill you," said Gaston.

"Oh, yes, you were."

"Maybe so. But I wouldn't have been happy about it afterward."

They stood there for a moment, on either side of the brick wall, two men smoking in silence. The Frenchified cigarette was harsh and bitter, like a Turkish coffee, Moonis imagined, sipped slowly in a Parisian café with a prostitute leaning her head on your shoulder.

"I've never even caught a sniff of France," said Moonis.

"It smells like rotten eggs," said Gaston.

On the edge of the yard, one of the guards, his face cut with shadows from overhead, was watching the brig while he chewed the cud. It was Handler, the new man. There was something sinister in his posture, like he was paying too much attention.

"How long do you suppose the bastards will keep me here?" said Gaston.

"The winter wheat is ripening. They'll let you out for harvest. Maybe sooner if you learn your lesson."

"And what lesson is that?"

"If I knew that," said Moonis, "would I be in this place?"

"We are, both of us, I am afraid, incorrigible malcontents. But beyond that, your problem is obvious to anyone with a brain. You should have let me win, and you know it. But what was it that forced your hand to advance your bishop? Pride."

"What in hell do I have to be proud about?"

"That is the question, no?"

"Here." Moonis tossed what was left of the pack through the bars and heard it slap onto the cement floor before he pushed himself off the wall. "I don't feel right smoking the cigarettes of a man in the brig."

After taking a few steps, he thought better of it and returned.

"Can I just have one more for the night?" said Moonis.

"Screw yourself," said Gaston.

The only tolerable thing about the LCM was the books. The company had confiscated a library from an abandoned rural college and put the volumes in a truck they drove from center to center for the edification of the detainees. When the truck arrived at the farm, Moonis haunted the thing, removing stacks at a time. Above the front door of the barracks was a yellow lightbulb, swarmed by moths and oversized mosquitoes. At night, when he wasn't playing chess, Moonis would sit outside and read by the yellow light, moth shadows flitting across the page like images rising from the text.

He had just cracked open his book when footsteps approached. Moonis looked up to see the new guard, standing before him. Handler was a tall, long-jawed man, with a cracked-tooth smile stained red. A billy stick hung off one side of his belt, a holstered gun hung off the other.

"He tried to kill you, and you give him a smoke," said Handler. "Someone tried that on me, I wouldn't give him nothing."

"Probably a better plan." Moonis had learned in his two LCM terms to always stay guarded with the guards, to say as little as possible without being disrespectful, and to keep his bile down.

"They say you was selected. Is that true?"

"A long time ago."

"Still, that must have been something. That must have been some damn thing. What's that you're reading?"

"Just a book," said Moonis.

"Anything good?"

"Dostoyevsky."

"Russian, huh?" Handler spat a crimson lump into the dirt. "You sure it's safe to read that commie stuff?"

"He died before the revolution."

"That really matter?"

Moonis couldn't tell if Handler didn't know enough to know better or was saying something strikingly profound. He thought on it a bit. During this second stint at the camp he had already punched through *Crime and Punishment* and *The Brothers Karamazov*. Dostoyevsky would have been dangerous no matter when he was born, whether he was a gambling czarist or a raving revolutionary. Just holding his books felt like a little shot of rebellion.

"Have you read him?" said Moonis.

"Hell no. After what them Russkies did, just the idea of them makes me sick. I had family in Saint Louis. The name's Jim." Handler spit again, wiping a crimson streak from his lips with the back of his hand. "Can I ask you something, Moonis?"

"You have the gun."

"What the hell you doing here?"

"My file's in the office."

"I don't mean the official why. There's always an official why. But you was selected. Krist. A Negro boy selected, that's something. And then the Dean, he says you're the best mechanic he's ever seen. He says if there's a problem with a tractor, if there's a combine motor that needs fixing, go get Moonis. And your overtime's off the chart, even though your teeth are still white. With the way you work, and with a bit of cud, you could fill two guaranteed jobs without a sweat. So why are you here?"

"I don't do well with bosses."

"You like guards better?"

"Evidently."

"And you give cigarettes to the man who tries to kill you."

"Is that against the rules?"

"Probably. There's always a rule against something. Look, I don't got much power here, being low man, but if the time comes, maybe I can do something for you. Don't know what, but I'll keep my eye open and if I get a chance, I'll do something. I believe in work, and I know a worker when I see one, whatever the color of the man. I'll take care of you, don't you worry. Enjoy the commie book."

Moonis nodded and lowered his gaze to the page.

I am a sick man. I am a spiteful man. I am an unattractive man. I think my liver hurts.

Funny, after the fight with Gaston, Moonis's liver did hurt.

He looked up from the book as Handler walked away. He thought about the offer and wondered why it felt less like a gesture of kindness and more like a threat.

4
CAPTAIN KYRK

"I expect you learned a valuable lesson," said Garth. He sat languidly in the chair, speaking calmly to Raden's girl as the men outside the cabin bolted bars onto her windows.

"And what lesson is that, other than not to escape on foot?"

"How good you have it here."

She looked around.

"Inside is better than outside, trust me," he said. "The D-Lands are a savage place. Any way you try to escape would be the wrong way. That's why we've taken your shoes, to protect you."

It wasn't Moonis who had saved her from would-be rapist Jake, it was Culbert—big, lumpy, shy Culbert—who had woken with a start, heard something soft and strange behind the cabin, crept around to investigate, and was just in time to see the flash of light on the crest and hear the scream before it was choked off by a fist at the throat. Jake was holding her by the neck with one hand while lowering his pants with the other when Culbert tackled him. After Culbert's call for help, Garth, uncharacteristically rumpled and sour, had showed up with two other men and told Culbert to put her back in the cabin while they dealt with Jake.

"I wouldn't want to be in Jake's shoes right about now," said Culbert as he pulled her down the rise.

"Little Garth's a real tiger, hey?"

"You don't know the half of it, miss. I played football till they kicked me out of school, and I learned early the way they look don't much matter. It's all in the doing, and that Garth, he does."

Now she and Garth were in the cabin, having one of their amiable chats, and she didn't know whether to be grateful to be still unviolated or disappointed to be still in her prison. But she didn't want to show her disappointment or her gratitude. Instead she wanted to act petulant and hard, not too difficult a trick, because petulant and hard was exactly what she had become.

"While I'm here, I thought I should warn you," said Garth. "Things might get a little crazy in a few nights."

"You mean crazier than being kidnapped and imprisoned as a sex object for some drug-running thug who is afraid to visit my room?"

"Raden isn't afraid. He's on the road. Business. Even a place as wild as the D-Lands needs discipline. Raden is the discipline. And he's also the reward. Which is why he decided we should have a party for the men. They need a release."

"What about my release?"

"We're bringing in some girls from the other side. We could bring one in for you if you'd like."

"Are the girls kidnapped, too?"

"Bought and paid for. We take pride in giving value."

"Except to me."

"How's your breathing, Cecily? It seems easier. And your skin color is darker. I'd suggest there's some value there. But I wanted to warn you about the party. I'm glad there are bars now. Things sometimes get out of hand."

"Sometimes?"

"Yes, you caught me. Things will get out of hand. The men have been in camp too long. Culbert will guard your cabin through the night."

"Poor Culbert."

"We'll make it up to him. Hunker down and try to ignore the things you hear. It won't be pretty."

"Pretty fabulous, I'd bet."

***

Kyrk was tall and bald, with aviator sunglasses that shone blankly like an insect's eyes. There wasn't much with regard to women that he hadn't perpetrated, and so he thought he understood the gender—its fears, its wants—but still he was surprised when he first heard the moaning from inside the shower. It was quiet enough so that only he could hear it, standing guard by the open doorway, quiet enough so that he had to wonder if it was merely a figment of his own hungers. But no, Raden's girl was moaning, softly, as if there were someone in the stall with her, the moans slow and deep-throated, rising in volume and pace to a breathless crescendo that weakened Kyrk's knees.

She left the shower building a few moments later as if nothing had happened, her long black hair stringy with wet, her head bowed, her robe tied, the bucket of shampoo and soap in her hand. But what was that quick glance she shot at him before she began walking back to her room? And was her rear shaking in a subtly different way, as if itself an invitation?

***

"So how did a guy in a white shirt and tan pants who knows every book reference I throw out end up in the D-Lands with a bunch of ruffians?" said Raden's girl on one of Garth's nightly visit.

"Ruffians? Is that what they are? Why, that almost sounds genteel. Powdered handkerchiefs, velvet jackets."

"Perhaps I misspoke. Barbarians."

"Bare-chested savages from the north with knives in their teeth, pulling down the temples of a decadent Rome. Yes, I do think that fits better."

Raden's girl smiled. These talks with Garth had strangely become the highlight of her day. It was the one thing she might miss when she escaped.

"Life didn't quite work out as I had planned," said Garth.

"I detect a note of self-pity."

"I was a Ventura District boy for the first decade of my life."

"Fancy. And in the second?"

"My father lost his trust fund. First, bit by bit in the market, and then by trying to make his losses back in some Ponzi scheme that took the rest. Next thing you know, he had a guaranteed job selling insurance in a rotten part of Hartford and I'm the new piñata at the local guaranteed school."

"Poor baby."

"I think the cruelest thing is to have expectations in your life. When they get snuffed out, you never really recover."

"Tell me about it."

"Your family had money?"

"We had potential. My brother was selected."

"Moonis, right?"

"Yes, how did you know?"

"It's my job to know. How'd that whole selection thing turn out?"

"Not so good for any of us."

"Well, at least you're here now."

"A captive concubine amongst a barbarian horde."

"You know what I love about the D-Lands?" said Garth, his voice losing the tinge of fussiness that was usually there. "There's no them, no us, no high, no low, no black, no white, no guarantees. Equality has a taste I've grown used to out here. You might learn to like it, too."

***

It came to Kyrk as clear as a summer rain, in the midst of another spell of shallow moans that could only barely be heard above the patter of water. Among the oohs and aahs that poured like soft lead through the shower's open door and into his ears came, ever so softly, a single *Oh, Kyrk* that prickled the hairs on the back of his neck. And then another. And then, as her breaths shortened and the register of her passion lowered, *Oh, oh my God, Kyrk, Kyrk.*

Leaning against the brick of the wall, Kyrk gripped the ivory handle of his gun so tightly his finger slipped onto the trigger and the damn thing went off, wham, just missing his foot and silencing immediately the exhalations coming through the thrumming of the water.

He looked around guiltily from behind his aviators, as a few heckles and shouts were called his way. He cursed them off, but he didn't feel chagrined. Instead he felt emboldened.

The whole camp knew that Raden never visited the girl, that she was kept as a prisoner, locked alone with only her nightly chats with Garth, which would hardly be enough to gain her any satisfaction. Of course she would have needs, of course she would dream of Kyrk fulfilling those needs for her.

He spat a red glob of cud onto the shallow mined by the bullet. Her desire for all he had to offer was as natural as a porcupine.

***

"You'll be involved in the festivities, I suppose," said Raden's girl as she walked with Garth around the yard. Lights were being strung, walls were being painted, a goat was being fitted onto a spit.

"On nights such as this, I do my best to stay far out of the way."

"No whoring for you? That seems such a waste of opportunity."

"I retain old-fashioned notions of love and courtship."

"That must be hard out here."

"I has its . . . challenges. But one never gives up hope. Were you ever in love?"

"Once," she said. "Clyde."

"Clyde?"

"My brother's best friend. He was so handsome, blond and broad, a football hero."

"Every girl's dream," said Garth, a touch of bitterness in his voice. "What happened to the hero?"

"He was sent away to an LCM, and that was that. When he came back, we both were changed. He had shrunken and I had grown and we didn't match up anymore."

"That's almost sad."

"Isn't it, though? Clyde Sparrow. He would have run through a brick wall for me."

"Smart guy."

"Dim as a board, actually. He knew his way around an electrical circuit, but I think he read a book once and decided once was enough. He works a guaranteed job in a diner now. Still, he did love me. Sometimes you take that for granted."

"You should be able to. And you can, here."

"The obsession of a barbarian king is not love. There's no love here. Just violence and sex that's bought or stolen."

"There's more on this side of the line, if you look. Equality, fraternity, maybe even a certain kind of liberty."

"I'm a prisoner."

"You're a guest for now. But I've found my place here, and you might, too. Sometimes you look for it all over and then find it in the most surprising location."

"That would be a surprise."

"It surprised me. My Ventura years had ruined me for a guaranteed job, and nothing else was available to someone in my position. So I stayed one step ahead of the sweepers until I found Raden."

"That sounds almost romantic."

"Power is romantic, it moves worlds. Even better, it changes you. Raden's power doesn't just cover his part of the D-Lands, it spreads from border to border and deep into the incorporated territory. The berry that you were buying in Chicago came through him. And it's a good thing you're not on the other side of the river anymore, because he's strangling the flow to Moline and Chicago and anyplace else in the incorporated lands."

"Why?"

"He has his reasons. The fat cats in the Ventura Districts believe they control him, when all along he's controlling them. He's a strong man who's only getting stronger, a new breed of man for a new age. And he wants you, Cecily. You should feel honored."

"Yeah, well, screw him, Garth."

"That's the idea."

5
"GOOD AS THE BEST"

With his back to the counter, Clyde Sparrow spat on a burger sizzling atop the flat grill. He expelled the spit so neatly the act was invisible from behind, but the little yellow blob landed smack-splat on target. Quick as the hawk itself, Clyde popped a slice of cheese over the patty and covered it with a metal bowl.

"You want onions with that, Bob?"

"And pickles. Don't forget the pickles."

"Coming right up."

A yellow-haired man with broad shoulders, Clyde wore a white shirt with the sleeves rolled up. His apron was white, his bow tie black. A white garrison cap with the words "Toddle House" embroidered on the linen was cocked at a jaunty angle. In the outfit he was every inch the Toddle House man and he took seriously his duty to expectorate and serve.

Clyde dipped his spatula into a metal bin of sautéed onions and dropped a clump onto the grill to heat. He sliced off a corner of a great bar of butter, slapped it onto the hot metal beside the onions, and pressed an open bun on top of the resulting slick. He lifted the basket out of the fryer and hung it to drain. His movements behind the counter were as practiced and efficient as a piece of modern dance, animated by a hate buried so deep in the breast it could be confused with contentment.

The Toddle House, with its outside spotlights and its cheerful neon sign, was a brightly lit haven along the dark of a Chicago street thick with gray, grim-faced figures marching in lines from or to their guaranteed jobs. Open all hours of the day and night, and with a mere ten seats at the counter, the tiny diner only required one guaranteed job to staff the evening shift, and for six years that shift had belonged to Clyde. A series of green-and-white signs set behind the counter educated the customers in all things Toddle House.

Refills on **COFFEE** Are Always **FREE!**

When the cheeseburger was bunned, topped with onions, squirted with ketchup, and layered with pickles, Clyde salted the fries and heaped them next to the burger. The plate spun on the stainless-steel counter, stopping only when the red-and-gray Toddle House shield was set precisely opposite the customer. In a place as tiny as a Toddle House, it was the details that mattered. Without asking, Clyde took Bob's half-empty Toddle House cup to the great twin coffee urns set between the milk-shake machine and the grill.

"Ah, short, dark, and lovely," said Bob when the cup, full and steaming, appeared again before him. "Just the way I like it." Bob, the sole customer at the moment, was a definite Bob, heavy, with red cheeks and pronounced jowls. His billy stick was set on the counter next to his blue peaked hat. The shoulder strap of his Sam Browne belt gleamed. "I'm going to need the caffeine tonight, Clyde," he said as he poured copious amounts of sugar and cream into the coffee, "what with the overtime they're making us put in."

"Anything exciting?"

"Krist, I hope not. Some new witch hunt by them narcotics boys."

"What a bunch of cards," said Clyde, shaking his head.

The silver bell above the door brightly tinkled and in walked Patti, a tall and skinny woman, with long black hair and a sharp nose that cut like a prow. She grinned, showing off long gums and crooked teeth, until Clyde gave her a warning look and nodded her toward a seat at the far end of the counter. Patti's narrow eyes focused on the cop as she wiped her nose with the back of her hand, then she quietly followed Clyde's direction.

"They're making a big push to stamp out the berry," said Bob, taking hold of his hamburger.

"What do they have against pie?"

"This ain't pie, Clyde. They say the berry is deadlier than heroin. Word has come down we need to make a point and we need to make it now. The action's been going on all week. Tonight it's our turn. I'm already dead tired, but the overtime's good and the rent is always due."

"Tell me about it," said Clyde. Over the years Clyde had collected a series of catchphrases that allowed him to talk with the customers without saying anything. *What can I do you for? Coffee? Pie? How would you like that? Coming right up. Tell me about it. You got that right. Can I freshen that coffee for you? Thanks for the business. Come again.*

Bob lifted the burger, took a bite, smacked his lips as he chewed.

OUR WORLD FAMOUS BURGER: ONLY $1.50!

"What can I do you for?" said Clyde after he had shifted over to Patti's side of the counter.

"You and me, we need to talk," said Patti, her voice secretive enough to draw attention. She was wearing work pants and a work shirt, the top buttons of the shirt undone, showing off collarbones that pressed hungrily out of her pale flesh.

"Coffee?" said Clyde. "Pie?"

"Yeah, sure. Both. Listen, Clyde, I got this dope about—"

"Coffee coming right up. Is apple okay?"

"Apple?"

"For the pie."

"Oh, right," said Patti, glancing at Bob the cop. "What about blueberry?"

"We don't have blueberry. Coconut custard. Lemon meringue. Cherry. Banana."

"Peach?"

"No peaches this time of year."

"How about apple? You got any apple?"

"Yes," said Clyde, a sigh in his voice, "we have apple."

"Sounds good," said Patti, glancing again at the cop.

"Coming right up."

Clyde grabbed a mug from the rack on the wall, just beneath another sign.

OUR WELL KNOWN SCRAMBLED EGGS: ONLY $1.25!

He filled the mug with coffee and put it in front of Patti, along with a gleaming set of cutlery. As Clyde pulled a piece of pie from beneath the Plexiglas riser, Bob stood from his stool, slipped his billy stick into the loop hanging off his belt, and set his cap.

"I don't know how you do it, Clyde," said Bob.

"Do what there, Bob?"

"Make your hamburgers so moist. It's like magic. Best burgers in town." Bob started patting his pockets. "What do I owe?"

"Get on now. You know your money's no good here."

"A burger that good deserves something."

"Your thanks and your service are enough. Go out and crack some heads for those narcotics boys."

"Will do." Bob sucked his teeth, patted his stomach. "Much appreciated, Clyde."

"Thanks for the business. Come again."

After the policeman had rung the bell on his way out, Clyde, still holding the pie in his hand, stared at the door for a good long moment. "What's fifteen percent of nothing, Pats?"

"That's math, man, how should I know?"

"Well, I'll tell you what it is. That clown comes in once a week for his free meal, and fifteen percent of nothing is what he leaves me for a tip."

"I guess he reads the sign."

"Fuck the sign."

NO TIPPING, Please!

Clyde spun the plate in front of Patti, who stared at it for a moment without reaching for her fork.

"What's the matter?" said Clyde. "You don't want pie?"

"I don't know."

"Everyone loves pie."

"But something's missing, don't you think?"

"Yeah, yeah, I got you." Clyde leaned down and opened a drawer beneath the counter. When he stood up again, he slipped a small Toddle House bag next to the pie.

"Thanks," said Patti, opening the bag, jamming it to her nose and giving it a heady sniff before slipping it into a pocket in her pants.

"Ten bucks for the whole candle—coffee, pie, and reefer," said Clyde.

"Can I owe you?"

"Hell no, you can't owe me." Pause. "What's the matter now?"

"I was thinking ice cream."

"Ice cream?"

"I'm just saying," said Patti. "A scoop of vanilla always goes nice with pie."

"Ice cream."

"Yeah."

"That will be another four bits. You want the pie heated, too?"

"But not too hot, like you do sometimes. Just warm and gooey."

"Coming right up," said Clyde.

Even though the counter job was guaranteed, it didn't pay enough on its own to make it through the month—most guaranteed jobs didn't. The joke was the only thing a guaranteed job guaranteed was hunger. You could work and almost starve, or refuse to work and get sent to an LCM where they booted you, forced you to work harder than a dog, and almost starved you anyway. So, like everyone else with a guaranteed job, Clyde had found a second, nonguaranteed gig to make ends meet. His manager always told him good counter work meant satisfying the customer, and Clyde took the advice to heart. You wanted a burger, Clyde would give you a world-famous burger, moist and delicious. You wanted reefer, Clyde would give you something so fresh and rich it was like breathing sweet oblivion itself.

TODDLE HOUSE Serves the Nation!

"The thing we got to talk about," said Patti as Clyde placed the pie on the griddle and covered it with the metal bowl, "is an opportunity what's fallen in my lap."

"It's funny how things like that fall into your lap."

"Hooper wants a car."

"Who doesn't?"

"A specific car."

"Since when do you need my help to steal a car? You've been doing it since you were twelve."

"This one's different."

35

"How so?"

"It's kind of sort of in one of the Ventura Districts."

"Pats."

"The money is good, man. Pissing good."

"Forget about it."

"It's a big score," said Patti. "I never had nothing this big and this rich. It would be my greatest boost. My moaning Lisa. And did I mention the money?"

"I don't trust a thing about Hooper. He's a liar and a thief."

"One sort of goes with the other."

"You've got to stop running his errands."

"This ain't about him, it's about us. It's about snatching for ourselves a bit of what they'll never give us fair. I haven't driven something with real power since I mustered out of the army. I'm tired of low-rent jalopies, I want something that shakes my leg when I shift them gears."

"I don't go in for statements anymore," said Clyde.

"I remember when you busted one of them V-District assholes with a single punch, stole his beer, stole his shoes."

"Good times, huh?"

"We was kings then, and you was the best of us."

"Well, you don't have a number on your shoulder."

They had caught him selling long-distance phone calls, stolen with a contraption he had built based on a whistle given away in Cap'n Crunch cereal boxes. When he connected the contraption to the phone and blew the whistle, a perfect 2,600-hertz signal went over the line, switching the call to the long-distance servers without any charges. This was after his mom had lost her guaranteed job because of the drugs she was taking for her ruined back. Clyde was stupid and hungry, but he built the contraption and made the sales and put food on the table. And then, somehow, out of nowhere the Homeland Guard surrounded his house with howitzers, like he was a D-Land terrorist instead of just a hungry kid looking for a quick buck. They sent him up to Lancaster,

Wisconsin, to work the zinc mines. Six months, as short a stint as they had—dubbed a "vacation" by the more experienced laborers—but it had left its mark. When he came home, his ankle ached every time it rained, and all that was left of his mom was the cat. Since then he'd kept out of trouble and kept his job. It wasn't much, he knew it, but it was all he had.

TODDLE HOUSE: GOOD AS THE BEST!

Clyde upended the bowl from the grill and flicked his spatula beneath the pie. He slid the oozing slice onto the plate before leaning over the freezer. He gently placed a scoop of vanilla atop the pie so that the melted sweet cream would cover the top surface like icing and pool along the edges.

"It's a cakewalk," said Patti, her mouth now full of pie and ice cream. "Hooper's getting us in. All I need is an electronics guy, and you're the best."

"Was. Now I flip burgers."

"Clyde? I need this."

"You get nabbed in a Ventura District . . . Krist, that's federal stuff. There's no telling what—"

The bell above the door tinkled. Patti turned to get a look at who was interrupting her begging.

The man in the doorway—tall and thin, rich dark suit, gray fedora, pinched face, a bad case of the oily sweats—coughed so hard his whole body contracted into a C. Then he coughed again. Clyde and Patti watched as the man lowered his chin and stepped to the opposite end of the counter and slid onto a stool. The man stared down at the stainless-steel counter, his hands clasped and sweating before him, waiting for something. Waiting for Clyde.

Patti looked at Clyde, Clyde looked at the man, and then both turned to face the sign above the tiny Kellogg's boxes.

NO LUNGERS SERVED!

Clyde didn't know much in the world for certain, but he was certain that the son of a bitch in the V-District suit and fancy fedora wasn't from this part of town. And he was a lunger, too, no doubt about it, coughing out his blood-soaked windbags onto Clyde's spotless counter.

6
THE LUNGER

"Coffee," said the V-District lunger without looking up at Clyde.

The man's voice was hoarse from the cough, a familiar hush of sadness and sickness. Lungers all sounded the same. Clyde stood with his hip against the edge of the grill, leaning as far from the man as he could lean.

"You see the writing on the wall?" said Clyde.

The man coughed into his fist and then raised his gaze to take in the signs. "Why are your scrambled eggs well-known?" said the man. "Are they the friendly sort?"

"That's not the writing I mean."

"Your hamburger is world-famous, apparently," said the man. "But the eggs are only well-known. What's wrong with your eggs?"

"Nothing's wrong with the eggs. Fresh as the morning, they are."

"Then why are they not as famous as the hamburgers? It's enough to give a chicken a complex."

"What do you want here, joe?"

"Coffee."

The man looked at Clyde like he knew something Clyde didn't, before lowering his gaze to stare again at his hands. Sweat oozed from beneath his hat. Oily drips slid down his temple, his nose. A drop slapped onto the counter. The heat from the grill roasted Clyde's back and he felt revulsion and pity harden into a shard of self-disgust that lodged in his kidney.

"Coming right up," he said finally.

He took a cup off the rack and filled it from one of the urns. With long arms he placed it on the edge of the counter along with a spoon, and then backed away, quietly, as if the man were hiding nitroglycerin in his hat. When Clyde was as far as he could get from the man while still standing inside the diner, the man took a napkin from the chrome dispenser and wiped his face with it.

"Krist," said Clyde under his breath.

"A guy like that shouldn't be in a place like this," said Patti, her mouth full of pie.

"You think I want him here?" said Clyde, not caring if he was loud enough to be heard at the other end of the counter. "They should keep all the V-District lungers in the damn V-Districts. Let the society bastards deal with them."

"You got that right," said Patti.

"He should be sitting in one of those fancy-assed sanitariums they got up there, sipping champagne with his peach pie, and leaving us in peace."

"Maybe we should let the boys at Tunney's know."

"And have a mob banging at the door with pitchforks? Forget about it. They'll burn the place down with him in it and then where will I be? A guaranteed spot out on the street. He'll drink his coffee and get the hell out and that will be the end of it. The sweepers will get him eventually."

The man cupped the mug in both hands and brought it, shaking, to his lips. Before he could put it down again, he started back with the coughing. Coffee spilled all across the counter. The man grabbed another napkin and put it to his lips. The napkin pinked.

"Holy Krist," said Clyde as the bell above the door tinkled and jingled.

The woman in the doorway was tall, thin, with copper hair and a tight dress, pale legs, red spiked heels, lips like maraschino cherries, crushed and wet. Helen. He'd known her since she was a chubby teenager when he was still in primary school, but she'd grown into a heart-stopper for sure, Helen, a vision of the kind of woman for whom you'd give up everything and a day, just to grab tight her arms and mash your lips onto hers. Fortunately for Clyde, it didn't take that much.

Her face stayed as impassive as the coffee urns while she surveyed the tiny room. She slipped onto the stool one over from Patti. "Hey, handsome," she said to Clyde.

"Coffee? Pie?"

"No pie."

"The pie's pretty good," said Patti. "But they don't got no peach."

"Well then, definitely no pie. And my special order, sweetie. I've run out."

"You picked some up last week."

"And they worked fine. But right now I still have half the night left and I'm about ready to fall over."

"If your father maybe put down the bottle and did some shoveling, you could take a break now and then."

"Are you preaching or selling? Because if I want a priest I can knock on the back door of any church and get all the priest I can handle."

"Remember when Clyde was ripe for anything?" said Patti. "Remember when he was the crazy child, the blond fox? Remember when he took on them Anteaters from 469 all by his lonesome?"

"That was before the bow tie," said Helen. "The bow tie changed everything."

"You're right," said Patti, laughing with a donkey bray. "It is the bow tie."

"He's become a preacher, and the Toddle House is his church. Hallelujah and pass the home fries."

"Coffee coming right up," said Clyde.

"Holy water in stainless-steel urns," said Helen.

Clyde ignored Patti's laughing as he headed down the counter toward the rack of cups.

"Hey, mister," said the lunger in the suit with his hushed voice, speaking now to Clyde's back. "More coffee, please."

"Haven't you had enough?" said Clyde without looking behind him.

"Refills are always free," said the man.

"So that sign you can read."

"I want my free refill."

Clyde turned and placed his hands against the edge of the counter. He took a moment to examine the mess in front of the man. Empty cup. Wadded napkins, wet with sweat and blood and spittle. Puddles of coffee beading on the stainless-steel top.

"You spilled more than you drank," said Clyde. "No refills allowed if you got the shakes so bad you can't lift the cup to your lips."

"Where does it say that?"

"The fine print. It's time for you to go, joe. They have all kinds of fancy coffee shops in the Ventura Districts."

"I didn't come for the coffee," said the man, just as one of his sweaty hands darted out and grabbed Clyde by the wrist. The man's grip was so tight and cold it was like being grabbed by a corpse. "I came for you, Clyde."

Clyde, his heart suddenly hammering, had to jerk his arm twice to free himself from the gray, sweaty hand. As he backed away and wiped his wrist on his apron, he glanced up at Helen and Patti to see what they had seen. Nothing, or everything—he couldn't tell.

"Refill, please," said the man.

"What the hell do you want?"

"You know what I want."

"I don't know a damn thing, joe."

"Refill."

Clyde stared at the man's sick little smile until the man clasped his hands together and lowered his gaze. Clyde wondered how the man knew his name. Had he heard Helen or Patti use it? He tried to trace back the conversations and then gave up because it didn't much matter. Whether he heard it or knew it before he came in, this V-District bastard was nothing but a finger of doom pointing right at Clyde's face. Clyde hesitated a moment before he picked up the soiled napkins and threw them in the basket. He took a rag and wiped the counter sparkly and threw the rag in the basket, too. Then he filled the man's cup with coffee.

"Thank you, Clyde."

Clyde immediately headed to the sink beneath the middle of the counter and scrubbed his hands raw with soap and a brush.

"It took you long enough," said Helen when Clyde came back with her coffee and a Toddle House bag, which he placed alongside the cup.

Helen pushed the bag to the side, gave it a pat, and lifted the coffee to her lips. The steam rose across her face like a soft filter on a camera lens, blurring the lines carved by her hard life, turning her breathlessly young again.

"You look tired," he said quietly after she put down the cup, and the weight of age returned.

"Not for long," said Helen.

From the Toddle House bag she took out a green pill. She stared at the pill in her right hand as if contemplating her own existence in the shimmer of jade. Clyde leaned forward to pull a water glass from beneath the counter. Patti hunched over, as if protecting her pie. The lunger on the far side of the counter held his coffee cup in his right hand without making any effort to drink from it. The four of them stayed stock-still, as if within a somber ill-lit painting and Clyde, for a moment, felt they had all been there, just like that, forever.

Helen broke the spell by swallowing the pill. She downed it with a swirl of coffee before Clyde could fill the water glass. Patti stabbed the pie and shoveled in a forkful. The lunger shook the coffee to his lips, spilling more than he took in.

"Good as new," said Helen before she looked up at Clyde's face and then traced his gaze to the man sitting at the other end of the counter. "Who's the lunger?"

"I don't know."

"Poor thing, but he shouldn't be here, spreading it."

"There ought to be a law," said Patti.

"There is a law," said Helen. "The Toddle House law, right up there on the wall."

"Damn lung-chucking, law-breaking lunger," said Patti.

"But it was Clyde who served him," said Helen. "I guess you could say it was Clyde who broke the Toddle House law."

"Are you two having fun?" said Clyde.

"You know what they should do?" said Helen. "They should send them all packing, just sweep them off the streets and boot them into the D-Lands."

"That's the ticket," said Patti. "Let the zombies have at them."

"You might as well leave a sick baby in the desert to die," said Clyde.

"Figures Clyde would take their side," said Helen. "We all know he's got a soft spot for lungers. Don't you, Clyde?"

"Are you done with that pie?" said Clyde.

"Not yet," said Patti.

"Well, hurry it up. I need the seat."

"The place is empty."

"The night rush is coming. Finish and scram."

"I got to go anyways," said Patti as she forked the last piece of apple filling smeared with sweet cream. "I got that thing to work on. How much do I owe you?"

"Ten fifty."

"Right, right, yeah." She reached into her pocket, pulled out a bundle of bills and change, spread it out on the counter. "I got four, five, five fifty-eight, five fifty-nine."

Clyde pulled it in like it was a poker pot. "You'll owe me the rest."

"Thanks, Clyde. You'll think about it?"

"The thing for Hooper? I thought about it already. No. Never. No."

"Maybe you'll change your mind."

"Smarten up for once."

As Patti shambled out of the diner, Helen fiddled in her purse and took out a cigarette. Clyde pulled a pack of matches from his apron and snapped one into fire.

"What's Patti up to?" she said after she took that first delicious drag.

"Trouble, as usual, but not any trouble that involves me. You coming over tonight?"

"If you want."

"I want."

"It could be late."

"Just wake me up. Am I paying this time?"

"You're paying."

"Someone ought to make an honest woman of you."

"Who?" Helen's laughter rose like a cavalcade of balloons. "You?"

"Why not?"

"Don't tell me you love me now, Clyde."

"What the hell does that have to do with anything?"

"You're the last of your kind, the man with one true love."

"That's long gone."

"Sure, Clyde. But let's not forget what we are, on both sides of the counter."

"You know what, Helen? Someone ought to make a less honest woman out of you."

She paid in full and left a tip. Helen always left a tip, not that she didn't get it back in the end. He watched her go, her arched back, her thin arms swinging, her head high like she knew something. What the hell had that whole exchange been about? Had he just proposed to a mawk? Krist, it was the Ventura lunger that was getting to him, knowing his name, smiling that smile. Just his presence in the diner changed all the damn equations.

The man turned to look at him from the other side of the Toddle House and lifted his cup.

"Refill, please."

7
LYDIA

Once the government started subsidizing the wages of workers in guaranteed jobs to keep employment full, it needed assistance in paying the government's own employees. President Krist was the first to find responsible corporate citizens willing to do their share in rebuilding the nation. Since then, private-public partnerships had become an essential component of the new economy. Poultry inspectors subsidized by Tyson. The Securities and Exchange Commission subsidized by J.P. Morgan. And the narcotics boys in Chicago bought and paid for by the good-health folks at Balthazar Pharmaceuticals.

That right there for Clyde was the problem.

Clyde held a white Toddle House bag against his tattered black raincoat as he hurried along the gray city street, filled with night-shift workers heading home on foot or bus or bicycle. Neon slashed through the darkness, heralding this cheap bar or that residence hotel offering refuge from the sweepers. It was a pinched economy, never resting, fueled by guaranteed jobs, three shifts a day filling the never-satisfied demand for work. And from the windows up and down the street and high in the residence towers came the dancing light of the eternal blue eye, blinking and winking out its entertainments as it kept watch over the city.

Clyde stayed close to the brick walls, avoiding the cones of arbitrary brightness spreading out beneath the street lamps, practicing a modicum of stealth as if someone were following. Someone probably was. Every time a Homeland Guard gunship cruised overhead with its blinding spotlight, he reeled into shadow.

That damn V-District lunger.

***

"I'm dying," had said the man after Helen left and they were alone in the diner.

"Congratulations," said Clyde.

"I'm dying fast and I was told you could help."

"Oh, I'll help all right, joe. How about a double order of onion rings topped with chili and cheese. That ought to put you over."

"I was thinking of something smaller, redder."

"Who the hell are you?"

"The name's Dunlap. I know your name, I figure you ought to know mine."

"What, they don't have any pharmacies up there in the Ventura Districts? You can't get hold of the fancy drugs no one down here can afford?"

"Those drugs are not berry."

"So you came to the Toddle House hoping to find the most illegal thing in the whole damn city on the menu."

"The fellow I was seeing on the west side got closed down two nights ago."

"It's tough all over, joe, but there's no berry here."

"That's not what Amber said."

"Who?"

"Are we telling jokes now, Clyde? I have a joke for you: my last lung X-ray. The radiologist called me a leopard."

"I've got nothing for no one I don't know."

"But you know me. My name's Dunlap. Amber sent me."

"I don't know any Amber."

"Sure you do, Clyde. You live with her."

"I live alone."

"In a house. With her daughter."

"I live alone."

"I'm dying, Clyde."

"Join the club," said Clyde. "You just have a head start on the rest of us."

But there was something in the man's eye that put the whole thing over, some well of good humor, like his condition was just the latest of all the jokes that had been played on both of them in this life. The lunger didn't look at Clyde like a customer, not like Helen looked at him or he looked at Helen, and he didn't look at Clyde like most V-District bastards looked at Clyde, as if he were a blank piece of bark. No, the lunger looked at Clyde like they were fellow travelers, despite their dissimilar places in the new economy. Look at what we're doing here, the man's eyes said. Look at the games we're forced to play. The joke's on us, it has always been on us, and the only thing for it is to do what we have to do, with the resignation of the damned.

Clyde had made the sale—twelve tiny pea-shaped husks, shriveled and cracked, pathetic little things halfway already to dust—and had charged the V-District wahoo a wad and a half.

But now, on his way home, he avoided the spotlights and scanned the street behind for some of the Balthazar-sponsored narcotics boys. Ever since the zinc mine, he had promised himself to be safer than safe, to only deal with those he knew, but that was blown now all to hell. If they weren't following him yet, it wouldn't be long.

***

He turned off the main road and tucked his chin as he made his way along the uneven walks of the side street. The houses in this part of town were two-story clapboard jobbers, set on narrow lots with barely a shoulder's width between them, ill lit, weathered, sad with age and neglect. They had been built as single-family houses in a different era, and then were carved into multi-family dwellings to accommodate the influx of workers from the disincorporated territories. But now single apartments were too pricey to afford on guaranteed wages, so the apartments had been whittled again into tiny rooms with a shared bathroom, telephone, and kitchen.

The guarantee against homelessness didn't guarantee a palace, but a room of one's own kept you out of the clutches of the sweepers charged with keeping the streets clean and the LCMs full.

Lydia was waiting for him in the shared kitchen when he came home. The table was covered in oilcloth, the white paint on the cabinets was chipped, the yellow telephone on the wall tilted unevenly, the air smelled of boiled cabbage and burned oil. From the closed doors of the rooms along the hallway he could hear the muffled sounds of televisions droning. Lydia, small for her thirteen years, sat at the table with a book. She was swathed in flannel, her hair loose, her eyes shining unnaturally, as lovely as a spring morning someplace other than here.

"What are you doing up?" said Clyde.

"Just reading."

"You should be sleeping."

"I'm not tired, and I like to stay up late when I can. At night, when the others are sleeping or watching their shows, I can just drift along with my book and the sounds of the words in my head and it's like I'm drifting on a raft in the center of a cool, clean lake."

He took a bundle covered with wax paper out of the bag. When he opened the streaked white door of the communal refrigerator to put the bag away, a waft of rot greeted him. The racks were littered with wilted vegetables, spoiling milk, half-eaten sandwiches, the leavings of unsatisfactory meals shoved down during commercial interruptions.

"I brought two eggs, a cooked hamburger, and a roll for your breakfast. Where's your mother?"

"I don't know. I think she met someone. She put on extra perfume after her shift today, so she may be out on another date. She's had a lot of dates lately."

He took a small plate, put it on the scarred linoleum floor, opened the wax paper and dropped onto the plate three chunks of raw ground beef. A thin black cat with a white face and one white paw appeared as if summoned by magic. The cat rubbed Clyde's leg as it slipped toward the plate. A sniff and a lick and it started in on the meal.

"I need to talk to your mother," said Clyde.

"I'll tell her, Clyde. I don't know why you don't take her out on dates. She's pretty, isn't she? And she likes you, you know that. You two would be such a wonderful match. And then I could have a room to myself and read all I wanted without my cough bothering anyone. Wouldn't that be wonderful, Clyde?"

"I'll make you some tea."

He filled the kettle from the sink, put it on the rusting gas stove to boil. From one of the cabinets he took out a mortar and pestle.

"Mother bought some cookies and put them in the jar," said Lydia. "Only one a day, she said. I'm not very hungry—I had apples for dinner—so you can have my one with your tea. I've been saving it for you."

"I ate at the diner. You have it."

"Are you sure?"

"Sure I'm sure."

From his pocket he took out a Toddle House bag and dumped its contents into the mortar. Four little desiccated berries. He looked into the bag, shook out what dust remained, and started grinding the dried berries into a pale-maroon powder.

"What you reading now?" he said.

"Something by Jane Austen. Mother got me the book from the library. That's a funny name for a writer, isn't it? Jane. Charles is the name of a writer, Herman or Henry David. Jane is a nurse, or a horseback rider, don't you think? I have a friend Jane in school, but she's not allowed to come by. There are lords and ladies in the book, and big houses, and lots of food. So much food. The main character is Elizabeth, with big brown eyes, like cow eyes, I suppose. She's a bit of a prig, but my guess is she'll get married in the end. In the books I want to write, the hero will always get married in the end. That's just the way it should be in a book, don't you think, Clyde?"

"I don't read much."

"Did you ever?"

"Just comic books."

"Reading is the most wonderful way to spend the day when you can't get to school."

"No school today?"

"This morning the cough got worse the harder I tried to quiet it. And then, with the doctor's appointment I had this afternoon, Mother told me just to stay beneath the covers and cough it out."

He poured the pestled powder into a chipped teacup, filled the cup with boiling water, put in a spoonful of sugar, then another, stirred. He filled a second cup from a flask in his pocket and brought both cups to the table, along with a white cookie from the cookie jar. He pushed the cup with the steaming pinkish liquid toward Lydia and placed the cookie on its saucer.

"Just like high tea in merry old England," said Lydia.

Lydia lifted her cup with two hands and held it there. Clyde lifted his with his pinkie out and they clinked before she began to drink.

"Yum," she said.

"What did the doc say?"

"I'm not getting better," said Lydia.

"That's too bad."

"But I'm not getting worse, either. The X-rays aren't changing. He says it's like a miracle. It is a miracle, isn't it, Clyde?"

"Sure. A miracle."

The cat jumped up onto the table, dropped into its haunches, and started licking its paws. Lydia sipped her tea, wincing at the bitterness even with the sugar. She put the cup down, took a bite of the cookie, broke off a small piece, and fed it to the cat.

"What did my mother do this time?" said Lydia.

"She's going to get me killed."

"She means well, Clyde. You know she means well. She just gets confused. I'll make sure she talks to you."

Just then Lydia's cup began to rattle in its saucer. The cat jumped off the table as if being chased. Clyde and Lydia looked at the rattling cup, then at each other, then back at the cup until Clyde reached out gently and touched its rim, quieting the rattle.

"Don't," he said.

"It just happens."

"You can't let it just happen. They don't like things that are . . . different."

"But I am different."

"Quiet. Mrs. McGillicutty is right down the hall. People talk, you know that."

"All except you, Clyde. Is your friend coming tonight?"

"Yes."

"I'll be quiet. I'll try not to cough. I know I make her nervous."

"No, you don't."

"I make everyone nervous. I actually like it, the way all the busybodies back away when I cough. It's the only time I don't feel small. It's like I know something they don't know. And I do. I'm going to be swooped up and saved like in one of your comic books. But I don't make you nervous, Clyde. Why not you?"

"You're just a kid."

"No, I'm not. I'm fourteen. Well, almost fourteen. And that's not a kid. Juliet was almost fourteen when she married Romeo. Did you know that, Clyde?"

"No."

"See?"

"And you remind me of someone," said Clyde.

"What was her name?"

"Cecily."

"Did you love her, Clyde?"

"Sure I did."

"Was she the love of your life? I bet she was. I bet it was wonderful to be in love like that. To hold each other and read each other poetry. Love sonnets. You know there are fourteen lines in a sonnet, just like Juliet was almost fourteen. Do you think there's a connection?"

"How would I know something like that?"

"What happened with you and Cecily?"

"Finish your tea and go to bed."

"Whatever happened to the love of your life, Clyde?"

8
TUNNEY'S

There were moments when Clyde caught the merest intimation of what the world could offer, and it tore at his heart.

His bed was so narrow that on the nights Helen stayed over she ended up crawling like a bug atop of him in her sleep, her leg over his hip, her breasts pressed into his chest, her lips on his neck. It wasn't an expression of love and connectedness, just a contorted grab at comfort on too small a bed in the too-hard night. But still, Clyde, staring into the darkness, could imagine that in another time and place the woman with her lips on his neck would be motivated not by comfort but by love, and that the fear in his gut would be replaced by some mute satisfaction of what he had made of his life.

It wasn't too hard to imagine, it wasn't too much for which to ask, and yet it seemed as if the whole of what the nation had become was driving him away from such a moment, blocking him and shoving him and ripping it from his grasp. As if there were a grand conspiracy of fate and man to keep him right where he was, droning and desperate with a job that didn't pay enough, in a room that wasn't big enough, with a mawk instead of a lover in his bed, stuck dead in a life that was limited at every turn.

No wonder he hawked on the fat cop's burger.

Slowly, carefully, like a child undoing a chain-link puzzle, Clyde extricated himself from Helen's twining limbs and slipped out of the bed. The room was so narrow he had to walk sideways between the bed and the chair, where he had left his white shirt and bow tie, to get to the bureau. He pulled open a drawer and pulled out a pair of black pants. When he was fully dressed, he slapped a slouch cap on his head.

Sometimes when Helen stayed over, if he stayed quiet and didn't beg, he pulled himself a freebie in the morning. But this night he had to meet a guy and he doubted she'd still be there when he got back. Too bad, because these days rolling around the sack with Helen was the only thing that eased the ever-tightening knot in his gut.

***

With full employment, and the three-shift system of guaranteed jobs, the Illinois Liquor Control Commission, subsidized by Pabst, allowed the city's bars to stay open all hours. It didn't make sense to close up at two when the night shift had just been whistled off work at midnight, not as long as there were workers still desperate to drink away their wages in joints as raw as Tunney's Tap.

"Hey, it's the Toddle House man."

"Yo, Clyde."

"Hey, boy."

"Where you been, Clyde?"

"Didn't think you'd make it tonight," said Patti, sitting morose and alone at the bar, three empty shot glasses surrounding her mostly empty glass of beer. "Not when Helen slipped into the diner. Since when do you have enough for her and a drink?"

"I'll have enough when you pay me the five bucks you still owe me."

"I'm a little pinched."

"Not too pinched to buy yourself a drink or four."

"A woman's got to breathe."

Tunney's Tap was a crowded storefront bar with an Old Style sign hanging over the door, like every other bar in the city. It didn't look like much from the outside, and on the inside looked like less. The wood on the tables was scarred by cigarette and knife, the green painted plaster on the walls was pitted and flaking, the long bar itself was rubbed pale by elbow and rag. Ripped upholstery, flickering neon beer signs, a skittery jukebox filled with sap songs approved by the RCA-subsidized music censors, the smell of piss coming from the bathroom. But the space was ill lit and thick with smoke, so it had that going for it. The only things that worked like they should in Tunney's were the taps and the cigarette machine. Home.

"You see Hooper?" said Clyde, shouting over the pallid strains of the latest croon on the jukebox.

"He's here somewheres," said Patti. "In fact he's been looking for you."

"I don't doubt it."

"You think about it more?"

"No."

"Thanks for nothing."

"This place is lousy with termites who would jump at the chance for an easy score."

"They're all losers."

"True."

"And all they know about alarms is setting them off. Buy me a drink."

"Get lost."

"I told you I was pinched."

Clyde slapped a fiver onto the bar and signaled Tunney to bring over a round. When the beers came, along with their little brown companions, the two old friends lifted their shot glasses.

"Fuck yourself," they both said before downing the shots and banging the glasses back onto the bar.

Clyde picked up his beer glass and his change. "I need to find Hooper."

***

He elbowed his way through the crowd—his crowd, the very neighborhood crowd that had been following him all his life. He had gone to school with this same group, or with their kids, drank with them, screwed most of the women at one time or another, fought with most of the men at one time or another. He had been coming to Tunney's Tap since before he was legal, and its very familiarity was like a bone caught in his throat.

Hooper was holding court at a table in the corner, making time with Marie, one of Cecily's friends, who Clyde remembered as a stick-thin waif running around the neighborhood with pigtails and a frog. Now she was all curves and lips and explicit willingness.

"Hi, Clyde," she said brightly.

"Get lost," said Clyde.

When Marie left, hurt face and sassy hips, Clyde took her seat across from Hooper. Hooper's hair was short, his jacket was plaid, his tie was narrow, his glasses were tortoiseshell. You could tell he was happening even without the gold watch or the toothpick in his teeth. He was three years younger than Clyde, which somehow always pissed Clyde off.

"I was wondering where you been, son," said Hooper.

"It just took me a while, is all," said Clyde.

Hooper took out an emery board and started in on his nails. "That's what I figured. We always know where to find the Toddle House man. Let's have it."

Clyde took a wad of bills from his pocket and started peeling off twenties.

"And the vig," said Hooper, checking a cuticle. "Don't forget the vig."

"It's there."

"I'll believe you." Hooper scooped the bills and, without counting, stuck them into a plaid pocket. Then he went back to his nails, a rub here, a dash there, working on them like it mattered. "What do you think of Marie?"

"Nice girl."

"I hope not too nice. I'm going to make her ears bleed tonight."

"Your singing ought to do it." Clyde leaned forward and lowered his voice. "I need more."

"Good luck on that."

"You know I'm good for it."

"Where you been, slim? The narcotics boys have been slamming down hard on anything berry. Two of our runners on the north side just got penned, which means we're already out what they owed."

"But you still have some."

"Some, sure. But with the heat, and with the way Raden's new boy has been squeezing our supply, the price has shot through the moon."

"What kind of new boy?"

"Some middleman Raden set up to run his trade in the city. The heat is on and supplies are scarce and getting scarcer. Here on in, it's all up front."

"Where does that leave me?"

"Shit out of luck, son."

"Look, Hooper. I made a new contact. A District contact."

Hooper's disinterested gaze rose from his nails. "How did someone like you meet up with someone like that?"

"A mawk in the same house as me set it up. He'll be back and he'll bring his rich lunger buddies, too."

"Intriguing."

"We're sitting on something big here, a whole new market, and the prices we can charge them Ventura wahoos—Krist, Hooper, if you can hook me up with Raden's new boy, or front me enough to get this new line going, we can sit back and watch the money pour in."

"How much will you need?"

"Bushels. You help me set this up and I'll cut your piece extra thick."

Hooper considered for a moment, his face working like a calculator before it spit out the answer. "No can do. Raden has set limits on my amounts and my markets. He plays the tune, all I can do is dance to it."

"My main chance comes in and you're dumping all over me."

"That's life, son. Some of us are here to fuck Marie, and some of us are here to be shit on. You got the wrong end of the stick, is all."

"Okay, fine." Clyde sat back in exasperation, took out his wad, started counting, and then just tossed it onto the table. Everything left from what the Ventura lunger had given him. "Just let me have as much of the berry as this can buy."

"You're not getting it," said Hooper. "What I got is spoken for. You've always been small-time to me, Clyde. I know you only got into the berry for the kid. I'm a sentimentalist, so I let you have a bunch or two on credit, but sentimentality only goes so far with the narcotics boys or with Raden. The heat is on, I can't do retail no more, and you, son, are definitely retail."

"I'm not your son."

"I always liked you, Clyde."

"Now why are you lying to me?"

"Because there might be a way to work out an arrangement. For the good of the girl, you know."

"Spill, you creep."

"Is that nice? Here I am trying to help and you're giving me the evil eye."

"Spill."

"Well, you see, there's this car."

9
BLOWOUT

The bus from the border town arrived at Raden's camp just as the sky darkened, pulling into the yard with repeated bleats of its horn—a prison bus, painted green, with cages over its open windows. The men charged out of their cabins hooting, shooting guns into the air. They lined up along the bus's flanks, sucking their teeth, sucking in their guts, as the women pounded the cages with their fists and called out come-ons learned from the hard streets. The driver sounded his horn a final time before yanking the lever that opened the door. And so it began.

As the women, one by one, stepped down from the bus, partners were grabbed without much howdy-do, and there was a humped moment of quiet when the first, most urgent necessities were taken care of with a fast spit and a quick double thrust. Then the men hitched up their pants and the women opened any bottles handed to them and the party suddenly exploded in all earnest.

A band played outside the dining hall, loud and fast and sweaty. The beer was cold, the fires were lit, the goat was sliced, the women

danced like sirens in the yard. Before long the rousing beat was punc-
tuated with gunfire and screams, the crunch of fistfights, the squeals
of naked women running for their lives, peals of laughter, roaring
motorcycles spinning around the yard, shrieks of horror and delight,
the crackle and bang of Roman candles thrown into the fire, detonat-
ing with fountains of sparks that burst into the sky and blotted out the
stars themselves.

And in the middle of all the mayhem and madness, Kyrk hiked
onto his cycle and drove it with a couple of whoops all around the yard,
and then right up to where Culbert was sitting morosely by the door to
the cabin of Raden's girl.

"How is it?" said Culbert, his voice blurred by what he had been
smoking. "Krist, it sounds wild."

"Hog wild," said Kyrk. "There's a girl with tits so big you're fighting for air the whole time she's riding you. And she's riding you, let me
tell you, like you was a Harley and she had someplace to be. I swear
if I didn't come hard enough to blast her off my carcass I would have
strangled right there in my socks."

"That's the way I always wanted to croak it, with a tit stuffed down
my throat. What's her name?"

"Sheila."

"Big Sheila."

"She's waiting on you. I told her Culbert's the one for her."

"Can't hardly. I'm on watch."

"I'll take over," said Kyrk, climbing off his cycle. "Go on."

"I can't. Garth said—"

"That flamer? Who the hell cares what he says? We got hot and
cold running girls out that bus and he's probably mooning over some
movie-star photo in his cabin, and not no girlie one, neither. Take your
ride and hurry on back. I'm tired and my back aches. That Sheila, she
plum wore me out. I could use the rest."

"I don't know."

"Go on, fool, afore I change my mind."

Culbert closed his eyes and imagined those magic breasts choking the life out of him, and without even realizing it he was rising from the chair. As Culbert staggered toward the party, Kyrk spit red and sucked crimson teeth and watched him go. Then he pulled a knife from his pocket, clicked it open, turned to the door and leaned his head upon the wood.

"Knock, knock," he said, a song in his voice. "It's you-know-who. We been circling this for a while, you and me, but the time for circling is through."

***

Culbert was curled asleep around his chair when the camp stuttered to wakefulness under the rising eye of the sun. The bus was still parked in the yard; the goat, still on the spit, was a burned carcass of bone. Garth stepped around the sleeping lug and knocked on the door, once, twice.

"You in there?"

No answer.

He kicked Culbert and then the wood of the door before opening it wide and discovering the truth of things.

Kyrk was sprawled in a drying puddle of blood on the floor. His eyes were glassy, his feet were bare, his holster was empty, his bike was missing, and Raden's girl was gone gone gone.

10

MISSING

"They can't find your sister," said the guard Handler in the mechanical shop about a week after the fight with Gaston.

Moonis, holding a wrench the size of a salmon and with his forehead smeared with grease, rolled himself from beneath the old Ford combine, a squat red thing with an external seat and a bent threshing wheel in front. The shop was a riot of hammer clangs and the screeching of drills bearing through metal. It was almost time to bring in the wheat they had planted last fall and the shop was in the final throes of preparing the machines required for the harvest. The combines they used in the LCMs were piles of crap held together with bobby pins and spit, and the spit keeping them together in this LCM was primarily Moonis's.

"They track family of the laborers in the office," said Handler, squatting down beside Moonis. The guard rubbed his long jaw and looked to the side, while continuing to speak low enough so that he couldn't be overheard among the grinding and banging. "Policy, you know. Keeps the grip tight. I got hold of your file and it turns out they can't find your sister."

"What are you doing paging through my file?"

"I told you I'd look out for you."

"They made a mistake. My sister has a guaranteed teaching job on the north side of Chicago."

"That school told them Cecily Fell, she ain't filled that job since last year."

"Then she's at another school. She's a teacher."

"Not anymore, at least not according to the district records," said Handler. "She vanished from their books, and the feds don't have no record of a guaranteed job for her since she left the school."

"Last I heard from her she was still teaching, complaining about some principal, like usual."

"That's a long time to be out of touch."

"I thought it best to make myself scarce to her. The government thinks discontent can be catching."

"I'm sorry to have to bring you the bad news," said Handler. "I just want to help, like I said. If there's anything else I can do, you let me know."

Moonis watched Handler saunter away and then slid back beneath the combine. He fitted the wrench onto the lug he had been working on and kept it there for a moment without twisting. That son of a bitch Handler, poking uninvited into his file. And those sons of bitches in the office, poking uninvited into his sister's life. It was enough to make him want to bite someone's head off.

But when he started thinking about his sister losing her job and disappearing, his heart started charging and he had to close his eyes. He saw Cecily the way she was when their mother left, the skinny little thing who sat quietly by Moonis, holding in the tears with her certainty that her big brother would always take care of her. And he had intended to, more than anything in the world, until the world got in the way.

But maybe it wasn't the world. Maybe that deranged Canadian was right and it was nothing but his pride, his foolish damning pride, which caused him to start his little fights with everyone who looked at him aslant. And what had all that pride gotten him? Nothing but a ticket to a metal boot, while Cecily worked herself so hard she thinned into vapor. He started counting all the ways he had failed his sister and then stopped when the self-loathing grew strong enough to close his throat. He took the wrench off the nut and threw it out from under the combine as hard as he could.

The wrench spun wildly across the cement floor before it slammed against something flush and stopped dead, accompanied by an anguished howl that rose as if from the very bones of Moonis's sorry life.

***

The Dean was shuffling paper in his office when they brought Moonis in. A bluff, thick man with a red face, the Dean was really a warden, but that sounded so penal, and it was repeatedly stated in public pronouncements that the LCM system was not about punishment but instead about teaching the benefits of hard work to those still doubting its importance to the nation. Thus it was not Warden Reischel who lifted his gaze to take in the grease-smeared figure before him, but Dean Reischel, with his kindly eyes and unlit pipe. Sometimes he even wore a corduroy jacket with patches at the elbows.

"Moonis," said the Dean. "Good to see you. Sit down. That's fine, you can go," he said to the guards, waving them out of his office. "Sit down, son. Sit."

Moonis dragged his booted ankle toward the chair, dropped down, rubbed the wooden arms of his chair nervously.

"There was a little trouble in the shop, I hear. Some nonsense about a wrench flying crazily across the floor?"

"The thing slipped out of my hand like it was alive," said Moonis.

"These things happen. Don't you worry. No harm done, except for Preston's leg, but he's a worthless idler anyhow. So what can we do for you, son? More books? A little extra ration? Maybe we can transfer Gaston to a different center, if that would make you more comfortable, after the unfortunate episode in the barracks. Just tell me what you need and we'll get it for you."

"I need to be released," said Moonis.

"I see, yes. Any particular reason why?"

"A family issue."

"You're an orphan, aren't you?"

"My father's dead, yes. My mother I don't know about, I haven't seen her since I was a kid. But I have a sister."

The Dean looked at Moonis, opened a file on his desktop, took out a paper, and examined it. "We don't have a record of you receiving a recent communication from your sister. No letter, no phone call." He paged through the file. "In fact we don't have record of anything from her in over a year."

"That's the point, Dean. I'm worried about her."

"Any reason why you should be?"

Moonis considered spurting out the whole Handler story about information in the file and then thought better of it. It didn't pay to play the stooge in camp, especially with a guard. And if the file noted Cecily as missing, then the Dean certainly knew it. "I just think she's in some kind of trouble. I need to help if I can."

"Well, Moonis, we appreciate the family feeling in Archer Daniels Midland LCM 204, we surely do. We all love our sisters. Why don't you come to see us after the harvest and we'll talk about trying to get you in touch with her then. But right now, we can't let you go."

"How has my behavior been, Dean? What kind of laborer have I been?"

"Excellent, Moonis. You're a maestro with an engine. We don't know anyone else who could keep our combines and tractors running like you do. That's why we're willing to provide you with any comfort you might seek. In fact, we were thinking of arranging a visit to the women's LCM down the road for a few of the boys after the harvest. Wouldn't you enjoy that?"

"I've done the calculation," said Moonis. "With the amount of overtime I've logged, and with the service award I would be due based on your recommendation as to the excellence of my work, my term should already be completed. Pursuant to Title 18, Section 179, I'm entitled to leave once that happens."

"No need to quote statutes, Moonis. We're friends here, aren't we? We don't need statutes coming between us."

"I'm here because of a statute."

"You're here because you need to be retrained. And your retraining is going quite well."

"Then let me go."

"Why don't we agree to talk about this after the harvest? The company is putting tremendous pressure on us. Our yields have not kept pace with their expectations."

"The combines are crap."

"We have a quota to meet."

"Which your bonus depends upon."

The Dean's kindly eyes crinkled like the cracking of surface ice on a frozen lake. "I'm sorry, Moonis, but as much as we all care about family bonds, we just can't spare you."

"But I have the right to—"

"You have the right to work. Under the Grand Constitution of the New American Government, that's the only right any of us have. Had you learned this before, you wouldn't be here now. If you want to quote statutes, we can quote statutes. Section 179(d)(2) allows us to extend your term of service in the forced-labor system for certain violations of LCM protocols. And we've been keeping an especial record in your case."

The Dean took a paper out of the file, ran his finger down the page.

"Oh, my," said the Dean. "Insubordination, thievery, gambling, assorted acts of violence, severe language violations. Did you really say that to one of our guards? Is that act even possible? And we'll have to add your fight last week and today's unfortunate incident with the wrench. I must say, I'm shocked at all this, Moonis, shocked. These infractions could add at least a year to your term, enough to cover two more harvests and a winter planting. And based on this information, I might have to change my overall evaluation of your service to 'unco-operative,' which would add even more time. Do you now understand your situation here?"

"Yes, I do," said Moonis. "Quite clearly."

"See what happens when two reasonable people reason out their issues? You are making such excellent progress that it would be a shame to halt the retraining midstream. Now, Moonis, we've been having trouble with the clutch of the '71 John Deere."

***

Sitting on the chair outside the barracks door, bathed in yellow light, a book in his hand, Moonis paged through the volume without reading the words, all the while fighting to keep down the bile.

It wouldn't do this time to give in to his pride and do something stupid, no matter how satisfying. It wouldn't do to burn down the Dean's office with gasoline cribbed from a combine. It wouldn't do to wring the Dean's fat neck until his eyes bled prettily. Every time Moonis had failed Cecily, it was because he had jumped for the easy satisfaction over the harder, more uncertain road. Each time before, he had felt gloriously self-righteous in burning down his life and yet she was the one who had suffered the consequences. Like she was suffering now while he wasted his days in this damn labor camp. But if she was in trouble, then he wouldn't fail her again, not this time, not today.

"Cigarette?"

Moonis looked up to see Gaston standing in the doorway, offering a pack of the Gauloises. "You learn your lesson?"

"No, but harvest is coming."

Moonis took a cigarette from the pack, leaned into the light Gaston offered, breathed deep the harsh taste of someone else's freedom.

"If you were going to escape from this little slice of heaven, Gaston, how would you do it?"

"Pride again?"

"Something more pressing than pride."

"Sex then?"

"Family."

"Too bad. Sex is the better reason, except maybe sex with family, which would be the best of all."

"I keep forgetting you're Canadian."

Gaston stood there for a bit, smoking, considering. "Escape, it is simple, yes," he said finally. "Just run off during the harvest. We are so spread out, there is no one to stop us. But then, of course, to where would we run? There is nothing out there but more labor camps and more fields. The city is far and the D-Lands are worse than this place without doubt, unless it is death we are running to. And with the ankle shackle slowing us down, they would undoubtedly grab us before we reached our destination. I think an escape attempt from here is futile at best, a meaningless gesture and nothing more."

"I've always been a great admirer of the meaningless gesture. Anything else is just plain expedience."

"But I have found that violence," said Gaston, "it almost always helps. If you kill someone, everything changes."

"How so?"

"If you kill a man in a labor camp, they must by law send you back to the city for punishment. The ankle weights are just for the LCMs. In the city you would have normal shackles, which are far simpler to crack compared to the boots. And then, while they are moving you back and forth from courthouse to jailhouse, if you grab a stone with a sharp edge and smash in the head of a guard, then maybe you can run to a whorehouse with a friendly madam named Ethel, then to the basement of a warehouse by the shore, then pay your way onto a cargo ship moving back and forth across the lake, and jump off in Canada where an old girlfriend with thick lips and breasts like kumquats she waits."

They smoked together in quiet, Gaston in the doorway, Moonis letting the plan sink into his bones.

"Kumquats?"

"Nothing wasted."

"You've thought about this," said Moonis.

"A little maybe. Now and then."

"And all you need is a willing victim to kill."

"Yes, that is the catch." Gaston spent a moment quietly with his cigarette before saying, "You perhaps want to play another game?"

Moonis laughed and shook his head. Across the yard he saw Handler leaning on a fence post, smoking, staring at the two of them.

The guards at the LCM weren't federal agents with all their hard-edged training, but instead rent-a-cops hired by the corporate sponsor. Some of the hired men used the uniforms and guns to puff up their chests; you crossed them, you crossed their inflated self-images and there was hell to pay. But most were a decent sort, just trying to get through the day without losing their guaranteed jobs, like everyone else. Some even went out of their way to talk civilly to the detainees, to let them know they were all in it together.

Handler, however peculiar he might be, was apparently one of the good ones. In his own twisted way he wanted to be helpful. But they weren't all in it together. Handler got to sleep outside the gates. Handler got to screw his wife on the couch at night. Handler didn't have an Oregon boot clamped to his ankle making every step an agony. And yet Handler's desire to be one with the labor gang, his sad need for solidarity, could be a useful thing.

Gaston's plan of violence was as unhinged as his chess game, but Moonis began to see a way out based on Handler's equally unhinged desire to be helpful. He plotted the steps in his head like in a chess game—bam, bam, bam—with each move inducing Handler one space closer to where Moonis needed him to be. It was devious and unfair and dependent on exploiting some kernel of spiritual need in the guard, but it laid out as clean as a flagstone path across a sylvan field.

He leaned back in the chair, leaned his face into the book, read the words mindlessly as he worked it out. For it to succeed, Moonis couldn't initiate anything; he had to keep his head down and wait. He would lie back until Handler, feeling cloaked in his goodness, with his own agenda of redemption, approached him.

Moonis didn't expect he'd have to wait for long.

11

HARD RED WINTER

Moonis Fell trained as a mechanic at McGraw-Hill Guaranteed Secondary School 774. After his selection, he had expected to study physics in the Ventura District school to which he had been assigned, had even spent the summer in the library reading book after book on the subject. But before the end of the eighth grade, when he was unceremoniously shipped back to his public school in Chicago, which only taught skills useful for guaranteed jobs extant in the city, he discovered there were no jobs requiring knowledge of quarks or theories about the big bang.

So instead of learning about the clockwork of the universe, Moonis learned everything there was to know about the inner workings of your basic internal combustion engine. He had spent years in school and in guaranteed jobs, as long as he could keep them, with his head beneath the raised hood of an automobile or underneath the chassis of a truck, sometimes working dawn to dusk without ever seeing the sun. Now, in the bright afternoon, beneath a cloudless sky, he sat atop the red Ford combine as it churned through a rippling sea of amber wheat stretching to the far horizon. The wild expanse of it filled him with joy.

Floating through this beauty, a red bandana over his mouth to keep wheat dust from his lungs, somehow felt like freedom to him, no matter how absurd the concept might seem to outside eyes. Yes, he was a forced laborer in an LCM with a shackle on his ankle, yes, he was here to be reeducated in the hard truths of hard work, yes, he was little more than a slave in the great machineries of the nation and Archer Daniels Midland. But still, being here, in these fields, on this machine, was the inevitable result of all his choices and, instead of raging against his fate, he accepted it with an open heart.

And, he had to admit, he loved it, all of it: the work, the tractors and combines, the fields. He somehow felt that in tilling the soil, planting the seeds, watching the earth split apart to deliver its bounty, he was finally playing a role in the great game of the universe. He should have been a farmer. He would have been a good farmer, at least before all the farms were snapped up by the agricultural trusts for the benefit of the nation.

But as he moved forward atop the combine—slowly, elegiacally, rolling through these fields of wheat as he harvested and threshed—he also looked about with a touch of sadness. The law allowed only two terms in an LCM before more serious methods of reeducation were applied, and he was already on his second stint. After today, no matter how it turned out, this pleasure would be taken from his life and never would he be allowed to taste of it again.

In the distance he spied a long dusty tail make its way across the dirt road toward his field, led by the truck to which it was attached. The guards did a regular round of checking on the laborers. Every hour or so they drove into the fields, stepped out of their trucks with their rifles, and made notes of the progress and any mechanical difficulties. It was the responsibility of the guards to make sure the laborers were meeting quota.

Now, as the truck approached, Moonis took the combine out of gear, raised his goggles, lowered his bandana, and waited. The truck turned and headed across an already-harvested portion of the field right up to the combine. When the truck stopped, Handler stepped out with a rifle in one hand and a clipboard in the other. He spat a crimson blob to the side; a long string of red saliva dribbled from his lips.

"I'm well ahead of schedule," said Moonis loud enough to be heard over the idling engine. "I've been riding this combine like a neighbor's wife, relentlessly and with much satisfaction. Did you get it?"

"Like I said. But it wasn't easy, I'll tell you that. And with the secretary coming back sooner than I thought, it was a closer thing than I wanted."

Moonis slid off the seat and climbed down the ladder affixed to the side of the combine. He propped his left foot on the front tire and waited as Handler fished a key out of his shirt pocket and handed it, headfirst, to Moonis. Moonis slid it right into one of the two slots in the huge oval ankle weight, turned it, and did the same in the other. When both locks were undone, he laid the key on the tire and pulled the heavy lead thing apart. The pieces thudded onto the dirt.

"Hot damn," said Moonis. He slid the iron brace from around his boot, turned, and threw it as far as he could into the field. "That thing is a curse on the world."

"A combine's going to get jammed on that."

"Hell if I care."

"There's a car waiting for you on the main road, a blue Chevy. My brother-in-law. He don't talk much, but he's all right. He's got a change of clothes for you and he'll take you to the other side of town. From there you're on your own, but there are always semis heading north to the city. My brother-in-law, he'll give you an address to send the money."

"And I'll send it, too. You know I will."

"I do know it, Moonis. But I'm not doing this for the money. You find your sister. You find her and take care of her. We need to take care of our kin. That's a religious thing beyond the understanding of the Dean and them others. I got no choice but to help."

"You don't know how appreciative I am, Jim," said Moonis. "Thankfulness is welling through me like a golden wave of sunshine. You don't expect to find people like you in a place like this."

"Be grateful enough not to get caught. I need to get back before they miss the key. My rotation gets me to the office before the next guard shows up here. By the time the alarm is sounded, the key will be safely locked up and you'll be on your way."

"That sounds fine as cake."

"Go on, now."

Moonis tossed off a smile before he took a step away from the combine into the tall stalks of wheat, and then another step, and then quickened his pace until he began to run. His left leg pained him with every stride, but even so it felt so light without the metal boot it was like he was flying through the sheaves.

The very act of running, along with the strange impression that freedom itself was spreading out like a path before him, filled him with a sensation spiritual in nature. This whole skein of events, from the fight with Gaston to the disturbing news about his sister to this brilliant opportunity for release and redemption, was seemingly linked by a force far greater than himself. And as for Handler, the strange, betel-chewing Handler, who had been so easily led to this point by Moonis's carefully laid-out series of gambits—bam, bam, bribe, bam—it was almost as if Handler had been doing the leading, guiding Moonis to this very point. As if Handler were part of some great plan at work in the churning maelstrom of the universe.

Moonis turned in the middle of his headlong run to wave fond farewell to fate's sweet emissary. And there he stood by the combine, Handler, in his brown uniform, the rifle now raised into shooting

12

RUNNING GIRL

Scarves of dust floated across the roadway until torn asunder by the wheels of the racing motorcycle. The racket of the engine fell onto thicketed fields all about, flushing twists of birds into the flat gray sky. A single track stretched vastly behind as Cecily Fell reeled in the flat ribbon of ruined road.

The past, with all its treachery and false idols, was receding with ever greater velocity even as the future remained wholly indistinct. Cecily was caught between the dead and the yet unborn, surging forward in a cocoon of nothing but noise and wind and speed. Her mouth was dry, her hands were cramping, her boots, too big for her feet, rested on the motorcycle's pegs. She leaned forward, squinting through aviator sunglasses as the wind rushed across her face and whipped her hair.

Every few moments she glanced into the round side mirror. Except for the track of her tires, the road behind was empty of any sign of humanity. They would expect her to head east, flat east, back to the incorporated territories and some semblance of safety. But what safety was there for her in Moline? Raden owned the border town, and swaths east all the way into Chicago. And Raden was shutting off the berry faucet. There was only imprisonment and rape, or sickness and death, back there for her. The single way for her was to head deeper into the D-Lands. With every mile chewed through on the motorcycle, she grew ever more lost to them.

The sun told her she was headed someplace west and south, which was all she needed to know. At the intersections of rural roads she turned first left, then right, and then left again to make her trail harder to follow. Where exactly she was going wasn't any longer important. Away was important. She felt like she was outracing fear as well as her past, and it felt good, it felt right; her cocoon in the midst of speed itself felt safe.

Until the engine sputtered and kicked and died and she coasted to a sad stop by the side of the road.

***

She rolled the bike forward, ever forward. The metal monster that had seemed hopped-up and alive as it roared along the cracked and pitted road was now a dead sack of cement unsteadily perched on two narrow wheels as she struggled to keep it moving.

It wasn't like she had forgotten about gasoline. She had checked Kyrk's tank before leaving—it was mostly full—and she had taken what cash was in Kyrk's pocket to buy herself some more. She'd thought by now she'd have found a station still pumping, but each town she passed through—miserable carcasses that once sported generic names like Conesville, Columbus Junction, Winfield, Fairfield—was as deserted as the next. The filling stations were all dead, the few vehicles on the road had already been siphoned dry. Only the occasional face on the wrong side of a shattered window, staring out as she motored by, let her know the ghost towns contained more than ghosts. But no gasoline.

Her tank had emptied about eight miles southwest of what had once been Libertyville, on a stretch of road going nowhere and taking its time doing it. She thought of turning around and trying to find someone to help in the small town she had just passed through, but thought better of it and kept going. Distance was safety, and this narrow rural road was as anonymous as dirt. If she could find a place to hide out and wait, maybe look for a safe ride to someplace farther away, she might outlast Raden's search.

But the going was slow and her feet, loose in Kyrk's oversized boots, were forming blisters that felt as large as toads. Leaning the bike against her thigh, she lifted each leg in turn and pulled off the boots. She fitted the boots in the gap between the seat and the rear tire guard and pressed them tight.

As she pushed the lifeless hunk of metal forward, shards of the dead land dug into the bare soles of her feet.

***

There were a few dented cans of vegetables in the farmhouse's pantry. She used the knife Kyrk had been holding to slash the top of a can of green beans, then tilted the can to her lips, drinking deep the sweet salt of the packing water inside. It was lovely, the taste, after all the dust and effort, even as it made her all the more thirsty.

The farmhouse was long deserted, its glass windows still intact but its porch overrun with vegetation and its yard prairie-like with tall grasses. She left a slim trail of blood from her sliced and bruised feet as she walked through the empty rooms with their faded furniture and bare floors. She found an abandoned pair of girl's shoes with little black bows, too small to fit her wounded feet. Above a useless sink and a rusted soap dish sat a cracked mirror with the silhouette of a young woman at its crown. The face staring back at her through the fractured glass was as inscrutable as a mask. The faucets in the house were dead, the propane tank in the rear was empty, and whatever wasn't canned in the pantry had been scattered and devoured by rodents. She had seen a raccoon ambling away, fat and unhurried, when she had leaned the bike against the propane tank to keep it hidden from the road, so there might have been some other food scraps still around, but nothing she wanted to hunt for.

Tired, she set a chair by a window with a view of the road and forced open the sash to get some air. She stuffed green beans into her mouth as she kept watch. The bright afternoon was thick with the sound of birds and the rustle of small animals beneath the floorboards. It wasn't anything like the monstrous disincorporated lands that used to terrify in her nightmares. In the quiet she imagined a life out here, wandering from abandoned house to abandoned house, picking abandoned pantries clean, finding abandoned shoes that fit, slipping into abandoned clothes left for the moths.

She'd be one of those wraithlike figures peeking through the windows in the small farm towns she had passed through. Every day would be an adventure, every day would be a treasure hunt. Concerned only with finding food and shelter and water and gasoline, no longer would she be struggling to reach some grand height in order to salve a childhood wound. No longer would she scramble madly to rise and become something new because her mother had left her and her brother had failed her. She had forever been defined by the inviolable levels in the incorporated territory. What would she be, free of such a system, without all the feverish striving? She closed her eyes and let the possibilities wash through her and smiled in her sleep.

She jerked awake at the sound. Something on the road, something coming, something loud. She slipped down off the chair, peeked her head above the sill, braced for the sight of an army of motorcycles.

But what she saw was an old pickup with a blown muffler and rounded lines, blue, battered, covered with dust. It was coming from the direction in which she had been headed. As it passed, she caught a glimpse of the driver, old and gray with a trucker's cap perched awkwardly on his head. She watched the truck pass, watched the plume of dust behind it rise and fall.

***

About three hours later, in the fading afternoon light, the truck made its noisy way back along the very same road. Cecily was now behind a tree on the roadside opposite the house, waiting for just that truck. She peeked around the tree, saw the truck's battered blue body with its headlights like kindly eyes coming toward her. She pushed herself to standing, removed the sunglasses to show off her eyes, and stepped out from behind the thick brown trunk. She waved the truck down with a little shake of her hand.

The driver veered the truck to her side of the road, stopped, looked her up and down, smiled. Cecily couldn't help but flinch at the sight of him. His teeth were long in his mouth, his cheeks ghost-white, his eyes hollow.

"What are you doing all the way out here, missy?"

"I suppose I'm a little lost," she said.

"I'd say. Where you headed?"

"I don't know."

"More than lost then, aren't you? What happened to your shoes?"

"Gone."

"I suppose you're hungry, too."

"I could eat."

"You're just a bundle of good news, aren't you? The name's Millard."

"Cecily."

"There's a market about forty miles away or so, up the road to a big old oak and then to the left. Only one in the territory. Set up by them folks at Yeager's farm. They don't got much variety, but it's mostly fresh what they got, and not glowing, so you'll keep your teeth. You can get some provisions if you got money. I'm just coming back from there."

"Pick up anything good?"

"They save the spoiled stuff for me, because it's what I can afford. When did you last eat, Cecily?"

"I had some green beans not too long ago."

"Old, pale beans from a can, I'd bet. And before that?"

She shrugged. She didn't want to say too much. She just stood there, one knee pointed at the other, and waited. The way to play it with a man like Millard was not too hard or fast. The way to play it with a man like Millard was to let him make up his mind.

"I know better, and I'm already regretting it," he said finally, "but get on in if you want and I'll fry you up something."

"Are you sure, Millard?"

"No."

"I won't be any trouble."

"So you say. Now, it won't be no feast. I'm not much of a cook."

"I'm sure you're pretty good."

"You just stay sure until you start the eating. You can spend the night in the barn, if you need to, but then you got to go. Okay, Cecily? You don't want to be hanging around, not near me."

"No, sir."

"I live alone for a reason. Out here it's better living alone. No telling what someone else brings with them."

"Yes, sir."

"You don't got the sickness, do you?"

"No."

"You look bright-eyed enough. Come on, then."

She didn't move, just stood there, looked down and then along the long road ahead of him.

"What else is on your mind there, Cecily?"

"I've got a motorcycle."

"Well, that's just something, isn't it? And no gasoline, I'd reckon."

"No."

"You got any money?"

"Some."

"Some will do," he said, with a long-toothed smile.

13
BROOME OF THE SYSTEM

Captain Broome's boot heels clicked sharp as a thumbtack in the eye as he strode into the Toddle House. Tall and pig-faced—the remarkable porcine man, with a corkscrew dick, no doubt—he was preceded by two Guardsmen, who flanked the front door as he entered.

Broome's entrance was the most pomp that Clyde had seen at the diner since the mayor stopped in on his way to reelection. "Just here to press the flesh and maybe grab a nightcap," had said the mayor with his grotesque politician's smile when he appeared, accompanied by pale-faced aides and a slew of photographers. A picture of Clyde in his bow tie standing with the mayor, a frosty-white milk shake between them, had made the inside pages of the *Tribune*. But Clyde suspected that this visit by Broome, in his black uniform with twin silver bars, shiny boots, and the insignia of the Homeland Guard on his hat, would not end with flashes and handshakes.

"What can I do you for, Captain?" said Clyde, avoiding looking into Broome's cold gray eyes. When dealing with rabid dogs and Homeland Guardsmen, it was best to avoid eye contact.

"Coffee," said Broome. His voice was as soft as cold eel in jelly, crushed like autumn leaves under a predator's foot.

"Pie with that?"

"Just the coffee, Clyde."

"Coming right up."

There were two other customers at the counter, a mechanic in his overalls eating a hamburger, and a woman fully dressed in her shabby best, nursing her tea to kill a slab of the night. By the time Clyde came back to the counter with Broome's coffee they had started the process of detaching themselves from the diner, shoving in burger and slurping down tea, pulling bills from wallets to pay the check. Clyde would have beat them out the door if he was on the other side of the counter.

"How long have you been working here now, Clyde?" said Broome when they were alone.

"About six years."

"Ever since you got back from the camp?"

"This was the guaranteed job they set up for me."

"How do you like it?"

"I like it fine."

"I bet you do, putting the feed bag on every shift, no doubt. And it pays for the roof over your head. A job, a home, a full stomach. What more could a man want?"

"Nothing."

"That's right, nothing." Broome rolled the dial on the toothpick dispenser, picked up a toothpick with his blunt fingers, worked the pick between his molars. "So maybe it didn't work out so badly, nabbing you for that phone thing like we did."

"I think of you every day."

Broome took a sip from his cup, put it down, stared at it. "Did you spit in my coffee, Clyde? It tastes more bitter than usual. Like you added your bile to it."

"It's the beans."

Broome pushed the coffee away, slowly, until the cup and saucer tipped over the counter. Clyde didn't move to catch it, didn't even wince at the smash-splash, or as the hot coffee spattered on his pant leg.

"I think you spit in my coffee, Clyde," said Broome.

"I wouldn't do that, Captain."

"Why not? I'd spit in yours."

"I'll get you another cup." Clyde turned to pull a cup off the rack, took it to the two great urns.

"There was an unfortunate incident in the northern Ventura District last night," said Broome, and when he said it the cup beneath the brown flow from the urn began to tremble. "A break-in at one of the houses in the Newport Estates development. Do you know the place, Clyde?"

"The District is Greek to me, Captain. I didn't grow up in it like you did."

"A large carport on the property was opened from the inside and a car was stolen."

Clyde kept his gaze down as he brought the coffee to the counter. "Have some cream, it cuts the bitterness."

"A blue Lamborghini. The way import licenses are today, the car is quite rare and very valuable." Broome took the stainless pot of cream and poured. The curls of white swirled like a storm. "The neatest trick was the way the alarm was bypassed. The alarm company said the wire splices were so beautifully done it was almost like a work of art. You studied electrical circuitry at school, didn't you, Clyde?"

"What do I remember from back then? I'm just a hash-slinger now."

Broome took a sip of the fresh coffee and nodded. "Better. You going to clean up the mess?"

Clyde stood there for a moment, trying to figure what mess Broome was talking about, before he nodded and headed to the storage room off to the side. He came back with a broom and dustpan and began to sweep up the shards of cup and saucer.

"Funny thing about the theft," said Broome. "They reached the carport through the main house—more like a mansion, I suppose. The place was filled with art and silver and all kinds of jewelry in the upstairs bedrooms. Gold, diamonds, a veritable fortune. They took none of that. They were only after the car."

"Dumb thieves. Who would have figured?"

"But the most telling note was in the kitchen. It's a beautiful kitchen with all the latest appliances. They have one of those Amana Radaranges that can boil a brain inside a skull. And the fanciest refrigerator on the market, a big commercial-grade unit. And here's the thing, Clyde, and I know you'll like this. When we checked out the inside of the fridge, some of the stuff had been eaten. There were gnawed-on chicken bones, a handful gouged out of a peach pie, a bottle of beer open and half-gone."

"Only half-gone? That tells you right there the joes weren't from this neighborhood."

"Not joes—joe. There was just one thief in the kitchen—we can tell from the footprints on the carpet. Just one."

Broome looked at Clyde as if there was some significance in that fact, like there was some significance in all these facts. Clyde stooped down to sweep the shattered china into the dustpan and dump the pieces into a can. Still beneath the counter, he pulled out his flask and downed a swallow.

"This was maybe after his confederate left with the stolen car," said Broome, "leaving the one thief to wander the house. I can see him walking around, touching this, touching that, like he was in a museum. Can you see it, Clyde?"

"Not from down here."

"I wonder what he was thinking. Do you have any idea, Clyde, what he was thinking?"

"Probably wondering where the beer was," said Clyde, as he wiped the coffee-stained floor with a towel.

"Right you are," said Broome, "because he ended up in the kitchen. And when he was finished with his feast from the refrigerator, he did the most extraordinary thing. There was a cake on one of the lower shelves, a big birthday cake, all frosted up, white and sweet and covered with buttercream roses. And get this, Clyde, the son of a bitch pissed all over it."

When Clyde stood up, Broome was staring straight at him.

"Why would he do something like that, Clyde? I can't wrap my mind around it."

Just then the door pressed open and an old woman walked in clutching a heavy bag. Broome swiveled on his stool, one of the Guardsmen shifted over to stand in front of her. The woman stopped, eyes suddenly alert to the danger, and slowly backed away, closing the door behind her. Broome turned back to Clyde.

"Can I freshen that coffee for you?" said Clyde.

"Coffee only, right, Clyde?"

"Coming right up."

As he refilled the cup, Clyde wondered why he had pissed in that big silver refrigerator, turning the white buttercreamed dream cake into a yellow soggy mess. What had driven him to it? Something about wandering about that house in the bright light kept on to deter burglars, the spaciousness, the paintings on the walls, the silver picture frames framing the smiling perfect family, the fucking perfect family, the fireplaces, the ceilings so high, the privilege so evident. He wasn't feeling a bitter envy so much as a disgust. In the midst of all that excess, that nauseating glut, the only sane response was to piss on the cake.

"Anything else, Captain?" said Clyde when he came back with the coffee. "The pies are good."

"Do you have peach?"

"No peach this time of year. At least not for us."

"Too bad. Sometimes a man's got a hunger for peach pie." He took the cream and poured more into the cup. "They didn't get away with it. Turns out it was too much car." He took a noisy slurp of the coffee. "On the way out of the District, the guy driving the Lamborghini accelerated into the wrong turn, lost control, and slammed into a post. Totaled the thing. It's kind of funny when you think about it. That car was worth a hundred thousand dollars, and all those idiots got was a ten-minute joyride."

"Idiots is right."

"The car was empty when the private guards came. The driver must have been picked up by his confederate, the pissing man. But based on the blood we found, the driver broke his nose on the steering wheel. You see anyone with a busted-up nose lately, Clyde?"

"Can't say as I have."

"I actually thought I'd see you with a bandage across your face."

"Sorry to disappoint you."

"We still can't figure out how they got in or out of the District, but we're working on it, checking out the photos from the entry gates. I'll be looking at them personally. It's only a matter of time."

"Keep at it, Captain. As they told me over and again in the LCM, hard work pays."

"One more thing. In the busted-up Lamborghini, along with the blood, we found this." Broome slipped open a pocket from his jacket, pulled out something white, slapped it on the counter.

A Toddle House bag.

"Any idea how it got there?" said Broome.

"Read the signs," said Clyde. "Our hamburgers are world-famous. People often take them to go."

"How about the marijuana that was inside? Is that to go, too?"

"We only sell what's on the menu. You want waffles, we have waffles. You want tuna salad? Ham salad? Meatloaf? Pie? We have anything you want, so long as it's on the menu."

"It will be tough on anyone we pop for the crime. A full term in an LCM at the least, more if it's a second stint. You know, Clyde, maybe I'll jack you into the station, grab a sample of your urine, compare it to the yellow buttercream we bagged from that cake. Unless, of course, I don't."

Clyde's eyes narrowed. Broome was playing him, dribbling out the facts of the aborted theft drop by drop. Clyde had assumed Broome was searching for a reaction, a tic of guilt to expose itself on Clyde's features. But Clyde had been wrong about that. The whole time Broome had pretended to hold all the cards, but he really held nothing. And he needed something. That is what it meant when a Guardsman was suggesting that he might do you a favor: he needed something from you and he needed it bad.

"What are you looking for, Captain?"

"Other than peach pie?"

"Yeah, other than the pie."

"You hear from Moonis lately?"

"Moonis? Moonis Fell? No. Hell no. Last I heard he was on that LCM downstate. What does he got, another year at least?"

"He won't be getting out at all when we find him."

Clyde started laughing but stopped when Broome trained his pale death's-head gaze on him. "You lost Moonis?"

"He escaped," said Broome.

"Don't they boot them down there?"

"Oh, they boot them all right. He found a way around it."

"He always was a bit too clever for his own good."

"Not that clever. He murdered a guard to get free."

"Moonis?"

"Drove over him with a combine."

"Our Moonis?"

"The guard's head popped off in the thresher and was carried up the conveyer. They found the ugly thing atop a load of winter wheat."

"Imagine that."

Broome pushed his coffee away, and kept pushing until it crashed onto the floor. He rolled the dial on the toothpick dispenser, five, six times, grabbed what came out, and stuffed the picks into a pocket.

"You let me know if you see him," said Broome as he stood.

"You can count on me, Captain," said Clyde.

Broome headed to the door and then stopped, turned around. The smile on his face was as cold as his eyes. "Just so you know, and maybe to encourage your cooperation, it was Moonis."

"It was Moonis what?" said Clyde.

"Who tipped us off about the phone hacking, who landed you in an LCM. It was Moonis."

"No, it wasn't."

"Something about getting you away from his precious sister."

"Go to hell."

"Ask around about him," said Broome. "See what the word is on the street. Find him for me."

"And if I do?"

"Maybe the Lamborghini thing will remain unsolved."

"What do I care about that?" said Clyde. "It was just a pleasant story to me. But, Captain, I know this girl—just a kid, really—who's got the lung disease, bad. Her mother can't afford the Balthazar drugs, and I was wondering—"

"No."

"I thought you might have—"

"You screwing her, Clyde? You pumping it to that little girl as she coughs blood on your neck? There's nothing hotter than a desperate lunger."

"She's just a kid who caught a bad break and—"

"You make we weep."

"I don't want you to weep, I just want it done. You've been after Moonis for a while, haven't you? You've been out for his blood more than half your life."

"Find him for me, Clyde, and I'll get the girl all the Balthazar cocktails she can handle. I'll get her the newest and best. You find him and I'll cure the hell out of your little friend."

"And what will happen to Moonis?"

"You know exactly what. And truth is, Clyde, after all we've been through, him and me, you can't say he doesn't have it coming."

14

TODDLE HOUSE MAN

As Clyde left the diner at the end of his shift, white bag clutched close, his long black raincoat draped over his white shirt, bow tie, and anger, he thought about what he had agreed to do for Broome.

Clyde was so used to lying to cops and Homeland Guardsmen that to find hard truth you could simply take every word he said to the bastards and turn it inside out. He had absorbed the rules of the LCM in his gut and they were simple and inviolate: avoid the sick bay, don't lick your plate, and never turn snitch if you don't want a shiv in your gut. Moonis and Clyde went back farther than sin and they were both stuck on the raw side of every deal. Turning in the likes of Moonis Fell would cross every line he had laid down in his soul, so of course he had been lying.

But Broome had said that it was Moonis who ratted him out and the story made enough sharp sense that Clyde immediately believed it to be true. What the hell then did he owe Moonis Fell, other than the tip of his boot? Not a damn thing. If Clyde actually did find Moonis, they'd have to drag Clyde's hands away from the son of a bitch's throat for Broome to have the satisfaction of killing Moonis himself. Clyde was shuddering at the sweet sensation of Moonis's neck collapsing beneath his angry fingers when he heard: "Are you the Toddle House man?"

Clyde stopped and turned and stared. An old geezer leaning against the wall of the diner lurched upright. The man was clean-shaven—his clothes were a step above the neighborhood average—but there was something wan in his appearance, something desperate.

"You're the Toddle House man."

Clyde didn't remember serving the man and wondered what the old man wanted, until the geezer started hacking away and Clyde grew sick with the knowing.

"I got nothing for you," said Clyde as he started to flee—not running, because running would draw attention on the streets—but walking with a determined stride. "Nothing."

"But you're the Toddle House man," said the old man, following now. "I have money. Lots of it."

Those six words would have normally stopped Clyde in his tracks, but not tonight. "It doesn't matter."

"You know what I need."

"I have nothing for you," said Clyde, keeping his pace even as the old man fell back.

"Help me, please."

"Nothing."

Overhead, a Homeland Guard gunship, its triple rotors slicing through the night sky, appeared with a rush of sound, painting Clyde for a moment in its hot white beam. He stood stock-still, as if pinned by the light, until it slipped behind him.

Clyde turned around and spied the old man now on his knees, looking into the sky, his gray pallor bleached by the gunship's spotlight. Clyde thought of turning back, helping the man up, dragging him to a side street before the sweepers got hold of him, but then what? He knew what the old man wanted, and knew he couldn't get it for him. They would take the old man eventually, maybe tonight, and maybe they'd take Clyde with him if Clyde stopped to help. Now was not the time to be taken. There never was a time.

Across the street, he saw a woman, old and sallow, raising an arm, hailing him as if he were a taxi.

Krist.

He ignored the hell out of her call as he veered off the main road. He took a roundabout way to the house, turning here, turning there, coming upon it with all his sly, as if the house itself were on the look-out for him. He lurked outside for a moment to see what new threats awaited. The small front porch was empty. The blue lights blinking from within the windows cast a spell of quiet on the neighborhood.

He slipped through the front door as quietly as he could. At the end of the hall with multiple doors on either side, he could catch a slice of the shared kitchen. Lydia was at the table, her book in front of her, drinking a cup of tea and talking, always talking. Krist, how that girl could talk. She was talking to her mother, no doubt. Good, he had a raft to unload on Amber. But not yet.

He walked quietly to his room, slid the key in the lock, slipped inside. The tiny, suffocating space was dark, the curtains were drawn, the television was on, the soundtrack of its turgid police procedural could barely be heard above the snoring. Patti was atop the bed, asleep.

Clyde snapped on the light.

"Huh? What?" said Patti, awakening with a spasm.

"I brought you a burger," said Clyde, tossing a bundle covered in wax paper onto the bed.

"Good. Yeah. Thanks." Patti, in T-shirt and panties and socks, kept her head as immobile as possible as she sat up on the bed. Her sharp nose was disjointed, her eyes were swollen black. Blood beneath the skin had purpled her cheeks. "I was just—"

"What did I tell you about the bed?"

"Yeah, yeah. I'll sleep on the floor tonight, but you weren't using it and my face hurt." She unwrapped the wax paper around the hamburger, grabbed hold, took a bite, spoke while she chewed. "Geez, I'm hungry. What about a beer?"

"What about it?"

"Any word on anything?"

"Broome came into the diner."

"For a hamburger?"

"You left your reefer bag in the car."

"I wondered where that was." She took another bite, then spoke while the mess of bread, meat, and pickle sloshed around in her mouth. "I'm going to need some more, by the way."

Clyde shucked off his coat, tossed it onto the chair, loosened his bow tie. "And Broome knows about the injury. He's probably got his minions out searching the neighborhood for a broken face."

"You think I can pass?"

"Holy Krist, Patti, you look like you've been kicked by a mule."

"What are we going to do?"

"Keep you here until we can get you out of town."

"I'm sorry, Clyde. I really screwed it this time. I'm so sorry."

"Yeah."

"It was the pedal, it was jerky. I was turning a corner and the car just kind of shot forward and next thing I knew I was off the road, heading for that tree. It was great, too, for a second, all that power. It was like flying. And then I wasn't flying no more. God, I could really use some reefer."

"You got any relatives somewhere not here who could put you up?"

"I have family in Minnesota. On a reservation. I'm a piece Chippewa."

"Get out of here."

"No, I am, really, like a full quarter on my mom's side."

"No, I mean get out of here and get up there. It'll be safer."

"There's nothing up there, man. There's a lake and nothing. I'd rather stay here."

"In my room?"

"Why not? A tube, a bed . . . well, a floor. What else is in the bag?"

"It's not for you. Hey, Pats, you hear anything lately about Moonis?"

"Moonis? No. Why?"

"Just asking."

"Moonis? What the hell does he have to do with anything?"

"I'm going to Tunney's tonight to see what's what. I'll fill you in."

"Hooper will be there."

"Better we find him than he finds us. Just stay quiet and in the room. First, I need to go to the kitchen, give a mawk a piece of my mind."

"You'll give her a piece of something, I bet."

Back in the hallway, Clyde could see Lydia still at the table, still yakking. He took a few steps forward and then stopped. Something wasn't right. She was quite animated in her conversation, like she was sometimes with him, but that wasn't the way she was with her mother. With Amber she was sullen, more exasperated than anything, but here she was sparkly and—

"Oh, Mr. Sparrow."

Behind him, from an open doorway in the hall, an old woman in a ratty robe, bent at the waist, gray as a ghost, was peeking her head out. With her size and posture, her head was no higher than the doorknob.

"It's a little late for you, isn't it, Mrs. McGillicutty?"

"I was staying awake for you, Mr. Sparrow."

"What did I do this time?"

"You know we all share a single toilet down here. We can't do much about the smell, but it is impolite to spend too much time in any one session, no matter the difficulties. It's been hard to get in all day. And really, with the way the walls have been built, every grunt and obscenity can be heard clearly throughout the hall."

"Grunts and obscenities?"

"This is just common courtesy."

"I only got back from work five minutes ago," said Clyde.

"Oh, I know it's not you, Mr. Sparrow. It's your friend."

"My friend?"

"Staying in your room, listening to the television, hogging the lavatory. The raccoon. And you know the policy on guests."

"Yes, I know the policy on guests."

"I could report you."

"I appreciate your discretion, Mrs. McGillicutty."

"Now if you could be so kind as to—"

"Of course."

"And she should wear a skirt in the hallway, too," she said, clutching her robe ever tighter. "Walking around in just her underthings. There is propriety."

"I'll tell her. Who is in the kitchen with Lydia?"

"A man."

"A policeman?"

"Oh, no, just a man. And he was looking for you."

"I bet he was," said Clyde. "Thank you, Mrs. McGillicutty."

"I'm just trying to be helpful, dear."

The old woman's head disappeared and her door closed and Clyde was left wondering whether he should head for the kitchen or straight out the door.

If it wasn't a cop or a Guardsman, that meant it was either a lunger looking for the magical Toddle House man, or one of Hooper's goons looking for payback over the busted-up Lamborghini. Hooper had spent a load getting the District passes for the heist, and he couldn't be happy about the results: money sunk, heat breathing down his neck, and no car. Either way, it would make more sense for Clyde to just turn around and beat it the hell out of there. But at the same time, he couldn't just leave whoever it was alone in there with Lydia.

He shucked his shoulders in preparation for something not good, not good at all, and then stepped forward.

"Well, it's about time," said Lydia as he walked through the doorway, her smile broad and devoid of fear. "We've been waiting for you. We're having tea. Do you want some tea? We all have so much to talk about, don't you think?"

"Hello, Clyde," said the man sitting across from her, leaning back in his chair, the cat sitting calmly in his lap as he scratched its back with one of his big hands.

And what Clyde felt just then was everything, the very blood of life: love and sadness and fear and hate, along with the bitter taste of all his pallid years. Clyde was speechless for a moment, hurled outside of this room and this moment by the shocking wave of emotion that rolled through him.

"Nothing to say, Clyde?" said Lydia.

"Hey, Moonis," said Clyde, finally and banally. "How are things?"

"Oh, just fine, Clyde. I'm feeling as dandy as a rich man at the opera."

"I heard you had left your camp."

"I suppose you did."

"What are you doing here?"

"Looking for you," said Moonis.

"That's funny," said Clyde, "because I was looking for you, too."

"Well, imagine that," said Moonis, his bright grin as wide as the poisoned Mississippi. "Fate is smiling like a baboon on us both."

And that grin was enough right there to spark all those emotions into the sweetest, most satisfying of rages. Next thing anyone knew Clyde was leaping across the table, scattering teacup and cutlery and cat, grabbing at Moonis's throat, feeling it squash like a sack of shit within the girdle of Clyde's livid anger.

15
LONG TOOTH

Cecily looked at her plate and felt a gag rising in her throat. Overcooked rice covered with a saccharine brown stew, accompanied by some slimy green concoction, maybe okra mixed with kale mixed with cow snot. The noxious quality of the food made her yearn for Paulo's ceremonial meals at Raden's compound, but Cecily didn't complain. She was actually touched by Millard's generosity.

"It's delicious," said Cecily.

"No, it's not," said Millard, smiling in the lamplight with those long teeth of his. "I know what good food is, and this is a crime. I used to go to a steak house in Springfield when I was still in a guaranteed job. I'd have to save up for months, but it was worth it. Cuts of meat as thick as a fist, and creamed spinach. I liked the creamed spinach, especially. Something about it made me feel like I was really living. Creamed spinach. Even the name is rich. But I lost my taste for the finer things. Spending too much time out here will do that. Now the only meat I get is what I kill. How's the stew?"

"Good."

"You lie pretty, Cecily. The stew meat's older than it should be—it's cool down in the basement, but not cool enough for the varmints to keep—though I cook it through and then cook it more to kill what's ailing it. How'd you find the shower?"

"Frosty."

"I pump the shower water right up from the creek, so it's best not to drink it. I tried to set up a way to heat the water, but the tank kept bursting. You get used to the cold."

"The creek is clean?"

"I been showering in it for a decade and I'm still here, and with most of my teeth, too."

Millard lived in a small one-room cabin in front of a grove of trees that had grown around a twist in the creek. The cabin smelled faintly of the sweet rot of old age. A barn that had once been red listed between the house and the water. Cecily's bike was in the barn, standing alongside two tanks, one for gasoline and a larger one for water.

"How long have you been here, Millard?"

"More than ten winters. I got tired of working for someone else, tired of being hungry and cold on guaranteed wages. Figured I could be hungry and cold out here without the work getting in between."

"Is it as bad out here as people say?"

"It's not good, I'll tell you that, and not easy. There's no law, no order, no convenience stores to sell you your chips. I miss the chips. And you got to make your own whiskey. But then again, there ain't no rich folk giving orders and making you feel invisible. Sometimes a man, he just can't take one more order, you know, before bursting. That was me."

"You sound like my brother."

"You got a brother? Does he know where you are?"

"He's in an LCM somewhere in downstate Illinois."

"That's too bad."

"I thought I'd wander a bit and then maybe look for him."

"Anyone else who might be able to give you a hand? Any of your people know where you are?"

"No one knows. No one but you."

"You're running from something, I can tell that."

"Yes."

"Well, don't worry. I'm not telling no one."

"I've made some mistakes in my life," said Cecily.

"That's the past. Here on in, let's say your slate is clean as the first day of school. Finish up and then I'll pour us some prairie dew, what I call my homemade corn liquor. I don't get many guests, so it's worth a toast."

"Thank you, Millard. You know, I was feeling bad about things, about the whole damn world. I guess you could say I made a mess of my life for all the wrong reasons. But to meet someone out here like you, someone who goes out of his way to help someone he doesn't know and without asking anything in return, it restores something."

"That's nice of you to say, but I ain't that noble. You'll be paying for your gasoline. They charge me enough for it."

"I wouldn't want it any other way."

"And you're sleeping in the barn, like I said. I get enough of that prairie dew in me and you looking like you do, you'll be safer out there. I'm not as old as you think. Now, about that snort."

He cleared the dishes into the sink, set a filled mason jar and two chipped teacups onto the table, and sat back down. With great ceremony, he opened the mason jar, took a sniff, let his eyes flutter. Then he poured the clear liquid into the two cups, about a shot and a half each. "Go on," he said. "Ladies first."

She had just lifted the teacup to her mouth when she heard the faint roar of distant engines, a pack of them.

She dropped the cup; shine dashed across the table.

***

They swarmed like bees, the beams from their headlights skipping across the house, the barn, the trees that surrounded the creek. When they finally cut their engines, they formed a circle in the space between the house and the barn. Millard rushed out of the rear door with a rifle in his hand and was promptly slammed hard from behind. The gun skittered forward as he fell. One of the men pulled him up by his collar while another pistol-whipped him twice. Millard was on his knees, blood pouring down his face, when Garth walked into the circle of light.

"Is she still alive?" said Garth.

"Who?" said Millard between gasps for breath. "What?"

"The bike's here," said one of the men. "In the barn."

"The cabin's empty," said another.

"Where is she?" said Garth again, his voice calm. "What did you do to her?"

"Nothing," said the old man, but his head turned slightly to the left and Garth turned his in the same direction, peering now into the dark woods.

"Is she out there hiding? From us?"

"I don't know."

"Oh, you are something, but you're stupid, too. You knew she was Raden's girl, you'd been told at the market. And yet you couldn't help yourself. What was the plan? Give her a hitch, give her a meal, ply her with your liquor?"

"I'm nothing but an old man," said Millard, crying now. "I didn't do a thing."

"Yet, maybe. Put a gun to his head, Paulo."

Paulo stepped into the circle of light and pulled a gun from his belt.

"Are you listening, Cecily?" said Garth, louder now, broadcasting his voice to the woods. "Do you hear? We don't mind you bashing in Kyrk's head—some people need a little bashing now and then—but you shouldn't have run. I told you not to run. I'm going to count to five, and if you don't appear, we're going to shoot this old bastard's face right off his skull. Ready? One."

The moment was soundless except for the old man's sobs.

"Two."

He didn't get to three before they heard a rustle in the woods. One of the bikers twisted his handlebars so that his headlight shone at the sound. And there she was, Raden's girl, coming through the trees, hesitant and haughty all at once. They all watched silently as she walked barefoot into the circle.

"Came to save the old man," said Garth. "That's almost sweet. You imagine yourself noble, I suppose."

Cecily didn't say anything. What was there to say? She had run, she had been caught, her fate was sealed.

"Follow me," said Garth. "I want to show you something."

Garth walked past the old man, still sobbing on his knees. Blood poured in a delta off the old man's scalp, rolling through one of the hollow eyes that stared up at her. *I'm sorry,* she mouthed to Millard before following Garth into the house.

***

She could see the anger in the hunch of Garth's posture. He wouldn't even look at her as he trooped through the living area of the small house, grabbed the lantern off the table, and headed to a door, which he flung open. The door led to a set of steps, narrow, dark, and steep.

"You think the bars we put on your windows were to keep you in?" said Garth, as he began to climb down the stairs, the boards creaking beneath his feet.

Cecily halted at the open doorway. Something didn't feel right, something didn't smell right. The sweet rot was stronger here, darker, fresher.

Garth stopped and turned his head to stare up at her. "You have no idea where you are," he said before turning again and resuming his descent.

Cecily didn't want to follow. She wanted to run, to madly flee from this man and this house and that smell. But something in Garth's tone dragged her forward and down, down.

"This isn't Chicago," he said when he reached the bottom and walked into the basement room, disappearing for a moment from the angle of her sight, even as his light spread across the dirt floor like a stain. "This isn't even Moline."

Left alone, she hurried after him, down to the dirt. Then she stopped and looked around and took a step back and then another until she bumped into something hard and slimy and she jumped and let out a scream.

"Welcome to the D-Lands," said Garth.

The basement was small, cramped, damp, windowless as a tomb, stinking of rot and death. And hanging from the rafters were things, long things that it took her a moment to identify in the dimness as carcasses—one of them swinging, the one she had bumped into. Each had a hook in its neck, each had its skin pulled free. But these were not the carcasses of deer, or rabbits, or hogs caught in thickets. These were the carcasses of men and women and the tender young. Some were mere skeletons with bits of dried meat still clinging to the bone. Others were halfway flayed, as if in some sort of scientific demonstration for the damned. The sight and smell and truth of it threw her to her knees.

"Your friend Millard is a hunter," said Garth, "and what he hunts is you. He uses his truck to pick up the lost and the wandering, poisons them with his prairie dew, lives on the meat and the spare change in their pockets."

A shot rang out from outside the house.

"At least he did," said Garth, "until he ignored the warning and put you in his truck. This is what is out here. This is what they have left for us in the disincorporated territories. Don't ever forget that the only thing between you and these rafters is Raden."

"I'm going to be sick."

"I don't doubt it," said Garth. "I saw the pots. How was the stew?"

***

After she had wiped the vomit from her lips, he took hold of her arm and led her up the stairs, through the main room of the cabin and out again through the rear door. Millard lay facedown in the dirt, half his head now blown away. Garth led her past the sight as if it were as simple a thing as a daffodil in the spring.

He took her into the center of the yard and stopped. Just outside the circle of light was a figure, so vaguely lit its silhouette was barely discernible against the night sky, but what she could make out was biblical in size, savage in stance. Goliath in the Valley of Elah.

"He's waiting," said Garth. "Go ahead."

And she did.

16
A LIVE-GROWING OAK

Three old friends with the weight of history and disappointment hanging around their necks were huddled together within the twilight between soft memory and hard reality. A garden of forty-ounce bottles of Pabst, most of the bottles now emptied, was planted among them, a dissolute nighttime tableau of low-rent liberation. They had grown up together, fought and laughed and raised hell together, and though they had failed separately, each of them, in a way they had failed together, too, because failure was built into the DNA of their lives, like puberty and death. And whatever thing it was that bound them together, it was forged within the walls of the building behind them.

"Who remembers that Mrs. Popolio, with the blue hair and the evil eye?" said Moonis, in a ribbed T-shirt over a pair of orange LCM work pants and LCM boots.

"Ninth-grade English," said Patti. She shivered and took a pull from one of the tall bottles of beer. "Tougher than boiled meat."

"I heard she was kicked out of the nunhood for being too severe," said Moonis.

"All that stinking grammar," said Patti. "Truth was, I never could tell the difference between a preposition and a Protestant."

"According to Mrs. Popolio," said Moonis, "the only one of the two it was okay to hang was a Protestant."

McDonald's Guaranteed Secondary School 774 was erected in an age of extravagant governmental waste. Built of brick and cement, designed with undue care and frosted with stern decoration intended to stiffen the spines of the youth within its halls, it had originally been named after a poet from the old nation, with grandiose ideas of what America could be. But in the grand march of progress the poet's name had been chiseled off the great granite lintel above the front entrance, replaced with a metal plaque denoting the current corporate sponsor. Beneath a single live oak growing all alone, the three friends, who had attended the school when it was named after a textbook publisher and not a hamburger stand, lay in the dirt or leaned against the trunk, shielded from the spotlights of passing gunships by the dark-green canopy.

"But what I don't get with your whole crazy story, Moonis," said Patti, who had slumped her way through the hallways of that building for six years, cadging cigarettes, blowing off assignments, slipping out to blow dope under this very tree, "is why that guard would spring you just to kill you."

"It's the golden puzzle, it is," said Moonis, "but I wasn't going to stop and figure it out right there and then with a gun pointed at my face. I dived into the wheat just as the bullet zing-zanged where my head would have been. And then he started laughing as he kept firing, firing, firing. He was firing at where he thought I'd be, under the reasonable assumption that I was racing away as fast as I could race. But running was never my way, right, Clyde?"

Clyde, sitting up against the tree trunk, had the same blond hair as the golden boy who had killed time in the classrooms inside that building until he could show up for football practice. He glared for a bit, like an angry jack-o'-lantern, before taking a long swallow from a big bottle. He was getting to the dregs, more warm spit than beer, but whatever beer was left he sure as hell needed all of it.

"You chopped his head off," said Clyde.

"I just put the thing in gear and set it on its way," said Moonis. "It was the combine that did the chopping."

"But Moonis had no choice if the guard was shooting," said Patti, her nose crooked beneath its bandage, her face swollen and black like a rotting fig. "It was, like, self-defense."

"Just like," said Moonis. "In fact, Patti, that's exactly what it was."

"See, Clyde, he didn't have no choice."

"We all have choices," said Clyde.

"I cheerfully admit to working like a fiend to escape that LCM," said Moonis. "But killing that guard was not part of any plan, just a pleasant necessity."

Patti laughed, a bray that caused Clyde to wince and look to see if it had been overheard. Patti and Moonis clinked their bottles.

"It doesn't much matter whether you planned it or not, does it?" said Clyde, his bitterness cutting through the laughter.

"To me it does," said Moonis.

"But not to him."

"No, I suppose not to him, but we'd be hard-pressed to consult him on the matter."

"And not to them, either. They're going to hunt you down and kill you, no matter what."

"They're going to try." Moonis slayed the rest of his bottle, tossed it to the side. "And tell me this now, Clyde. Are you going to help them?"

"They don't need my help. That Mrs. McGillicutty was on the phone the minute we left."

"An iron grip around my throat wasn't exactly the greeting I was expecting," said Moonis.

"What were you hoping for, Moonis, hugs and ribbons?"

"That would have been preferable. And thank you, Patti, for pulling him off my carcass."

Patti lifted her bottle in acknowledgment.

"But I should have known better when I saw Broome and you chatting like old friends," said Moonis. "I was coming to see you directly, when I peeked in the window of the diner and there he was. What were you two hatching?"

"Plots," said Clyde.

"Cemetery plots?"

"Clyde wouldn't do that," said Patti. "He's the last one that would plot with Broome. Clyde's stand-up."

"Are you stand-up, Clyde?"

"Sure I am," said Clyde. "It's just a matter of who I'm standing up to and what I'm standing up for."

Clyde drained the slurp at the bottom of his bottle, tossed it atop the other empties with a clank, and grabbed another. The forties had been cold when he picked them up at the all-night deli, but they warmed outside and warmed even more with the holding, so the key was to drink as quickly as you could once you opened one. He poured as much of the new bottle as he could stand down his throat, choked down his swallow, and banged the back of his head against the tree. He was feeling a swirl of emotions that were enough to give him a headache even without the beer.

"This place is smaller than I remember," said Moonis.

"They built a stack of apartments on the old football field," said Patti. "And then a Chinese place, another bar."

"But the building seems smaller, too."

"I bet it seemed tiny when you came running home like a little lost dog from that Ventura School," said Clyde.

"Coming back after the selection wasn't Moonis's doing," said Patti. "They booted him out, you know that."

"Things just never work out for Moonis, and it's nobody's fault," said Clyde. "Like the guard without a head. Nobody's fault."

"Drink some more beer, Clyde," said Moonis. "Maybe it will drown the bee buzzing up your ass."

"And it doesn't have a reason to be there? And I don't have a reason to choke you blue?"

"This isn't like you, Clyde," said Patti. "You and Moonis were like brothers, man. What's going on?"

"Rumor and innuendo."

"Not innuendo," said Moonis. "My God, Clyde, anything but innuendo."

"Broome told me it was Moonis who snitched on my phone operation. That it was Moonis who had me sent up to the LCM in Wisconsin. Is that true, Moonis?"

"Broome's an asshole," said Moonis.

"I know he's an asshole. No one knows he's an asshole like I know he's an asshole. But that doesn't mean it's not true. You know how cold it gets in Wisconsin?"

"If a Guardsman's lips are moving, he's lying," said Patti. "Why would you believe Broome?"

"Because it felt true," said Clyde.

"But it's not, is it, Moonis? It can't be. Tell him it ain't so, Moonis. Tell him."

Moonis picked up a fresh forty and twisted off the top. The bottle sighed sadly.

"Why would Moonis have done something like that?" said Patti. "I don't understand."

"Because I wasn't good enough for his precious sister," said Clyde.

"That's crazy talk, Clyde. Moonis wouldn't have done something like that for . . . Moonis, tell him you wouldn't have done such a . . ."

Moonis raised his bottle and let the beer flow in unimpeded glugs down his throat.

"He can't deny it," said Clyde.

"Oh man," said Patti.

"He isn't even man enough to lie about it," said Clyde.

"Things were complicated," said Moonis. "I was confused."

"Moonis, man, that just wasn't right," said Patti. "We take care of each other, we don't rat on each other to Broome."

"I know it," said Moonis. "Who knows it more than I know it?"

"What the hell are you doing here, Moonis?" said Clyde. "You're a wanted man, maybe the most wanted man in the state. And based on what that guard was up to, they wanted you dead even before you set the combine on his ass. Why bring your mess to us?"

"Because I need your help, Clyde," said Moonis.

"My help?" said Clyde. "Like I would ever help a betraying sack of shit like you."

"It's not about me, it's about Cecily. She's gone missing."

"She's got that guaranteed teaching job in Uptown."

"Not anymore. She's missing. I don't know why, I don't know how, all I know is that she's missing, and I need to find her. And I can't do it without you."

"That's a joke, right?"

"I was going to look for her myself, that's why I was running from the labor camp. But they're searching for me now, so I can't really go around in orange pants, asking questions, making waves."

"Buy a pair of slacks," said Clyde.

"I'll do it, Moonis," said Patti. "You just tell me what to do and I'll do it. I'll do anything."

"I know you would, Patti," said Moonis. "But you're on the lam yourself and your face right now is like a confession. I need Clyde."

"They're going to kill you, Moonis," said Clyde. "And if I'm helping you, they're going to kill me, too. It's not enough that you ruined my life, now you want to end it?"

"She's in trouble, I can feel it."

"Find someone else."

"I'll pay you."

"I don't want jack from you, joe."

"I spent my life never asking anyone for anything. And while that's gotten me nothing but spit, it still, for some reason, always felt like a fair trade. But my sister needs me now, and I need to change. So here I am, on my knees, Clyde, begging for your help."

"You're not on your knees, you're on your ass."

"I'm on my knees figuratively. I'm opening my raw need to you, Clyde."

"How does it feel?"

"Surprisingly good."

"Why me?"

"Because you love her. Because you've always loved her. And despite it all, Clyde, you are a servant of your love."

"No."

"Clyde?"

"Screw you, Moonis, no."

"Clyde?"

II
WANDERERS

17
SPADE WORK

Clyde put on a suit. It was an old suit, brown as bark. His mother had bought it for him before his criminal hearing. Fat good it did then. But when he came back from the LCM, there it was, hanging like a corpse in his mother's closet, along with all her faded print frocks and stockings scarred thick with darning. He only wore the suit to funerals and church, which meant he only anymore wore it to funerals.

Clyde couldn't find a tie without a stain, which bothered him not at all. He never liked ties, the way they dripped down like a napkin tucked into your collar. He knotted his Toddle House bow tie instead.

He slapped on his slouch cap and took it off again. That was a jockey's cap, fine enough for a cold night with a hot mawk, but this play needed something with authority. He still had his grandfather's fedora, a chocolate Borsalino with silk lining and the lingering scent of Aqua Velva. It had been jammed in the back of some high shelf when he cleaned out his mother's room. Its brim was as wide as the South Side. It fit the way he would have to dance to get this done right.

He couldn't be just some guy who worked at a Toddle House; to find Cecily Fell, he'd have to be the Toddle House man.

"Remember, you're not asking for me," had said Moonis from inside the dank hole they had buried him in to keep him safe. "You're asking as a friend, an old friend from the old neighborhood. You've been wondering what happened to her. You just want to make sure she's okay."

Not too hard a proposition, since Clyde was an old friend from the old neighborhood. Moonis had been his best pal growing up on the city's West Side and Moonis's sister had always been there, a thin, quiet presence that had barely registered until one day Clyde looked up and his heart seized as he realized that for no reason, and for every reason possible, he loved her. And Clyde wouldn't be lying when he said he wanted to be sure she was okay. From the first, that had seemed to drive his emotions, the need to care for and protect all of her—those thin legs, those narrow wrists, those sad, haunted eyes that seemed steeled for some dark future—to be the guardian of her wary dignity.

Cecily Fell. Crap.

The name meant something to him, like the sound of a prayer to a penitent or a sure thing to a degenerate gambler. She was the chipped plaster saint in the devotional corner of his soul. Cecily Fell. He put on the hat, adjusted it to shield his eyes. He hadn't known she was missing, but now that he did he was going to find her. It didn't matter what she thought of him anymore. He had loved her, and Moonis had asked it of him, and that was enough.

***

Clyde took the elevated train toward the Loop and switched to another heading north. The passengers were grim-faced, exhausted, the default expression of the bottom tier of the new economy. He didn't have to act to fit in.

Cecily had worked at a school in Uptown, a neighborhood filled with hillbillies up from Appalachia. They had come seeking those golden guaranteed jobs. There were jobs, all right, but the gilding turned out to be not so shiny.

Vienna Beef Guaranteed Primary School 298 was a three-story brick building with tall windows and a green roof. It was surrounded by cement and ragged tufts of weeds. The mortar between its bricks was pocked and broken, the paint on its window frames was peeling, a playground with rusting swings and a collapsing jungle gym was set off to the side. But the flagpole was straight as rain, and the flag flapped proudly.

"Cecily Fell," said Clyde to the receptionist in the school's main office. Her face was flabby, her hair was high, and the caution that sliced into her eyes when he said the name told him something. He didn't know what, but something.

"Who are you, exactly?" she said. Her voice twanged like a plucked banjo.

"A concerned friend."

"You're not the police, then."

"Do you want me to be the police? I could be the police if you wanted me to be the police."

"Do you have a badge?"

"No, but I do have the hat."

The slightest of smiles. "I'm sorry, but Miss Fell doesn't teach here anymore. She hasn't taught here for almost a year."

"Why not? What happened? Tell me the story, Flora."

Her eyes shifted; Clyde followed her gaze. A small blonde woman, slight and timid and holding a stack of files, was staring wide-eyed at the two of them.

"Blink," he said to the blonde.

"Perhaps you should talk to the principal," said the receptionist.

"I've heard that before," said Clyde.

"Could you take this man to Mr. Bullock's office, Maureen?" said the receptionist.

"This way please," said Maureen.

As Clyde followed the blonde woman around the front desk and into a hallway, he could hear the receptionist pick up the phone.

***

The principal's office was large and tidy, and gave Clyde the creeps. He had spent enough time in the principal's office at good old 774 to be able to hear the cries and pleas that had bled into the bland space. *I didn't do it. It wasn't my fault. Suspension? Don't tell my dad, please.* Krist.

"Cecily Fell," said Clyde when he was situated in the disciplinary chair.

"Miss Fell hasn't taught here since last June," said Principal Bullock, a small balding man with a compensating mustache. He worked a pipe in his mouth, hiding within its wreath of smoke.

"She left voluntarily?"

"Let's say she and I both decided it was better for her to find employment elsewhere."

"She was a cock-up as a teacher, I suppose."

"Oh, no, she was wonderful. The children loved her. But there were pedagogical issues."

"Teaching Russian to the little brats?"

"Not quite."

"But something like that?"

"Why are you asking about Miss Fell, if I may ask?"

"I'm a friend, an old friend from the old neighborhood," recited Clyde.

"So you're not here in any official capacity."

"Only in my official capacity as a concerned citizen able to kick up a ruckus."

The principal puffed for a bit. Clyde sat quietly and said nothing and let the quiet build its own expectation. This Mr. Bullock wanted to talk, wanted to get out his side of the story, which meant there was another side that Clyde would have to find somewhere else.

"Cecily had certain interesting ideas about teaching civics," said Bullock. "I spoke to her about it numerous times. And there were complaints from some of the parents. We are not a Ventura School, Mr. Sparrow. There were certain ideas that we believed were counterproductive."

"Such as?"

"Did someone ever tell you that you could do anything you wanted if you put your mind to it?"

"My mother used to dish out something along those lines."

"And how did that work out for you?"

"I get it. She buttered up the kids and so you canned her."

"Let's say we chose to go in a different direction. Our mission is to prepare the children for their eventual places in the unfolding future of the nation, and we pursue that mission with utter seriousness. I can't divulge any further details that factored into our decision. I'm sure you understand."

"I understand very little, because I went to a school just like this one, but I know a ram job when I see one."

"You have the wrong idea."

"Let's say I don't think so."

"This is not a place for fairy tales and she knew what she was risking. Miss Fell was a guaranteed employee, and under the terms of the Federal Guaranteed Employment Act we could terminate her employment for any reason or for no reason at all. Whatever reason we did or did not come up with, it was sufficient."

"So what you're saying is you're legally safe."

"Yes, that is what I'm saying."

"Any idea where she shuffled off to?"

"No, I'm sorry. Nothing. I'd like to help you."
"Oh, I bet," said Clyde.

***

The Montrose Arms, not far from the school, was a C-shaped brick structure with bars over the windows on the first two floors. The court-yard of the place was filled with life—dogs leaping at birds, squirrels scampering, pigeons flocking to tossed crumbs, bottles tilting down into shaking gray gizzards. Kids too young for school played together in the dirt as their mothers, off work on parental exemptions, sat on benches and looked on. A clot of the young and able-bodied milled insolently about the entrance. Clyde had never seen these specific slack-ers before, but he knew what they were all about, looking for an angle even if the only available angle was trouble. They gave Clyde the collec-tive eye as he shifted his way through the group and into the entrance.

The fourth-floor hallway was long and lousy with doors, door after door. He knew the way it worked: one window to an apartment, except for the washrooms, which needed no window at all, just a fan moving the stink into the hallway. Next to every washroom was a phone. This had once been a luxury building, but luxury was now reserved for the Ventura Districts north of the city or the high-rises linked arm in arm on the Ventura Coast lakeside. After the disincorporation, this build-ing had been carved up to grab as many guaranteed-housing checks as possible.

Apartment 416B, Cecily's last known address. From inside he could hear the sound of a television swallowing the hours with sound and little fury.

He knocked and heard a high-pitched screech, like metal grinding on cat. He knocked again.

When the door opened, a grizzled man in socks, boxers, and a T-shirt stared, his belly slack, his eyes red and weary. The room behind him was dark and smoke-filled, the shades drawn, the blue eye of the television blinking.

"Yeah?" said the man.

"Cecily Fell," said Clyde.

"Who the hell?"

"She lived here."

"Well, she ain't here no more, pal."

And then from inside, over the sound of the television, that shriek again. "Who is it, Harry? Who's there?"

"It's just someone," he shouted back.

"What does he want?"

"Someone named Cecily something."

"She's not here," came the screech. "Tell him she's not here."

"I told him," he shouted back.

"Cecily Fell lived here," said Clyde. "This was her address."

"Maybe, who the hell knows?" said the man. "We been in this dump since last April. The longest decade of my life."

"Send him away," came the screech. "We're watching a show."

"Pipe down," he shouted back. "It's a rerun. The husband of the other girl did it. I'm being neighborly, here."

"Then tell the neighbors to stop screwing in the middle of the night. All that banging, I can't sleep."

The man looked at Clyde with suffering in his tired red eyes. Look at what I have to deal with, he said without saying. Can you believe this crap?

"Did the lady before you leave any forwarding address, or anything at all?"

"These places, the way they are now, in and out and in again, who the hell knows who anyone is? Hey, wait a minute. I know you?"

"No, you don't."

"I think I do. Take off your hat for a minute."

Clyde slipped off the hat and smiled quickly, as if for the flash of a photo machine.

"I do know you," said the guy, his eyes brightening. "You're the Toddle House guy."

"How the hell? Have you been to the diner?"

"It's your picture. I know you from your picture."

"Who is it, Harry?" came the screech. "What's going on?"

"It's the Toddle House guy."

"Who?"

"The Toddle House guy, from the picture over the mirror."

"Really? Imagine that. Tell him I want a milk shake."

"Like you need a milk shake."

"What does that mean?"

"It doesn't mean nothing."

"What the hell does that mean, you son of a bitch?"

"I don't understand," said Clyde, interrupting the lovemaking. "You have my picture?"

"It was up when we got here, on the wall, and Mildred was too lazy to take it down."

"I heard that," came the screech.

"Let me show you." The man left the door open as he retreated into the dark, smoky room. When he came back, after much shouting and ballyhoo, the man was holding a yellowing patch of newspaper with dingy strips of tape attached. *Mayor Bartholomew and Clyde Sparrow of the Toddle House in West Garfield Park share a milk shake on the eve of the election.*

"That's you, ain't it?" said the man.

"That's me, all right," said Clyde, feeling his heavy shoes lift from the floor as if his chest were filling with helium. "Imagine that. She saved it. Thanks for everything, joe."

"Harry."

"Suit yourself."

"Hey, buddy," said the man as Clyde walked away. "Will you sign it for me?"

Clyde stopped and turned around, doffed his fedora, and smiled like he was touched. He came back to the open door and snatched the newspaper clipping from the man's hand.

"Don't be ridiculous," said Clyde as he shoved the photograph into his hat.

***

When Clyde stepped outside the building, his mind wrapped in dreamy gauze, the courtyard was empty, except for one lone figure, sitting on a bench, his back to the door. The loiterers, the little children and their mothers, the old and the infirm, the dogs, all had disappeared. Even the birds had flittered away. It was as if a wild boar with great angry tusks had waddled out of the jungle and scared off every other beast on the land and in the air before bowing low at the water hole to drink.

Broome.

Parked at the mouth of the courtyard, its camouflage pattern like a splash of insane modern art on the gray city street, was a Homeland Guard personnel carrier with two armed Guardsmen leaning against its haunch. Clyde, shaken back into the hard reality of his situation, fitted his hat more firmly on his head before walking to the bench and leaning his forearms upon the top stave.

"I figured I'd see you somewhere along the line, Captain," said Clyde. "That school receptionist had betrayal in her eye."

"Where is he, Clyde?" came the husk of a voice, dark and desiccated.

"I don't know."

"He was at your building last night."

"If you know that, then you also know I tried to kill the son of a bitch for you."

"I don't need you to kill him for me. I just need you to turn him over."

"So you can have the pleasure yourself. I get it. But don't worry your silver bars over it. He escaped from me last night, he won't escape from me again. What do you know about Cecily Fell?"

"His labor officer was looking for her, part of their normal update of prisoner files, and she came up missing. Somehow Moonis got word of it and tried to get released. When that didn't work, he killed the guard and ran."

"Moonis and Cecily grew up pretty much on their own. The mother ran, the father worked two jobs and drank himself into a stupor every night. Moonis cooked for his sister, cleaned for her. He was her protector. If he thinks she's in trouble, he'll move heaven and earth to help her. I find the sister, I'll find him. And then I'll sic you on him like a rabid dog."

"Clyde, I must say, I didn't expect to see so much initiative out of you."

"I pay my debts."

"Just so you know, a reward has been posted."

"Is that a fact?"

"For any information leading to the murderer's capture. Donated by Archer Daniels Midland. They sponsored the camp he escaped from. Twenty thousand dollars."

"That's a lot of money," said Clyde.

"You could buy your own diner with that much money, have saps in bow ties working for you. Everything could change."

"I know what twenty thousand dollars is."

"The phone call we received mentioned a woman with bruises on her face, like a raccoon, a woman who had been hiding in your room until she burst out in her underwear and broke up the fight. Broken nose, maybe?"

"That Mrs. McGillicutty has quite the imagination."

"Just so you know your choices."

"I get it."

"On the one hand, on the other hand. And then there are the drugs for the girl."

"I said I get it. I'm going to serve him up to you as neat as a slice of pie. But to do it I'm going to need something from you."

"Nothing too inconvenient I hope."

"A Ventura pass."

"What the hell?"

"Just a hunch I have. Something that doesn't jibe in the timeline. I think this Cecily, she's made the jump. If I want to follow, I'll need a pass. But not a service pass. I won't get anything that way. All access."

"Getting above yourself, Clyde?"

"I'm getting something, and you're going to help me do it."

Broome took a book out of his pocket, wrote up the pass, signed it, pulled it. "You get two weeks."

"Two weeks will be jimmy," said Clyde.

"Let me just tell you this, as a friendly warning. I find another yellow cake stinking of piss somewhere in a Ventura District, I'm taking your head."

***

Clyde leaned up against a wall with his hat low, chewing a stick of Wrigley's he had bought at a newsstand, waiting. He wasn't worried about the sweepers, not with Broome's pass in his pocket. He was free to waste the day propping up a wall and chewing gum, free to loiter. Wasn't that the sweetest damn word in the English language? Loiter. It rolled off the tongue like a fresh oyster.

The bell rang and the kids swarmed out of the front doors of GPS 298, running, flying, shouting, pushing. Some raced home, others made a beeline to the sad, sagging playground. They laughed and cried and plotted. Clyde and Moonis and Patti had once been just like that, full to bursting with life. Kids were always kids; it was what happened to them later that was the crime. Clyde stayed leaning against the wall, chewing and loitering, letting the sun lick his face like a happy puppy.

The school stayed closed and quiet for a time, as if the place were already empty, until a lone teacher pushed open a door, looking nervously about like she was the point in a jailbreak. Then a few others. Then a trickle. Then a gush. The woman he was waiting for was in the gush, her head down, eyes low, hoping she wouldn't be noticed among the streaming crowd.

"Oh," she said when he grabbed her arm and halted her escape. "It's you."

"You're not really surprised to see me, are you there, Maureen?" he said to the small blonde from the office, the one who had stared when he had said Cecily's name.

"I don't . . . I'm sorry . . . I need to . . ."

"How about some coffee?"

"I can't."

"There's a place right down the street."

"Really, Mr. . . ."

"Call me Clyde."

She pulled back at the name. "You're Clyde?"

"That's right, I'm Clyde. So how do you like your coffee, Maureen, one lump or two?"

***

They found a booth in a diner a block and a half from the school. There were streaks on the Formica, the silverware was spotted. Six years in the game and now Clyde noticed these things.

"Why was Cecily fired?" he asked right out, before they even ordered. Clyde had a lot of questions about Cecily. Was she still just as pretty? What did she say about Clyde? What good things did she say about Clyde? What did she say about Clyde? But he started with this.

"What did Mr. Bullock tell you?" said Maureen.

"She was teaching the kids to grab for the stars when only dirt's in reach."

"That was part of it," said Maureen, burying her face in the menu.

"What was the other part?"

"I'll just have a coffee."

"What was the other part?"

She looked up at him without an ounce of her previous timidity. "She liked you, Clyde. You were the last real boyfriend she ever had. After that, it was always something else."

"The other part."

"We were friends. Not great friends, you know, but work friends. We had drinks together sometimes, and we both had the same ambitions. She had a red dress she let me borrow. It was long on me, but I loved the color. Don't you think we need color? We're required to wear muted tones at work. That's part of the dress code at Vienna Beef Guaranteed Primary School 298."

"Is that why she was fired? The color of her dresses?"

"She was starting to cough in class."

"Krist."

"Yeah."

They sat there for a moment in quiet. When the waitress came, Clyde ordered a couple of coffees. "You want pie?" he said.

"No, thank you," said Maureen.

"I think I'm going to have pie. You have peach?"

"Not this time of year," said the waitress.

"They got it in the V-District."

"Get it there, then, why don't you."

"They teach you to snap gum like that in waitressing school? Forget the pie. Just the coffees. And some clean spoons. These look like a rat rubbed its ass on them." When the waitress left, Clyde sucked his teeth for a moment. "How bad was it?"

"Just starting."

"Are you sure, then? Maybe it was just a parched throat. A couple of mentholated drops and all is well."

"We work with children," said Maureen. "The school can't wait to be sure. The kids tell their parents, and the parents go right to the superintendent. You cut it off early or there's hell to pay."

"So that's good, right? So maybe it was nothing, right?"

"If you want to think so, sure."

"And she stopped work in June?"

"That's right."

"You heard from her since?"

"Not really."

"Is that a yes or a no?"

"No."

"So you don't know if it has gotten worse."

"Does it ever get better?"

The waitress brought the coffee. It was watery, weak, and bitter at the same time. It takes art to so foully ruin a cup of coffee. It doesn't just happen, you've got to work at it.

"You know what this joint needs?" said Clyde.

"What?"

"Me." Clyde set the cup down. "So here's something interesting maybe you can help me with, Maureen. You say Cecily stopped working at the school in June. But when I checked out her apartment, the new tenants said they had moved into the place in April. So the question I have is where was she living between April and June?"

"She moved."

"Where to?"

"I don't know exactly. She moved in with someone."

"Before or after the cough started?"

"Before."

"Who was he?"

"His name is Brad."

"Brad. Like the nail."

"What are you doing, Clyde?"

"I'm trying to find her."

"Why?"

"Why do you think?"

She swirled a spoon in her coffee. "She told me once her brother was selected. Is that true?"

"True as pain."

"Wow. That's something, isn't it? I should remember him."

"It was a long time ago."

"What did he look like?"

"Then? He was a skinny little black kid with thick glasses. Not an athlete, like most of the others."

"I think I do remember him. Tall for his age, right?"

"That's him. He was something like a genius then."

"How about now?"

"Not so much."

"It's quite a thing, isn't it, to get selected like that. For your brains. But there's more than one way to skin that fish."

"You going somewhere with this?"

"Cecily wouldn't date anyone from here. And believe me, they tried. Every teacher took a shot, single or married, it didn't matter, but no one from here was good enough. Just like you weren't good enough. She talked about her brother being selected and the promises he made and the way that didn't work out. But she was determined to keep those promises for both of them anyway. She was going to be selected the only way she could."

"Sounds filthy."

"It's as old as the Bible. Ruth hiking up her skirt as she gleaned from Boaz's field."

"I don't know from the Bible."

"Too bad, it's a handy little book. There's not a thing in the world it can't justify."

"So I'm guessing this Brad isn't from around here. I'm guessing this Brad is some Ventura District wahoo with all kinds of cash. Probably went to Harvard, probably plays golf at the club. So tell me, Maureen, how does a girl from here meet a specimen like that?"

"There's a place," she said. "There's always a place."

18

Selection

Consider the caterpillar.

Within the imperfect darkness of his hideout, Moonis was doing exactly that. He lay with his hands behind his head on a bed of rolled, moldy carpets, surrounded by mop heads dried stiff as bone, by metal shelves bowed by the weight of foul liquids sitting in rusting tins, beside a toilet bolted to the floor but without water or seat. And in this wasteland, beneath the site of his greatest triumph and enveloped by the very stink of his worst failure, he considered the caterpillar.

It crawls along a vast horizontal landscape on stubby legs, its tender belly scraped by rock and thorn. Huge heedless creatures scamper by as the caterpillar searches for stray bits of leaf or tufts of grass to gnash with its mandibles. The entire scheme of the universe, all its quirks and quarks, its quasars and black holes, every force that sends all matter and antimatter and dark matter spinning and crushing, burning and dying, conspires to grind our little caterpillar inexorably into the earth.

And then, against the great weight of gravity's hand, the caterpillar lifts its little head, looks through its round glasses up into the bright-blue sky, and glimpses heaven, or as close to it as it will ever know: an oak tree with a lovely canopy of leaves, more food than our hero could eat in a hundred thousand days. It is the very live-growing oak, as a matter of fact, that rose outside the school in which Moonis was hiding.

If only, thinks the caterpillar, if only I could escape gravity's unbearable pressure and get from down here to up there. If only.

***

Every fall, as part of a nationwide demonstration of the continuing meritocracy in the incorporated areas, each of the nation's Ventura Schools selected one deserving seventh grader from the guaranteed system to study within its hallowed halls on full scholarship.

These selections were announced with great fanfare across town and country. Students in the guaranteed system spent their school years apprenticing in the technical or service sectors in preparation for the guaranteed jobs they would enter right after secondary school. But students at the Ventura Schools prepared for long years of university training in business management, in public policy, in the arts, in medicine and engineering and the hard sciences, before taking their rightful places in the leadership sector of the nation, at salaries that afforded them the opportunity to send their own children to the Ventura Schools. One child's selection was the kind of wondrous boon that could impact a family for untold generations.

More than a dozen years had passed since Moonis had been eligible for selection, yet he could still see the crowd that filled the auditorium in the building that squatted now stolid and solid above him. He could still see the video camera set up in the rear, could still see the television placed upon the stage, could still see the circular test pattern with the stern-faced Indian in full headdress, could still feel the pulse of possibility that snapped electric through the student body and within the boy with the highest test scores in the city, the boy with dreams of studying the swirling mysteries of the universe. And along with the pulse of possibility, Moonis could still feel the bitter anticipation of the disappointment he was certain to feel.

They selected athletes, they selected the wellest-to-do, they selected for raw beauty—it was as simple as that. They didn't select a Moonis Fell. Moonis's friend Clyde, the lithe and handsome football hero, had been scouted by the selectors; Moonis was as athletic as an aardvark. And ever since Moonis's mother had deserted her family, Moonis's father had struggled to keep the apartment heated and food on the table and liquor in his gut; there was no money in the larder for bribes to buy the recommendations from teachers and politicians that were necessary to push a name to the forefront.

No, Moonis had no chance, and he believed he had resigned himself to the raw impossibility of his ever rising beyond guaranteed status; but even so, on the edge of the announcement, he sat on the edge of his seat, blood buzzing with hope and yearning, as they all waited for a name to be called, a single name that would twist a myriad of destinies.

***

Moonis couldn't help but lose himself in remembrance of his churning emotions as he waited for the announcement, but he pulled himself out of the roil of nostalgia and returned to the caterpillar, climbing now that mighty oak.

The path is long and uneven, and every step is fraught with danger, yet still it climbs. Down is hunger and toil and the dark, careless tread of death. Up is sunlight and sustenance. Step by step it climbs, though with all its little legs it is more like stepstepstepstepstep by stepstepstepstepstep.

Maybe as it climbed, it could hear the long echoes of the cheers rising from the McGraw-Hill Guaranteed Secondary School 774 as the mayor's fat face blinked onto the television screen set up on the stage, and then the expectant hush as the mayor, in his gruff, flat voice began to list the names of the boys and girls selected to rise. One by one the names were read, one by one the schools across the city broke into riotous cheers, one by one the selected students were shown in shock and delight on the television screen, and one by one Moonis's chances turned ever more bleak. He had stopped listening out of frustration when he heard the gasp from all the seats around him. What, what had happened? And then he deciphered the words that had flowed meaninglessly just a moment before through his discouraged brain.

"Finally," had said the mayor, "selected from the McGraw-Hill Guaranteed Secondary School 774 in West Garfield Park, we have seventh grader Moonis Fell."

***

The cheers poured down upon him like moonbeams and candy corn, a roar so loud it pressed him into his seat even as he struggled to rise. A future writ clear and sad in the gray carbon of pencil had, with the simple calling of his name, been erased syllable by syllable and replaced with a rainbow.

He would never have gotten to his feet if Clyde and Patti, on either side of him, hadn't pushed him to standing. He looked at Clyde, expecting to see bitter disappointment on his friend's face, but saw only a shining expression of sincere delight that would stay with Moonis all his days. Moonis wouldn't remember sliding out of his row or walking down the aisle, he only remembered the slight stumble as he tripped on an untied shoelace while climbing the steps.

Next thing he knew, he was standing on the stage between Principal Brooks and Mrs. Popolio, standing in front of the entire student body, standing there like a triumphant Roman hero returned from the Punic Wars as his image was relayed by the cameras all across the city.

Maybe that is close to what the caterpillar feels as it begins to chomp the leaves in its new oaken aerie. It has made the impossible climb, has risen to great heights, is certain there is nothing but green foliage and glorious satiety to mark the rest of its now-magnificent life.

Poor deluded caterpillar.

19
FOSBURY'S

A window slid open on the metal door in the dank, narrow alley, revealing the crimson teeth of a betel chewer and a jaw that shook in disapproval.

"Private club," said the bouncer.

"I'm wearing a suit," said Clyde.

"The wrong suit."

"My mother got me this suit."

"Date your mother, then."

"So now I'm supposed to take dressing advice from a rhinoceros?"

"Private club, pal."

"What does it take to get in?"

"More than you got."

"What about you take a gander at this?"

Clyde reached into his jacket, and the bouncer's lips curled at the possibility of cold cash. Instead of a wallet, Clyde pulled out the pass. The bouncer grabbed hold of it, pulled it inside the window, and shut out Clyde.

Clyde spit as he waited.

A moment later, the door opened wide. "A pass from Broome?" said the bouncer. "Krist, pal, why didn't you say so?"

"I'm not your pal," said Clyde, snatching back the pass. "Call me sir and we'll call it square."

"Yes, sir."

"Is Brad in tonight?"

"You know Brad?"

"Good old Brad."

"Not in yet, not in lately. Right this way, sir."

"Ballyhoo," said Clyde.

***

The bouncer ushered Clyde down a dimly lit stairwell. At the lower landing, an old man sat on a stool in front of a black curtain. From behind the curtain Clyde could hear the sound of a brighter world: laughter, the tinkling of glass, a jazz standard being sexily sung. But just as he was about to push through the curtain, the man on the stool slapped a walking stick into his chest.

"Welcome to Fosbury's," said the old man, lit with a sinister blue light. The man was kindly of voice, but there was a squint to his eye that made you want to check the walking stick for nails. "That'll be twenty-five."

"I have a pass," said Clyde.

"How you got through the door is your concern, but the band needs to eat."

"What about the girls? Do they pay?"

"It's ladies' night."

"But it's not Wednesday."

"Don't get out much, do you? Twenty-five."

"That include a drink?"

"For the band, maybe. Let me give you a piece of square, friend. If you're sweating the cover, you're in the wrong place."

"Oh, I'm in the right place." Clyde pulled out the wad he had taken off the lunger, licked his thumb, thumbed out five fives.

"You're new here, so I'll gift you some other pieces of square," said the old man as he stuffed the bills into a pocket. "Don't say you're a lawyer. They don't take to lawyers. Or a writer, heaven forbid. Businessman is good. Banker is better. Your daddy being rich as sin is always the best, even if it's not true. Hell, it's mostly lies down here, one way or the other. But it's no lie that all of them girls, they like the breeding. Use big words, it don't matter if you use them right. Four syllables, they'll be licking their lips. Eight syllables and they're licking something else. I know a guy with a suit as plum ugly as yours found a pretty just by saying 'semiautobiographical.' You might want to remember that. Semiautobiographical. It's a nice way of saying you're lying."

"Is that it?"

"You'll pay to learn the rest like everyone else."

Clyde nodded a bit, steeling himself for his entrance.

"Semiautobiographical," said the man just before Clyde pushed through the curtain.

***

Clyde found himself in a place so unlike the ragged familiarity of Tunney's Tap it was like being in an alternate universe. Candlelit tables, beautiful people dressed beautifully, spotlights bouncing off the sweat of the musicians and the jewelry on wrist and ear. Fosbury's was a supper club from a different era—a time before the atomic explosions, before the Grand Constitution and the closing of the D-Lands and the graying of American life—with waiters in tuxes swerving between tables as they carried goblets of champagne, and crystal lowballs with rye concoctions sporting cherries speared to bright slivers of lemon.

A zinc bar ran up one side of the place, bottles glowing in a rain-bow of toxic colors; a jazz trio swung softly on a stage against the other side, with a pretty lady singer warbling high and sweet. The place was polished to an edge of cool so sharp it cut. Best of all, even at the late hour—well past midnight, because Clyde had worked his shift—women were everywhere, good-looking women, packs of them, flash-ing leg and smile and sloping tops of breasts. There were men too, of course, well-dressed men, mostly older, some beefy, some outright porkers, but none of the men were alone, each had someone into whose ear they purred and whose chests they ogled.

You could feel the promise of sex in the place, like the walking line of the upright bass, like the sizzling of the neon art on the walls, like the plaintive wail of the saxophone released into its solo.

"Wowza," said Clyde.

He spied that Maureen from the school, who had told him about the place, sitting at a table with a glass of champagne and some middle-aged guy with a slick blue suit and slicked-back hair. At the school, she had seemed the little blonde mouse, but in this place, with those high black heels and her lips painted like bruised plums, she was something else entirely. Hunger brought out the best in her. She glanced up at Clyde and shook her head slightly before aiming a bright smile at her Ventura mark.

Clyde slipped over to the bar, took a stool, took off his hat, ordered rye over ice from the skinny barkeep. He thought he'd have a moment to enjoy his drink, scope the place, figure out a plan for learning what he needed to learn. He must have underestimated his attractiveness, because he wasn't settled for half a minute before he was besieged.

***

First, Sharon—pretty, slight, sharp-eyed in a clever, knowing way—sidled up beside him. Then two more joined the party: Roberta, big-boned and athletic, and Veronica, tall and blonde and cold as the rocks in his rye.

The women stood around and said sweet things and batted eyelashes and waited for Clyde to buy them drinks, which he did. It was a revelation, having Sharon and Roberta and Veronica flock to him— good-looking, interesting women, the kind who never toddled over to Clyde at the Toddle House or at Tunney's. He had slipped through the surface of a mirror into some other, brighter world, where he mattered in a way he didn't matter outside it.

They chatted amiably, the four of them, about the music, the weather, the latest shooting in the news. And Clyde was ever so charming; it was surprisingly easy to be ever so charming when charming women were hanging like bats on your every word. He felt somehow taller here. His eyesight was better. His jaw was more firm. And all the time as they slurped and gabbed, he could sense the three women were getting closer to asking the big question, the only question that really mattered in a place like this. It shimmered like a ghost between them.

"So, Clyde," said Roberta, finally giving voice to the ghost, "what is it that you do?"

"Oh, this and that," said Clyde, suddenly and surprisingly nervous.

"Which this," said Sharon, peering over her bubbly pink drink, "and which that?"

"Well, I'll tell you one thing," said Clyde, holding up his rye and admiring the rich brown color. "I'm not a stinking lawyer."

"Thank God for that," said Veronica, and the four of them laughed and laughed.

"Well, what exactly, then?" said Roberta, bearing in relentlessly, like a linebacker.

"Food and beverage," said Clyde.

"How's business?"

"Everyone's got to eat."

"That sounds exciting," said Veronica. "I can't get enough of big business."

"And I can assure you my business is big," said Clyde.

The laughter was undeserved and all the richer for it.

"Do one of you lovelies," said Clyde, "happen to know my friend Brad?"

"You know Brad?" said Sharon.

"We're old friends. We grew up in the District together."

"I like your tie," said Veronica, reaching out her slim, pale hand and stroking the knot. "You don't see many bow ties in a place like this."

"My haberdasher swears by them," said Clyde before silently counting the syllables. "Haberdashery. Prestidigitation." With each new word their eyes seemed to grow wider. "So has Brad been in lately?"

"No," said Sharon with a little pout. "And he promised."

"When was the last time you saw him here?"

"Months maybe," said Roberta.

"Was he alone?"

"He's never alone for long," said Sharon. "We all love Brad. He's the life of the party."

"Enough about Brad," said Veronica, her hand now flat against his chest, spreading a delicious cold. "Let's talk about Clyde."

"Careful, Clyde," came a woman's voice from behind him. "Veronica's liable to reach inside your shirt and pull out your liver."

Sharon and Roberta and Veronica backed away as if being approached by a bear. Clyde turned, and there stood Helen, red hair done, iridescent green dress matching her shoes, slim and sharp and dressed in a way Clyde had never seen her dressed before, like a glass of pure class poured from a crystal decanter.

"We were here first," said Veronica.

"But I'm here best, so totter off and find someone new," said Helen. "Shouldn't they totter off, Clyde?"

Clyde, still staring at Helen, felt something slip inside, some veneer of politeness plastered over a hidden longing that infuriated him. "Don't you look sharp."

"I always look sharp," said Helen.

Clyde politely gave the other three women the brush-off. Sharon shrugged, Roberta's eyes narrowed in anger, Veronica leaned forward and kissed him smack on the lips. Even her lips were cold.

In the sensual freeze of that kiss, it came to him with utter precision, the path to being here for real, in this place, in this world, not courtesy of a Broome-supplied pass but through a piece of his own devising, a play as clean and hard as a glass of rye. Use the twenty thousand to buy a diner, turn it around as only the Toddle House man could, take the profits and buy another and then another until all his lies were true and he could stand here with Sharon and Roberta and Veronica—lusciously vanilla Veronica, heartlessly cold Veronica—so he could stand here and tell the lot of them to go straight the fuck to hell.

***

Helen and Clyde sat with their drinks at a table in the corner, heads leaning close so that they could hear each other above the band. Whatever joy he had been feeling at having slipped into this other world had turned into a bitterness as hard and bright as a diamond.

"Wholesome little slag heap you found for yourself," said Clyde.

"You seemed to be enjoying yourself," said Helen.

"That Veronica is something."

"Something you couldn't afford in a million years."

"I save up enough of what I'm paying you, I might be able to buy a night."

"Charming. How'd you get in?"

"Charm."

"What are you doing here, Clyde?"

"What is anyone doing in a joint like this? I'm looking for someone."

"And here I am. Now what?"

"You think I'm here for you?" said Clyde, a nasty laugh slipping out between gritted teeth. "You think I'm chasing a mawk to a bordello?"

"That's not what this is."

"Nice dress. Expensive?"

"What do you think?"

"You never wore a dress like that for me."

"Once they get the stink of fried onions in them, Clyde, it never gets out."

"So that's the game. You make me shovel out my hard-earned green for a shack-up, and then you turn around and spend it on a piece of slink to attract the slime at a joint like this."

"They're not slime."

"But they're not us. At a bordello at least the merchandise gets paid. What do you get here for spreading your legs? Free drinks and a chance to suck a rock of fool's gold."

"I'm playing the angles, Clyde. Just like you. You sell drugs, what do I have to sell? But don't get yourself in a hissy. I'm aging fast; the street agitates the time in you. Pretty soon they'll stop letting me in. You want to make an honest woman of me then?"

"You deserve better than these slick-haired creeps."

"I deserve something, all right."

"I'm looking for someone maybe you know. His name's Brad."

"Brad? Yeah, I know Brad. We all know Brad. He's the goddamn life of the goddamn party." Helen rubbed a finger on the edge of her glass. "So, as always, it's all about Cecily. Krist, aren't you the lovesick sap."

20
THE SPOILS

When we left our caterpillar hero, crawling about in the consciousness of one Moonis Fell, it had made the long, dangerous climb up the thick oak outside McGraw-Hill Guaranteed Secondary School 774 and reached larval nirvana. There it sits, gnashing verdant leaf, free from loping paw and hoof, hidden from the sadistic chubby fingers of your basic human toddler. Life has seemingly reached a pinnacle of perfection for our many-legged friend.

But the world is never as we most fervently hope. Even in this leaf-strewn sanctuary, gravity presses down, not just binding the creature to leaf or limb but also threatening to send it hurtling from unimaginable heights. And though in the canopy there be no wandering doe or hedgehog, up here there are predators of a more savage kind, wild winged things searching with ravenous eyes to pluck our hero from the leaves, to encase it in their awful beaks, to suck it down into dark pits of acid, where it will succumb to a death both painful and . . .

This whole caterpillar contemplation wasn't idle, but was instead an analysis limned with a fierce necessity. From the caterpillar, Moonis was seeking to learn how to survive and change in the face of immutable force. The whole of his life he had been caught in a scheme ever more brutal than gravity, because it had malice in its heart. But now, fragile and desperate and wanted by the law, he had to change to survive. He had taken a first step by asking, nay, begging, for help from his old friend, Clyde. And strangely, the begging itself felt liberating. Yet there were more steps he needed to take, and the caterpillar apparently had an answer so simple and yet so revolutionary it was hard to ignore.

The caterpillar spins a cocoon around itself, hunches inside, and through time and effort and intense pain transmogrifies into something new, something long and light and handsome as a jewel, a new creature that slips lightly among the varied currents of air to stay aloft. That is the way of the caterpillar: adapt to beat the system.

Moonis had tried to adapt, all those years ago in the time after his selection. It was an era of great promise in his life and he fully expected to leave the Ventura School different than when he arrived. He would grow silver wings sparkling with knowledge and fly to the stars.

But that plan had worked as well as a fist to the face.

***

The beatings came as regularly as the short yellow bus that met him at the checkpoint each morning and drove him to the hallowed halls of the George Washington Ventura School.

They came as regularly as chapel each morning in the school's great Gothic church, attendance at which was mandatory, even for the Jews.

From some it was an elbow in the ribs, from others it was a tripping and a kicking amidst peals of laughter, from still others it was as mild as a gob of spit launched from a few feet away, the parabola of its flight sweet enough to be studied in the advanced physics class he was taking, before it landed splat on his cheek.

It was a venerated tradition at Ventura Schools nationwide to treat selected students like dirt, part of the V-District's great culture of fun. But Moonis, selected not for his athletic prowess or his beauty, and notably black in a sea of white, was handled especially harshly. And one boy in particular, a broad-shouldered brute with a pug nose, took an especially savage interest in his new classmate.

The boy's name was Edward, and his pounding fists landed in rib and gut as regularly as the bells that sent students scurrying along the stone walkways that crisscrossed the school's main square.

***

Moonis had grown up with his classmates at McGraw-Hill Guaranteed Secondary School 774. They were neighbors, they all respected his abilities. And, truth was, anyone who wanted to pick on the tall, gawky kid would have had to answer to Clyde. So Moonis had little experience with which to process what was happening to him at the George Washington Ventura School. He loved the classes, even if the teachers were cold and imperious, even loved the uniform he had to put on each morning like a superhero costume, but he didn't know what to do about the violence.

"Nothing is what you'll do 'bout it," said Mr. deGroot, who drove the bus that picked him up from the checkpoint each morning and dropped him off each afternoon. DeGroot was a round, squinty-eyed man, absolutely hairless, with a guttural accent and a rumpled blue uniform. "I see boys from guaranteed areas always coming back on this bus with blood and bruises and broken bones. The trick is to duck when you can, and when you can't, just to take it."

"But I don't want to take it," said Moonis. "Maybe I'll fight back. Why can't I fight back?"

"Well, for one, they're stronger."

"How do you know?"

"So skinny you are, young Moonis, they're all stronger. Besides, the boys in them schools won't pick fights they can't win. That's just the way they're taught."

"I still don't want to take it."

DeGroot stopped the bus and turned around. He kept his eyes on the other selected students in the back, sitting in tense silence or hurriedly scribbling their homework, as he said, urgently, "Do what I say. You stop the minding and take it. That's the way of it for folk like we. They have their business, and you have your business. You can't let their business get in the way of your business. You keep your eye on your prize and find yourself a bucketful of ice."

"I thought I already won my prize."

"Oh, no, young Moonis. Them sons of somgums, they make you earn it every day."

And they did, every day. He would come onto the bus with a busted lip, a noticeable limp, he would climb the steps hunched over to protect a rib that was cracked beneath one of Edward's blows, and all the time Mr. deGroot counseled him to do nothing. Nothing.

And Moonis, young Moonis, knew that Mr. deGroot was right, that the driver had his best interests in mind when he dished his advice. And yet something in Moonis wouldn't allow it, would prefer disaster, which is what he found instead.

***

"Do you ever play Risk, Mr. deGroot?"

On their way to the school, Moonis was in his usual seat on the bus, directly behind the old hairless driver, speaking quietly so that only he could hear.

"Risk?" said the driver. "I don't got time for gambling."

"It's not gambling, it's a game of world conquest."

"Ah, a perfect game for your classmates before they end up playing it for real."

"The players sometimes make deals not to attack each other and sometimes they break their word."

"That sounds less like Risk and more like life."

"We play that game, too. But when I play Risk with my friends from home, if someone breaks your deal, the game changes and suddenly the object is not to win anymore but to destroy the betrayer. And not just in that game, but in game after game. And the thing is, with that understanding, no one breaks their deals."

"I don't like where this is going."

"It's just an idea of how maybe to stop what Edward is doing to me."

"That's the problem," said deGroot. "You don't stop it. You take it until he stops it. It's not your game, it's his game. The only way to play is not to play. Get through school, get a job, become big man, and then you can change the game. Not now. Now you keep your head down. High trees catch much wind. Stay small, stay quiet. Take it with a smile."

But Moonis had other ideas. He thought then he understood the caterpillar's lesson: change, adapt, become something bright and new. Faced with the clean brutality of the Ventura boy, Moonis would spin around himself a cocoon of his own fear and injury, and let time and violence and self-loathing do its work, before he emerged as something different, something fierce and terrifying in its own right.

"I know you're not listening no more to deGroot," said the bus driver.

"I have a plan," said Moonis.

"Of course you have a plan. And what is this plan of yours that can only lead to ruin?"

"I'm going to propose a deal to Eddie Broome," said Moonis, "that the creep won't dare to reject."

21
THE VENTURA COAST

The building gleamed in the sun, broad-shouldered and blond against the bright-blue sky. Limestone, glass, steel—it rose like a hard monument to light and promise. Unrolling white and smooth on the other side of Lakeshore Drive was the beach—exclusive for residents of the zone—and then the lake itself, stretching out to the far horizon, catching bits of the sun like a blessing gently gifted to all the high towers on Chicago's Ventura Coast.

Clyde had to pass through two checkpoints just to get to the stretch of asphalt and curb outside the building's entrance. He looked up at the tall pillar of luxury and imagined Cecily standing inside, staring out her window at the lake, as if she had finally found, in that view, fulfillment of all the promises made when her brother was selected—that beach, that sky, that infinite stretch of fresh water. She had a glass of champagne in her hand, a slight smile on her lips, and her eyes were dead. Dead as yesterday's dream.

He fixed his hat and headed inside.

***

The doorman was trussed up in green and brass, sporting epaulettes and a peaked hat like a little toy soldier. He eyed Clyde for half an instant before taking his full measure.

"The servant's entrance is in the back."

"I'm not a servant," said Clyde. "Leastways not here, not today."

"Whatever you are," said the man, rising on his tiptoes, "your entrance is in the back."

"I don't think so," said Clyde, taking out his pass. "Is Brad at home?"

The doorman read the pass, raised an eyebrow.

"Let's have it," said Clyde.

"I haven't seen Mr. Illingworth this morning."

"What about a girl, good-looking?"

"They're all good-looking."

"Dark, thin, name of Cecily."

"Cecily?"

"That's right," said Clyde, picking up a hint of humanity beneath the doorman's preposterous costume. "Cecily's the kind to say hello when she comes down each morning, to ask about your day and mean it."

"Are you a friend of Cecily's?"

"An old friend."

"She hasn't been around."

"For how long now?"

"A month or so," said the doorman. "Maybe longer."

"Got you. Illingworth?"

The doorman looked at Clyde like they were both suddenly on the same team, and this Brad, this Bradley Illingworth, was a little piece of gristle caught between his teeth. "Twenty-third floor."

"Which apartment?"

"There's only one."

"Must be nice," said Clyde.

In the elevator—bright lights and stark steel walls and a camera in the corner—Clyde shucked his shoulders and sucked his teeth. He successfully resisted the urge to shine his shoe on the calf of his pant leg, though it was a struggle. Guys like the doorman, guaranteed-job slobs even with their pretty costumes and pretty airs, Clyde had been dealing with all his life. He knew cold the role he was playing with that type. But he felt his nerves snap as the elevator rose with a swish of authority to the twenty-third floor. Who would he be in Bradley Illingworth's presence?

***

His knock on the single door in the small marble lobby of the twenty-third floor was answered by a dapper old man, Filipino, by the looks of him, in spats and a red vest.

"Yes, please?" the man said in a high, accented voice.

"Cecily Fell," said Clyde.

"Miss Cecily? She no here. Sorry."

"You know where she is?"

"No, no."

"Well, maybe Brad does. Tell Brad I'm here to see him."

"You friend of Mr. Illingworth?"

"Oh, yes. Great buddies. We were in the war together."

"There was war?"

"Every day, pal. Just tell Brad that Clyde is here."

"Follow me, please. Clyde, yes?"

"Yes, Clyde," said Clyde.

The man led Clyde to a wood-paneled room stocked with books, and paintings of golf courses. There was a desk, there were leather arm-chairs, there was a bar. On the bar were three crystal decanters, filled. Clyde took off his hat and scratched his scalp.

"Something to drink as you wait, yes?" said the man in the vest. "Brandy?"

"And a cigar," said Clyde. "Let's not forget the cigar."

Clyde was standing at the window with a snifter and a stogie, taking in the very same view he'd imagined Cecily enjoying with those dead eyes. He didn't much like the cigar, but the brandy, Krist, that was something. Rich and sweet, like a fistful of silver. He could get used to the brandy, and the view, and the old Filipino polishing his shoes. And maybe cold-blooded Veronica waiting in the bedroom, chilling his bed in anticipation. How many Toddle Houses would a life like this cost? He'd have to buy a chain, he'd have to be a mogul.

He felt just then, looking over the edge of the lake, like he was peering over the edge of some precarious perch.

***

"Clyde, is it?"

Clyde turned without haste to see a man in his shirtsleeves leaning against the doorjamb, his narrow black tie hanging beneath an open collar. Thin, rumpled, curly black hair, a sardonic smile on his handsome, unshaven face. At first Clyde thought this might be another servant, but when he saw the old Filipino standing nervously behind the man, Clyde knew. Life-of-the-party Brad.

"How's the brandy?"

"Quite good," said Clyde, sticking the 'quite' right in there like it was as natural as breathing.

"And the cigar?"

"A bit rough, that."

"They were my father's. He passed away a number of years ago and I haven't replaced them, so they're past their sell-by date."

Clyde looked at the cigar as it smoldered like a trash dump in his hand.

This Brad walked into the room and gestured to one of the over-stuffed leather chairs. As Clyde sat, Brad moved toward the bar. He added ice to a cut-crystal glass, poured himself something amber from one of the decanters, and then sat himself. He lifted his glass in a toast, took a gulp, nodded.

"You're looking for Cissy," he said.

"Her name's Cecily. What does she call you?"

"Brad. Any special reason you're looking for her?"

"Do I need one?"

The man looked at Clyde, took in his old funeral suit, his scuffed shoes, the bow tie, the fedora sitting on the table. "What game are you in, Clyde?"

"Food and beverage."

"Lucrative?"

"Everyone's got to eat."

"Where'd you go to school?"

"Does it matter?"

"It always matters."

"Not Harvard," said Clyde.

"Good for you. I'm a Yalie myself."

"Go Tigers," said Clyde.

"Bulldogs."

"Whatever."

Brad laughed and downed another swallow, and Clyde caught himself wanting to be liked by this man. Was it due to the man's evident charisma—he could see how Cecily could fall for his rumpled charm—or was it due to some pathetic need within Clyde's own makeup? Clyde had the urge to punch this Brad in the face at the same time he freshened his drink.

"I'm sorry, but I can't help you, Clyde. As a matter of fact, I'd like to know where Cissy is myself. About a month and a half ago, she just left."

"Just like that?"

"Isn't that the way of it in romance? One moment things are going swimmingly and then, bang, it's over. You could say our relationship had run its course. And then there were other issues."

"What other issues?"

"That's a bit personal, don't you think?"

"For me it's as personal as blood."

"I see. So let me guess, Clyde," said the man, smiling wryly. "You're an old friend from the old neighborhood. You went through public school with Cissy out there in West Garfield Park. Maybe you were a little in love with her. Who wouldn't be? And now you've gotten wind somehow that she's fallen into opportunity. With her brother out of the way, you figure you're the one to stake your claim. So you put on your bow tie and make your move. Is that it?"

"What do you know about her brother?"

"Dead, I hear."

"Is that what you hear?"

"Isn't he?"

"I'm not here to stake a claim. That would be a bit mercenary for the likes of me. Like I said, I didn't go to Harvard. What about her health there, Brad? Was that another issue?"

"Her health? Can I be frank, Clyde?"

"Try to be Brad, Frank."

"Her health wasn't good."

"And all those Balthazar drugs you were able to buy with all your money, they did nothing?"

Brad finished off his drink. "They apparently only work if the disease is not so far advanced."

"So you kicked her onto the street."

"That's not the way it played out. If you must know, I wanted her to stay. I wanted to care for her. I loved her, Clyde. I still do." He looked Clyde right in the eye, his gaze like a gob of spit. "That I know you understand."

"Where'd she go?"

"Off to cure herself. She was looking for a miracle, and no matter how much I loved her, she wasn't going to find it here."

"What kind of miracle?"

"Some new treatment somewhere. Something alternative, something holistic."

"Something berry?"

"Do you know the consequences of even talking about it?"

"Where did she head off to find it?"

"I don't know. She went off without telling me. Just left a note and went."

"Did you keep it?"

"I burned it. It could have only gotten her in trouble."

"And you've stayed in town the whole time?"

"That's right."

"That doesn't quite check, Brad. Your friends at Fosbury's say you haven't been around."

"I haven't been around to Fosbury's because I want to forget her. If I go there, all I'll do is think of her. She sort of sticks in the mind, but you know that, don't you."

"Maybe I do."

"You're going to keep looking for her, aren't you? Tell me you're going to keep looking for her."

"I'm going to keep looking for her."

"Good," said the man. "You're a tenacious sort, I can tell. Somehow you got into Fosbury's and somehow you got up here and there's no way someone like you should have gotten to either place. You might find her at that. Here, take this." He reached into his pocket and pulled out a wad of cash.

"I didn't come here for that."

"Take it, Clyde. Don't be shy. You'll use it to find her, I know you will. Go ahead, take it."

Clyde thought a moment before snuffing out the cigar and taking hold of the cash. But before Brad let go, he looked Clyde right in the eye.

"And if you do find her, Clyde, you need to do me a favor."

"There's always a catch, isn't there?"

"Will you tell her I love her?"

"You want me to tell Cecily that you love her? Me?"

"Yes, Clyde, you. Could you tell her that for me, please?"

"Sure thing, Brad," said Clyde, smiling like a wolf before snatching the money away and stuffing it in a jacket pocket. "And you can trust I'll make sure it goes over like peaches."

***

Clyde, leaning against the stone edge of a doorway and squinting from the sunlight bouncing off Illingworth's building, caught himself daydreaming about wiping the counter at the Toddle House. Krist, even his daydreams had turned tepid. He should at least have been fantasizing about cold sex with that ice queen Veronica, or tossing the winning touchdown pass, or crapping money out his asshole, something productive. But at least here he could loiter in peace; there were no sweepers sweeping clean these fine streets.

Apparently in the Ventura Districts loitering wasn't a problem. Everyone had something fabulous to do. What fabulous thing Clyde had to do was to wait.

Every now and then, the doorman from across the street looked behind him and shrugged. Clyde checked his watch. His shift started at four; something would have to happen soon. But even just the long wait told him something. It was a weekday, and Bradley boy wasn't bustling off to work. Bradley boy wasn't bustling anywhere. A life of leisure. He could see the attraction for Cecily—money, style, good views, better brandy, lazy days. And what could Clyde ever have offered?

The stink of grilled onions.

He had better things to do with his day than stand out here like someone else's sore thumb. He needed sleep—he hadn't had a good night's shut-eye since Moonis returned—and he needed to hit up the Laundromat, and he needed to find a new source of berry for Lydia. The girl's mother hadn't seen fit to come home the last few days and Lydia's coughs were among the things keeping him awake at night. Clyde didn't know how he had become responsible for the girl, but he felt the obligation squeeze his chest with every damn cough. Yet here he was, burning hours on this sterile Ventura street.

He had almost bought the whole act up there on the twenty-third floor, the young scion still in love with the commoner, like something out of a bad Brit movie they showed weekends at the Rialto. Clyde had wanted to lap it up, along with his brandy. Talking man-to-man with a V-District slick, he could feel himself being sucked into aspirations. But there was that one discordant note, a loose string plunked on a guitar.

The thing that had struck Clyde in Moonis's story was the guard turning around and trying to kill him after making a show of helping him escape. Who would so want Moonis dead that he'd go to all that trouble? It made no sense. But then good old Brad went ahead and assumed the killing had already happened. What it meant Clyde had no clue, but maybe keeping an eye on Brad would give it up.

The doorman stepped out of the building's entrance and gave Clyde a nod. Clyde slipped deeper into the doorway until he was covered by shadow. A moment later Bradley Illingworth, in a gray suit with collar buttoned and narrow black tie knotted tight, took a long drag of his cigarette in the doorway, looked left, looked right, tossed the butt, and headed off.

When it was safe, Clyde tipped his hat to the doorman and followed.

***

This street, that street, holding back as Bradley boy stopped at a stand to buy a pack of cigs. At first Clyde had to stay far behind, but as they headed west, into an area of fancy stores and exclusive restaurants, the sidewalks grew thick with the well-heeled and high-hatted and he could stay closer. Until they joined the line heading through the checkpoint gate and into the business district.

It was always easier getting out of a Ventura District than into one, but even so, Clyde's handwritten pass from Broome was flagged and he was pulled to the side as his mark kept walking.

"Broome gave you this personally?" said one of the private guards at the gate.

"I'm on Guardsman business, joe, and I'm in a hurry."

"This doesn't look right. Maybe I should call this in, just to be sure."

"And maybe you should start looking for new guaranteed work," said Clyde. "I hear they got shifts slopping shit in the stockyards."

He got free of the gate just in time to see Brad turn a corner. Clyde did a quick hop-step-dash to catch up. As he turned the corner himself, he stopped and backed up and pulled his hat low.

Bradley boy was meeting someone outside a bar. The man was dressed in pants as tight as Brad's, a tie just as narrow. His hair was short and neat, his glasses round and tortoiseshell, his jacket plaid. The two men looked like they shopped at the same store. Clyde could just catch them bat a few words back and forth before they entered the saloon together.

Clyde didn't go in after them like a good detective would. Instead he leaned against a wall, took off his hat with one hand, and twisted an ear with the other. He tried to put it all together, tried to figure out how any of it could make any sense, and came up as empty as his bank account.

Why the hell was a Ventura slick like Bradley Illingworth swapping drinks with a goddamn hood from Tunney's Tap like Hooper?

22
MACHETE

Moonis was no longer waiting in the foul basement of his old school. He had stepped out into the night, a baseball cap pulled low, and slipped through a warren of streets as familiar as the bones in his hand, until he found himself hunkered beside a garbage bin in a trash-strewn alleyway behind, of all places, Tunney's Tap, inside which, in his time, Moonis had spilled enough beer to drown a mongoose.

Moonis gripped a rusted gardener's machete as he kept watch on the bar's rear entrance, shallowly lit by a yellow bulb incarcerated in a metal cage above the door. The air about him reeked of rot and foul, of spilled beer and vomit and sardines. Here, now, in this stinking alley, hiding from the law as he searched for his missing sister, Moonis Fell was living in the fallout of his deal, just as deGroot had seen as clear as the sunset.

"You must always remember, young Moonis," had said the wizened bus driver in his Old World accent, "if we give them the opportunity to kill us, they will. That is what they are trained for, to kill us."

"He's just a boy," said Moonis, "like every other boy."

"He's one of them, and you, sadly, are not. I fear, now, you never will be. Because this Edward Broome, he has a father. And this father, he has power. And so whatever problem you cause this boy with your so-called deal will be solved by the father."

And deGroot had been right—of course he had been right, about everything, right as death.

On his humiliating return to McGraw-Hill Guaranteed Secondary School 774, Moonis had expected that a fuss and a muss would be made of the boy who had been selected and then, with unprecedented swiftness, sent home again. But as he limped through the doors that seemed so suddenly small to him, no one paid him any mind. As he dragged his books through the narrow hallway, no one called out his name. When he took his seat next to Clyde in the Arithmetic for Bookkeepers class, no one asked what he was doing back or remarked on the bruises staining his face. The teacher droned on and the students jotted figures in their practice ledgers as if his presence there was as common as air.

Only Clyde looked straight at him, neither joy nor sorrow on Clyde's face, and without the least hint that he would have made a better show of it had he been selected, even though he surely would have. No, Clyde simply passed to Moonis in his slight sad smile a knowing resignation, like what the hell could either of them ever have expected?

***

The rear door of the bar opened to the alley. A woman stepped out, hesitant, searching. Tight dress, high heels, hair up, nice legs, arms bare.

"Moonis?" she whispered loudly enough for him to hear. "Are you there, Moonis?"

"Who's looking for him?" said Moonis.

"It's me, Marie. Remember? Cecily's friend."

Moonis stood and slipped from behind the garbage bin as he slipped the machete into his belt. "Marie? Were you the one with the red pigtails and the frogs?"

"I've grown. Clyde didn't tell me who was out here, but to get me to go along he said it had something to do with Cecily, so I hoped it would be you. When did you get back?"

"A few days ago."

"Did you do what they say you did?"

"I've done everything they ever said I did, but not the way they said it."

"That's good enough for me. If you see Cecily, give her my love. I miss her. I'd like to chat, but Clyde says I need to skedaddle before Hooper comes out looking for me. He's in the middle of something, he'll be out in a few."

"What did you promise Hooper to get him to come outside?"

"Oh, you know."

"I apologize, Marie. You're better than that."

"I was. Are you going to hurt him?"

"Not if I don't have to."

"Well, don't hold off on my account. He's not the gentleman he looks like."

"Everyone in Tunney's could have told you that."

"They did, I just didn't listen."

"You have grown, Marie. You're a whole different shade of red."

"If you get a chance, Moonis, look me up sometime."

"Where would I do that?"

"Usually here," she said with a tinge of sadness before grabbing her arms and hurrying out of the alley.

Moonis took the machete out of his pants and patted his head with the flat of the blade as he watched her walk away on those heels. The last time he had been with a woman was during a social with the women's LCM down the road from his. There was an inmate named

Joan, not half the looker that Marie had turned into. *Is something the matter?* that Joan had said. *Yeah, something's the matter,* he could have said back. *I drank too much and my ankle is killing me and you look like a gander flapping her stinking beak with every "Oh, oh, oh."* Of course he didn't say anything, he just turned her over and kept on trying.

He stared after Marie's retreating figure, and continued staring even after it disappeared. Krist. He needed to get something to eat and he needed to find some fresh clothes and he needed to find Cecily and he really, really needed to get laid.

***

He scooted back behind the bin, squatted again within the stink, and tapped his thigh with the machete as his mind veered once again to the caterpillar. Turned magically into a beautiful butterfly, it seemingly cheats gravity as it flaps its canvases of color and flits thrillingly among the flowers. Yet if our airborne caterpillar grows tired from all that flapping, it drops. Bam. Even as it beats its wings, it hasn't beaten anything. Gravity's brutal and unwavering force will eventually grind it to dust.

Was the problem the particular adaptation or the very idea of adaptation itself? And this was Moonis's insight, in that alley, behind that garbage bin behind Tunney's Tap. Adaptation required acceptance, and the hell with that. To adapt was to submit and Moonis was simply too ornery to ever grow a set of wings. Our caterpillar, instead, needs to find a way to exit the brutal system completely.

Maybe it could simply will itself to freedom. Maybe with enough concentration the caterpillar, through the intricate workings of its tiny brain, could fight to suspend the laws of the physical universe. And maybe as it engaged in the titanic effort, with its eyes shut and its mandibles tensed in the determination, it would begin to float, to rise just a bit, as all the loose detritus of the world about it did the same. And even without knowing, because its concentration would be so intense that all other sensations disappeared, it would finally, in its slight rise from the hard surface of the earth, float free, even if only for a short and glorious moment, free of the forces that had subjugated it through the entirety of its small and striving life.

***

Moonis fell back to the surface of the earth when the back door of Tunney's opened once again. This time it was Hooper stepping into the fetid alley, backlit into silhouette until the door slammed shut and Moonis could see him clearly in the sallow light. His jacket was plaid, his tie was narrow, his glasses caught a sheen of yellow that hid his eyes. He held a bottle of Old Style in one hand as he unbuckled his belt with the other.

"Marie, you minx," he said. "Get the hell on over here."

Moonis crouched lower and slid back until fully in the shadows.

"Marie, come on, don't make me chase."

Moonis waited as Hooper, now holding on to his undone pants, hopped around in a circle, edging ever closer to the garbage bin.

"It will be worse for you if I need to chase." Hop, hop, swig of beer, hop. "Come on, Marie, I'm horny as a—gaaak!"

The bottle fell to the ground, smashing into bits, beer foaming wildly about it. Moonis, standing now behind Hooper, tightened his grip around Hooper's neck.

"What the hell?" Hooper said hoarsely, weakly. "Goddamn—"

"Shut up, Hooper."

"Whoever the fuck this is you better—"

Moonis lifted the machete and showed it to Hooper, and Hooper shut up.

Moonis spun him around, grabbed him by the lapel of his jacket, slammed him up against the garbage bin with a loud metallic rattle.

Hooper looked up through his glasses first in puzzlement and then in recognition and then in abject terror.

"Let your pants drop," said Moonis.

"Moonis, what are you going—?"

Moonis pulled him forward and shoved him back into the metal bin with a violent rattle. "Just do it."

Hooper let go of his pants and they swarmed around his ankles. Protected now from a kick, Moonis jammed the business edge of the machete into Hooper's neck.

"You know that I'm a notorious fugitive," said Moonis.

"What are—?"

Moonis pressed the machete. "Just say yes, Hooper."

"Yes."

"And you know why I'm wanted by the law."

"You escaped an LCM."

"And why else?"

"The guard," said Hooper, pulling back his neck to ease the pressure of the blade.

"Did they tell you what I did to that guard?"

"I don't believe any of—"

"Just yes or no, Hooper. This isn't some revival meeting."

"Yes," said Hooper.

"Good," said Moonis, pressing the rusty blade so deep into Hooper's flesh a line of blood formed. "So, now that we understand each other, you're going to be as sharp as the edge at your throat when you answer my next question. Where the hell is my sister?"

23
THE ABYSSINIAN

The police stopped the van with the usual lights and hullabaloo just outside of Somonauk.

Somonauk was a tightfisted town barely holding on to a couple of bars, a diner, and a gas station among the husks of low brick buildings that comprised its out-of-business district. Most of the surrounding farm fields were tended now by a Monsanto LCM, and so the town now tended only to the LCM guards and the few family farmers who had foolishly held on to their land and were slowly going broke and going dead. Clyde could imagine the Saturday nights: distressed, grim affairs fueled by hard liquor and frantic sex, with only the promise of a drunken, dreamless sleep keeping the festivities from tipping over into despair.

Fun times for Somonauk.

Patti had filled the tank at the gas station while Clyde bought some sandwiches and sodas at the Country Kitchen and a six-pack at the bar next door. They had visited the filthy filling-station toilet before resuming their trip west. Maybe that's why they were stopped; they were strangers who had come through a strange town in a strange van and couldn't find a better place to piss than a gas-station toilet. What could be more suspicious?

"Where you folks headed?" said the cop, a short, swarthy hedgehog, who snuffed twice before speaking.

"Moline," said Clyde from the driver's seat. He was wearing his jacket and bow tie. His left arm was hanging out the window.

"Border town," said the cop before another double snuff. "What business you got in a border town?"

"General relaxation," said Clyde.

"This your van?"

"You bet."

"Hoffman Retirement Village?" said the cop, leaning back to read the printing on the van's white flank.

"I have a guaranteed job in Chicago taking the biddies to bingo," said Clyde.

"Can I see the registration?"

"Was I going too fast?"

"Just hand over the registration."

"I don't think I was going too fast. You think I was going too fast, Pats?"

"We was keeping it to the limit," said Patti in the passenger seat. "Calm as horseflies."

"What's with her face?" said the cop.

Clyde turned and looked at Patti, the bandage still on her nose, her cheeks now more yellow than black.

"Bad boyfriend," said Clyde. "We're taking her to Moline to cheer her up."

"That's a strange place for it."

"We heard the wine out there in Moline has a piquant bouquet."

"Registration," said the cop. "Now."

"Here you go, pal," said Clyde, pulling a folded-up paper from his shirt pocket and handing it over. "I'm sure this will do."

The cop unfolded the paper, gave it a read, took off his hat, and scratched his head. "Broome, huh?"

"So why don't you just get back in your little toy car," said Patti, "burp up that donut you just ate, and leave us on our way."

A stifled cough came from the backseat, then another, then a chain of coughs, full-blown and desperate.

"Who's the girl back there?" said the cop.

Clyde turned around and flashed Lydia a smile as she jammed two hands over her mouth, trying to strangle her coughing fit. Clyde had no choice but to bring her along. With her mother still missing, that Mrs. McGillicutty had placed a call to Children and Family Services. The social workers in their uniforms had already come looking for her. Lydia had escaped their grasp by hiding in Clyde's room, but if she stayed in the house without her mother, the do-gooders would get her eventually. It didn't go well for underage lungers sent to the orphans' home.

"She's my niece," said Clyde.

"I'm sorry," said Lydia in between stifled coughs.

"She's got a cold," said Clyde. "Playing in the rain or something. Is anything about the pass not clear?"

"Oh, it's clear all right," said the cop. "Who's that all the way in the back?"

"He's with us."

"What's with the hair and those clothes?"

"He's not from here," said Clyde, looking at Moonis in the rear-view mirror. Moonis's hair was combed out and wild, dark-brown spectacles were clipped onto his glasses, his shirt—bought by Lydia in a thrift shop, along with the clip-ons to aid the disguise—was a loosely fitting splotch of blue paisley.

"He's an Abyssinian," said Patti.

"An Aby-what?"

"He's just visiting," said Clyde.

"Does he speak English? Hey, pallie," said the cop to Moonis in the backseat. "You speaka da English?"

"Sure, sure," said Moonis, a wide, stupid smile on his face. "Two, tree, Pepsi-Cola, please."

"Get the hell out of here," said the cop. "And on your way home, take the northern route and keep the hell out of Somonauk."

"You don't need to tell me twice," said Clyde, reaching out the window and snatching back the pass before slapping the van in gear. "I've had friendlier muggings."

Clyde kept watch on the cop as they accelerated forward, the black-and-white shrinking madly in the rearview. He couldn't shake the sense that an army of bullets would soon be chasing them down the highway. He missed being enveloped by buildings and people, by the walls of his room. In the city, everything was formed and neat, the lines were starkly drawn, the expectations were clear as the ice in a glass of rye. In the wide-open spaces of the boonies, anything could happen and nobody would be the wiser. You could drive by a freshly covered grave and suspect not a thing.

But after what Hooper, with a machete at his throat, had spilled to Moonis, there was no choice but to travel through a succession of hick towns, each hickier than the last. They had nothing in their pockets but a lousy pack of questions, and the answers, it seemed, were all in Moline.

***

Bradley Illingworth had come into Tunney's, so Hooper's story went, looking for a lunger fix. Why some V-Coast rich kid with clear eyes had chosen Tunney's for his drug buy, Hooper couldn't figure, and the whole thing was suspicious enough for Hooper to send the kid packing, until Brad said he wasn't coming for himself but for Cecily Fell. To Hooper, that was another matter altogether; Cecily had always been a sweet kid, and this Brad said they were in love. It was such a romantic story that Hooper promptly overcharged him for a small bag of berry.

Soon Hooper was selling Brad recreational stuff along with his berry—first coke and then heroin, all at inflated prices. It was a rich little deal for Hooper, until good old Brad showed up at Tunney's one night strung out and shaking, looking to score without any cash at all. His family had cottoned on to his slumming love life and his rampant drug abuse, and, shocked more by the former than the latter, had cut off his stipend and frozen his trust accounts. He was on the outs, he said, and on the rocks, and Cecily was getting sicker. Brad was desperate.

Desperation is never good business, Hooper had told Moonis. To get rid of good old Brad, Hooper wove a tale about the berry in the border town: how potent, how plentiful, how cheap. He could see Brad's eyes light up, not just at the easy score, but at the opportunity, too. Hooper figured Brad would take Cecily west to score that cheap berry and to remake his fortune, purveying the drug to V-District lungers. At least that would be the plan until Raden got hold of him.

Raden didn't take kindly to anyone elbowing in on his business. Border towns were the very edge of things. Border towns were where people went to disappear. Hooper figured a soft mark like Brad wouldn't last a week in Moline.

But a couple weeks later, Brad sauntered into Tunney's with two of Raden's hoods at his side. And there was something different about him, something calm and dangerous. He wasn't a buyer anymore, he was a supplier—the supplier. In a few weeks' time, Bradley Illingworth had gone from a penniless addict to Raden's new boy in Chicago. Any berry sold on the city streets had to go through him.

How Hooper had gone from scamming Brad to fronting for him, Hooper didn't know, but what he did know was that Brad had left Chicago with Cecily, hit the border town hard, and had come back without her.

***

"Abyssinian?" said Moonis as they sped away from Somonauk.

"It just came to me," said Patti. "I read it once in a comic book."

"Batman?" said Lydia between coughs.

"*Conan.* And truth is, Moonis, it seemed to fit the shirt."

"Who the hell told you to dress like a clown anyway?" said Clyde.

"I like the shirt," said Moonis.

"You said you wanted him to look like anything but a prison laborer," said Lydia. "That's why I combed out his hair and picked up the sunglass clip-ons. He looks so dashing now, like Romeo at the ball. When I saw that shirt in the thrift shop, I knew it would be perfect."

"For a freak show," said Clyde.

"At least he don't look like his picture," said Patti. "That was the point, right?"

"What does it matter anymore? It won't be but twenty minutes before that cop scratches his suspicions by getting on the horn to Broome. And when he describes the Abyssinian in the backseat, that will be the end of that. Broome will see right through the hair, the shirt, the fake accent."

"O Romeo, Romeo," said Lydia. "Wherefore art thou Romeo?"

"In the backseat of a stolen van, twenty minutes from getting pinched," said Clyde. "We would have had a better chance in a car with dark windows and a three-nine-six under the hood. Why the hell did you steal a Kraut van, anyway?"

"It was there," said Patti.

"Didn't you see the writing on the side?"

"I wasn't reading it, I was boosting it."

"It might as well say 'Capture Me.' When we get to Moline, we're going to have to paint this thing."

"Can we paint it pretty?" said Lydia.

"Any color you want, I don't care."

"We'll paint it pretty and give it a name," said Lydia. "I've never had a car before, but when I dreamed of one, it always had a name."

"Paint it what you want and call it what you want, just so long as it's not white and you can't see the letters sticking through. Patti, you go with her. Find some second-rate chop shop that will do it on the sly. Moonis and I will hit the streets searching for Cecily."

"They'll be looking for Moonis," said Patti. "It's safer if you and me, we do the thing."

"It's my sister," said Moonis.

"Sure it is, but—"

"It's Moonis's sister," said Clyde. "The story's as simple as that. He'll be able to find her the quickest. And whatever we do, we're going to be quick about it. I got three days to get back or they're taking my job."

"Oh no," said Moonis, his voice as flat white as the color of the van. "Not your job. What will the Toddle House do without you?"

"A two-time loser on the run from the LCM is giving me guff about a guaranteed job? Krist, won't this be a party, and in a freaking border town no less."

24
THE FREECOAST

In the margin between no and yes, between long-standing and free-flowing, between the inert and the radioactive, between the dead and the quick, in these margins lived the relocation refugees. Teeming within a strip of Moline hard by the dead river, tired and tempest-tossed, forever looking over the blighted waterway to a deserted land they still plowed and planted in their dreams, they were a tribe of their own, with flowers in their hair.

The practical pragmatists, who still saw shine in the New America, had already radiated outward in caravans of buses, forsaking their pasts for guaranteed jobs in the swelling cities of Chicago and Detroit, Seattle and Denver and Austin, swarming the streets, swamping the markets for housing and food, turning their new homes crowded and gray with their grime.

But when the voices in opposition to the great migration rose in volume and violence, the buses stopped, restrictions were issued, and further guarantees were made to keep the remnants close by the border. By then all that remained were the disturbed, the clairvoyant, the unreconciled, along with their children, curly-haired waifs with glimmers of the future in their wide, innocent eyes.

They slouched in high boots or pranced in bare feet. Their piercings gleamed in the sun. They wore their denim pants low and their shirts open. Amulets from the old land hung about their necks, and babies peeked out from slings set between their swinging breasts. They were the wretched refuse of the disincorporated, estranged from all but their historic yearnings, with their own lingo, their own law, held together by sex and drugs and slogans shouted to the wind—"Self-determination is nonnegotiable," "Free the Freecoast Eight," "Nothing succeeds like secession"—along with the howls of electrified guitars that scratched the eardrums of a nation still swaying to the sweet tones of Ventura District crooners.

They were home neither here nor there, rebels with no cause but their own rebellions. And their hearts, one and all, belonged to the wasteland.

***

Moonis Fell, with his hair combed out and eyes hidden by the brown clip-ons, in blue paisley shirt and orange LCM pants, looked around and felt a surge of affection for these lost and forgotten, one and all. Something about the energy of the parade, the snarl in the music, the defiance evident in every aspect of the writhing scene, vibrated like truth in his bones.

"Stinking bunch of nut rolls," said Clyde.

"Ever wonder what they think of you," said Moonis, "with your hat and your bow tie and your jaw tense as rock?"

"They only wish they looked so sharp."

An old woman stumbled through the crowd, her clothes mere rags, her face weathered and raw with time, a stack of cards in her gnarled hand. As she approached Clyde, she staggered forward. Clyde caught her before she fell.

"Easy there, old-timer," he said.

The old woman looked up at Clyde with rheumy eyes and held out a card, which Clyde dutifully took before the woman shambled on. Clyde looked at the card, thumbed his hat higher on his head, and then handed the card to Moonis.

A picture of a woman, half-naked, chest spilling out of her top. But the text advertised not a hooker. *Top jobs with fully guaranteed wages. Must have papers. No experience necessary. Join the RCA team.*

"Imagine that," said Clyde. "A prime player like RCA has so many jobs to fill out here that it's hiring lady bums to scare up workers."

"Moline, Moline, the land of guaranteed promise," said Moonis.

"Makes you wonder who the hell's promising what."

"Jobs," said a tall, weedy man with a beard and bare feet, handing out his own set of cards. "Jobs ripe for the taking. Best company. Guaranteed wages."

Moonis snatched an offered card and took a look. "General Electric. Maybe we should salute. I heard something about this somewhere. Jobs in the borderlands are fully subsidized, with a bonus for every new hire. It's the government's way to keep the remaining refugees from pouring into the homeland. Out here you make a profit just by hiring."

"Sweet racket."

"All the rackets are sweet, Clyde, if you're on the right side of them."

"Guaranteed job, easy hours, come and get it," said a teen with floppy blond hair, floating shirtless through the crowd on roller skates.

"Hey, pal," said Clyde, grabbing not a card but the kid's wrist, spinning him into an orbiting circle. "Where can a guy score something stronger than an aspirin out here?"

The kid looked up at Clyde. "You new here, bull?" he said.

"The name's not Bull."

"With that G-man lid? You want to score a job, I can help. Other than that I got nothing."

"I already got a job," said Clyde.

"Then I got nothing." The kid yanked his wrist from Clyde's grasp and skated on.

"He thought you were blue," said Moonis.

"Me, a cop? Why, I've never been so insulted in my life."

"If Cecily's here, maybe she found friends. Take off the hat and turn down your hard-boil. Try to fit in a little."

"I don't want to fit in. With a crowd this bunk, I want to fit out. I never wanted to fit out so much in my entire life. Let's just find Cecily fast and get the hell out of here. My bet is that a bit of stiff detecting, along with a couple of stiff rights, will get us some answers, not some flower-dancing with the rest of these banana trucks."

"If you want to learn, you need to be ready to listen."

"You need to be ready to knock heads."

"Different shirts, different paths."

Clyde cocked an eye at Moonis with his wild hair, his dark glasses, his blue paisley shirt. A man in white with paint on his face and beads around his neck skipped down the road toward the river, banging all the while on a drum. A woman handed out flowers. An old man, his gray hair pulled into a ponytail, walked by smoking weed. Moonis looked like a card-carrying member of the passing parade.

"They're searching for you, Moonis, and more than just the Guard. Someone was out to kill you on that LCM."

"You think I don't know it."

"Okay then," said Clyde. "We'll do it your way, apart. Just meet up with Patti and Lydia at the diner when we said. Don't be late."

"Don't worry."

"Now get the hell out of here, you're crimping my style."

Moonis smiled. "What style is that?"

"Haven't you heard?" Clyde tightened his bow tie. "I'm the Toddle House man."

Clyde watched Moonis nod twice before heading off. There was an extra bounce in Moonis's walk, something energized and different. Or maybe it was just his limp.

"Hey, hat man. You on the level?"

The shirtless kid on roller skates was back, circling around, close enough to speak softly but far enough away that Clyde couldn't knock him off his skates with a slap to the head.

"Not your level," said Clyde.

"I know a guy might have a lead on what you were looking for."

"Is that a fact."

"Take this," said the kid, handing Clyde a card. "Tell him JoJo sent you."

Before Clyde could respond, the kid was racing off, swerving through the crowd as he made his getaway. Clyde looked at the card. It promised the usual top job, this time working for Chrysler. Krist. They were all in on it.

He turned the thing over and saw an address scrawled in the margin and a single additional word: *Dion*.

25
FREAKS

Moonis examined the surrounding spectacle from behind his dark clip-ons. A woman without shoes was juggling bowling pins, a kid with a harmonica and a guitar was singing old Okie folk songs for tips. From a stage down the road, electric guitars squealed as refugees danced like waterfalls. The blue sky was empty and clean; the sun was bright with promise. There were no sweepers, no cops; no one much was working and no one gave a damn. It was as far from an LCM as Mars.

Behind him, Clyde, in his stiff-necked getup, was talking again with the skater kid handing out work leaflets. Clyde didn't look so much like he came from the big city as out of a black-and-white movie from another era. Moonis felt a kick in his gut for abandoning Clyde—it reminded him of all those years before, when Moonis had left Clyde and Patti and Cecily behind to rise to the Ventura School. He had the urge to take Clyde's hand and lead him through whatever wall existed between him and this dazzling scene, but Clyde would balk. He once had been as open as anyone to the wide possibilities in the world, but life and the system had closed him off to them. Now he was Clyde, always Clyde, doomed forever to be Clyde.

But Moonis looked around and felt strangely at home. He could lose himself here, and if there was a trace of Cecily to be found among these refugees, maybe losing himself here was the only way to find it. In a deserted grass field, weedy and pocked with tents, a group clad in orange robes sat together in the open. A bald man with a long beard seemed to be leading the group, but no one was paying him much attention. The color of the robes almost perfectly matched Moonis's pants. It was a place to start.

He took off his paisley shirt and tied it around his waist. He felt the heat of the sun warm his bare chest like a mother's hug as he headed into the field. When he reached the group, he found an open patch of grass and sat beside a woman in her early twenties, with a black velvet band tied around her neck. He twisted his legs into a position to mimic hers and hummed along with the chants of the rest of them, faking it like someone making up words to a song on the radio. A joint was being passed from hand to hand. When it came his way he took it and sucked at it greedily.

The glowing tip of the joint shortened and sparked.

***

"Do you have any food?" said the woman next to Moonis after a long bout of meaningless chant. She had long straight hair, brown and shining, and pale skin. The pupils in her pretty eyes were the size of pennies.

"Not a thing," said Moonis. "I'm sorry."

"Don't be sorry."

"What about a store, isn't there a store?"

"There are plenty of stores."

Her eyes were not so much vacant as open, open to anything. Deep, shimmering pools of brown with flecks of light. He wanted to dive in, as if the answer to every mystery in the whole of the universe were submerged within those pools.

He took a photograph from his pocket, a picture of Cecily on the first day of her teaching job. Cecily had posed, all pretty and prideful and scared. He stared at it for a moment, saw Cecily cock her hip in the photograph, and then handed the picture to the girl.

"She's pretty," said the girl.

"She's my sister. I'm here to search for her."

"She looks sweet."

"She is," said Moonis, taking back the photograph.

"What's her name?"

"Cecily."

"What's your name?"

"Moonis."

"I like your name. Moonis. And I like your pants. I'm Trout."

"I'm new here, Trout, but wherever I've been, there's always someone who knows everyone."

"Jarvis," she said, laughing. "You're talking about Jarvis."

"Where can I find this Jarvis?"

"Around. He's always around. Everyone knows Jarvis."

"RCA's hiring, according to the guy handing out cards," said Moonis. "You could get a job."

"Why would I want to do that?"

"For the money. For the store. For the food."

"Are you working for RCA, Moonis?"

"No," he said.

"Do you want to? Are you jumping up to give your soul over to RCA?"

"I'm a little confused, here, Trout. What's the point of all this sitting and chanting?"

"Point?"

"Yes."

"You are confused. My maharishi told me Chandra was in ascendance and now here you are."

"I never met this Chandra," said Moonis.

"Chandra is the lunar deity. I'm supposed to seize the opportunity of her rising to nurture my emotional side. Do you want to make it, Moonis?"

"I need to find my sister."

"Well, you won't find her here," said Trout, pulling out another joint.

***

They returned together to the field, hand in hand, each in their own glow of understanding, and sat again with crossed legs and eyes closed. There Moonis stayed until the sounds tasted sour in his mouth and his knees turned into lizards. He looked at Trout, sitting prettily, her voice sweet, lost in her own mind. To say good-bye would jerk her away from a place of peace and contentment, and so he left without a word.

The grasses of the field writhed with bursts of color, a living landscape painted by Van Gogh. He followed the road down to the riverfront, floating along walkways made of air, passing card players, a row of rough wooden hovels, a circus tent whose stripes were pirouetting.

Down by the Mississippi, a heron stood on the quay, playing a ukulele, colors flying like little birds from the sound hole. A giant frog in a wool cap sat on the stone wall, fishing, a bucket glowing on the wall beside him.

Moonis raised a hand to shield his eyes from the light pouring out of the water. The river was blazing, as if there were a fire raging somewhere beneath the thin surface. From his fingertips, swirls of color spiraled, blending into the radiance of the river so that he couldn't exactly tell where his flesh ended and the river began.

The light was made even brighter by the darkness on the far bank beyond the ruined span of the bridge, a darkness that moaned into his ears. It sounded like the wind having sex with the water, like trees birthing and swallows dying and the keen of pure truth.

It was the most beautiful sound he had ever heard.

He took out the photograph of Cecily. He was able to look beyond the shiny finish into the scene on the street, and from within that scene Cecily smiled at him and told him it would be okay, that she loved him and trusted him and forgave him. "I know you're coming," she told him. "All I need is a sign."

Something in his stomach lurched, something huge started crawling. As his bare stomach distended he could make out a shelled insect, with plates on its back and a thousand legs, scuttling inside.

He instinctively knew the vile insect inside him was his loneliness. He missed her, the girl in the photograph, he missed his sister. And he missed his mother, who had run away. And he missed his father, who had stayed and worked like a dog and drank like a fish and died. And he even missed Patti and Clyde, though he had been with them that very day. The insect of loneliness had been growing in his gut for years, ever since his selection and great failure. Somehow he had become acclimated to the monster's presence, but now, suddenly, it was rising up his throat, anxious to be released into the world. The vile thing was climbing so high it threatened to choke the life out of him.

He fell to his knees, and leaned over the water, and threw up the loneliness, and when it hit the water, with all its legs spinning, the hard-shelled thing swam away. It swam past the island that rose like a garrison in the middle of the river, and continued swimming toward the far bank, toward the desolation, toward the moan that called to his heart, swimming so fast and sure it was as if it knew where it belonged and was as determined as death to get there. As if the solution to its pain were there, over there, on the other side of the foul, burning river.

Moonis Fell watched the great arthropod swim away, just a fading blip of darkness within the river's glow, and he felt serene, and loved, and at one with the river and the world on either side of it.

Man alive, he thought, the weed out here is pretty damn outstanding.

***

The old man was sitting on a folding chair not far from the quay, sunglasses on to protect him from the river's glow. In front of him, set on a milk crate, was a flat piece of cardboard colored into a chessboard. The old man, his dark face glowing with a swirl of red, his beard long and tangled and weaving itself into knots, was studying the position of the pieces on his board as if much of the universe could be explained in the array of bishops and pawns.

"Move the horsey thing," said Moonis.

The old man didn't look up as he pursed his lips over teeth that moved like caterpillars inside his mouth. "Don't be talking on something you know nothing about."

"I know chess."

"That don't mean you know anything 'bout the game I'm playing." The old man rubbed his jaw, moved his knight. "Press on, son. You're in my light."

"I'm looking for Jarvis," said Moonis. "Do you know Jarvis?"

"All I know for sure is you smell like sex, and you in my light."

"I smell like sex?"

"You been eating tuna fish, boy?"

"No."

"They you go. Other than that, I can't say a word."

"Why can't you say?"

"Because strangers cause me trouble, they been causing me trouble my entire life. Was a stranger that took my teeth, was a stranger that took my wife. I got no truck with them. And I know you're not from 'round here or you'd know better than to stand in my light."

"So you don't want to play?"

"Do it look like I was sitting here, hoping some fool would come around and start talking about horsey things? Horsey things. No, sir, I got better ways to waste my time."

"You must like playing with yourself."

"Don't be sassy. I suppose the only way to get rid of your shadow is to show you a thing or two."

"I suppose so."

"Then get your ass down so as I get my light back. You don't mind if I play white."

"Be my guest," said Moonis, sitting on the ground.

"Good," said the old man as he began to set up the pieces. "Because it was going to happen whether you minded or not."

***

The game was a massacre.

Moonis could hear the lamentation of the old man's bishops and pawns as he brutally wiped them off the board. It was like the old man was offering him the game, square by square, move by disastrous move, and Moonis took full advantage. Blood flowed like oil as he slaughtered the old man's army. The old man said not a word through the butchery.

"That didn't take long," said Moonis.

"Course it didn't," said the old man, "the way you was playing."

"I won, didn't I?"

"They you go."

"You weren't playing to win?"

"I was playing to play."

"The point of the game is to win, old man. Everybody knows that."

"Yeah, and what else does everybody know? That the sun rises and the moon sets? That crime don't pay? That happiness can be pursued? That sex is better than shitting?"

"I don't need to hear about your troubles on the pot."

"Not that it's none of your business."

"So, we were talking about Jarvis."

"You were talking about Jarvis. I was talking about chess. Set them up, boy."

"Wasn't once enough?"

"Maybe this time you'll play right."

"You're on, old man."

"I ain't old," said the man as he replaced his pieces on the board. "I'm just well seasoned."

***

It began with the old man moving forward his king's pawn. Moonis didn't hesitate and within three moves he was back to pressing his attack. But he concentrated more carefully on the board this time, trying to divine what the old man was up to even as Moonis again gained a dominant position. And then the old man moved his knight, and a sound sparked in Moonis's head, a series of notes like a sweet smiling song from a violin.

The old man's move wasn't a good move—it took the knight from the center of the board and weakened the old man's defenses—but there was something about it. The move was—what word would Moonis use?—playful. The shift up and to the right, balanced against the position of the other pieces, was like an artistic gallop. And the horse seemed to grin into it.

"Are these pieces making faces at you?" said Moonis.

"Not at me," said the old man. "They's just pieces. But I don't smoke none of that wack they lace up with government poison."

"What kind of government poison?"

"Not everyone thinks that's what it is, but whenever did the government start caring about our spiritual development? About opening up our consciousness? Your move."

Moonis could take the knight or attack the suddenly weakened center of the board. But his own knight was nodding at him. And he realized if he skipped that knight to the opposite side of the board, there would be a lovely symmetry with the old man's move, as if the pieces were playing not against each other but with each other. Of course it would leave a pawn undefended and open his own position to attack. And more deeply, it would violate the whole construct of chess as it had been played for two thousand years. But with the melody from the violin still echoing, Moonis felt the peculiar urge to improvise a little jazz, right there on the board.

He made the move, looked up, saw the old man rub his jaw.

A bishop to the right, a rook to the left, a knight swooping into the middle of it all. And suddenly the pieces weren't fighting tooth and tongue, they were dancing, prancing across the board in a ballet of form and movement, with threats and feints and breathtaking symmetry. The pace quickened, the positions swirled, the music grew more complex. Moonis laughed at the play, and the old man laughed with him, and the pieces seemed to rise into their moment, leading Moonis forward step by joyous step.

And in the drugged and overheated crevices of Moonis's consciousness, he began to glimpse a way of being in the world different than his two default modes of battling or succumbing. Maybe here lay the answer to his caterpillar quandary. Maybe the caterpillar needed to step outside the system of win and lose, up and down. It was only a glimmer of the possibility of an idea, but it struck him hard and filled his soul with a bright green light.

He was still trying to make sense of it all when, within this coordinated dance of chess, the old man's bishop sliced across the board and murdered Moonis's cavorting queen.

***

Moonis was taken aback for a moment by the slaughter, as if some new rule had been violated. But he replayed the dance of the pieces in his head, and this time the brutal move didn't feel like a betrayal so much as a thing of beauty, like the suicide of Lady Macbeth, with all its pain and sweet inevitability.

"That hurt," said Moonis.

"I had no choice," said the old man.

"I know. It was the next step in the dance."

"I still hated to do it."

"Anything else would have been false."

"I'm Digger," said the old man.

"Moonis."

"That's about right. You got something in your eye there, Moonis."

"A sty?"

"A beam. That Jarvis you looking for? He can be found sometimes in that tent up the road."

"The circus tent that was spinning like a top?"

"Only spinning when you're wacked. Now why you need a chump like Jarvis?"

"I'm looking for someone and he might be able to help me find her." Moonis took out the picture, handed it to Digger, watched as the old man's face lit with the blue light of recognition while spurts of yellow flame flicked from his scalp.

"What's she to you?" said Digger.

"She's my sister."

"Imagine that."

"You know her."

"I know a lot of people."

"But you know her."

"Let's go see what Jarvis has to say."

"Aren't we going to finish the game?"

"We already done that," said Digger. "Come on, boy. I'll take you to the circus. And I'll watch your back, too, because with Jarvis, it will need watching."

26
GEEKS

"You ever stand on the riverbank and stare up at the stars and wonder what we're doing here?" Dion, a long-haired geek in leather pants with no shirt and a belt of silver medallions, smoked a reefer as he stood behind the counter of a shoddy storefront shack called Puberty, selling comic books, pornography, and inebriants. "It puts everything in perspective." Inhale. "You want a hit?"

"I'm here on business, joe."

"Suit yourself, man."

Exhale.

"Those stars," said Dion, "so damn far away and brighter than your soul, can make you feel small, tiny as an ant, which is a nice feeling for a change. We're so wrapped in our own little heads, our own little heads, our own little heads. It's a revolution just to step outside for a bit."

"You stepped outside, all right," said Clyde.

"And not just out of my head, but out of this whole false construct they've built around us. You know what you see when you step out of everything, man? Out your head, out your clothes, out of the little boxes they stuff you in?"

"I'm trying not to imagine."

"You see freedom, man, freedom. You need to try it sometime." He took another hit, closed one eye, and stared with the other at Clyde. "I knew a preacher once with a bow tie. He tried to save me. Talk about a job with heavy lifting. Are you a believer?"

"Sure I am. And you know what I believe?"

"What's that?"

"That you couldn't scrape up a bag of berry if I put a gun to your head. Maybe we should try."

Dion stared a bit, the emotions on his face washed to a fearful blankness for a moment before he started laughing. Like everyone else Clyde had met in this wacko border town, Dion talked too damn much about nothing at all, while getting nothing done. The storefront was empty except for the two of them. A place that quiet left Dion a lot of time to smoke reefer and jack off, while imagining himself fast as the Flash. Puberty. Perfect.

"Are we doing business," said Clyde, "or are we just talking?"

"You want to get down to hard business?" said Dion. "Okay, here's the business." Inhale. A moment looking at the shortening tip of his smoke. Exhale. "No matter what JoJo said, I can't get you no berry. I can get you bam, barb, bop, blow, blond, or the ever-popular bud. But no berry."

"Then what good are you?" said Clyde.

"Now that's a question worth pondering. That's a question for the stars. But berry is out. They've locked up the supply."

"Who?"

"Look, it's dangerous even to be talking about it. So if you're done here, I got to get back to work."

"That's right," said Clyde, looking around the desolate storefront. "Before your customers start a riot. If you don't know nothing about nothing, who might know something?"

"Ruby, maybe."

"Where do I find this Ruby?"

"In a bar called Big Brother, by the bridge. But it's a rough spot and she's a tiger."

"I'm from the west end of Chi-Town. I think I can handle a girl named Ruby." Clyde took a picture out of his pocket, placed it gently on the counter, turned it around, pushed it toward the man. "You ever see her around?"

Dion put the joint in his lips, picked up the photograph, squinted before smiling in recognition.

"Did she come in here looking to buy?" said Clyde.

"Not here. And not buying, if you know what I mean."

"No, I don't know what you mean."

"If anything, she was selling."

"Selling what?"

"I'll show you."

Dion stepped out from behind the counter and headed to the pornography wall. Amidst the breasts and thighs and perky buttocks was a bin with a stack of flyers. Dion took one, looked it over, handed it to Clyde.

It was an advertisement for a strip club in Old Moline, the ScuttleButt, the name surrounded by pictures of a dozen dancers, each picture fronting a great gold star. Clyde looked down at the paper, up at Dion, who was smiling like an idiot, back down at the paper. Then he saw her, in the corner, naked leg out, jaw tilted up, name listed as Cinnamon. And Clyde's face stayed flat as brick even as his stomach tightened in disappointment, followed by disappointment at his own disappointment. The world is hard, all of us sell what we need to get by, no one is immune, and yet—

"'Oh, Cinnamon, let me in,'" sang Dion. "But you're out of luck, man. Cinnamon, she wasn't there last time I hit up the ScuttleButt. But when she was, damn. Talk about the stars shining brightly."

***

Clyde stood in the shadows of what had been the Iowa–Illinois Memorial Bridge, a hulking structure that once leaped across the great turn in the course of the Mississippi but now reached only a third of the way before vanishing, as if it led not to the far bank, but to some other dimension. The Homeland Guard had bombed the span in the midst of the relocation riots, along with all but one of the other bridges in the then Quad Cities, in order to keep stark control over everything that went into and out of the disincorporated territories. What had once been Davenport and Bettendorf on the other side of the river were now only unreachable ruins.

But the vestige of the old bridge had not gone to waste. On its surface a crust of lean-tos and tables sold vegetables, meats, fish pulled from the radiating river—"tooth-stealers," the old folk called them— along with moth-ridden clothes, ratty furniture, pillows infested with fleas. But the most prized items in the market were the smuggled fragments of the lost life scavenged from the ruined cities that loomed across the waterway. In the telling of tales over the fires that pocked the surface of the bridge at nightfall, these lost cities of Iowa loomed as a mythical land of joy and plenty.

The streets, they said, the streets of Bettendorf were paved with . . .

Beneath the bridge's span, surrounded by a shining pack of motor-cycles, a saloon leaned off one of the bridge's enormous pillars, like a drunk leaning off a lamppost, about to collapse into a pool of his own vomit. It was a twisting, uneven structure, covered by unreadable graffiti and clad in wire fencing, with great black cords and gray pipe snaking through walls and into various windows to connect it to the city's power and water. A hissing neon sign affixed atop the doorway blinked on and off, on and off, the name of the bar shining red above a huge blue eye.

BIG BROTHER TAP

The door slammed closed behind Clyde, quieting the crowd for a moment as it turned to stare at him in his getup. Even the singer on the stage, a big-boned redhead backed by a drummer and a bass player, stopped plucking her guitar for a moment and tilted her head. Clyde sucked his teeth and stared back at the longhairs and motorheads. Let them try to figure him out. A moment later, bored already by the sight of him, they all turned around and went back to their business, except the singer, who kept staring even as she started again with the strumming.

He stepped to the bar on the right side of the room and surveyed the scene. The lighting was uneven, the space was thick with smoke, the vests of the cyclists sported a skull with wings, and the T-shirts of the longhairs radiated color. On the graffiti-scarred walls, neon beer signs glowed nostalgically, each for a brewery dead in the D-Lands— Falstaff, Hamm's, Griesedieck Brothers, Muehlebach, Goetz Country Club, and, most reverently missed, Budweiser. It was almost enough to bring a tear to the eye of someone not raised ninety miles south of Milwaukee.

A couple of the women fit his image of this Ruby, hard-eyed types sitting next to muscle, in denim or leather. When his drink came, rye on the rocks, Clyde turned away from the room and asked the barkeep.

"You see this crowd?" said the bartender. "Whoever's here is here for Ruby."

"Busy girl. Which one is she?"

"The one onstage."

Clyde nodded like it was as obvious as rain before downing the rye. Without turning, he listened to the voice, rough as ground glass, rich with pain. She was singing about freedom won and love lost and loneliness, and it sounded like she knew what she was singing.

When the song ended, with a clatter of claps and bottles banging on tables, she started in on another. Clyde turned and watched her strum and sing. Between verses she watched him watching. He wasn't surprised that at the end of the set she made her way straight to him.

"I been waiting on you, darling," she said, hitching onto the stool next to Clyde. She smiled at him with surprising warmth. Her mouth was wide, her eyes were wide, her wide nose was freckled. Everything about her was oversized, and her copper hair was wild about her face. "But I didn't think you'd be alone. Where's your friend?"

"You've got the wrong party, sister."

"Do I?"

"The name's Clyde."

"It doesn't really matter."

"You know a kid named JoJo?"

"The dog-faced boy?"

"JoJo sent me to Dion, who sent me to you."

"I once broke a bottle over Dion's head. Since then he's sent noth-ing but trouble my way. How do you like my singing?"

"It's a little rough."

"Thank you, darling. Hey, Levon," she said to the barkeep. "Pull me up my bottle."

When the bottle came, a half-emptied fifth of Southern Comfort, she grabbed it by the neck. "Let's get down to business, Clyde."

***

They sat at a table in the corner, where Clyde had a view of the door, and they drank the rock-candy whiskey and talked and joked. When

Ruby laughed, it came from deep inside and rattled the walls before she choked it off with a drink. The way she drank, it was clear she could drink him under the table, and her smile let him know she'd take full advantage of him when she did. She had rings on her fingers and bangles on her wrists and was as alluring as a rattlesnake with an apple in its mouth. She was electric.

"You're a dangerous man, Clyde, and you don't even know it. I always had a thing for dangerous men."

"I bet you scare them more than they scare you."

"Ain't that the truth. Chicago, right? Your accent is like a bumper sticker on your ass."

"Where's your accent from?"

"Texas."

"You're not a refugee."

"You ever been to Texas?"

"How long you been in this freak show?"

"A couple years."

"Why here?"

"No swing band is paying me to sing in something slinky in your hometown."

"I sure as hell would pay to see that."

"You and me both, brother. Hell, all I ever wanted to do was to sing, but I didn't fit where I was from. I drifted a bit, hitched here and there looking for gigs. It never clicked until I landed here. Whatever I got, they seem to take to it, so here I stay. At least for the now."

"It's getting old here in Freaksville?"

"I thought at first it was the promised land of milk and freedom. But you know, it's not much different than Texas when you cut down to the bone. There's always a system. What are you looking for, Clyde?"

Clyde leaned forward, lowered his voice. "Medicine."

"There's a pile of pharmacies in Old Moline."

"They don't have what I need. Do you have what I need, Ruby, or are we just playing games here?"

"Oh, I have what you need, Clyde. And I got this, too."

She took a small bottle from a pocket in her shirt, opened the lid, shook something into her palm before rolling it onto the table. A single berry, red and bright, brighter than any berry Clyde had ever seen. From the pucker of its skin, he could tell the strange fruit had only started to wither. He picked it up, rolled it in his fingers, brought it to his nose, and smelled the bitterness, a scent astringent enough to burn the disease right out of your soul.

"Fresh from the farm," said Ruby. "But you need to know what you're getting into, Clyde. This is treacherous stuff."

"I've handled it before."

"Not this stuff, baby. This is tariff-free."

"I don't get you."

"Jarvis has us going on about how grand it's going to be once we get the Establishment off our asses. Free this, free that, Freecoast. But that's only half the problem. Out here, we rely on our links to the other side, but they are utterly controlled."

"By who?"

"Godzilla."

"Raden."

She flinched when Clyde said the name and then looked about. "He's like a bull standing on the shoulders of another bull. He controls the barter between here and there. Gasoline, artifacts, rutabaga."

"Rutabaga?"

"There's no rutabaga like D-Land rutabaga. And he controls the berry. Everything passes through him, and from everything that passes he takes a piece."

"That's the tariff."

"But for some reason he's closed the berry tap into Moline, and people are hurting. I'm hurting."

"You?"

"I sing like this 'cause I got no choice, and I learned to like it. But I was the sweetest little canary you ever heard before it hit me. How about you? You look clear-eyed and red-cheeked, and you haven't coughed once since you've been in here."

"It's not for me."

"Tell me the sad story."

"It's for a girl."

"I'm blowing my nose."

"She's just a kid, Ruby. Krist, I'm not even related. She's just a kid I've been stuck with that's got it bad."

"They're all just kids." She lifted the bottle, gave it a shake, then put it on the table, pressed it toward him. "On the house, darling."

"But that's yours."

"Get it while you can, Clyde, the situation you're in. There's just a few doses in there. If you come back tomorrow, same time, I'll see if I can rustle a full load for you. It will cost."

"It always does. So tell me, Ruby, what situation do you think I'm in? And why did you think I had a friend?"

"You're a dangerous man, Clyde. They're out after you, and you don't even know it."

"I'm getting the idea, though. Tell me something else. You get many Guardsmen in this joint to hear you sing?"

"Never."

"Well, you do today. A couple just came through the door."

"Oh, sweetie, you're just so adorable," she said, without turning around, "but they didn't come for me."

27
THE GREATEST SHOW ON EARTH

When Moonis stepped into the multicolored tent, having followed the old man up the road and through the flap door, it was as if he had stepped into some sort of alternative world of magic and merriment. Under the great expanse of canvas, amidst the competing strains of electric guitar and calliope, there were clowns clowning and gymnasts flipping and folks dancing on the dirt, along with stretches of those doing nothing but loafing and drinking, reefing, making out. And then there were the mimes.

Yeah, mimes.

Moonis had the sense that this place, this madcap madhouse, was the physical manifestation of the game he had played with the old man, a game with purposes and strategies beyond those he had ever before known to exist. Though his high was fading, Moonis could still see giant snakes of color snapping and slithering through the big top, and each massive flow of energy seemed to emanate from a single man, about his age, rock-jawed and mop-haired, standing on a drum at the center of the footprint, lecturing to a diverse group of youth and oldster both.

"Jarvis," said Digger before spitting on the dirt.

This Jarvis was a supernova of verve and vim, with vibrating colors swirling on his shirt and radiating across his aura. He waved his hands wildly and hopped atop the drum like a rabid ferret on Benzedrine, while he preached to the dazed, adoring eyes staring up at him.

Moonis stepped close to hear his sermon, the word according to Jarvis.

***

"We're bringing the big top tomorrow, my fellow circus freaks. Why a circus? Because people love the circus, man. Who doesn't love the circus? Wild animals, trapeze artists, clowns, mimes. Forget your Kalashnikovs; give me an army of mimes and I'll change the world.

"We tried it the other way, but it fell flatter than a pancake on the highway. It always will. Wave a sign, give a speech, and all you get is six hundred words in the *New York Times* on the 'So-Called Freecoast Eight,' buried in the City section, below the fold. In terms of creating a new reality, that gets us nothing. The *New York Times* is death to us. It's all about words with them, you know: let's cross words, let's analyze words with more words. Soon as you analyze a movement, man, it's dead. But send a troupe of mimes into a jailhouse to liberate a cell of political prisoners, and people get that right away.

"It's all about understanding the media, man. The circus is meant for TV, and I don't mean all those bullshit political shows like *Meet the Press*, you know, where you get a New Democrat and a New Republican arguing back and forth, this and that, this and that, yeah, yeah. What's that shit? We want to be prime time, we want to be the variety shows, the sitcoms, we want to be the shit where people are looking at it and digging it. A game show beaming into the eyeballs of every working slob with a guaranteed job in the incorporated areas. That's what moves the world."

***

As soon as Jarvis spied Moonis standing amidst the crowd, his brows lifted in recognition. He cut off his talk and leaped toward Moonis like he had been expecting him, like Jarvis and Moonis were the oldest of pals.

"Welcome, Moonis, welcome," said Jarvis. "Trout told me you'd be coming. What a lovely girl, you know what I mean? I know you do. And it's good to see you, too, Digger. You don't come around much."

"I know a circus when I see one," said Digger.

"Exactly, man. Exactly. You came at a good time. We're in the middle of organizing something big, something that will blow the doors off this whole fucking town."

As Jarvis spoke, Moonis felt the power of the man, a charisma and energy almost sexual in its intensity, like a sirocco at midnight. Jarvis could capture you with a single smile, for when Jarvis smiled at you, you wanted nothing more than to earn it, to widen it. Moonis had never felt anything like it.

"I'll be with you both right after I finish with these rookies. Meanwhile, grab something to drink, something to smoke. Have you met Sylvie? Oh man, Moonis, you need to meet Sylvie."

"Watch your pockets," said Digger after Jarvis skipped away, talked to a man and a woman, and then jumped back onto his drum. The man he had talked to headed out of the tent. The woman, a blonde with a wide smile and hollow eyes, walked toward Moonis.

"He's after something," said Digger. "He always is."

"I don't have much for him to steal," said Moonis.

"You got pants, don't you?"

"Hello, baby," said the blonde. She pulled his face down to hers and kissed him wetly. She tasted fresh and bright, a sprig of mint. "I'm Sylvie."

***

"See, Madison Avenue people think like the circus all the time. No matter what the people are watching on their precious televisions, the admen are selling something else. The show is text. The subtext is buy, baby, buy. You can't step out your door without those boys stuffing something down your throat. Tide, Cheer, Dove, Brillo, Hellmann's. Hell, man, enough. It's time they start buying us.

"That's why the long hair. I mean, shit, you know, long hair is just another prop. You go on TV and you can say anything you want, but the people are looking at you and they see a bunch of sex-loving, dope-loving beatnik weirdos doing nothing but screwing and drinking and slacking, and they shake their heads, but deep inside they're thinking, hey, man, there's a choice.

"I mean, who the hell wouldn't want to get in on that? Our text is life is fun, life's a gas, party on. Our subtext is burn, baby, burn. Trust me, burning is always an easier sell than buying. For one thing, it takes less cash.

"So picture this, all right. An army of pretty little mimes in white face, white shirts, short plaid skirts. But they also got pints of pigs' blood in little plastic bags. A cop goes to hit one of them, right. When he lifts his stick, she takes her bag of blood and goes whack, over her own head. All this blood pours out, running bright red down her pale mime face, staining her virgin-white shirt. And the fucking cop is left standing there with his jaw on the floor. Now that says a whole lot more than a picket sign.

"People come down and look around and holy shit, what the hell is going on? Blood all over the fucking place, smoke bombs going off, shouts, and flares. Yeah, man, that's the circus. Let the *New York Times* take a picture of that. That's page one, above the fold. That's the nightly news. You convince them you're crazy enough, they'll pay you to let them leave you alone. And that's what we're fighting for, the right to be left the fuck alone. So tomorrow we're going to be so crazy they'll leave us alone for decades, man. We're going to rage in a new age. Power to the people, man. Refugee power. Free food, free drugs, freedom, hear that crazy bell chime, free the Freecoast Eight."

***

After his speech, and after conferring with a few of his followers, Jarvis danced over and put his arm around Moonis.

"Now what can I do for you, Moonis? Anything. *Mi casa es su casa,* man."

"It's a big *casa*," said Moonis, looking around, laughing.

"And this is just the bedroom. Hey, Sylvie, sweets, get our friend Digger something to eat. You hungry there, Digger?"

"I'll stay with Moonis," said Digger, rubbing his jaw.

"No, Moonis and I, we need to talk in private," said Jarvis. "Sylvie, get my man Digger something macrobiotic. Some spelt, some teff, a little agar-agar. And sprouts, grown right alongside our Hawaiian special grade A. You'll love the sprouts."

"I don't want no sprouts," said Digger.

"And a beer."

"Beer?" said Digger.

Moonis gave Digger a sign that it was all right, and then let Jarvis lead him toward the back of the tent.

"What did you think of the speech?" said Jarvis.

"It was a speech, all right," said Moonis. "It had enough words to qualify. But it felt like you were gearing up for a war."

"We're ready for it if it comes. In the guerrilla circus, you need to be willing to pay any price for the people's advancement."

"Advancement?"

"What do you think we're here for, man, kicks? Well, kicks, for sure, but more. It's time to carve out a system of our own in the midst of their crap. We're all outcasts anyway—you can dig that, right? I notice you limp. LCM?"

"They sent me up twice after deciding once was not enough."

"What did you do?"

"It was what I didn't do that pissed them off."

"Then you do dig it. We're already self-contained, self-centered, self-involved, self-regulating. It's about time we are self-determined, too."

"I just can't get my head around paying 'any price,'" said Moonis, shaking his head. "That doesn't sound like getting away with it. That sounds like a politician sending others into combat."

"Do I look like a politician?"

Moonis spied a large group just behind them now, the same disciples who had been listening to the speech, their eyes still starry, following the two of them as Moonis and Jarvis made their way to the back of the tent. Suddenly the scene didn't seem so playful anymore—more programmed, determined, the manic playfulness of wound-up dolls.

"Someone always ends up in charge," said Moonis. "That's just the fate of things."

Jarvis laughed. "Lighten up, man. Trout said you were looking for someone. How can I help? I am your servant."

Moonis doubted that, but he took out the picture anyway and handed it over.

"Dig that, man," said Jarvis. "Who is she to you?"

"My sister."

"Yeah, I recognize her, of course I do. You don't forget someone who looks like that. Except she hasn't been around in a while. That's what happens in a border town: people drifting in, and then drift-ing out again. But I'm wired here. I'll pass the word that her brother is looking for her. I'll get you some answers. But in exchange, you're going to have to help us."

"Me?"

"Oh yeah."

"I'm nothing and no one," said Moonis. "I can't even help myself."

"Dig it, man, everyone's got a part to play in the circus. See, here's the thing. It's okay for a cop to crack the head of a mime, but heaven help us if a mime is cracking the head of a cop. As soon you pick up a gun, you're worse than history, man, you're irrelevant. On the other side, all they'll see is the threat, and then you've got nothing in your future but the wrong end of a tank. You get me, man?"

"Get what?" said Moonis.

"The same way we can't pick up a gun, we can't have a murderer in our ranks."

As Jarvis took hold of one of his arms, it came to him, what should have come to him sooner, what the forced playfulness and the forced smiles should have told him before, and he nodded into the truth of it. The gang behind was getting closer, some of the crowd members were holding juggling pins as cudgels. And behind them, the old man, Digger, was being held back from coming to his aid by two longhairs with leather vests.

"The answer is yes," said Moonis.

"Yes what?"

"You do look like a politician." He said it flatly, like it was the vilest insult he could hurl.

"It was a deal that had to be made," said Jarvis.

"My skin for what?"

"We give them you, we get our people out of jail. Our action tomorrow is a guaranteed success, the Freecoast Eight are as good as free."

"Power to the people."

"You got that right."

"As long as it's the right people. Where is my sister?"

"On the other side, man, good as gone. It's time to stop thinking about her and thinking about yourself. Do your time, man, come back to us, and we'll welcome you like a hero."

"I don't want to be a hero. I just want to find her. You might be playing their game like a master, Jarvis, but it's still their game."

Just as the gang got close enough to grab hold, Moonis slammed his elbow into Jarvis's jaw to free himself from the man's grip before sprinting toward the rear exit of the tent. The gang was shouting, charging after him, raising their cudgels. They were only a few feet away when he hit the flaps and shot out of the tent.

Six cops were waiting.

One tripped him.

A second kicked his face as he fell.

A third put his knee on Moonis's back while a fourth cuffed him.

And the final two just stood there, shaking their heads the way cops do when the inevitable stamps down like a boot on the face.

28
MOE'S EATS

"Where's Moonis, Clyde?" said Lydia, in the breathless voice she had when her lungs were tight as a drum.

"Don't know," said Clyde. He slid into the booth beside Lydia, took off his hat, rubbed his hands together. "I'm starving. I could go for a burger and maybe some chili, if it's hot enough. What about you guys?"

"What do you mean you don't know?" said Patti.

They were at the spot they all had picked out before Patti had dropped them off to do their detective work, Moe's Eats, in Old Moline, in the shadow of the courthouse. It was one of those stainless-steel joints that had been grilling burgers since Coolidge was president, the grill black with ancient grease, the counterman as old as the grill. The kind of place where the waitress wore pink and the men wore hats, with no freaky refugees in sight.

"You two were supposed to stay together," said Patti. "You were supposed to be looking out for him, Clyde."

"Yeah, well, it's not so easy. Moonis thought I was cramping his style. You want some tea, Lydia?"

Lydia stifled a cough and nodded, before the coughing got the best of her and she went into a jag.

"What were the plans you made with him?" said Patti.

"To meet back here."

"When?"

"Now."

"Krist," said Patti.

"Did you guys already eat or something?"

"This isn't right," said Patti. "You shouldn't have let him go off alone like that. The whole reason we're out here is to take care of him."

"It's his sister we're hunting, he gets to call the shots. Don't worry—Moonis is like a cat with iron boots."

"What does that mean?" said Lydia.

"It means don't be beneath him when he lands on his feet."

Clyde made a point of not telling them that he himself had almost been nabbed by two Guardsmen. He had been ready to whip out his pass right there in the bar, not expecting it to work based on the hard expressions on their Guard faces, when Ruby turned around, stuck two fingers in her mouth and whistled. A pack of motorcyclists with black leather vests stood, picked up on Ruby's slight finger twirl, and started a scene right there in the middle of the floor. The commotion was enough for Ruby to lead Clyde out the back door.

"Why'd you do that for me?" said Clyde.

"Because you're a dangerous man, darling," said Ruby, "and I got a soft spot for just that thing. You come back tomorrow and I'll have that load for you we talked about."

"You're something, aren't you?"

"Yes, yes, I am," she had said before he skedaddled out of there.

But Ruby had told him they were after Moonis, too, which was why he was as concerned as Patti that Moonis hadn't yet shown. Except what was he going to do, get all nervous and shaky in front of the girl?

"Hey, sweets," he called out to the waitress. "A cup of joe when you get a chance, and tea for the girl."

The bent-backed waitress in pink, with a white ruffled cap and support hose, brought the coffee and a cup of hot water with a limp tea bag on the side. As she was taking their orders, Lydia lapsed into a fit of wet and ugly coughs.

"What does she got?" said the waitress.

"A frog in her throat, is all," said Clyde. "It's not your concern. Just bring the grub and make it snappy. And while you're at it, maybe you want to launder your apron. I can still see last week's meatloaf."

When the waitress left them alone, Clyde looked around shiftily before slipping out of his sleeve the little bottle Ruby had given him. With one hand he popped the lid and shook four of the red puckered berries into the hot water. With a spoon, he smashed them against the side of the cup before dunking the bag and pouring in sugar.

"Tell me how that tastes," he said to Lydia as he slid the cup to her.

"Aaach," she said, after a quick sip.

"The bitterer, the better." He poured in more sugar. "Finish it up. How's the van?"

"Paint job's almost done," said Patti. "I let Lydia pick out the color."

"You name it yet, Lydia?"

"Not yet," she said, her voice still tight. "I thought Pete, I always liked the name Pete, but the new color doesn't fit."

"Keep working on it."

"So what was it like down by the river?" said Patti.

"Like a sideshow at the carnival," said Clyde. "Each freak trying to outdo the next."

"What about Moonis?"

"He fits right in."

"Maybe I should go look for him," said Patti. "Maybe I can get into places you can't."

"You can get into trouble down there, is all. If Broome got word of your bruises, he'll be looking especially for you. You stay with Lydia. Maybe buy us some gasoline cans so we don't have to stop at any stations on the way back."

"What are you going to do about Moonis?"

"I'm going to find Cecily," said Clyde. "Wherever she is, maybe he'll be there, too. Maybe he's with her right now, sipping champagne, waiting on me."

"You got any leads?"

"It turns out our girl Cecily got a gig out here dancing."

"Oh, how wonderful," said Lydia. "Beautiful costumes, tutus and tiaras. I took some lessons before Daddy died. I always wanted to go back, and Mother promised, but then I got sick. I loved the music, the movements. Pliés. Glissades. Sissonnes. Was she dancing ballet, Clyde?"

"No."

***

Clyde waited until Patti and Lydia left before he hit the pay phone with a jangle of coins the cashier wrung out of a five. He called the Chicago number and waited patiently on the rings. When the phone is in the hall, no one is jumping to answer the thing.

"Yes?" came a voice, finally, something old and scratchy and full of guile. "How can I help you?"

"Mrs. McGillicutty, is that you?"

"Who's this?"

"It's Clyde. Clyde Sparrow, from across the hall."

"Oh, Mr. Sparrow, I've been meaning to talk to you. The seat was left up again last night. How many times have I talked to you about leaving the seat up in the middle—"

"Many times, Mrs. McGillicutty. But I wasn't around last night."

"I see."

"Is Amber there? I need to talk to Amber."

"Amber?"

"Lydia's mom."

"Oh, I know who Amber is, Mr. Sparrow. Do you know where the girl is, that Lydia?"

Pause. "No, I don't."

"A girl like that shouldn't be on her own."

"What do you mean 'on her own'?"

"The girl's mother was picked up by the sweepers, you see. A few days ago. They said she was . . . well, no need to talk about it in polite society. She's being sent to an LCM. For two years, we've been told."

"Two years?"

"It is her second labor camp, Mr. Sparrow. Who knew we were living with a malcontent."

"Krist," said Clyde. "And this you mention after the thing with the toilet?"

"It is unsanitary, Mr. Sparrow. We must all be concerned about sanitation, especially in these times. The social workers have been here again looking for the girl. With the mother in a labor camp, they are twice as concerned about the girl's condition."

"What condition is that, Mrs. McGillicutty?"

"Her cough, Mr. Sparrow. Her cough. It keeps us all up at night with worry. It puts us all at risk. And it just so happens, my niece is looking for an apartment. With a proper disinfectant, this could work out quite well for her and the landlord."

"For everyone but the girl," said Clyde.

"Oh, Mr. Sparrow, someone came looking for you, too. Someone from the Guard."

"I bet."

"A captain. I'm supposed to notify him as soon as I hear from you. Where can I tell him you are, Mr. Sparrow?"

"You can tell him I'm minding my own business, Mrs. McGillicutty. You should try it. It might keep you from getting your nose bit off in the middle of the night."

"Who would do something like that?"

"No one knows," said Clyde. "That's just the point. Don't forget to feed the kitty."

29
POLECAT

The crowd at the ScuttleButt, a stone's throw from the Moline Ventura District, was a melting pot of Moline society, the rich and the poor, the disaffected, the freakish, the powerful and the outlawed, all drawn together by the unquenchable thirst to see women dance mostly naked and in high heels. In its own way, then, the ScuttleButt pointed, however hesitantly, toward a future of sweet national unification, predicated on the free flow of young tits and small bills.

"What are you looking at?" said Clyde.

"Someone I ain't seen before," said the massive doorman by the club's front door, who was examining Clyde like a wolf eyeing a hanging stick of salami.

"Why, I was here just a few weeks ago."

"I don't remember you, bub."

"Saw a girl named Cinnamon," said Clyde. "Scorched my eyeballs, she did."

"I still don't remember you."

"Stay off the booze, my friend. I sure as hell remember you. You were wearing some other shirt."

"The red one?"

"Yes, right. The red one. Is that Cinnamon on tonight? My God but she was something."

"She's gone."

"No," said Clyde, disappointment leaking from his voice. "Where?"

"Just gone. They don't check out with me when they leave."

"Well, I suppose she's got some friends inside."

"I wouldn't know."

"Who would?" said Clyde as he stripped a ten-dollar bill from his wad and stuffed it in the doorman's shirt pocket.

"Try Blaze. She's like a mother hen to the rest of them."

"Sounds a bit old in the tooth for my liking."

"But she sure knows how to shake what she's got."

"Then Blaze it is."

"Just keep your hands off the merchandise, bub."

"You don't need to tell me twice," said Clyde, straightening his bow tie.

Twenty minutes later, Clyde was in the Champagne Room for a private session. The room was small, swathed in red velvet, smelling of cheap perfume and old sweat and bleach. Clyde was sitting spread-legged on the couch. Blaze was leaning over him, lifting his hat so that she could rub her breasts on the top of his head.

"No need for that, sister," said Clyde. "You'll muss my do."

"But four out of five doctors agree it's beneficial to the scalp," said Blaze, weathered and overripe, with folds at her throat and a great mass of false blonde hair, which Clyde admired for the effort it showed. "You'll like it, I promise you that."

"I'm sure I'd like it—I like just thinking about it—but right now I'm in the mood to talk."

"Talk?"

"Sometimes a man is only seeking a few rare moments of companionship."

"It's your dime and your time, but it seems a tragic waste of twenty minutes. Still, it's anything you want so long as you keep your hands to yourself. You sure you don't want I mash your face with my rear end? That's quite popular with men in suits."

"As attractive as that sounds, I'd rather just talk," said Clyde.

"Talk about what? The weather?"

"Nah, let's talk something spicier. How about we talk about Cinnamon."

***

"They line up every morning, the poor little things," said Blaze.

She was sitting next to Clyde on the couch, one of her bare legs slung over both of his trouser legs, leaning close as she lightly rubbed a finger in his ear.

"Most of them are too far gone to be of much use, but still they come, all the sad-eyes, shaking with desperation as they cough out their lungs."

She had only agreed to talk about Cinnamon after Clyde showed her the picture and then told her the wretched tale of his unrequited love. Clyde had learned long ago that strippers had a thing for unrequited love, since it was how they earned their livings. Blaze insisted on sitting close and pretending at doing her job for the camera, though there were no microphones, so they were free to talk as they pleased.

"They come here because Diego has what they need, what we all need."

"You too?"

"Why else would I be strutting like this at my age, Clyde? I'd be sitting now by the river, drinking sweet tea and watching the sun set if I didn't need my daily dose. It's gotten so dear, you can't afford it on a guaranteed paycheck. But Diego, he's got a direct supply from the other side, pure and fresh. That's what brought Cinnamon. First time I saw her was when Diego led her into the dressing room. We all thought he'd gone off his rocker, the way she was, skinny and weak, hacking away, with that look of the lost. You know the way they get?"

"The sweats, the shakes, the bloody coughs."

"That was Cinnamon. We didn't figure anyone would pay to ogle a lunger that far gone. But Diego saw something and he was right. Damn was he right. She perked up quick with the berry, filled out nicely. The beginners take care of the back room and run errands in their apprenticeships, so she had time to get her strength back. But it wasn't long before it was on to the stage."

"Was she any good?"

"No." Blaze laughed, a good belly laugh. "The girl was so nervous she could barely piss, much less dance. She made it a point to let us know that this wasn't the real her. She was a teacher, her brother had been selected, she had a District boyfriend, but she got no sympathy from the dressing room. We all have our trail of tears."

"Not the likes of you, Blaze," said Clyde. "You have the world on a string."

"It will take more than twenty minutes to hear my sad tale. You want to get me a drink?"

"After the story."

"I'm getting thirsty."

"I get it," said Clyde. He peeled off a ten. "Go ahead and get a rye on the rocks for me and a champagne something for you to keep your bosses happy. I suppose you get a piece of every order you bring in, too. That's only fair. But be sure to come back. You're just getting to the good part."

After she left to pick up the drinks, he turned to look at the camera. He sucked his teeth, twisted an ear.

"I tried to give her some advice, some moves," said Blaze, back on the sofa by his side, cuddling close, holding on to her own drink as Clyde swallowed the rye. "I even spent some time teaching her the pole, afternoons before we opened, but in the end you're on your own up there, and she was, well, terrible. Nervous, stiff, fear like a stain across her pretty features. I thought it would get ugly. There are expectations you need to meet to work at the 'Butt. But here's the thing. Some girls, they gyrate onstage with nothing but heels and still they look like they're wearing armor. But other girls can stand there stock-still, wrapped in a sheet, and something about them makes them look so naked and raw it grabs at your gut. That was Cinnamon. And the jeezers, they lapped it up like she was born to it. And all the time he was looking on, a stupid grin on his face."

"He?"

"The Ventura boyfriend."

"Brad," said Clyde, like he was spitting out a curse.

She nodded. "A lot of the young ones come with someone tagging along, handling the money, keeping them under their thumbs."

"Sounds like a bunch of pimps to me."

"Something like that, maybe. But he was different, a Ventura operator who knew how to make friends. As Cinnamon rose the ladder of demand, he started sitting at Diego's table, telling jokes, slapping backs. That's where he was, keeping his eye on her, when it started. Another drink, Clyde?"

"Not yet."

"All this talk is getting me thirsty."

Clyde shook the ice in his glass like a couple of dice. "Let's get thirstier, then."

"He doesn't come in much. He and his band spend most of their time in an old tourist camp on the other side of the line. But Diego gets his product directly from him, and so when he shows up with his entourage, special arrangements are made."

"Who are we talking about now?"

"You either know or you don't know."

"I'm getting the idea."

"When he comes, Diego stops watering the liquor, the riffraff is kept out, and the girls are given bonuses to put on their best shows. So that night was a night like any night when he comes to town, until Cinnamon stepped onto the stage. You could tell right away, the way the place quieted, the way he leaned forward, by the expression on all their faces. Not the dreamy stares we get from most guys, but a different stare altogether. The way you look at a steak grilling on the fire. She wasn't doing anything fancy on the pole, but it was enough."

"With her it always was," said Clyde.

"Poor baby, missing his girl."

"I been missing her for a long time."

"And now you've come to find her?"

"That's right."

"Poor baby is right. Normally they were in and out in one night, here for business only—it was too dangerous for them to stay—but this visit, they kept coming back and coming back. They even closed the place down early one night and kept only her. The liquor flowed, and the girl danced, and money was passed to keep the boyfriend happy as they sat drinking together, laughing together, staring together at the girl on the pole."

"Nice friendly party. So let's get to the meat of it, huh, Blaze?"

"I think I could use another drink."

"You still got some left."

She threw back her head and swallowed what she had. "This is almost fun. Maybe we should get a whole bottle."

"Let's hear it."

"Another rye for you, Clyde?"

Clyde grabbed her wrist, bent her arm down, brought her face close to his. "Finish the story."

"What do you think happened to your old love, Clyde? He left and she left with him. Power attracts. Nothing's sexier."

"She's with Raden?"

"Lucky girl."

"Where?"

"Where do you think?"

"Where?"

She tried to pull her arm away, but he held on like he was holding on to something precious and long-lived in his heart. Blaze looked at him flatly and then looked up at the camera.

"You should have bought the drink," she said, just before the door slammed open.

30
THE SACRED SHOE

Moonis was locked in a cage of cinder block, concrete, and iron. His whole life had been about cages of one sort or another, and so it only made sense that he should return behind bars before his sad excuse of a life was finally extinguished. If character is destiny, then his character was that of a dog who crawls each night back into his foul, shit-stained crate.

The jail in the Moline courthouse smelled of piss that had soaked into the cement, of the body odor of too many inmates in too small a place, of poverty and violence and cleaning fluid and overcooked green beans, a scent so strong and furious it was as if it had its own DNA. The incarcerated were a mixture of the young and the incorrigible, along with a pack of refugees in red-and-white-striped shirts, milling about like a troupe of minstrels. One freak in sandals was sprawled in the corner, sleeping.

Moonis sat on a bench set against a cinder-block wall painted green. He sat beneath the cell's single narrow window. He sat apart from the rest, resigned to his fate. They were going to turn him over to Broome, and Broome was going to kill him; it was as simple as that.

And meanwhile, according to Jarvis, Cecily was lost in the D-Lands. She was out there in the radiating ruins beyond the river with the intransigent, the mutated, the bloodsuckers and brain-eaters. She was lost among the savages, and here sat Moonis, helpless as a lamb about to be slaughtered for supper, with nothing but barriers between him and her.

***

"Welcome to the Moline Hospitality Association," said one of the freaks. He was an older man, over thirty, with a receding crop of curly blond hair and a cherubic face. He gave a wry smile before sitting down uninvited next to Moonis. "As you are new to our establishment, think of me as your personal PX. What can I get you this lovely evening?"

"Solitude," said Moonis.

"Oh, you can get pretty much anything you want in here except that. Food, drink, drugs—sex, even, if you're willing to work at it— but not sweet solitude. That treat awaits you in the state pen. With the wrong attitude you can definitely get too much of it there, I can tell you from experience, since my attitude is apparently just wrong enough. But in here you are sadly stuck in the sloppy mire of our society. What infraction landed you in this pit?"

"Trust."

"Ahh, betrayal," said the man. "The bitterest fruit in the garden of injustice, and therefore also the most nourishing. What can better keep you warm and clothed through the cold winter of incarceration than betrayal? And who, perchance, played the part of the betrayer in your sad, sordid tale?"

"Do you know a dancing sack of crap named Jarvis?"

"Jarvis, was it?" said the man before calling to another of the refugees, a longhair lying on his back in the middle of the floor, his head resting on his hands. "Hey, Brother Always? This man says he was betrayed by Jarvis."

"That's what he does, man," said the freak on the floor.

"Let me take the wildest of guesses," said the first of the refugees. "You're Moonis Fell."

"I might just be."

"We heard there was a trade in the works. You for us. Seemed liked a fair enough bargain, as long as you were just a name."

Moonis looked around the cell and was only surprised by his lack of surprise. "So I suppose you fellows are the Freecoast Eight?"

"Five of eight. The other three are in the women's cell, which, let me tell you, puts a crimp in the sex part. I am your host, Big Words. We all have tribal names here, which better suit the image we are desperately and pitifully attempting to portray."

"And what image is that?" said Moonis.

"A merry band of tricksters, trying to impress the truth of reality into the minds of the masses."

"And what truth is that, Big Words?"

"That the world's a joke, man, and we're the punch line."

"The point being?"

"No point. Points are for basketball players. We're truth tellers, dig it? Now, the little lizard on the floor with the dazed eyes is Always Tripping."

The longhair raised a hand in greeting.

"That's his name and his condition. On the bench over there is Counting Error: he does the math, keeps the payroll, that sort of thing." Counting Error had short hair and tortoiseshell glasses and was biting the edge of his thumb. "Our organization is basically run on imaginary numbers. Last year, for tax purposes, we earned, in endorsements and salary, the square root of negative one. Funny how the banks didn't appreciate our efforts. Sitting there with the big furry hat, is the Right Reverend Somewhat Spiritual."

"My son," said Somewhat Spiritual in his deep voice. He sat still on the bench, his long hair bunched into streams of mud-caked braids that fell from a furry blue top hat. He was wearing a blue bandleader's jacket with gold trim on the buttonholes, the lapels, the epaulettes, the sleeves.

"And there, sleeping in the corner to escape the travails of his mind, fresh from the cuckoo bin—he's dark, he's manic when he's not depressed, he is the one and only Occasionally Committed. This, gentlemen, is Moonis Fell, who will be the instrument of our liberation once all the paperwork is taken care of."

"Thanks, man," said Somewhat Spiritual. "It's quite altruistic of you to get us out of here."

"I didn't volunteer," said Moonis.

"What instrument ever does? As the good book says, it matters not if the scalpel is afraid of the blood, it's still going to slice."

"What book is that?" said Counting Error.

"*Gray's Anatomy.* Liberation is what you are, Moonis, what you were made for. You're our Lincoln, dedicated to the proposition of making us free, and we are ever so grateful."

"They're going to kill me," said Moonis.

"Don't be so dramatic, man," said Always Tripping from the floor. "The Moline police are sweethearts."

"They're turning me over to the Guard."

"Well, in that case."

"It's not no biggie, there, Moonis," said Somewhat Spiritual. "As that good book says, none of us are getting out of here alive."

"What book is that?" said Counting Error.

"*The Tibetan Book of the Dead.*"

"Why don't you stick to one book?"

"Because, like the great late Walt, I contain multitudes," said Somewhat Spiritual.

"Did Jarvis give you his speech?" said Big Words. "You know the one." Big Words roughed up his voice to match Jarvis's manic bark. "'In the guerrilla circus, you need to be willing to pay any price for the people's advancement.'"

"He laid that on me like a wreath," said Moonis.

"He loves that speech, man. But it's funny how it never seems to be Jarvis paying the price."

"Jarvis is how we ended up in here, too," said Always Tripping. "One of his actions didn't go so well and we paid his price."

"But you're getting out," said Moonis.

"Out, in, what's the difference?" said Somewhat Spiritual. "It's just a matter of adjusting your brain. I can show you."

"Show him later," said Big Words. "The chime's about to sound, so first we need to dance."

***

At the chiming of the hour—an ominous tolling that slipped through the one open window and descended like a blanket of melancholy—they danced like fools.

Not Moonis, who wasn't feeling particularly dancish, but the rest of the tricksters—all but Occasionally Committed, who slept through the madness as if drugged. Somewhat Spiritual chanted and Big Words played air guitar, shouting out the riffs, and Always and Counting clapped as they danced, crazy and wild, like an Indian Guide tribe on greenies. They were unsuccessful in trying to pull Moonis into the circle, but one of the young kids joined them, stomping with his boots, a smile broad on his face. From down the hall came a similar wild music, working in harmony to their singing, and then a beautiful voice calling out some lovely lines of blues.

"Who's that?" said Moonis.

"That's Barely Dressed in the women's cell," said Always Tripping. "They join us in our hourly dance."

The spirit of the thing was infectious and, even anchored to the bench as he was, Moonis couldn't keep himself from joining in on the clapping.

"Come on and dance with us, Moonis," said Big Words. "Join the tribe."

"I'm too busy getting ready to die," said Moonis.

"But dancing can save your life."

"Truly?"

"No. But this is what we do, man, every hour on the hour. They think we're crazy and we wouldn't want to disappoint them. They hate the dancing so much they can't wait to get rid of us."

"So it's all an act, a put-on, a fraud."

"Never trust a trickster, Moonis, that's lesson number two."

"What's lesson number one?"

"Stay the hell out of Jarvis's tent."

***

"We need a thing," said Somewhat Spiritual.

"What kind of thing?" said Always Tripping.

"Anything, man. Just a thing."

"They took everything off of us," said Big Words.

"I got, like, a used wad of tissues," said Always Tripping.

"No, man, we need a sacred thing," said Somewhat Spiritual.

They were sitting in a circle in the middle of the cell: the four Freecoasters who were awake (Occasionally Committed was still sleeping), Moonis, and the kid who had been dancing. They sat as instructed by Somewhat Spiritual, with their legs crossed, their backs straight, their hands set in OK signs on their knees, like a statue Moonis had seen in the Art Institute back in Chicago.

"We need something with real meaning," said Somewhat Spiritual. "Something beautiful and universal."

"How about Euler's identity?" said Counting Error. "The most beautiful theorem in the universe—e to the power of i times pi plus one equals zero."

Somewhat Spiritual thought about it for a moment, nodding as if he were digging the strange mathematical purity of the equivalence, until he said, "How about a shoe?"

"Here you go, man," said Big Words, taking off a brown leather tie-up thing.

"Good," said Somewhat Spiritual, taking hold of the shoe and giving a quick and painful sniff before holding it well away from him. He closed his eyes for a bit and then opened one. "I don't suppose anyone's got peyote. It goes easier with peyote. No? So it's the shoe and only the shoe." Somewhat Spiritual shut again his eyes and began humming to himself.

On the floor, in the circle, Moonis looked around at this gang of freaky refugees, worshipping a ripe old shoe. These tricksters were unlike any prisoners he had known before, and he had known too many in his life. They were goofy and wacked yet seemingly in total control of their situation. How was it possible for the prisoner to control the prison? He had joined their magic circle to find out.

"The only jail that matters is the one in our own minds," said Somewhat Spiritual. "The only true prisons are the ones we've built around ourselves. They can wrap us in chains and we can still be free if we let our minds soar, dig it?"

"Dig it," said everyone else in the circle, Moonis joining in belatedly.

"We might be jammed stuck in this courthouse cell, but worse is the way we are stuck alone in our own individual prisons, sentenced for crimes against our own souls. But there's a route to liberation, my brothers. Lean close and let me elucidate the path. This is the sacred Shoe of the Satchel Mouth."

"My shoe?" said Big Words.

"Just go with it," said Always Tripping.

"As a dream catcher snags your dreams, the Shoe of the Satchel Mouth will absolve you of your crimes, so long as you confess of them openly and from the heart. In so doing, you will free your spirit to soar over the clouds into the great blue yonder, like the great shoe itself, flying through the heavens on silver wings."

"My shoe now has wings?"

"He's on a roll."

"Do you dig it?" said Somewhat Spiritual.

"We dig it."

"I'll begin." His eyes still closed, he took in deep breaths as his body began to shake, almost as if the shoe itself, this Shoe of the Satchel Mouth, was vibrating him with its awesome power of absolution.

"I am a fraud," said Somewhat Spiritual finally, in a voice coming from deep in his chest, strangely different than his usual voice. "I pretend I understand the mysteries of the universe when I understand nothing. I just make shit up. But because I'm a black man and my voice is low, people think I'm deep, and I let them. Why? Truth is, because it gets me laid. The ladies, they come to me with true hearts looking for divine help, and all I do is bed them down. It's despicable. I'm despicable."

"Weren't you just ministering to my old lady the night before we got arrested?" said Always Tripping.

"I merely read Trout her horoscope. Her moon is in ascendance. It is a ripe moment for change."

"And then what?" said Always.

"The past is past," said Somewhat Spiritual. "I have confessed my crimes and suddenly I feel lighter. I feel like I can float away. Hold me down, brothers, hold me down."

Moonis on one side and Big Words on the other grabbed Somewhat's shaking arms to keep him from floating away like a helium balloon. And then the shaking subsided and Somewhat Spiritual opened his eyes. "I don't think I've ever felt freer," he said. "The damn thing works."

"I got to talk to you about my old lady, man," said Always.

"Now is not the time," said Somewhat. "Now is the time to pass the shoe."

And so it went. One by one the confessions poured out as the great Shoe of the Satchel Mouth, with all its healing power, was passed from hand to hand around the circle.

Big Words: "I have squandered my talent in exchange for worthless beads of experience. I am a writer, a novelist, I have worlds to create, and yet I've turned myself into a dancer, a prancer, a trickster, a tripster. I have succumbed to my fears of living up to my promise by spending all my efforts at not even trying. I am a disgrace to what I once might have been."

Always Tripping: "You know how we make fun of the Establishment, the moneymen. You know how we declare ourselves free of the shackles of commerce. Well, that's crap, man. More than anything I want to be rich. I want to be high, too, sure, but I want to be high sitting by the pool, with a butler. Man, I want a butler. And the rest is just me knowing I'll never have one."

The kid with the boots: "I robbed a liquor store, that's why I'm here." *Why'd you rob that store, man?* "For the money." *What were you going to do with it?* "Buy liquor."

And then, after the ritual of confession and absolution had made its way around the circle, one startling admission after the next, the shoe was passed to Moonis.

Moonis knew it was just a shoe, some knocked-around brown work boot off Big Word's foot, not some almighty artifact, and yet when it was handed to him by Counting Error he could feel a power in it, as if the faith of the others had imbued it with some sort of authority. He held it out in front of him and closed his eyes and let the power he felt in the shoe slip through his hands and arms and into the center of who he was.

It was confession time and Moonis had so much to confess. His whole life had been one crime or another: a crime against his potential, a crime against his family, a crime against work and order, a crime against the state. But with his sister lost in the D-Lands, his failure to protect her and care for her through the whole of her life seemed just then his greatest crime, and that was what he was about to declare to the circle. But something stopped him. It felt as if the shoe itself were riffling through the sheaves of his days to come up with the crime for which Moonis was most in need of absolution. And when the words came out, compelled by the shoe itself, they surprised Moonis as much as the freaks around him.

"I killed a man," said Moonis.

"Whoa," said Big Words, scooting back just a bit.

"Crunchy," said Counting Error.

"What did it feel like?" said Always.

"It was sort of a self-defense thing," said Moonis, backtracking immediately out of habit and fear, unsure from which dark crevice within him that confession had burped, but at the same time feeling a true and honest pain. "He was out to kill me first."

"Well then, man," said Always Tripping. "What else could you do?"

"Maybe nothing else," said Moonis, tears pressing at his eyes, not just from the guilt, but also from gratitude that this thing he hadn't yet dealt with had been slapped into his face by the Shoe of the Satchel Mouth so that he could come to grips with it. "But still, I killed him.

He had been turning me so I would end up dead for some unknown reason, but at the same time I had been turning him for my own purposes. We were both using the other to get what we wanted, and because of that, one of us was going to die. That I ended up killing him only means I am a better killer than he was. So it's not enough to say I had no choice. I killed a man. That's why I'm in this cell, and that's why they're going to kill me. And maybe they're right to do it."

"What's happening?" said Occasionally Committed in the corner, sitting up suddenly from his sleep, rubbing his face. "What's going on? And who is that holding Big Word's shoe?"

"That's Moonis," said Somewhat Spiritual. "He killed a man."

"Wow," said Occasionally Committed.

"You know, that sounds like a name to me," said Big Words.

"It surely does," said Somewhat Spiritual.

"Hey there, He Killed a Man," said Big Words. "Welcome to the tribe."

31
REUNION

They threw Clyde out of the ScuttleButt face-first and without the caress of gentleness.

Two club bouncers with busted noses and ears like toads each grabbed an arm and a leg, pulled him out of the Champagne Room, dragged him down the stairs—Clyde's head banging on each riser—lugged him through the primary dance emporium, and tossed him like a sack of garbage onto the asphalt beyond the front door.

Clyde's hat landed first, his shoulder landed second. He screamed into the pain as he rolled over and looked up at the blob sitting on a stool by the door.

"I told you not to handle the merchandise," said the doorman.

"Is that him?" came a voice from the shadows. Clyde turned his head toward the sound as two rough-hewn hard cases with black shirts and tattooed faces stepped into the light.

"That's him all right," said one of the hard cases, this one the size of a refrigerator.

"We've been looking all over for you, Sparrow," said the other, thin and tall and ugly as a scarecrow.

"I knew it was you, bub, the one my pals was looking for," said the doorman, "because I don't got a red shirt."

"Well, aren't you the little gumshoe," said Clyde, sitting up, dusting off his suit. "What do you creeps want?"

"Come with us and you'll find out," said the Scarecrow.

"I don't want to know that badly."

"It ain't a suggestion."

Clyde picked his hat off the ground, pushed himself to standing, rotated his arm to stretch out his shoulder. "I don't care what it is. Unless you put a gun to my head, I'm going my own way."

"Well, in that case," said the Scarecrow as he pulled a revolver from his belt. "Your friend ended up in the courthouse jail; we'll deal with him when we can. But you we can deal with in the here and the now. Let's go."

"Later, bub," said the doorman. "And next time you'll know to keep your hands to yourself."

"Next time you won't be getting a tenner from me," said Clyde. "You'll be getting a shiv in your gut. It'll be a treat watching you fly around the parking lot like a popped balloon."

Clyde looked around and considered his options, but the barrel of the gun, now pointed at his head, cut the options short. He raised his hands and let the hard cases lead him around the building to the ill-lit parking area spread out behind.

A small truck stood alone in the corner of the lot, its rear doors open. Inside the trailer was darkness, nothing. Inside the trailer was his death.

"I have a pass," said Clyde as they marched him to the truck. "An all-points pass signed by Broome."

"Who?"

"The head of the Guard in Chicago."

"Too bad this ain't Chicago," said the Refrigerator.

"The pass is good in Moline, too."

"Ain't nothing good in Moline," said the Scarecrow. The hard cases both laughed at that.

"You work for Raden, is that it?" said Clyde, hustling for an angle.

"Shut up," said the Refrigerator.

"It's a good thing we ran into each other, then. I have a message for Raden."

"He don't want your message."

"Yes, he does. I have to deliver it personally, and he won't be happy you killing the messenger before it's delivered."

"So Raden won't be happy. Nothing different there. He's not a happy guy."

"Where are you taking me?"

"You'll see."

"Wherever I'm going," said Clyde, "I'm not getting in that truck."

Something smacked Clyde's head so hard it drove him to his knees. Half his brain filled with a white flash of pain.

"I said shut up. Now stand."

Clyde struggled to standing. Slowly he turned to face the two men.

"Get in the truck," said the Refrigerator.

"No."

"What are we going to do about this?" said the Scarecrow to his pal.

"We're just going to have to—"

At that moment something roared to Clyde's right. Both of Raden's goons turned their heads toward the sound, and their eyes suddenly lit up like Christmas candles. Before they could react to the light, something large and yellow powered through and, with a double crack, like twin bolts of lightning, sent both goons flying.

It all happened too quickly for Clyde to process. One moment he stood with the gape of death behind him and two men and a gun in front of him. In the next moment, after a flood of yellow and a furious roar, before him lay only the open expanse of the parking lot.

Stunned and scared, Clyde looked to his left and saw the two men flung onto the asphalt—one writhing, one not, while a snub-nosed van idled, its bright-yellow paint job glowing madly in the night. From the driver's window, Patti stuck out her head and flashed her crooked-toothed smile.

"You getting in?" she said.

***

"It sure is yellow," said Clyde as they drove away from the club, toward the center of town.

"Do you like it?" said Lydia.

"Love it," he said, his voice drained of any emotion.

"They had a brighter yellow, like a lemon yellow, but I thought this one, school-bus yellow with a little bit of orange, was just perfect. I've always thought of school buses as magical, whisking you off to enchanted lands of learning."

"That's not the way I thought of school." He glanced back at Lydia as he said this. How do you tell a girl her mother is in an LCM for a full stint? Fast, like pulling off a Band-Aid, he supposed. But not now, not yet, not with so much still to do.

"Did you learn anything?" said Patti.

"Not in the classrooms, that's for sure," said Clyde.

"About Cecily."

"Yeah, I learned something," said Clyde. "I also learned where Moonis is."

"Where?"

"In the courthouse jail." Clyde rubbed his jaw as he remembered the dark maw of that truck, the roiling darkness where he had been headed just a few moments before. "What were you doing there, Patti, in the parking lot, when those two lugs were about to skin me alive?"

"Waiting for you, is all. The paint job was done when we got to the garage so I figured we'd pick you up when you was through with your lap dance. It didn't take much asking around to figure out where you were going. Good thing we were there, huh?"

"Yeah, good thing."

"Who were they?"

"They work for Raden."

"Krist, Clyde, what have you gotten us into?"

"A pile of it. Grade A. And I'd be facedown in it, too, if it weren't for you and Lydia."

"We were lucky."

"No, it was more. You're always saying we need to take care of each other. It's just a shock to see it clear for once."

"Don't make nice, it pisses me off. So what's the plan?"

"The plan is, we're going back to Chicago."

"What about Cecily?"

"It's beyond us now, Pats. We're heading back to Chicago and fast, soon as I can get Moonis out of the clink."

"How are you going to do that?"

"I don't know yet. Did you get the gas cans?"

"They're in the back."

"Good. We might need to make a detour on the way home. Now stop right here," said Clyde. "You see that nice policeman on the corner? He's going to take me to Moonis."

"Do you know him?"

"Not yet." He fished his wallet out of his pocket, took out his license and the pass from Broome, put them in the inner band of his hat, and handed the rest of it to Lydia. "Hold on to this for me, will you, kid?"

"Sure, Clyde," said Lydia.

"Where's your family from?"

"My mom's from Decatur. My mom's sister still lives there. I have a cousin a little younger than me. We visited them a couple years ago."

"Maybe we'll visit them again on the way home."

"Why would we do that?" said Lydia.

"Beautiful Decatur? Why not? There's so much to see and do there. You feeling any better?"

"A little, yeah."

"I'll get more tea for you as soon as we spring Moonis. I found a source. You'll like her. She's a singer."

"A real live singer? Is her voice lovely?"

"That's not quite the right word, but it sure is something. Okay, Patti, as soon as I get going you pull out of here, disappear for a bit, find a place for you and Lydia to sleep the night, because nothing's going to happen until tomorrow. Tomorrow morning, you use the money in my wallet to fill up the tank and the gas cans and then take this little yellow beauty down to the courthouse. Try to park someplace you can be seen from the entrance and wait for us."

"Be careful," said Patti.

"That won't get it done, will it?"

Clyde stepped out of the van, slammed shut the door, fixed his hat.

He watched as Patti drove the van away, then he shook his head. School-bus yellow, what a mess. The only thing worse than having the printing on the side is having the damn van as bright as an overripe orange. Lydia might as well have raised a neon sign blinking on and off with the words "Catch Me Now."

And yet as the van drove off, he felt a strange elation. Clyde had been looking after his own skin for as long as he could remember. Whatever trouble he had been in, it had always been up to him to get himself out of it. Who would have expected that it would be Patti who eventually stepped up for him? Maybe Moonis would do the same, too.

Maybe Helen. Maybe even Lydia. Maybe the world was different than the stinking jungle he imagined it to be.

Maybe not, but it was sweet to think it for a moment.

The cop on the corner was leaning on a post, catching a moment with his cigarette. Tall and thin, redheaded and freckled, he seemed amiable enough for Clyde's purposes.

"Hey, pal," said Clyde. "You know how to get to the courthouse from here?"

"Head down that way, take a left on Seventh, a right on Sixteenth, a left on Fifth, you can't miss it."

"No offense, joe, but that's a lot of numbers and I was never any good at math," said Clyde before he cracked the cop with a shot to the jaw.

***

Clyde's step was jaunty as they led him, hands cuffed behind his back, down the hallway in the courthouse basement. He had already been fingerprinted and photographed, just like years before when he had been busted for the phone hacking, but he wasn't a sniveling pile of regret and fear this time. This time he smiled for the camera. "Get my good side, boys," he said.

"We don't take ass shots," said one of the cops and they all cracked up at that, even Clyde.

There's a difference between being acted upon and being an actor, and Clyde was learning the power of one over the other. On the way down the hall, they walked him past the women's cell, with a strange assortment of freaks and prostitutes and drunks locked inside. One of the prostitutes hooted at him as he passed by.

"I'll be back for you ladies later," he said out of the side of his mouth. And then, noticing one of the freaks was wearing next to nothing and looking good doing it, he said, "That girl is barely dressed."

"So you know her," said one of the cops.

"What?"

Just then the hour chimed and all hell broke loose.

"Damn refugees," said one of the guards behind him. "I can't wait until we get them the hell out of here. They make me sick to my stomach."

"You and me both," said Clyde.

When the cops finally threw Clyde into his holding cell, a pack of freaks was dancing in a crazed circle in the center, clapping hands and shouting out as a tall man in a furry top hat and blue-and-gold hussar jacket sang and chanted. A few surly inmates huddled in the corner while a couple of younger kids laughed and stamped their feet at the display, one even joining in. And among the gyrating dancers, there was Moonis, twirling and clapping like a fool, as if the few hours Clyde had left him alone in Moline had turned Moonis into a relocation refugee himself. What a sap. Clyde hadn't gotten himself arrested a moment too soon.

Moonis's eyes widened when he saw Clyde in the cell, but he kept dancing as the guards locked the door and stood for a bit, glaring at the display. One of the guards banged the bars with his billy stick, shouting at the freaks to quiet down, but they kept at it, raising the pitch of their insane song in response. The guards shook their heads and muttered as they beat a retreat.

Clyde sat on the bench beneath the window, leaned back against the green wall, tilted his hat low, and waited. A moment after the craziness ended, Moonis dropped heavily onto the seat beside him. His smile was wide, his dark skin glistened, his paisley shirt was heavy with his sweat. They stared at each other for a moment, friends forever and now almost strangers.

"So," said Clyde, "how was Freaktown?"

"Enlightening," said Moonis.

"So it appears," said Clyde.

"I learned more than I expected," said Moonis. "Including that Cecily's on the other side of the river."

"I learned the same thing, but my way. And also what she was doing in Moline."

"And what was that?"

"Stripping for berry."

"No."

"Yes."

"Krist," said Moonis. He sat in quiet for a long moment, digesting the image of his sister on the pole, and everything that had led to it.

"Don't beat yourself up about it, pal," said Clyde finally. "We all need to breathe."

"I suppose we're headed to the wrong side of the line," said Moonis.

"Well, that's not going to happen. She's with Raden, Moonis."

"Raden?"

"He controls everything coming in and out of the D-Lands. He's the worst kind of gang leader, huge and vile and violent, with an army of his own. That's who wanted you dead at the LCM, and that's who just tried to kill me, too."

"You?"

"His thugs tried to stick my carcass in the back of a meat truck. I survived by the skin of my teeth and by Patti's chestnuts. Raden is more than we can handle, and the D-Lands are more than any of us bargained for. I'm heading back to Chicago."

"To the Toddle House?"

"A job's a job."

"Then what are you doing here, Clyde?"

"They know where you are, Moonis. They're coming for you. I came to get you out and save your life before I went on home." Clyde looked around the cell, at the bars, the walls, then spun on the bench to take a gander at the window above them. "There must be some kind of way out of here."

"There is," said Moonis, nodding at the pack of freaks. "Through them."

32
FREE-FOR-ALL

The armies were to face one another on the streets surrounding the courthouse of Old Moline. Shield and gas mask versus long hair and tie-dye. Billy stick versus slogan, gun versus rose, tear gas versus tear. It would be the furthest thing from a fair fight; the police and Homeland Guardsmen wouldn't stand a chance.

"It's not enough to merely free our political prisoners," had said Jarvis to the mob before the action began. "That would be a page-four item beneath the indiscriminate dips and dives of their precious stock market. We need a visual, something to shake awake the masses. So we don't give up when our people are released, we keep going until we prompt their overreaction. Cue the paint, cue the pandemonium. We're missionaries, bringing the word to the masses, and we don't stop until we see the fucking horses. Got it? The blood will put us on page one, but horses will preempt the prime-time movie of the week, and that's what shakes the world. We make our mark, here and now. Freedom for the Freecoast, here and now."

With Jarvis's exhortation ringing in its ears, the proud rabble surged south from the refugee zone with song, with flower, with pots of paint of every color. Protesters swarmed through the streets, over wooden barriers, around cars, a great mass of complaint and purpose, the artists among them turning everything in their path into a riotous paisley swirl.

Onward they marched, tributaries of tribes merging into streams that merged ever onward until they were a great river of self-determination, as mighty as the poisoned waterway that marked the boundary of their exile. They flowed forward, an inexorable force flowing forward, until, one and all, they were face-to-face with the forces of the Establishment cordoning the courthouse.

The police and the Guard brandished their shields, their weapons. Gunships buzzed the skies.

The refugees waited with elbows linked, singing, chanting, the rear guard slapping their wild colors on whatever was at hand, walls and hydrants, street signs, an empty cop car, a yellow van sitting patiently across from the courthouse. As brushes swiped the van on all sides, laying down a wild kaleidoscope of color on its yellow flanks, a woman with long black hair and a bandaged nose popped her head out the front window.

"What the hell are you freaks doing?" she said.

"Painting," said one of the painters.

"Why?"

"We're leaving our mark all the way to the courthouse."

"Including on our van?"

"Welcome to the show."

"Okay, that's cool." She looked left, right, then lowered her voice. "You got any reefer?"

Just then, as if a fuse were lit through the whole of the crowd, a great jeering cheer arose from its collective throat when the cordon of Guardsmen and police broke apart and the heroes of the day emerged, a pack of freaks in close order, walking toward freedom, the Freecoast Eight in all their glory, red-and-white-striped shirts on the men, the bare legs of Barely Dressed, raised fists, Somewhat Spiritual's furry top hat and blue military jacket.

As soon as they had slipped through the line, the cordon around the courthouse tightened again, and the eight continued toward the crowd, clasping hands above their heads, acknowledging the cheers as their names were called one by one like heroes of another age.

"Somewhat, Somewhat Spiritual."

"Go get them, Always."

"We missed you, Barely."

"Big Words, Big Words."

The newly freed were given their moment until a shout went up, and the cheers turned to bellows, and in an act of glorious ferocity the refugees charged, first surrounding the eight with their affections and protections, and then, heeding Jarvis's call, continuing on, rushing like a brigade of light, right at the heart of the police and Guardsmen.

The cordon lifted its shields, fitted its masks, bowed its helmeted heads, as onward they came, a sea of battering rams racing to breach the castle doors. And the Establishment line was just about to break when, from the front steps of the courthouse, behind the cordon, something was shot into the air with a mighty whoosh, some brown oblong baseball of a thing.

At the sound of the whoosh the violence stilled, the refugees stopped their charge and stared silently up. The brown oblong thing rose in a graceful arc, letting out a strange ch-ch-ch as the refugees silently followed its majestic flight—first, rising, the slightest, loveliest hesitation at the apex, and then the sweet accelerating fall, until it slammed into the asphalt with a pop!, unleashing an odorless cloud that drifted along the main street before its burning, noxious fingers reached the noses and eyes of the rabble.

And suddenly, quick as that, it was on, a free-for-all of swinging shields and thrown paint, of police being swarmed, and refugees hauled to the ground by the locks of their hair, and billy sticks flashing in the great blue sky.

Whoosh, ch-ch-ch, pop! Whoosh, ch-ch-ch, pop!

The canisters came down like hail. And protesters were running crazily like football kick returners amidst the smolder and violence. And smoke drifted until the courthouse itself was cloaked in it. And refugees were on their knees, hacking at the pain in eye and throat. And blood—pigs' blood and human blood both—was everywhere.

Whoosh, ch-ch-ch, pop!

It was an almost perfect little war zone, warming the cockles of Jarvis's malignant little heart, just awaiting one final touch for the snapping and whirring cameras.

And then, as if cued by the great director of chaos and confusion herself, came the horses.

In the midst of the madness and the mayhem, two of the freed Freecoast Eight slipped from the pack and through the crowd, accepting the cheers and pats on their backs as they made their way, the broad one pulling the tall one, toward a van that had once been yellow and was now a great splash of wild, indiscriminate color.

33
SMOKE

"Let's get the hell out of here," said Clyde as soon as he and Moonis jumped into the van, but Patti, her head turned, simply stared at the two of them, her jaw loose.

Clyde, sitting in the front next to Patti, was wearing sandals, white pants, a T-shirt with wide horizontal red stripes—as un-Clyde-like an outfit as could be imagined. Moonis, next to Lydia in the middle seat, was wearing some sort of blue-and-gold bandleader's jacket over his orange pants and paisley shirt, with a furry top hat on his lap. It wouldn't be long before the guards discovered that Occasionally Committed and Somewhat Spiritual, though ordered released by the judge, were still sitting in the cell, while two dangerous prisoners had gone terribly missing. Someone would pay for the screwup, and Clyde wanted to be long gone when the piper made his call, but Patti was flummoxed into stasis.

"What are you looking at?" said Clyde.

"I don't know," she said, "but whatever it is, it smells god-awful."

Clyde took a sniff of himself, and his lip curled like cauliflower was boiling somewhere. "Think of what that freak is doing to my suit right now. Get going, they'll be on to us sooner rather than later."

"It's just you're a sight, you are. Though Moonis, you look good."

"Like a real dandy," said Lydia. "That hat is quite becoming."

"Becoming a corpse," said Clyde. "Let's go go go."

Patti started the van, popped it into first. The van was surrounded by wisps of gas and the meandering tail of the crowd and so it took longer than Clyde was comfortable with for Patti to turn the thing around without running anyone over. As they started heading away from the courthouse, a bearded geezer appeared in front of them like an apparition in the smoke.

Patti slammed on the brakes, and the van lurched to a stop just an instant before slamming the old man into tomorrow. The old man leaned forward and peered through the windshield like a biblical prophet.

"What the hell is he looking for?" said Clyde.

"He's looking for me," said Moonis.

Moonis opened the side door, and the old man came around and ducked his head in. "I thought that was you," said the old man. "Jarvis won't be pleased, you outside like this."

"Screw Jarvis."

"That's about right," said the old man. "Where you headed, boy?"

"Same place I've been heading since I had a weight on my ankle," said Moonis. "To my sister."

"You know where she is?"

"Now I do."

"It's a hard place to be lost in."

"Then I need to find myself a guide."

"I been there and back again," said the old man. "I lost more there than you ever had."

"Are you volunteering?"

The old man rubbed his beard. "I'm just saying I know the highways and the byways."

"In or out," said Clyde. "We've got places to be."

The old man looked at Clyde. "Who's that?"

"That's Clyde," said Moonis.

"He coming too?"

"No," said Moonis. "He'll be taking the van back to Chicago."

"Well, in that case."

As the old man climbed into the van with his pack, Clyde saw a small group of men wade through the smoke toward the courthouse, hard-case motorheads like the two who had shanghaied him in front of the ScuttleButt. When he took a closer look, he recognized one of the men, better dressed than the others, curly dark hair, unshaven jaw.

Krist, it was that Bradley Illingworth from Chicago, now tied hard into Raden and looking for him.

"Can we get the hell out of here, please," said Clyde.

As the van lurched forward, the roar of the engine drew Brad's attention. Clyde could see his arrogant eyes taking in the wild-colored flanks instead of the figures in the window until, bam, the van shot down the road, out of Brad's view and away from the fight.

"Where are we going?" said Patti.

"Moonis?" said Clyde.

"Digger?" said Moonis.

"There's a way into them D-Lands about thirty miles west of town," said the old man. "An illegal ferry I used couple of years ago. You could drop us off at what's left of the old route over to what was once a place called Muscatine. We can make it to the ferry from there."

"Is that all right with you, Clyde?" said Moonis.

"Right as rain," said Clyde. "As far as I'm concerned, the sooner we get the hell out of this burg, the better. But I have one more stop to make first. Patti, you know where the old bridge is?"

"The one with the market on top?"

"That's the one. Head on over. I need to say good-bye to a girl."

***

The Freecoast was eerily vacant, just a shell of what Clyde had seen the day before. The more political and felonious of the refugees were still rampaging up by the courthouse while the more cautious were locked inside their tenement shacks, holding close their children, hoping to weather the certain backlash to come. There was always blowback after one of Jarvis's actions, explained the old man, but this time the leaders in the Moline Ventura District were going to demand more than a show. There was going to be blood, there was going to be counterrevolution.

When they arrived at Big Brother Tap, the lights were off and the neon was no longer flashing. The metal link fence around the joint was padlocked with a chain, the links of which were as big as a fist. Ruby, in a purple coat fringed in pink fluff, was sitting on her guitar case outside the padlocked entrance, a suitcase by her feet.

"Stop here and get in the back," said Clyde to Patti. "I'll drive the rest of the way." Then he hopped out of the van and ambled over to Ruby.

"Hey, darling," she said, not getting up. "You've gone native."

"Aren't I the merry fellow."

"I worried you weren't going to make it, what with the festivities in the old town, but I guess you learned to blend in."

"Just until I can delouse. Going somewhere?"

"Anywhere. This place is played, Clyde. Can't you feel it?"

"I felt it as soon as I set foot in it."

"I was hoping you could maybe give me a ride out."

"We're headed to Chicago by way of Decatur."

"That'll do."

"The girl I was telling you about is in the car. What you gave me helped her. You said you'd get me more."

"I know I did, darling, and I tried, for her and me both. But that door's been closed, that door's been burned shut. Famine's coming."

"I guess we'll have to get some inland."

"Don't count on that. There's plenty on the other side, waiting to be plucked as easy as a guitar string, but Raden's made a deal with the devil."

"What devil?"

"The narco police. The word of the day is 'embargo.'"

"Those Balthazar bastards," said Clyde, looking at the small figure of Lydia, sitting in the rear bench seat in the van.

He thought about the cop in the Toddle House, taking his free burger as he talked of working overtime for the Balthazar boys. He thought of Cecily dancing for her berry at a dump like the ScuttleButt. He thought of Broome and his bribe of Balthazar drugs. They controlled the money. They controlled the cops and the landscape and the crap they shoved at you on the television and the crap they advertised between the crap they shoved at you on the television. They controlled every aspect of his life, and he had let them, because the fight for survival was enough to wear him to the bone. But when they started controlling a young girl's very breath . . .

"The new world's like the old world, Clyde," said Ruby. "There's nothing to do about it but sing the blues."

"There's always something, Ruby."

A few moments later, with Ruby sitting in the rear next to Lydia, Patti in the middle seat with the old man, and Moonis up front, Clyde drove down the road parallel to the river. He was still tasting the bitterness of his anger as he gritted his teeth and accelerated into a right turn, a turn that took them onto the causeway that led to the island squatting smack in the middle of the river.

***

"This ain't the way," said the old man.

"It is now, pops," said Clyde.

"That ferry we talked about is the other way out," said the old man. "That island ahead is the Guard Arsenal."

"Yeah, well, plans have changed."

"Where are you going, Clyde?" said Patti.

"Where I should have been going all along."

"To the Guard?" said the old man.

"He wouldn't," said Patti.

"He is," said the old man.

Clyde ignored the rising tide of panic after that, Patti's braying and the old man's harrumphing and Lydia's calling of his name. Clyde knew where he was headed and why, and he wasn't going to let anyone force him to swerve.

"If you're turning me over," said Moonis, softly enough to keep his words from the rest, "I guess that will only make us even."

"We'll never be even," said Clyde, looking dead ahead through the windshield. "That's the way it is with old friends. Someone is always keeping score."

"What did Broome promise you?"

"Money."

"Is that all?"

"And medicine for the girl."

"Now that's more like it," said Moonis. "It's always healthy to drape betrayal in good intent."

"Like you were taking care of Cecily when you sent me away? What about me wasn't good enough for her, Moonis?"

"You were too much like me. We both were stuck. I wanted more for her."

"Well, that's what you got, all right."

"What's happening here?" said the old man. "You're going to let him do this, Moonis?"

"Clyde has to do what he has to do," said Moonis.

They rolled in past the golf course and toward the great metal gate that fronted the arsenal. Two Guardsmen, in full battle gear, stood behind the fence. Two more were in the guardhouse. Clyde brought the van to a stop as one of the Guardsmen unslung his rifle and stepped to the van.

"You can't be here, folks," said the Guardsman. "Turn yourselves around and head on back to the relocation area."

"I have business inside," said Clyde.

"It doesn't seem likely, sir, in such a vehicle."

"What's wrong with my vehicle?" said Clyde.

The Guardsman hefted his gun. "Turn around, please, before we are forced to take action."

"Who's in charge?" said Clyde, taking out his pass from Broome that was jammed into his pants pocket. "And where the hell is he? Because whoever it is, that's who I'm here to see."

34
FIRE

Moonis thought of jumping from the van as Clyde drove them into the maw of the Guard Arsenal. He imagined himself tearing across the island, clasping together his hands as he broke through the swirling surface of the poisoned water. Except Moline, now wreathed in smoke, wasn't safe for him, and neither were the brutal lands on the other side of the river. And neither, for that matter, was the river itself.

So he didn't jump and he didn't run. Instead he let Clyde have his rope, even if it would end up laced around Moonis's neck. Maybe it was a sad bit of faith in an old friend, or maybe it was the sense of justice being played out in their respective lives. If betrayal was in the works, then who was more justified to be betraying him than Clyde?

"This ain't right," said Digger.

"Let it go, Digger," said Moonis. "We're in Clyde's hands now. In Clyde we trust."

"That ain't the way it's written on the penny," said Digger.

"Clyde knows what he's doing," said Lydia.

"He better," said the woman Clyde had picked up and introduced as Ruby. "This isn't a play park for folks like us."

"It don't take a genius," said Digger, "to know not to go to no Guard Arsenal when you got a wanted man in your van."

"Well, then, we're okay," said Patti, "because Clyde ain't no genius."

Clyde glanced at Moonis and kept on driving.

The Homeland Guard Arsenal was deserted—of course it was. Pretty much the whole of the Guard had been called to Old Moline to keep the refugees from burning down the town. There were no jeeps barging up and down the road that bisected the camp, no Guardsmen marching on the parade grounds, only a skeleton crew manning the base.

As the van approached the large white headquarters building, where a Colonel McKenzie was supposedly now expecting them, Clyde slowed. And then sped up again, past the barracks and the rows of tanks, the gunships in their hangars, and through a park toward the northwest corner of the island. Beyond was the northern expanse of the river and beyond that, the ruins of Davenport.

Only a pair of armed men stood before the wooden post barring the entrance to the old railroad bridge. Clyde pulled the van to a stop well before the guardhouse.

"That's the only bridge to the other side," he said for all to hear. "As far as I can figure, that's the only way over for Moonis and the old man. Any illegal way across, like that ferry into Muscatine, is going to be controlled by Raden. Moonis and the old man wouldn't make it halfway across the river before they each got a bullet in the brain."

"You might have a point," said Digger.

"I'm going to see if I can bluff a way over with my pass and the colonel's name that I got at the front gate. But here's the thing. I'm going with Moonis and the old man, because Cecily is there, and because I've known Moonis my entire life, and because there's berry over there, and because if I flip another burger I'm going to rip out my own throat."

"You don't have to," said Moonis.

"If I had to, I wouldn't," said Clyde. "Now, Patti, I'm going to need you to take Lydia to her cousin's place in Decatur."

"Why Decatur?" said the girl.

Clyde twisted the rearview so that he could see her. "Your mom's been picked up by the sweepers, Lydia. She's being sent to an LCM for a year, maybe two."

"Why? What did she do?"

Clyde hesitated a moment before saying, "I don't know."

"Then it's not true," was all the girl could say. Moonis looked behind him and saw the girl's face fall into a mask of blank. It reminded him of the numbness he felt when his father told him his own mother had up and left.

"The social workers in the uniforms came looking for you again," continued Clyde. "They asked about your cough. You don't want to go to an orphans' home with your cough. You'll be better off with your cousin in Decatur."

"No, I won't," said the girl before burying her face in Ruby's shoulder.

The singer put her arm around her.

"When I get back," said Clyde, "I'll bring a bushel of berry and stop off and make you some tea, I promise. Patti, you'll tell the Guard that we forced the three of you onto the island. They'll believe you, because anything else would be flat crazy. Once you're out of here, you'll drop Lydia in Decatur and then take Ruby to Chicago. How's that sound?"

"Suicidal," said Patti. "Which I admire. Except I'm going with you and Moonis."

"I need you to take care of Lydia."

"We're in this together, the three of us," said Patti. "We always have been. No reason to break up a winning strategy."

"What the hell have we ever won?" said Clyde.

"Is it true about my mother?" said Lydia, her forehead still on Ruby's shoulder.

"Yes, I'm sorry. Mrs. McGillicutty told me just yesterday."

"I bet that old biddy couldn't wait to tell you."

"As a matter of fact."

"I'm going with you, too, Clyde."

"It's too dangerous."

"You're not my mother. You can't stop me. Is there really berry there?"

"More than you could pick," said Ruby.

"Maybe I'll be able to breathe there. Maybe there I won't be sick all the time. Maybe I'll dance again."

"We'll take care of her, darling," said Ruby. "I promise."

"You're coming, too?" said Clyde.

"It's as good a place as any for all of us, I suppose. And what was I going to do in Chicago? You think my act would go over there?"

"I don't know what to say," said Clyde.

"Say nothing, darling. Just go out there and wave your pass and see how it goes."

Clyde turned to look at Moonis with the wryest of smiles on his lips and the resignation of the damned in his eye. In that instant something in the universe cracked open for Moonis Fell, and in the narrow cleft he glimpsed some new, sublime possibility of how to move forward in the world.

"Okay with you, Moonis?" said Clyde.

"Do I have any say?" said Moonis.

"Not much."

"Then it sounds just about right."

Clyde put the van in gear. As they approached the mouth of the bridge, one Guardsman stepped out, and then the second Guardsman. Both lifted their guns. Clyde stopped the van a few yards from the men, climbed out, and strode forward, waving his precious pass.

There was a moment of discussion, a moment when all three turned to look at the van, another bout of discussion, and then Clyde and the two Guardsmen headed for the small guardhouse. When they were inside, the door closed behind them, and only their silhouettes could be seen through the dusty windows.

***

Moonis observed all this from within the van and behind the churning of his thoughts. He had always felt more than just a little bit superior to his oldest friend. Moonis read everything he could get his hands on while Clyde rotted his brain with beer and whores and television. Moonis had fought his existential battles tooth and nail while Clyde flipped burgers with a seemingly endless contentment. Moonis had been selected. (Yes, in his bones Moonis still lived on that pathetic fact.) When Clyde said old friends are always keeping score, Moonis knew exactly what he meant, and in Moonis's scorekeeping, Clyde was always falling short.

Yet Clyde had decided to go with Moonis to the D-Lands out of loyalty, and love, and a sense of obligation to a sick girl to whom he had no obligation other than what he felt in his gut. And Patti and Ruby and the girl were all ready to follow him, no matter the risk to their own skins. All of it was true and beautiful and it touched Moonis like a slap in the face. It made him think that—

One of the guard shack's dusty windowpanes suddenly blew out as a soldier's head slammed through the glass before being pulled back inside. Moonis jumped into the driver's seat of the van, kicked the clutch, and jammed the idling engine into reverse, ready to back the hell out of there amidst a sea of bullets.

But it wasn't a Guardsman with his rifle blazing who stepped out of the door when the ruckus was over. It was Clyde, a rivulet of blood streaming from his short blond hair. He smiled and raised a finger before heading back inside.

A moment later the wooden gatepost rose and when Clyde came out again, a pack was slung over his shoulder, a pistol was in his belt, and he carried two rifles and a crate of bottled water.

"We ready?" said Clyde after Digger had pulled open the side door to take the weapons and supplies.

"What the hell happened in there?" said Moonis.

"They didn't believe me when I said I had already gotten permission." Clyde slammed shut the side door and hopped into the front passenger seat. "They started to call that colonel. That was a mistake."

Clyde closed his door and calmly looked straight ahead, as if they were about to take a simple drive in the country. And Moonis stared at his old friend, still in that ridiculous red-and-white shirt, with blood on his face and a strange smile on his lips. Seeing Clyde like this was like viewing him while high on reefer, where all became, in the firing synapses of the weeded brain, their archetypal selves. And Clyde's archetype, Moonis realized, was hero. Through the whole of his own life, Moonis had been nothing more than a dilettante whose failures had required the hero's call, and it was Clyde who had responded. Who could ever have imagined such a thing? But now, if heroism was needed to free his sister and build a life, maybe he had himself a model.

"What are you waiting on?" said Clyde.

"Just getting a better look at you."

"Don't look too long, Moonis. That call they made might have gone through before I hung up the line. The jeeps could be on their way."

Moonis slammed the van into first and jolted forward. As he passed the guardhouse, he caught a glimpse of the bodies in a pile on the floor. A single leg stretched out the door, shaking.

And then they were on the bridge, picking up speed. He upshifted and upshifted again until they were accelerating madly forward,

Moonis and Clyde, Lydia and Ruby and Patti and the old man Digger, all of them encased within the overpainted surfaces of that psychedelic van, accelerating forward and further, full of steam, barreling across the mighty Mississippi River, the great demarcation of their pasts and their futures, their hearts brimming with fear and hope and good intent, riding like hellcats into the unknown territory of the blighted D-Lands.

And into their glory.

III

WARRIORS

35
YEAGER'S FARM

Martha came to Yeager's farm when she was just fourteen, a runaway who had outrun the sweepers by crossing the river in the pitch of night on a stolen wooden rowboat, old, leaky, smelling of illegal walleye that would steal your teeth.

She had been tall for her age, gawky and nervous. Her blonde hair had been dyed black and hacked short with a knife, six small hoops hung from holes gouged with safety pins in her left ear, and her forearms were crossed with scars. In the D-Lands she lived off cans of food scavenged from shelves, water from backyard rain barrels, corn growing wild in the fields.

Life was simpler on the wrong side of the river—no rules, no sweepers, no shortage of abandoned books to read, no librarian to frown at her selections of Woolf or Dostoyevsky, and no stepfather with a bone-handled knife who had lost his guaranteed job and wanted her to turn tricks to pay for his whiskey. There were dangers, sure, but Martha had learned long ago to make herself small, and so she remained unnoticed, except by the black flies that chewed her flesh.

Always more comfortable with no one about, she survived an entire summer without ever being bored or lonely, scavenging in the mornings, reading in the afternoons, watching the sunsets, each day moving ever deeper into the disincorporated territory. It was not so much an adventure as a new life, and every day she felt more in love with the ruined land and her burgeoning freedom. And the love grew fiercer even as the nights grew colder, the feral crops withered on their vines, the burns on her legs from the river water turned to suppurating sores.

Cold and hungry, her cough thicker and wetter by the day, she was drawn off the road by a distant wisp of smoke rising like an invitation in the darkening sky. She followed a pitted dirt road that meandered through a dark wood toward the smoke's source. When she emerged slowly, cautiously, from beneath the canopy into dusk, she saw an old farmhouse with its windows lit, its siding freshly painted, the field behind it planted in neat rows. The sound of a piano drifted from the house. To her right, a pasture enclosed with wooden fencing was set before a red barn. It was a scene from a distant age, daubed on wood with iridescent paint by Laura Ingalls Wilder.

She clutched her bag close as she stepped warily toward the house, hoping to peek into a window just to see what life could be like inside such a place. As she approached, her foot caught on something and a cowbell rang in the distance. She moved forward, tripped slightly again, heard another cowbell. By the time she realized what she was blundering through, the piano music had died and in the house's doorway stood a man, squat, bald, ugly as a squashed melon, gripping a shotgun leveled at her chest.

"What you want around heya, girl?" said the man, with a high-pitched drawl.

"Nothing," she said.

"Then you won't mind turning round and scatting the hell out of heya afore you get a belly full of buckshot."

"Oh, you let her be, Thaddeus."

Martha looked up and saw a beautiful woman with gray pigtails, sticking half her body out a dormer window. "She's just hungry, can't you see?"

"Don't care none about that," said the man. "Close yo window, Stella, and leave this thieving scamp to me."

"Why, the poor little thing is just shaking with hunger."

"She ain't so little," said the man, "and there's plenty to eat on the other side, with all them prison farms. She needs to eat, I'm sure they'd be more than grateful to find a plate for her."

"You want to come in, little lady, and get a bite of food?"

"I don't want to be a bother," said Martha before loosing a cavalcade of coughs.

"That's a bald-faced lie," howled the old man. "You came here for no other reason than to be a bother. And you are succeeding mightily. I am so bothered I'm about to burst."

"We have some fried chicken left over," said the woman, "and a bit of greens. How does that sound?"

"I maybe could eat some," said Martha.

"She maybe could eat some?" said the man. "She's just full of surprises, ain't she? She maybe could rob us blind, too, and chop us up for stew when she's done."

"Don't be ridiculous," said the woman. "If she was eating fat old men, there'd be more than skin on her bones."

"Get on your way now, young lady, afore I shoot."

"Put down the gun, you old fool, and let her be. I'm coming down to make her up a platter. And some wild berry tea. With that cough, she could use some of the tea."

The man looked at Martha, raised his shotgun to get a fair bead on her, and then lowered the gun and shook his head, as if at the perfidy of the whole human race.

"Don't think I won't be watching your every step, missy," he said. "And don't think you won't be working twice for anything you'll be getting heya, because you will, I promise you that." He stepped to the side. "Now get in if you're getting in. We don't need no more pests inside than we got already."

The man's name was Yeager, Thaddeus Yeager. It was his farm, would always be his farm, and in all of Martha's life she would never meet anyone kinder or more true than the squat little man who had aimed a shotgun at her face.

***

It was now fifteen years after Martha's first appearance at the farm. Thaddeus Yeager was buried in the pasture, his wife was a demented invalid in the second-floor bedroom, and Martha had turned into a tall, earnest woman, with high bones in her cheeks and a fussing baby on her hip.

The baby let out a shriek, and a tiny hand grasped at Martha's shirt. She lifted him off her hip, looked at his angry red face, not so different than farmer Yeager's face all those years ago, and gave him a kiss. The baby's name was Peace and the imprint of Martha's kiss lingered in lipstick on Peace's forehead.

"It's a-comin', I can feel it . . . like a train it is . . . barreling right at us . . . downhill stretch of track," said Zephyr, standing bare-chested and bare-footed behind her, jeans rolled up past his ankles, a rolled cigarette between his lips. His voice was a barely discernible rush of words, as much a frantic bebop riff as a collection of meaningful sentences, with gaps where he spoke so softly and quickly you couldn't catch the words, only the melody. "And I'm not insinuating here, Martha, no, I'm not, the normal scratchy visit thing . . . This is coming raw . . . snap, like a thunderstorm rolling through the plains . . . crackle, torrents of rain and terror and frogs . . . Pop goes that weasel."

Zephyr was tall and handsome and calm as a snort of Benzedrine. He loved to work—no one could plow like Zephyr; when the horses got tired, he would pull the thing himself—and he loved to smoke, and to screw, and to run, and to screw some more. But most of all he loved to talk, and when he talked, he talked all in a whoosh.

"The kind of whoop-de-doo that changes everything . . . sex with the cosmos that fries your blood . . . and you know what I mean, I know you do . . . like when one of them aliens that come and visit . . . just waves his finger . . . Everything, it swirls up into the air . . . a tornado out of nothing . . . zowie-wang . . . and most times not for the better."

"You've seen aliens, Zephyr?" said Martha.

"Clear as Venus on a starry night . . . with Gene, out in New Mexico . . . crazy old New Mexico . . . stars and mesas and Mexicans . . . on our way from there to here . . . Little green guys they were."

"Green?"

"Green as lizards, Martha. Truth. Nice teeth they had, too."

Peace wasn't Martha's baby, but each of the children were the responsibility of all the citizens—"citizen" is what they called anyone who worked the farm—and so she cared for Peace exactly as if Peace were one of her three birth children rolling about the rolling hills. The red kiss on the baby's forehead reminded Martha of the heaviness of the day. It was only in preparation for these foul visits that she daubed on the makeup. It was like a mask; somehow it allowed the marauders to see her as they wanted to see her, while she hid her hatreds beneath the red and the rouge. She wiped the lipstick off Peace's forehead with her thumb before opening her shirt and putting the baby on her breast. He squirmed his mouth around before latching on, closing his lids only when the milk began to flow. As the baby suckled, Martha scanned the landscape with her pale-green eyes, wondering if the farm was ready for another appointment with the taxmen from hell.

The farm had grown like a wildfire from her first days. Over the years it seemed like anyone lost in the D-Lands sooner or later ended up at Yeager's farm, and the Yeagers, it turned out, never turned anyone away. Beyond the large fuchsia outbuilding with the huge double doors that served as dining hall, dance hall, rec hall, meeting hall, party hall, anything hall, there was a vast shantyfield of shacks and tents and makeshift domes. Even so, among the structures that had been erected around the newly incorporated fields were a large dormitory and a children's house that would soon need to be expanded. The community of citizens that had come to the farm as outcasts had worked there and grown there and danced there and left there and returned there and procreated there. Over the years they had become a great and boisterous extended family.

"Ask Gene if your mind balks," said Zephyr. "True as rain it is . . . Roadhouse bar, two girls from Topeka, me and Gene, soaking our brains . . . just off Route 70 . . . burning the day, making our moves . . . hoo-ha . . . when in they walk."

"The aliens."

"Olive-heads, you bet . . . chugging beer, smoking Marlboros . . . nickels in the jukebox . . . hitting on our girls . . . They liked Sinatra, they liked Perry Como . . . Old souls with grabby hands and white teeth . . . like skid-row drunks in downtown Denver . . . green as gangrene . . . and then they up and ask for beer nuts . . . how strange, beer nuts on Mars . . . And the barkeep . . . beefy and sour like sauerbraten in an old kettle . . . he goes, 'We don't got no beer nuts, only pretzels.' And these little green folk . . . guests of the nation . . . gnash their white teeth, and their fingers start to waving, and next thing you know . . . bazoom-kazoom . . . everything inside is swirling, in the air, tumbling, spinning . . . I was flying, Martha, with Gene and the chairs and the barkeep and the bottles . . . And these aliens are just sitting at the bar, drinking their beer, chattering away about how pretzels suck."

"The lesson, I suppose," said Martha, "is don't forget the beer nuts."

"That should be the seventh commandment, instead of what they got now, which I never did buy . . . A little adultery's good for the soul, my mama would have told you . . . But the way the air felt when all that was happening, in that bar, that's how it feels now . . . silvery, you know . . . like sucking on a dime while licking an electric socket."

As Zephyr kept talking, talking, Martha spied Enrique walking up to them from the hall. She pulled young Peace off her breast. The baby looked up at her with such shocked disappointment that it would have made her laugh if she had been in the mood for laughing. But she wasn't in the mood for laughing. The farm was ostensibly a place with no leaders and no laws, but in the end someone had to stand up and point the way, and somehow, against her stated desire, it always seemed to come down to Martha, the closest thing the Yeagers ever had to a daughter. In the midst of Zephyr's monologue, she thought, not for the first time, that she had been here too long, that it was time to take her children and venture deeper into the D-Lands, someplace away from the specter of the Guard and the reality of Raden and the weariness of responsibility, maybe to find a land no man or woman had gone to before.

"Take him, please," she said to Zephyr, passing the child.

"Yeah, man," said Zephyr. He lifted Peace high over his head and gave him a little shake that made the baby forget his deprivation and laugh. "Want to fly, little one? Want to buss the moon? Whose is he, anyhoo?"

"Does it matter?" said Martha as she buttoned her shirt and reflexively gathered loose strands of golden hair behind her ear. Zephyr gently tossed young Peace into the air before placing him like a football in one of his outsized, muscular arms and running off in swerves and dashes to the children's house, jabbering all the way.

"Any word on the radio?" she said to Enrique when he arrived.

"They're coming, is all, Miss Martha," said Enrique.

"I've asked you not to call me Miss Martha. I feel old enough as it is."

"I won't, Miss Martha."

Enrique, who had wandered onto the farm as a boy and now had the stirrings of a beard, had slipped into the role of unofficial foreman. They had scavenged a hand-cranked mimeograph machine from an abandoned school, along with boxes of stencil sheets and ink, and each evening Enrique posted the next day's jobs on mimeographed sheets in the dormitory and the main hall. The citizens, between their meditations, and their copulations, and their shine-and-drug-fueled naked wildings, somehow made sure each task was done before nightfall.

"Is the box prepared?" she said.

"Packed tight and ready to go boom."

"Good. The box might be our only chance to survive what's coming."

"That and your sweet smile, Miss Martha."

"You think I have enough makeup on?"

Enrique grinned. "You remind me of a mime I once saw in Guadalajara on the Day of the Dead."

"Perfect," she said.

36
TOURIST CAMP

Dawn in the D-Lands. Still early enough so that three stars could be seen in the sky.

The quiet that covered the landscape like a blanket was interrupted only by the sweet melodies of early birds and the uneasy chirping of their prey, along with the footsteps of the four as they made their way down the cracked and pitted road. Two of the four had Guard rifles at the ready. One, staggering forward on bowlegs creaky with age, had a gun in his belt. There was no light conversation, there were no orders barked, they each of them already knew what to do. To a person they didn't want to fight, but three of the four were ready to kill if the need arose, and the three figured the need would arise indeed.

The problem was the fourth.

Around the fire the night before, Digger had roughly mapped the landscape, and Patti, drawing on her short stint in the army, had laid out a rudimentary strategy. It was their first night in, and as Patti drew lines in the dirt, Ruby cooked up a couple of cans of beans and some potted meat, which Clyde had taken from the guard shack, in a pan they scavenged from an abandoned farmhouse. They were camped out just east of what had been Columbus Junction, a place Digger told them was close, but not too close, to Raden's camp.

Patti's plan had been simple enough. They would leave Ruby and Lydia with the van and a pistol a few miles from the tourist camp where Raden held court. The rest would head out at earliest dawn, walking down the road to the camp, and spend the day silently surveilling in the surrounding woods to find out where Cecily was kept. When the time was ripe, most likely after nightfall, they would slip in, make the rescue, and slip out before Raden's thugs were any the wiser. Then it would be a mad dash back to the van and back to the border, figuring out how to get over the river once they reached it.

No one said it was genius, but simple had its virtues, too, and each knew his part to play. Except maybe Moonis.

Clyde figured they could count on Patti, so long as she wasn't driving a sports car, and the old man seemed game enough, but Moonis was a cipher; who the hell knew what was going on in that brainpan of his. Their mad bolt across the Mississippi and into the ruins on the far side had seemed to unsettle him.

What had been the city of Davenport was now just the blackened memory of a town. The bare outlines of blistered buildings rose like specters from the rubble, the derelict walls jagged and piecemeal, silent memorials.

"What the hell happened to this place?" had said Patti in the midst of the desolation.

"I never got a clear story," said Ruby.

"Ain't nothing clear about it," said Digger. "And it's not a story you're gonna want to hear, neither."

"You were here, Digger?" said Ruby, her arm still around Lydia. "Before the fire?"

"It wasn't just a fire, it was brimstone, too. I was right in the middle of it when it all went to hell."

"And here we are," said Clyde, "a bunch of fools riding through the gay old town with a wheezing van painted every bald color under the sun."

"'Every ship is a romantic object, except that we sail in,'" said Moonis.

"Don't get stupid on me, Moonis."

"That's not me," said Moonis. "That's Emerson."

"What, did we go to school with him?"

"I did, you didn't."

"That's what we should call it," said Lydia.

"What's that you say, honey?" said Ruby.

"We should call the van the Every Ship. That should be its name. Everything should have a name."

"I like it," said Digger. "It's got heft."

"Just so long as it's got an engine and gasoline," said Clyde.

As the Every Ship picked its way through the destruction, along a path cleared in the rubble by Guard bulldozers, they could just catch glimpses of life in the relics. Something large and furry loped in the gap between two blackened walls, something dark peered out a cracked and whitened window. A mismatched, mangy pack of dogs scurried across the roadway.

"We're being watched," said Moonis. "Judged, even."

"By who?" said Clyde. "There's nothing here but rubble."

"And eyes," said Moonis.

"That's it for sure," said the old man with a cackle. "Rubble and eyes. Welcome to the D-Lands."

And right about then, even as he drove deeper into the land, Moonis had gone quiet. It wasn't a sullen silence, it was just a stillness, like he was cocooned in his own thoughts, which was a dangerous place for anyone to be. What Moonis was thinking on, and whether he could get out of his own way when action was required, remained a mystery.

As Clyde walked by his side down the dusty road, he hoped the answer wouldn't get them all killed.

The old man raised a hand and they stopped their progress. The road ahead bent to the left. It was as if the dawning hadn't yet reached that far; darkness oozed around the bend. The old man slipped into the woods to the left and Clyde and Moonis, in single file, followed him in. Patti waited a beat and then found a path through the woods on their left flank. Like the earliest inhabitants of the land, they infiltrated as silently as they could manage through the thick, weedy woods, steeling themselves for the carnage to come.

***

The old tourist camp was a ghost in the blurred morning light.

Clyde peeked out just over the crest of a rise looking down upon the collection of rustic cabins scattered around a dirt yard. In the middle of the yard was what appeared to be a makeshift shower house, with a rusted metal water tank perched atop the roof. To Clyde's left was an overgrown path that led from the cabins, through the woods, over a small hill, and then down to the river.

Moonis and the old man were hunkered on the other side of the path. Patti had climbed a tree behind them, with a view all the way down to the river, to make sure nobody came at them from behind. Their position was ideal for keeping an eye on the camp, but as the sky brightened, it became ever clearer that while the position might be ideal, the plan was crap.

The yard was desolate, empty of the swarms of bikes and trucks and tankers that should have been present. There was no army camped out here, no distressed damsel being held prisoner by a mob. There was only a single motorcycle parked by the shower house, a set of goggles hanging from the handlebars, which could have meant that no one was there at all. But the bike was enough to keep them waiting silently for something to happen. And so they waited, waited. A doe nimbly climbed from the river and nibbled at a leaf. The old man threw a rock. The doe bolted. They waited some more.

And then the door of a cabin slammed open and a naked woman ran out with a scream, breasts and buttocks bouncing as she sprinted away.

A moment later the door slammed open again and a skinny bearded man, also naked, sprinted out after her.

Was the woman laughing, crying, shouting with fear or with joy? It didn't much matter to Clyde; he wasn't going to sit tight and watch her beaten bloody or screwed silly on that dusty yard. One bike, one naked biker—the situation was clear enough to him. Clyde turned and signaled to Patti and then, with rifle in hand, he crested the rise and quietly made his way down the hill until he was in plain view of the otherwise-engaged couple. It turned out when it came to a choice between the beating and the screwing it wasn't either-or.

"Yoo-hoo," Clyde called out in the middle of the violent rutting. "Is that you, Ernestine?"

The woman, who was pressed against the door of the shower, pushed the man's head away from her as she jerked her reddened face toward Clyde. She screeched something and the bearded man turned and stared, his body still hard against the woman's.

"I hope I'm not interrupting," said Clyde.

"Who the fuck?" said the man, throwing the woman to the ground as he spun around, naked and enraged, to face the intruder. His teeth were red with betel.

"I just thought that might be Ernestine," said Clyde. "You never know where she gets to these days."

"Buddy," said the naked bearded man. "Are you ever in the wrong place." He started walking toward Clyde, not at an amble but at a determined gait, fast and direct.

"I don't mean to cause any trouble," said Clyde.

"Don't matter," said the man, his walk speeding up, turning into a run and then into a charge, "'cause you found it." He was wiry and strong and surprisingly fast. With his flock flapping and his arms pumping, he swallowed the gap like ice cream. And now there was a knife in his hand. Where did that come from?

"I'm just looking for my lost love," said Clyde, taking a nervous step back and then another.

"Come and get her," said the man, knife held like an ice pick, before lunging like a missile for Clyde.

Quick as a spasm, Clyde lifted the gun and slammed the man's face with the butt end. Clyde felt the electric shock of it in his bones. The naked bearded man dropped flat and unmoving, like a dead eel.

As Clyde looked down at the smashed mass of gristle and blood that had been the man's nose, the woman on the ground started cursing while she grappled to her feet. She stood naked in the yard, swaying and cursing. Not bad-looking, either, for a motorcycle mawk.

Clyde hefted the rifle and pointed it at her face. "Shut up, Ernestine," he said.

***

"What I want to know more than anything," said Clyde, leaning on the bathhouse wall, talking softly to the naked woman, who was sitting now on the ground, "is where the knife came from."

"Get me my clothes," she said.

"It's safer like this for now," said Clyde.

"What are you, some kind of perv?"

"Some kind, yes," said Clyde. The sun was bright in the sky. Gnats flitted about his face.

He heard an excited holler and turned to see Patti stepping out of what appeared to be the dining hall with a box held over her head. "Chili," she said loudly. "A whole case. We'll eat like kings tonight."

"And crap like mules tomorrow," said Clyde.

Patti had been foraging among the cabins and had already collected a pile in the middle of the yard: pistols, a shotgun, boxes of ammo, bottles of liquor, canteens, flashlights, leather jackets, food cans, coffee. Clyde examined the scene for a moment and then turned back to the naked lady.

"Was it hidden on him? Did you have it behind your back? How does a naked man end up charging at me with a knife? This is going to plague me for weeks."

"What are you doing here, rube?"

"Looking for a girl," said Clyde.

"Me?"

"Not you, Ernestine. Someone with a bit of class."

"Boy, are you ever in the wrong place."

He had tried talking to the man on the ground with the smashed nose. Clyde had picked up the knife, put it in his belt, and then leaned over, putting his questions hard and harsh, but all the bearded man did was spit blood. So he had left him to Moonis and went off to interrogate the naked woman. Even in the bright light, she was too good-looking to be in a place like this with a goon like Naked Knife Boy. Clyde was somehow disappointed in the way she had conducted her life.

"You know where that Raden went off to?" said Clyde.

"Go to hell," she said.

"You know when he's coming back?"

"Go to hell."

"I get the general drift," said Clyde, who turned to look over at Moonis.

He was sitting in a chair, leaning forward, talking to the bearded man, who was sitting on the dirt and staring up at Moonis out of a gnarly mass of blood. The old man, Digger, was standing behind Moonis, a gun in his hand.

"Ask him where a naked man gets hold of a knife," Clyde called out to Moonis, "and whether he's got any others nearby." Moonis glanced up at Clyde and gave him a signal to button it. Fine. Clyde was good at buttoning it.

Patti came out of one of the cabins holding up a pair of heavy black motorcycle boots. "Anyone need size twelve?"

Clyde looked down at the sandals he was still wearing from his prison break. "I'll take them," he called out.

"They're yours," said Patti.

"Whose bike is that?" said Clyde to the woman.

"Screw off."

"If you don't answer, I'm going to take this knife and spike the gas tank, which means no one's going anywhere on it anytime soon. So let's try it again. Whose bike is it?"

"His," said the woman.

"Does he have a name?"

"Blade. His name is Blade."

"Charming," said Clyde. "He must have been the cutest little baby."

"They left him to keep an eye on things."

"And he did a swell job of it, too," said Clyde. He looked around at the camp. Cozy little place. "So I guess that means they're coming back."

"They always do."

"You are just a bundle of good tidings, aren't you?"

Moonis was still leaning toward Blade, talking intently but quietly. And strangely enough, the bearded man seemed to be listening, and he was talking now and then himself. They were having a conversation. How do you like that apple?

"Whoo-hoo," shouted Patti as she walked out of one of the cabins, hoisting a wooden crate high over her head.

"What you got there, young lady?" said the old man.

"A case of dynamite," she said. "Someone was ready to have a blasting party."

"Just be careful you don't drop that thing."

"Don't worry," said Patti. "I got this."

"Yes, you do," said the old man.

The pile was growing. They'd have to strap some of the stuff to the van's roof. In just a few hours in the D-Lands they had already become accomplished scavengers. That said something about what it was to be human, but Clyde wasn't quite sure exactly what.

"So tell me this," he said to the naked woman. "How many are there with Raden? A lot, a little?"

"Enough to skin your sorry hides," said the woman.

"More than a hundred? Less than a hundred?"

"They're going to kill you and dance on your bones."

"You know what you need, Ernestine? A cheerier disposition."

"My name's not Ernestine."

"Then what should I call you?"

"Desiree."

"I've known a couple Desirees in my time," said Clyde, gazing out at the emptiness of the road that whipped by the tourist camp. "And none of them was named that in the cradle."

A shot shattered the quiet, and then a second, bam, quick as that, sending a flight of birds beating their wings as they climbed into the sky.

Clyde spun, his rifle up and searching, when he saw the old man staggering back, his smoking pistol still pointing at a body on the ground. The man called Blade was sprawled now face-first in the dust. In his outstretched hand, somehow, was another knife.

"How does he do that?" said Clyde to the naked woman, who showed not an ounce of mournfulness.

***

After the shooting, the old man took one of the liquor bottles Patti scavenged and repaired to the woods to drink the taste of killing out of his mouth. Moonis sat off by himself, lost in thought. Patti took the motorcycle down the road to retrieve the van. And Clyde kept close to Desiree as she prepared to leave with them. Moonis had made it clear that they wouldn't leave her alone in the D-Lands, and though Clyde was of another opinion, he went along. He might have gotten them over the river, but this was going to be Moonis's show.

"What are you going to do with me?" said the woman as she and Clyde walked to the cabin she had fled naked and screaming.

"Drop you off someplace safe as soon as we can," said Clyde.

"I need to get back to the other side."

"You and me both, sister. But until then it looks like we're chasing Raden, and since you've been out with them on their rounds, you're showing us the way."

"I suppose you're tired of living."

"I sure as hell am," said Clyde. "Aren't you?"

He entered the cabin with her and watched as she made up her face nicely, threw what she needed into a bag, and started dressing. Long black leather gloves, a tight fishnet top with leather straps that hid nothing and showed everything to surprisingly good effect, a black leather thong with handcuffs hanging down, pointy leather boots covered with straps and buckles. To top it off was a black leather cop cap with a shiny visor.

"You got to be kidding me," said Clyde after she put on her getup.

"It's this or nothing."

"It's as good as nothing. We got a young girl with us, for Krist's sake."

"What are you doing with a girl in the D-Lands?"

"It's a long story. Come on. We'll get one of those leather jackets Patti found and put it around your shoulders for modesty's sake."

"I never been all that modest."

"Time to start."

Just as they stepped out of the cabin, the Every Ship appeared in all its Technicolor glory, with Ruby driving and Lydia sitting next to her in the front seat. Patti was following behind with the cycle, round green goggles over her eyes.

"What the hell is that thing?" said Desiree.

"That's our ride, baby."

***

There were two metal barrels set up on frames on the edge of the yard. One was filled with drinking water, the other contained more than enough gasoline to fill the van, the motorcycle, and the extra gasoline cans Patti had bought. With all the fuel, they were good for another couple hundred miles.

When everything was filled and loaded, the cans and some of the cases lashed to the top of the van, Moonis and Clyde stood side by side in the middle of the dusty yard with the dead man still lying there.

"Why'd he go after you like that?" said Clyde. "Was it just general orneriness?"

"I don't know exactly," said Moonis. "We were getting along just fine until I told him my name."

Clyde looked at Moonis for a bit, and then started laughing.

"There's some gasoline left," said Moonis. "I say let's torch this stinking place."

"Torch it?"

"As a sign to Cecily that we're here, and we're coming for her. And as a sign to Raden, too."

"It's not like you to draw attention to yourself."

"You want to be above the fold, Clyde, you've got to put on a show."

"What's the fold?" said Clyde.

They burned the place to the disincorporated ground. The cabins, the large building, the makeshift shower house: burned, burned, burned. The fires were so bright they competed with the sun, and the smoke rose fat and black, each individual strain braiding with the others into a pillar so high it broke apart on the roof of the sky to deliver its message across the ruined landscape.

Moonis Fell was coming.

And then, with the smoke still pouring upward, they left the camp and drove down what remained of the road, following Desiree's uncertain directions: Clyde at the wheel of the Every Ship, the mawk beside him to show the way, Moonis and Digger in the middle seat, Ruby with the girl in the rear, and Patti rolling along beside them on the motorcycle like an honor guard.

The smoke billowed and the road unspooled and the van trailed a wild wake of color as it delivered them ever farther into the wilderness.

37
CARAVAN

Cecily heard the camp come alive at first light: determined strides over the rocky yard, tools thrown into trucks, orders barked, engines fiddled with and revved to the red line, shouts and curses, guns test-fired into the woods.

She put on her robe, tightened it around her waist, stepped out of the cottage in her bare feet, and walked down the path to watch the preparations. While the tourist camp was Raden's home base, there were always pieces of his army coming or going. In the days since her recapture—or maybe more accurately, her rescue from Millard's stew— she had seen much movement. Raden controlled a great swath of the eastern D-Lands and his control required a continued presence. But this looked as if the whole miserable pack of them was getting ready to head on out. And some of the men were bringing their women, which meant they'd be away for a while.

One of the men saw her standing there and stopped short, as if he had seen a wolf in the camp. He averted his gaze. "Hello there, Miss Fell," he said. "Fine morning, ain't it?"

"Yes, it is, Jake. Going somewhere?"

"Rounds. We'll be gone for a mite."

"How nice for you."

"Ain't no picnic." He murmured something else, backed up a bit while still looking down, and then limped away.

"Morning, Miss Fell," said another as he passed, giving a crimson-tinted smile. "You wanting some coffee?"

"That would be lovely, Blade, if you have the time to spare."

"Not no problem," said the bearded man. "I ain't got much else to do. I'm not going nowhere but back to bed."

"Oh, 'scuse me, I didn't see you," said a tall man, half his head wrapped in bandages, coming to an abrupt stop. The one eye not covered by the dirty white cloth was aimed at the ground.

"Good morning, Kyrk," she said. "Feeling any better?"

"Some."

"That's too bad," said Cecily.

She stood and watched the activity and waited for her coffee with a sweet sense of satisfaction. She liked the way she was treated at the camp now, with a certain awestruck respect mixed with the longing looks. It was amazing what happens to your place in the world when you smash some asshole's head with a chair leg. She should have done it sooner, she thought; she should do it every day.

***

After the terror at Millard's cabin, it had been a harrowing drive back to the camp on the back of Raden's cycle. He had said nothing to her when she approached him, barely acknowledging her presence as she followed him to the bike, and then he had ignored her as they rode back toward the camp.

Mile by mile she felt the will to resist him ebb out of her, as if it were leaking like blood from a wound. Raden was a huge mound of scar and gristle, a full foot taller than she, with a girth so massive Cecily could barely keep hold of his waist as they raced through the darkness on his cycle. When the inevitable rape came that night—and she didn't doubt that it would come that night—she'd decided she wouldn't struggle against it, she had nothing left to struggle with. Raden was too massive, too powerful, he had just saved her life, and she was still psychologically cracked by the sight of the old man's blown-apart skull. Resistance was impossible in so many ways. Raden had waited and he had won and now he would take his prize without a fight, as simple as that. Without any willingness in her heart, true, but without a fight.

By the time they pulled into the camp, Raden was well ahead of his army and he and Cecily were alone. He roared right through the yard and up the path to her cabin, killing the engine and kicking the bike forward on its stand.

And then . . . And then . . . Nothing.

He climbed off his bike, gave Cecily, still sitting there, a stare she couldn't decipher, like he was waiting for her to say something. Like he was waiting for an invitation. And when she gave none, he simply let his scarred and brutal face crack into a semblance of a smile before he trudged off, down toward the yard, leaving her shocked and relieved and slightly disappointed at the same time. Disappointed because nothing had been resolved, nothing had been changed, her fate remained in a strange limbo.

And yet, along with her shock and relief and peculiar disappointment, she also felt a tender sprout of gratitude. She had been helpless before Raden, as defenseless as a comatose lamb, and yet all Raden had done was smile and leave her safely behind. Gratitude. It was a strange and, frankly, unfamiliar emotion, for when had she ever before offered up gratitude that simply before. Yet it was also lovely, and innocent, and one of the purest emotions she had ever felt, untinged as it was with all her strivings. Gratitude.

That's when she decided she would no longer try to escape. She wouldn't give herself over to the brute, but out of respect for his saving her that very night, and then his act of grace by leaving her alone, she would accept for a time the boundaries he had placed around her. She would accept her life here, in this camp, among the savages.

And in so doing, and over time, she learned the strangest of truths: the struggle toward the heights might fill the heart, but in acceptance lies great power.

***

She was standing in the yard, a mug of coffee in her hand, watching the preparations continue, when Garth came to her with a box. He was wearing a white dress shirt and brown oxfords. He looked like an accountant.

"We're taking a trip," he told her. "We'll be gone maybe a couple weeks."

"I'll miss you all," she said.

"No, you won't. We can't afford to leave a pack of guards for you."

"I won't run," she said.

"I believe you," he said. "But we're leaving Blade behind to keep tabs on the camp and we'd need to leave the pack to keep you safe from him."

"Oh, Blade's sweet."

"Until you get to know him. Blade's got knives hidden every which way, some places you wouldn't believe. You think you've got him covered, and quick as that, you've got a shiv at your throat. And Raden wouldn't like that one bit if it happened to you. We're leaving within the hour." He opened the box, removed a pair of soft black boots, held them out to her. "Raden bought you these to make the trip more pleasant."

Cecily took the gift and felt the suppleness of the leather. "That Raden's a honey."

***

The very earth trembled as Raden's army rolled through a territory war-torn by time. Birds alighted with panic when the caravan approached, dogs rose on their hind legs and howled, terrified eyes dipped beneath the sills of shattered windows. Only a line of vultures on the outstretched branch of an oak calmly held its place as the army passed. Each in this world recognizes its own.

Cecily was somewhere in the middle of the pack, in the passenger seat of the big black pickup Garth was driving. They were in a line of tankers and trucks, surrounded by a swarm of motorcycles mounted by riders armed tooth to jowl, bandoliers across their shoulders, shotguns sticking out of their saddlebags. All about them was a riot of unmuffled internal combustion. Even so, Garth and Cecily kept the windows down so that they could feel the raw wind whipping.

"It's beautiful in its way," shouted Cecily, looking at the landscape filled with fields of invasive prairie grass, the sprouts of weed trees, houses subsumed in vine. "The way nature has taken back the upper hand."

"That's only temporary," Garth shouted back. "Raden will whip nature, too."

"He's not a god."

"Out here he's the closest thing," said Garth.

"I thought you liked the equality of life in the D-Lands. It hardly sounds equal to call one of you a god."

"Equality only goes so far. There is always the strong and the weak. That's part of nature itself."

"And what are you, Garth?"

"Smart enough to hitch my wagon to the strong. You might think about that."

***

Early into their second day of travel they stopped on the road, the whole wretched army, taking a break, allowing the cyclists to rest their kidneys while Raden, a pack of motorcycles, and a fuel tanker with a big red star on its side veered off the road and onto a rutted dirt path. Garth followed in the pickup.

"We supply drinking water and gasoline to scattered outposts," said Garth. "We're like a public utility."

"Accompanied by a marauding horde."

"It's the D-Lands," said Garth with a shrug. "We're headed to the Birkenheads, some sort of religious order. They buy our gasoline but get most of their drinking water from a well. For their sacraments and for the men, they use rainwater."

"Is well water safe out here?"

"They say they heal the water with their prayers. But I wouldn't drink any tea if it's offered. The Birkenheads have been cutting back on their gasoline purchases from us. Word is they're getting cheap fuel from one of the wildcat tanker outfits swooping into our territory from the north."

"Don't tell me big, tough Raden is afraid of a little competition? It sounds like American-style capitalism."

"That's not the way America works," said Garth. "Only the weak allow competition."

Three or four miles down the punishing road, winding through field and wood, they emerged from the shade of a stand of tall trees into a small farming compound. A curl of rustic huts bounded a grassy flat, all of it surrounded by swaths of agricultural fields, thick with differing textures and colors of green. Women with bright bandanas over their mouths stood up in the fields and stared at their entrance before hiking their skirts and running toward a large church-like structure. Children in those same fields stood still and stared at the intruders with flat black eyes.

"Wait here," said Garth after parking the truck. He reached behind to grab a clipboard in the backseat before joining Raden at the tanker with the red star, which was now parked beside a black barn with a metal silo.

Two older boys in dark pants and suspenders stood within the grass oval and disinterestedly kicked a ball back and forth as they stared at Cecily. Chickens clucked. Beyond the barn, pens were filled with pigs, and cows stood motionless in a fenced field, their udders swollen. A small patch of red glowed so brightly in the distance it looked like it was on fire.

Cecily climbed out of the pickup, stretched her back, breathed deep the air, thick with the twining scents of freshly sickled grass and manure. She gave a little wave to the boys kicking the ball. They stared back. A fire pit was dug in the middle of the oval and beside the pit a great wooden cross emerged from the ground with a rough lectern before it. There was something slow and tamed in the scene, domestic, peaceful. If she didn't know the truth, she'd maybe want to stay for a church service at the bonfire, to feel God's presence in a place so natural it seemed almost holy.

"The head man in the place is Birkenhead," had said Garth, "a preacher of sorts, Bible-thumper, so-called seer of prophecy. The women in the compound are his wives, all of them. The children, all of them, are his children. He is father, husband, preacher, taskmaster. When the children get old enough, he marries the girls and sends the boys off to wander the D-Lands. He lets a few stay to act as guards and enforcers, but the ones who stay are sworn to celibacy and sliced and diced to make sure they keep to it."

"Krist," said Cecily.

"There's only one rooster allowed in the Birkenhead henhouse."

She looked again at the boys playing with the ball and wondered when it would be their time to give up their testicles or be forced into exile. As she watched the ball go back and forth, she slowly realized they weren't actually kicking at it. Instead the ball was just moving back and forth between them, back and forth, as if of its own volition.

She was trying to figure how they managed that little trick when a man emerged from the church-like structure and walked down the path toward Raden and Garth. The man was fat, his overalls were hiked high, his hair was long and greasy. He had the waddling walk of an angry bear.

Behind him marched two mournful young men carrying shot-guns. She had an idea why they seemed so sad. Some of the women, their bandanas modestly raised to cover the lower parts of their faces, like old-time holdup artists, followed the three men in a pack.

Cecily leaned against the truck and lifted her chin to the sun. She closed her eyes, listened to the sound of the ball skittering back and forth, the chickens, the blur of men talking over by the barn. No mat-ter how the world turned, it always ended turning on men and their business. She looked again at the boys and their ball. It bounced back and forth and back without once being kicked at. How did they do that? With rubber bands? Like a yo-yo on a string? It was pleasant to watch and try to figure it out, like a parlor trick of some sort.

She was in the process of being mesmerized by the ball when she heard the crack, like a tree being snapped in half, followed by an inhu-man howl. She jerked her attention toward the men by the barn.

The fat, greasy man was now on the ground, howling. One leg was grotesquely splayed behind him, his knee bending in a way nature never intended.

Raden stood tall with a shovel in his hands.

The two mournful men had their shotguns aimed at Raden's scarred face even as an armory in the hands of Raden's men was aimed at the pair.

The women with bandanas over their faces were bending forward and then, one by one, falling onto their knees, keening, as if at some strange Irish wake.

And Garth, in the midst of this Mexican standoff, was now leaning over the broken fat man, talking casually, pointing at the numbers on his clipboard as if they were having a reasonable discussion over accounting principles.

For some reason his calm in the midst of the mayhem gave Cecily a secret thrill.

***

They beat the crap out of Birkenhead's mournful young sons with the son's own shotguns. They poured what Garth calculated to be the amount of wildcat gas purchased by Birkenhead onto the bright-red field and with a single match turned what had been a healing patch of berry into flame and smoke. They shot four of Birkenhead's pigs in the head—bam bam bambam—and tossed the dead sacks of meat by their short little legs into the bed of the pickup. And, for good measure, they set the great wooded cross aflame.

The women of the compound rushed with wails to the burning cross. Cecily expected the wives to grab buckets and douse their sacred symbol, but instead they fell to their knees before it, and lowered their bandanas, and keened and sang and prayed before the burning cross. Their eyes blazed with misery and belief, blazed hotter than the fire itself. But it was their mouths that stole Cecily's breath.

Now uncovered, these mouths were unholy rictuses of blackness and boils and blood, without a single tooth to add a gleam of hope. Toward Cecily the women turned their faces, scarred, ruined, monstrous, their mouths open festering sores, dark and gory. It was as if these mouths were the blackened eyes of some foul creature bearing down upon her. Bearing down upon her with such anger and hatred that she could actually feel the force of it, a force so strong it felt like an animal pressing upon her chest.

She tore her gaze away, fighting to fill her lungs, and looked up to see the compound's children, arrayed in the distant fields, staring at her with those flat black eyes. And she sensed the force she was feeling upon her chest was coming not from the horrifying mouths of the keening women, but from the children, their eyes, their hatred.

As the two boys in the oval stared at her like the rest of the children, the ball bounced back and forth, back and forth, as if of its own accord, back and forth.

***

When they finally made it back to the main road, the rest of Raden's army was staring off into the distance. A pillar of smoke was rising, billowing down and rising again.

Garth left the pickup and joined Raden as he stood with his men and watched. A soldier with a compass and an old map indicated the direction. The men stared at the smoke as if trying to decipher signals from some savage civilization. And then Raden spoke low to Garth, and Garth barked an order.

Four of Raden's most brutal soldiers hiked onto their bikes. They kicked their engines to angry life, circled around and blasted on down the road, the way they had come, side by side by side by side. Between the four they had five shotguns, sixty stone, seven eyes, eight wheels. Their names were Pestilence, War, Famine, and Fred.

"What is it?" Cecily said when Garth made it back to the truck.

"There's a fire. It's somewhere in the direction of the camp. We sent some people to check it out."

"What could have happened?"

"It might not be coming from the camp. Fires are common out here. And if it is the camp, it could have been anything, maybe even an accidental explosion. There was some gasoline in the tank, and dynamite in one of the cabins, and Blade's a reckless son of a bitch."

"But if it was set, who would be crazy enough to attack Raden's camp?"

"Someone with a death wish," said Garth.

Suddenly, with those words, Cecily was filled with a terrifying suspicion. She didn't say anything to Garth as the army climbed upon their cycles and into their trucks, and the engines fired to life, and the mob began to move toward the next stop on its rounds, but the suspicion stayed with her, until it turned into a possibility, and then a dead certainty.

It was Moonis, it had to be Moonis, come to the D-Lands to save her, like Orpheus diving into the underworld to save his love. Who else could it be? For who, in the whole of her life, had she ever known to have a greater wish to die than her darling brother?

38
DIGGER'S TALE

"It was a man in a uniform that told us the truth, surprising as that might sound," said Digger, sitting at the campfire the night after they burned down Raden's camp. "He was filling up his jeep at our Esso, with his hair all awry and his eyes like squirming toads. That's where we heard about the wrench."

The firelight flickered across his wizened face like some deep truth. He talked not so much to any of the other six sitting around the fire; instead it was like he was talking to his past, trying to get a grip on some great wound in his life. Yet the others listened, rapt. For them, he wasn't only telling his singular sad tale, he was reciting for them their own secret histories.

"The soldier, he said one of them grease monkeys high up in the silo dropped his tool, simple as that. The wrench bounced around, spinning and banging and falling, before ripping through a fitting, and the fuel from that giant missile, it just started spewing. Some hero boys dived into that silo to see what they could fix; this fellow, he headed

right to the motor pool. That's how he made it out alive before everything all went to hell."

∗∗∗

It appeared to Clyde that something had gone out of Digger with the
killing that morning. When the old man set out in the calm hours
before dawn, he was on an adventure, something to rile up aged blood
long past its prime. But then he had killed a man, and that the man
needed killing didn't change the root nature of the deed.

The old man had drunk himself quiet in the woods right after,
and kept drinking even as the six in the rainbow van, and Patti alongside on the cycle, continued on in search of Cecily, moving through a
landscape blighted and raw, every inch untended. They passed prairies
stretching into the limitless horizon, fields returned to the primeval
crops of wild rye, bluestem grass, milkweed—swaths of amber, as tall
as a horse's hind, that had covered the land when it was still wild and
well beyond the frontier.

Whenever they reached an intersection where the tracks in the dust
were less than clear, Clyde slowed, not for some impending traffic—
they saw nothing on the road the entire trip except for dog and deer—
but to find out where to head next.

"Any idea?" said Clyde.

"I think just straight," said Desiree, leather jacket covering her fishnet top.

"You think?"

"I don't know, maybe a left. Where are you going to leave me?"

"Depends on where he's going."

"There are still some communities hunkered down," said Desiree.
"Farm stuff, and drugs, crazy labs. Off the map. Raden makes a route,
buys their drugs, sells them gasoline and other necessities."

"And this road is it?" said Clyde.

"I think."

"She thinks."

"I seen that house up there before."

"It looks like every other wreck we passed."

"Where do they get their berry?" said Moonis.

"Mainly from a farm. Bunch of freaks."

"Is this the way?"

"I think."

"Is it far?"

"Not really."

"That's good enough for me," said Moonis. "Straight it is."

They saw scores of old homesteads collapsing into themselves, tombstones of dreams discounted, dismembered, disincorporated. A farmhouse stripped to its bones, its wooden clapboards pried and looted, only the skeleton of its studs and the sagging roof remaining in place. A barn, its bowed roof covered in moss, its commercial imperative still legible on a wall pale and weathered. An undifferentiated pile of burned rubble overtaken by vines, with an outhouse visible behind, teetering.

They had been driving for five or six hours, following in the tracks of Raden's army, and had dropped down into what had once been Missouri, before night threatened to fall, one of those threats you take seriously in a wild land without power, except from the sun. That's when they started looking for a place both safe and relatively comfortable to camp for the night.

It was Patti who found the spot. Clyde followed her in the Every Ship, around a farmhouse, over a rocky, overgrown yard, and into a ruined barn back a ways, so they would be hidden from the road.

***

While they set up camp in the barn, Clyde wandered through the house itself, exploring with a shotgun scavenged from the camp. When he returned, he tossed a faded blue-print dress to Desiree, who was standing by the fire, built with timbers fallen from the barn's half-collapsed roof, surrounded by a ring of stones.

"I found this in a closet," said Clyde. "Put it on."

"I am sure as hell not putting on no ratty leftover shift."

"You don't need to dress like a mawk out here."

"I'll dress how I want."

"And of all the outfits in the world, that's what you pick?"

"You got a problem with it?"

"You wear that because that's how they want you to dress. I know. I wore a bow tie and an apron for six years for the very same reason. But out here, they don't matter."

"They'll matter when they find you."

"But until then, you don't need to dress for them. Especially around the girl."

"Don't be such a daddy."

"She's not mine," said Clyde, "but she's my responsibility. And yours too, now. All of us, we're only here to take care of her."

"Do the rest of them know that?"

"It doesn't matter what they know. Put it on, Desiree."

She looked at Clyde for a long moment, her eyes narrowed, as if trying to figure out what the hell he wanted. "Gloria," she said finally. "The name's Gloria." She held up the dress and brought it to her body to check the size. "It should sort of fit."

"You bet it will," said Clyde, and it did. She looked good in it, too, wearing it beneath the leather jacket with her boots.

After eating a batch of the chili, cooked up right in the cans, and rustling up places for themselves to sleep atop the dried vegetation inside the barn, they convened around the fire, wrapping themselves in whatever they could find to take the edge off the night chill. Smoke rose through the ruined roof, blotting out the band of stars as bright as a diamond bracelet in the sky.

Ruby took out her guitar and sang a song about a bird, and then another about a flower falling in love with the sun. Her voice was sweet and sour both, and it felt right at home in the abandoned barn. While she sang, Clyde filled one of the cleaned-out chili cans with water to make Lydia a cup of tea with the last of the berries he had gotten from Ruby. The others stared into the fire, passed around some of the liquor Patti had scavenged, and tried not to be afraid.

And all that time, Digger stared into the bottle that he gripped in his fist.

"Have you been out here before, Mr. Digger?" said Lydia.

"In the D-Lands?" said Digger. "I had me a life, here. Had me a son here."

"Where is he now, your son?" said Moonis.

"Gone."

"How did he die?" said Moonis.

"Didn't never say he was dead. I said he was gone. Why else you think I came along on this fool's errand with you? I came back across that river to find him."

"Find him?" said Lydia. "Here, in the D-Lands? Where?"

"That's the question, ain't it? Don't rightly know the answer. But I can tell you something true, because I feel it in my heart: the farther we edge into the territory the closer he gets. And the closer I get to home."

"Were you a farmer, Mr. Digger?" said Lydia.

"Course not. What do I know about farming, other than it's too damn hard for the likes of me. No, in them old days we had us a business. Townes's Filling Station. That was when I still had me a family name. I was a Townes. We sold gasoline and ribs. This was on the eastern edge of Kansas, on the road to Lawrence. Tyrone was young and surly then, sharp as an ax and handsome as his father, but he didn't want to be on the outskirts of things, he wanted to be in the big city with all the sassy, where he could find himself the right kind of trouble. But we was strict with him, so he stayed with us, living behind the shop, pumping the gas and fixing the cars. My boy, he had a talent for tinkering. I smoked and sauced the meat. My wife, Rebecca, did the serving, counted the money, kept a little food store."

"Sounds dreamy," said Lydia.

"It was pretty damn sweet, yes, it was, young Lydia. And they came from all over to fill their tanks and their bellies, from KC, sure, but also from Leavenworth, Topeka, even Omaha. I smoked the best ribs west of Memphis, and had the trophies to prove it. I made my own sauce with real Kentucky bourbon, that made the difference right there. In fact I was saucing up a prize-winning rack the very day when the whole sky, it burst into flame."

***

"Tyrone was blown right off his feet by the force of the light," said Digger. "We rushed outside and just stared at that cloud, gray black, billowing up and out, like a living fungus on the horizon. We had been expecting something ever since that mess in Cuba, but why would the sons of bitches drop the big one in Ozawkie, Kansas?

"It didn't make no sense, until Toad Eyes in the uniform came through with his story about the wrench. I was ready to run right there, get us all the hell out the way of them X-rays, but the government, it told us to remain calm, that there was no danger, and Rebecca was always one to do as she was told.

"I reckon Wrench Boy didn't make it very far before they silenced him right up, the way they do, because we didn't hear nothing about a wrench as them war drums started hammering. And next time Tyrone called us out, it was to see them lines of smoke rising from the silos in Auburn, Osage City, Baldwin, the thin white plumes of them Titan missiles veering all over the place like fireworks spinning out of control.

And right after, bam, Saint Louis was hit. And parts of Nebraska, Iowa. Never knew them Reds was so hot to wipe out Cedar Rapids, did you? All that oatmeal, I suppose.

"That's when they started on the voluntary evacuations. The rivers feeding into the Mississippi from Iowa and Missouri were glowing hot from the bombs. Tap water was said to be clean, but folks was getting sick all over, which just fed the panic. They advised us to go east, over the river, to camps they set up in Illinois, Kentucky, Tennessee. We could come back to our homes when the land was safe again.

"I was packed and ready, Rebecca too, but not Tyrone. He said after knowing about the wrench, he didn't believe anymore any of their promises, that whatever we give up would be gone for good, sucked up by them that was going to make fortunes over our leavings. He wasn't going to let no one run him off our place and no amount of words was changing his mind. My boy.

"I looked at Rebecca, she looked at me. And then one by one we took our clothes out of them suitcases. There wasn't no choice, you understand. We was scared, the both of us, but our life was in that child.

"Right after the evacuation order, flocks of cars and government buses started coming through, folks headed east, away from . . . away from . . ."

"Away from what?" said Ruby.

"Shhh," said Digger. "Listen."

In the hush, they heard the distant disturbance of motorcycles and instantly they each knew what it was: death on a host of pale cycles, sent forth by Raden on a killing mission, rushing down the road to find them and murder them one and all.

39
THE BOX

Martha saw the children running away from the woods and knew what it meant even before the distant roar reached her like the cries of martyrs and the sad bleat of trumpets at the coming of the end of the world.

They arrived in a clamor and a cloud, an army of mercenaries with violence loaded into their saddlebags and sadism packed into their hearts, followed by a convoy of trucks and tankers. Martha cringed at the sight, and then straightened herself to greet the riders with hugs and her painted smile. But her warmest smile and tightest hug was for Raden, for whom she had put on the lipstick. Her job for the whole of the visit was to keep the monster happy.

"Welcome," she said, with her arms slung around the granite block of man on the lead cycle. "It's so good to see you again. Welcome."

"We brought you some pig," said Raden, in what might have counted as the most elaborate sentence he had ever delivered to her.

"Dead or alive?" she said.

"Stone dead."

"That will save us the trouble of slitting their throats ourselves. We'll spit them right up, but they won't be ready until near morning. Gene," she said to one of the citizens, "uncork a fresh jug of shine for our visitors. Get the fires started and strike up the band. It's time for a party. Oh, and tell Enrique to have Zephyr bring up the box."

This was the way it went down with every visit from Raden's army, not unlike the treatment of an ancient king visiting the duchy of one of his noblemen. First, a lone rider approached, like a page of old, giving word of the coming visit so that arrangements could be made. Then cattle were slaughtered, chickens chased and wrung, pies baked—rutabaga, apple, peach, in season—greens chopped, corn husked, cider tapped, tables laid out before a wooden stage so that the guests could have music during the feast. The wise always bow low to power. And at the same time, and most crucially, as far as Martha was concerned, the box was prepared.

As the riders unsaddled, Martha watched as they grabbed at cups of shine, handfuls of chicken torn from roasted carcasses, and beef ribs the size of their exhaust pipes.

***

"Where did you get the pigs?" Martha asked Garth as they stood beside his truck, apart from the upward-spiraling revelry.

Garth was the business end of Raden's operation, calmly setting out the delivery schedules for product Raden was reselling in the incorporated territories, along with the brutal payments the farm owed to Raden for the right to continue to exist. She had tried to charm him and befriend him, would have even tried to seduce him if she had thought it would work, but Garth was as cold and businesslike as the clipboard he carried. There was no such thing as a casual conversation with Garth because there was nothing casual about him.

"The pigs are from Birkenhead," said Garth.

"That was sweet of him."

"He had been shorting his orders and wildcatting his fuel. Raden convinced him to come back to the fold. It's funny how persuasive Raden can be with a shovel in his hands. If you want to thank Birkenhead, maybe send a wheelchair."

"We saw the smoke."

"There was a gasoline spill. He accidentally burned his berry."

"Accidentally?"

"How many exiled boys from his compound have you taken in?"

"Enough not to feel bad roasting up his pigs," said Martha. "We saw the other smoke, too. In the distance."

"We've already taken care of that."

She turned to look at the woman who had ridden in on Garth's truck. Tall and shapely, her skin like sweet coffee rich with cream, so beautiful she was hard to look at even without an ounce of makeup. She was sitting with some of the cyclists, as comfortable among the wreakers of havoc as a protected nun. She looked up, saw Martha's smile, misinterpreted it as intended for her, and smiled back.

"Is that the girl that was missing?"

"Cecily."

"Raden always had good taste. Where did you end up finding her?"

"With Millard."

"I was wondering why he hadn't been to the stand lately."

"He won't be coming anytime soon. Or anytime, actually."

"You can't say the fool wasn't warned."

"No, you can't say that. And it was long overdue anyway. There are changes coming, Martha. We're shifting our focus, which means you'll have to shift yours. We're all going to have to dig deeper."

"We?"

"We'll talk tomorrow, after the celebration."

"You're already bleeding us, Garth. You can't get blood from the dead."

"Tell that to the pigs."

***

The band started playing—two acoustic guitars, a makeshift bass, a ginger-haired drummer banging on cans—the shine kept flowing, a few of the visitors started dancing with their own women, a few of the citizen women danced with each other, a few of the cyclists joined in. Some of the citizen men took offense at the way some of the visitors started dancing with and grabbing at their current lovers. There were shouts and catcalls, boasts and clutching. Smile, Martha told herself, just keep smiling, and she did, even as the inevitable fistfights ensued. It was the usual start to a forced celebration with Raden's army; the trick was surviving it with as few casualties as possible.

But just as the festivities looked to be spinning out of anyone's control, just as blood was boiling to be spilled, Zephyr marched toward the tables, his lips moving as he kept up his constant monologue, the box perched like a hero on his shoulder.

When the riders noted the box's arrival, a religious holler rose from their throats, as if the Ark of the Covenant were being carried into the midst of the Israelites by one of the sacred priests reciting holy incantations. The raucous crowd, citizen and cyclehead both, gathered around and stilled their voices.

"We are lost in time, my friends . . . bereft and alone . . . except for this," said Zephyr as he laid the box upon one of the tables. "A cornucopia it is . . . black magic and voodoo, sprinkled with interstellar dust . . . wazoom . . . soaked with cockroach juice and witch's spit."

The box was made of wood, painted with swirls that seeped one into the other, a kaleidoscope of melting hues that glowed unnaturally.

"We are two-dimensional beings, living in a three-dimensional world . . . dig it . . . traveling unwittingly through a fourth dimension, dreaming of a fifth, and a sixth, and a seventh . . . and on and on . . . while all the time missing the dimension that matters most, the dimension of the now."

With a drumroll from the stage, Zephyr slowly raised the lid. And the scent, well, was there a mead ever sweeter, a leaf ever greener, a breast ever more ripe?

"Because wherever we are, we're not there anymore . . . an unsolvable conundrum . . . which is why, ladies and germs . . . ahem . . . we are necessitated to resort to inhaling the now."

At Yeager's farm, the citizens cultivated mellow weed and quick weed and weed that drove a sweet nostalgic longing like a stake into your heart. Yeager's Bud™, in fact, was the very weed that Hooper had sold to Clyde and that Clyde in turn had purveyed along with the burgers and milk shakes in the Toddle House. But the rarest of the crop, the most debilitating stuff, the weed that put the waste in wasted, the ruin in ruined, the total in trashed, was saved solely for the seasonal visits of Raden and his men. Once the carefully tended plants were picked and sorted and dried to perfection, the buds were heaped into cigar wraps, which were in turn twisted into spliffs the size of ice-cream cones. And then, just to be sure, the finished smokes were dipped in a special brew of barbiturate and hallucinogen so that one good lungful hit the head like a baseball bat and turned the brain into a warm bowl of rice pudding.

In the midst of his indecipherable monologue, accompanied by a walking jazz line from the makeshift bass and the dawdling beat of the ginger-haired drummer, Zephyr handed the gigajoints one by one to the voracious mob. And one by one the cones were fired to life and drawn down, down. And as the crackly sweet fog engulfed them all, the crowd, as if soothed not just by the smoke but by the slow music and Zephyr's blur of talk, mellowed. The rage dissipated, the arguments died, and eternal friendship, man, I mean it, eternal like forever, man, reigned supreme.

And Martha, smile still in place and without a joint, exhaled with the rest of them.

***

When Raden's men were dancing slowly to the now-slow, dreamy music, or humping naked atop piles of hay, or wandering aimlessly through the starry night, eating handfuls of roasted rolled oats coated with honey, or lying on their backs and staring with awe at the flowering moon, Raden's girl came to talk to Martha.

"You put on quite a party," said Raden's girl.

"Our old friends deserve the best," said a smiling Martha, being careful what she said to this woman. Raden's girl had run, had been recaptured, and now looked like one of them. That's the way it was sometimes with captives, they became more loyal to their prisons than their pasts.

"I didn't think Raden had any friends."

"He has you."

"He took me," said Raden's girl. "You know, in their current drug-induced delirium, you could probably kill them all right now, free the whole D-Lands."

Martha turned to look at her and noticed no ironic smile, just a frightening flatness. "We don't even like to kill our chickens," said Martha.

"So it's squeamishness?"

"It's not what we are. But even double-dosed, we couldn't kill Raden. His strength is beyond us. And he has allies to the west that would exact his revenge."

"Hey, Martha, have you seen Amazon?" said Gene, stumbling a bit with a jug of shine in his hand. Gene, who had come to the farm with Zephyr, was dark and handsome, with the saddest eyes. "I been looking for that sweet girl."

"Why don't you go to sleep," said Martha.

"I need to find her."

"I haven't seen her, Gene. But you know Amazon."

"Yeah," he said, "I know Amazon."

"Hey, Gene, you ever see any aliens in New Mexico with Zephyr?"

"Sure did," said Gene. "Who hasn't? I mean, New Mexico."

"Go to sleep, all right?"

"Okay, maybe." He staggered forward a bit and then stopped. "If you see her, tell her I'm looking for her."

"Will do," said Martha, and then, when he was gone, she spoke to Raden's girl. "It's an epidemic, men wanting to possess the very things that can never be possessed. Even here."

"Why would it be different here?"

"Because it is different here. No one owns anything at the farm. We all own everything."

"What is that, farm life according to Marx?"

"According to Yeager."

"How do you get by without owning anything?"

"Pretty damn well, usually, until someone like Gene wants to own a girl like Amazon—a girl too independent to ever allow herself to be owned—and then it just all turns sad. Either he gets over it, or one of them ends up leaving. Some of the best men I ever knew are gone because I refuse to be anyone's property. Their need to own is like a disease."

"I need a favor."

"Cecily, right?"

"Right."

"I know you're in a tough spot, Cecily. You tried to run, and ended up with Millard, and that didn't work out well for anyone. Especially for Millard. I would really like to help you, but I can't."

"I know."

"I'm responsible for all these people. We have thirty children. You might imagine massacring Raden's men in their sleep, but the most likely meat for massacre here is us. He'll pass in time, they all do, in time. Until then we have no choice but to work with him."

"I'm not asking you to save me. When Raden leaves, I'll leave with him, that's already in the stars. But I think my brother is somewhere in the D-Lands. His name is Moonis Fell, and he's coming to save me."

"The fire at Raden's camp?"

"When I saw the smoke, I knew it was him."

"Either he's not so bright or he's crazy as a rabid dog."

"He's the smartest person I've ever known."

"I guess that decides it."

"Raden sent some of his worst killers after him. If Moonis survives the night, I expect he'll end up here. And I need you to tell him something."

"His name's Moonis?"

"Tell him I love him, and tell him how grateful I am that he's come, and then tell him that I'm fine, that I'm happy, that I'm exactly where I need to be."

Martha turned to Raden's girl, looked into her sweet liquid eyes, put a hand on her cheek. She had seemed so self-possessed, this woman, while she sat with the barbarians, but now Martha could feel the sadness within her, the hopelessness pouring out of her.

"You're not where you need to be," said Martha. "Not at all."

"He's going to try to save me, and when he does, they're going to kill him. I'd rather die myself a thousand times. So I need you to tell him how happy, happy, happy I am, and then tell him to please go home."

40

DIGGER'S TALE CONT'D

Around the fire they sat in silence, their sight of the road blocked by
the walls of the old barn, as the song of their doom roared toward
them. Digger gripped his bottle tighter and pulled out his pistol. Ruby
pulled Lydia close. Clyde picked up the shotgun. Their frightened faces
glowed unevenly in the light of the flame as the ominous clatter of the
cycles closed in.

Clyde stood suddenly and jerked the pump handle of the shotgun. In the darkness, beyond the open door, catching just a bit of
the firelight before tossing it back, were two eyes, glowing red. Clyde
snatched the shotgun to his shoulder just as he realized the eyes were
canine. Behind them were two more, and then four more. A pack of
dogs was staring into the barn, staring at the fire, drawn by the smell
of chili meat.

Clyde looked at the dogs. The dogs looked at Clyde. Some of the
eyes outside looked vaguely human. The thunder of the cycles grew
ever louder, the pitch ever higher.

William Lashner

Then, quick as a breath, the sound of fear peaked in every way before dropping down, dropping deeper, the volume lessening as quickly as it rose. The riders had powered past the house without stopping. Clyde lowered his gun and smiles broke out. But when Gloria started to say something, Moonis put up a hand and they waited in silence, trying to detect any alteration of the motorcycles' path. When the sound died finally in the distance, they looked at each other, relief palpable on their flickering faces.

Clyde looked down at Moonis. "I guess they got your message," he said.

***

Moonis sent Patti out to make sure the riders didn't double back. And then, to calm the rest, he said, "Go on, Digger," with an encouraging smile.

"You heard enough of my blabbing."

"Please, Mr. Digger," said Lydia. "They don't teach us this in school."

"No, young lady, I'm sure they don't. But we all know history is real life prettied up with someone else's bow."

"Go on," said Moonis. "We could use the distraction."

"Okay, then." Digger put away his pistol and took a long swallow from his bottle. "Right after all that hell broke loose, the traffic started coming through, folks headed east, away from the fear. The government paid us to stay and fuel them vehicles to get them off the land, even gave us the gasoline for free, so we made a killing, filling the tanks of the long lines of cars, and them buses going out empty and coming back full. But soon the cars petered out and the buses were coming through less full, and then empty, and then they simply stopped, too. And for a while it seemed like it was just us out there on the empty road, listening to the wind whistle. We were like something biblical, the last people on earth.

"Until a truck showed up, a wildcatter selling gasoline, who took our money to fill our tanks again just in case someone else drove by. And then another truck came, taking some of the gasoline and leaving rain-grown vegetables we put on our shelves.

"Tyrone, he found himself an abandoned truck and spent his time fixing it up. When it was ready, he loaded it with some of our stock from the store and headed out on the lonely open road. When he came back, damn if he didn't have a pocketful of cash and a couple of live cows. We kept one for the milk and for the other I fired up the smoker. Suddenly, as if there were a telegram sent, folks appeared, bringing their own foodstuffs with them, and we had us all a feast like I never before seen.

"Don't get me wrong, things was mighty slow after the voluntary evacuation, but we sort of grew to like it slow. We could feel the sun beat down, feel the earth beneath our feet. Rebecca never looked lovelier, except for a nagging little cough. There was still law, and electricity in the wires, and water coming through the pipes that we could drink, so they said. And there was money, though most things was bartered, which kept the government out of it. But everything was different, too. Suddenly it didn't matter white or black, rich or poor, because all of us still on the land were all of them things all at once.

"And best of all our son, our Tyrone—going place to place in that truck, shaking hands, spreading news from one outpost to the next—he grew into himself. He became a man of the territory that the folks all looked up to. With the coming of the Grand Constitution, we was all certain that our decision to stay was a good one, that everything was going to get richer, and that my boy was going to rise. Mayor Townes, Governor Townes, Senator Townes. Why the hell not? He had found his place, we had all found our places. It was something like a paradise.

"But then came the Great Disincorporation."

***

Patti interrupted Digger's tale, returning with word that she had spotted nothing.

"That doesn't mean they're not coming back," said Clyde. "Once they find the ruined camp, they'll be burning up the road to get to us."

"We're going to need a lookout through the night," said Moonis. "Let Patti take the first shift. I'll relieve her in a couple of hours and go through until morning. Since you're driving, Clyde, you get to sleep. I'll doze during the ride."

Patti nodded, heading out again. Digger stayed silent for a bit, staring at the fire. Ruby put more of the barn's roof onto the circle of stones. The flames shot up from the shifting coals to embrace the weathered wood. A dog outside the barn yipped.

"I remember the disincorporation," said Ruby. "President Krist announced it on the radio. The water was uncertain, the upkeep was getting too darn expensive. It seemed to make sense at the time."

"To those on the right side of the line, sure," said Digger. "But to us it was like they was snatching everything we thought we could count on. There was going to be no electricity, no piped water, no law. The only government was going to be Guard patrols chasing any fools what tried to remain behind, and the crews to keep some of them roads passable to let the Guard do its work. And this time relocation was mandatory.

"Tyrone, he wanted to put up a fight, but I was ready to go, for Rebecca's sake. I guess I loved that woman so much that it turned me blind, because at first I didn't recognize the coughing as something serious or that the pretty sallow of her skin was what comes just before the dive. But come the time of the disincorporation, I knew. Remember, this was before they found the berry growing wild, and I thought maybe, on the other side, maybe in a decent hospital, maybe . . .

"In the end, Tyrone had no choice but to come along with us. His mother was sick, his father was taking her over the line, and the Guard was going house to house. They only let us fill one case each before putting us into a green bus with wires on the windows and driving us to one of them camps they set up to process the last of us. That's how we ended up in Davenport.

"They had ringed the city with a fence and left only one route over, the big bridge that ain't there no more. There was a line hundreds deep waiting to make the walk over the Mississippi. We stood in that line four hours, moving just a few feet, Rebecca getting weaker and weaker, stifling her cough when the Guard walked by. Then we learned the line was so slow because a doctor was picking out those with the sickness to ship to a quarantine camp. We knew what a quarantine camp was, we had seen the flickering images from the European war. That was the end of the line for us.

"We ended up in some office building, incredibly crowded with refugees. These folks in the office building had been there for weeks, they was part of a larger group of refugees herded into Davenport from all over the Midwest that decided, finally, to make a stand. Tyrone liked what he heard and became one of them. And me, what could I do? Was I going to desert my son? Was I going to let them take away my wife?

"The buses stopped coming, the line, it shortened and died, and soon all that was left in Davenport were those of us who were refusing to be pushed one step more. There were orders given, warnings over loudspeakers, they cut the food and water, but none of it mattered. We had been shoved far enough and had faith in the Lord and our God-given right to stay put. We sang songs of protest. Our spirits were high. At least until the Guard, with riot shields and helmets, came through them gates, made a line that stretched across the northern edge of the city, and began their march to the river.

"A few ran toward the bridge, where prison vans waited to drive them into labor or quarantine camps on the incorporated side, but the rest of us stayed, forcing the Guard to advance building by building, door by door. Then we fought back. Shots fired from abandoned buildings, Molotov cocktails served, burning cars sent hurling into the Guard lines that had suddenly stopped moving forward, that suddenly began to back up, until they broke in headlong retreat.

"There was a moment of silence, an eerie calm, until a roar of victory went up all across the old town. My God, hugs and cheers and hope ringing down like a cleansing rain.

"Until the bombing began."

***

Digger poked at the fire, coals sparked, flames rose. Within the center of the pile the wood was both charred and glowing, like the heart of some fierce force of destruction.

"The Guard gunships took down the city in waves north to south, block by block, not giving a damn about who was inside. There was no fighting it. Just waves of flame explosion coming ever closer. I had stayed in that town to save my wife, not to have them kill her with their bombs. When they came close enough to shatter the windows of our building, we headed out, Tyrone and me dragging Rebecca south, to the river, to the bridge, to the prison buses, to the camps.

"But when we got in sight of the bridge and the buses waiting to take us away, Tyrone, he hugged my wife, hugged me, and before we knew what was what, he ran back to the falling city, back to the bombs. I yelled at him, cursed at him, begged for him to come back, but nothing came of it. My boy, he just disappeared into the smoke.

"My wife and me, we found ourselves on a bus headed over that bridge just before they bombed it dead. And that was the end of our sorry little rebellion. A couple strangers in white jackets, they took my Rebecca away to the quarantine camp. And for three years I broke my back in a labor camp in Pennsylvania, shoveling sand for Owen-Illinois.

. Soon as I was free, I headed straight for Moline, going through them refugees one by one, begging for word of my wife or my boy. Nothing. Not a thing."

"That's just horrible," said Lydia, the tracks of her tears now catching the firelight. "I can't imagine."

"Neither could I, sweet Lydia," said Digger. "But that was the new facts of my life. I slipped in and out of the D-Lands a couple times, looking for word of my boy and finding nothing, but mostly I stayed in Moline, on the banks of the Mississippi, stayed there no matter how freaky the scene became, because every morning I could see it over the river, beyond the shattered bridge: the ruins of my past. They never bulldozed or flattened what was left of Davenport, they left them burned buildings as a warning. There is nothing over there but ruin, they was telling us. Your future is on the right side of our line.

"But all I saw in them ruins was hope. My boy was over there, somewhere, still fighting, and someday, I knew, he was going to make it to Moline to free us all. I knew it, I done knew it for sure.

"And then he did," said Digger.

***

"He came?" said Lydia, wiping her eyes. "Your son? Tyrone? He came back?"

"It was like seeing a ghost, but still it made my heart leap."

"Where did you see him?" said Ruby. "When?"

"Just a few days ago. I was sitting there at my normal spot, in sight of the river and them ruins, playing chess by my lonesome, when some raggedy-assed inlander with a limp and eyes wild from drugs sat down and played me a game of chess."

"And it was him?" said Lydia.

"It wasn't him," said Moonis. "It was me."

William Lashner

"Whatever the hell Moonis might be," said Clyde, "he's not your son. I knew his father. I knew his mother. I knew his mother's father."

"It don't matter," said Digger. "He sat down and I saw my son, Tyrone. He was in your eyes, Moonis. In your eyes I saw the man my son was destined to be."

"I was high on that wacked weed," said Moonis. "I was tripping."

"What you were don't matter, it was what you were going to be that I saw. And when Jarvis, he betrayed your ass, with me in the very tent filling my gut with Jarvis's beer, I knew I had failed Tyrone again."

"There was nothing you could have done, Digger," said Moonis.

"There is always something that can be done. And I didn't do it. That's why I followed your fool ass to the courthouse and then over the river. I'm here to protect you, Moonis. And after I killed that man this morning, the one trying to knife you in your heart, I been trying to figure out my feelings on it ever since, and this is what I came up with."

Digger looked into the fire and took a swig of whiskey.

"Killing that man was near to the greatest moment of my sad-sack life. I don't like that none, not one bit, but there it is. And there's going to be more killing necessary afore this is through, I know that, too. And I don't got no choice about it, not no—"

A single pop of gunfire came from outside the barn, and then a bam bam bam, followed by a yelp, a snarl, a scream.

Without a word Clyde grabbed the shotgun and sprinted into the night. Moonis followed, then Ruby. And pulling up the rear, scampering to the fight as fast as his rusted joints would allow, which wasn't fast at all, which was slow as pain, actually, scurried the old man, scurried Digger, determined once again to save the day.

41

OKAY, GENE

They sliced the pigs at dawn.

Raden's men rose from drugged sleep or stumbled out of sweet hallucination to find the carcasses belly-down on the tables, skin burnished mahogany by the fire, sweet juices leaking through gaps between the table slats. The men scratched their balls and pissed on the peonies and climbed into their pants and pulled at the crackly pigskin with filthy hands. They stuffed meat into their jaws until their cheeks grew shiny with lard. The night had been fat with dream and sex and laughter and death—yes, death; Raden's men didn't come with roses and rice—and now their stomachs would be grossly distended with pork.

What more could a man ever want except for more.

"You're going to have to plow under your berry," said Garth to Martha as they sat side by side at a table while Raden and his men dismembered and devoured the swine. One large oaf walked about gnawing a little brown piggy leg.

"But you taught us the planting method," said Martha. "You ordered us to turn three fields over to it. How are we going to pay you what you're demanding now if we kill the crop?"

"There's always a way," said Garth. "You'll find it. We have great faith in you."

This was the meeting Garth had promised, where his demands would be laid out and she would object and cajole and plead and beg. The whole dog and pony show of her bright lipstick and outsized hospitality was to help her object and cajole and plead and beg. But there was an edge to Garth this morning that let her know most of her dance would be in vain. And all the while they talked, Garth made sure that Martha could view the human corpse lying on its stomach on the ground like the pigs on the tables, its face rooting in the dirt.

"We have citizens here who need the tea to survive," she said. "They'll die without it."

"Harvest what you need for your own use—and maybe some to sell at your D-Land markets, we'll allow that—but the rest has to be destroyed. No berry will be allowed over the river."

"Why? It makes no sense."

"It doesn't need to make sense to you. There are plans in the works bigger than you can understand. There are steps being taken—not just on this side of the line, but in the highest levels of the Guard and the government—that will mean profound changes for the whole of the D-Lands. For the good of us all, we each must do our part. This is your part. The field needs to be plowed under by the time we return."

"When are you coming back?"

"Sooner than you might want," said Garth. "It could be within a week."

"A week?"

"And we might be staying."

"For a second night?"

"We were thinking of a more permanent arrangement."

"You can't stay here."

"If our camp is gone, we'll need a place to park ourselves for a time. We always have a good time here."

"We don't have room."

"Clear out the dormitory. Maybe the children's house, too."

"It's impossible."

Garth smiled and raised his palms. "That's not a word Raden understands."

"Buy him a dictionary."

"We're not giving you a choice, Martha, but even so, don't over-look the honor that Raden is bestowing by calling your farm his home. Things are changing. Raden's rising like a rocket ship. He's consolidating his power and strengthening his lines to the other side. You're either on board with a ticket to the stars, or you're left behind."

Garth looked over his shoulder at the dead man on the ground.

"It's a shame about Gene, isn't it?"

***

They buried Gene in the pasture. This was after Raden and his army had departed with a roar of a hundred tigers and a cloud of noxious exhaust. They buried Gene alongside Thaddeus Yeager, and the still-born Yeager babies, and the children who had passed from disease, and the citizens who had died in the course of their labors, and the citizens who had been murdered one way or the other by Raden and his ilk. You don't spend a decade and a half on a farm without becoming familiar with the ministrations of death.

"Okay, Gene," said Zephyr, shirtless as usual, talking in his low, manic mumble, as most of the citizenry of the farm, children included, and Stella Yeager in a wheelchair, assembled in a thick circle around the hole in the ground. Martha's face was scrubbed clean of makeup and pale with grief. "Roaring spirit . . . sad-eyed knight . . . seeking truth in

word and bottle . . . The trees dripping tears, the sun dimming in sadness . . . you and me, we been chasing this car from sea to city to prairie
. . . dogs howling at the humpbacked moon . . . and now that you have
the bumper in your teeth, how does it taste? . . . Like saxophones on
a summer's night? . . . Like the lips of another beat princess? . . . And
all we can say, standing here, left behind . . . What was the rush, boy?"

Martha shook her head at the waste of it all. The killing had been
as inevitable as dawn. Instead of going to sleep, as Martha had advised,
Gene had gone looking for Amazon. The problem was, he found her,
riding one of Raden's men, a huge redheaded beast named Bear Claw,
with a bushy beard. Bear Claw said Gene came at him with a black-
handled switchblade. Two cracks of gunfire, like two bolts of lightning
splitting the night, and good-bye, Gene.

"Drinking rotgut whiskey on the rocks of Big Sur," continued
Zephyr. "Making time with those college girls from Berkeley while
Charlie Parker blew out the stars . . . jabbing our fingers in the air
in a Times Square Automat, arguing on Kant and Kierkegaard and
Baudelaire . . . two weeks of bringing in the corn . . . Zephyr and
Gene on the loose . . . Toodle-oose, toodle-oo . . . this farm your final
paradise."

Raden had given Martha a quick hug before climbing on his bike
and charging back down the road. Raden's girl had merely nodded,
pretending they hadn't had their talk. Amazon herself had cried on
Martha's shoulder before riding off with the pack of them, her face red
and washed with tears. And Garth, well, Garth just whipped out that
clipboard.

"You'll make the arrangements like we talked about," he said. "The
berry gone and our beds ready."

"Do we have a choice?"

"There's always a choice," said Garth. "Shovel some dirt on Gene's
coffin for me."

Martha sensed the killing wasn't just a happenstance. With enough drugs Amazon was always willing, and the dynamic between her and Gene wasn't hard to figure with one good look. And Gene might have been besotted, but he wasn't a fighter. No one, not even Zephyr, had ever before seen Gene's supposed knife. But even if Garth hadn't arranged it, he surely didn't mind that it happened.

Nothing sets the tenor of a negotiation like a killing before the talking starts.

So this was a triply sad funeral for Martha. Good-bye, Gene. Good-bye, berry. Good-bye, any semblance of independence. There would be a citizens' meeting that night to figure out how to proceed, but there weren't any real options, as that hole in the ground proved.

"And where are you now, my brown-haired boy?" said Zephyr. "Buried with your dog-eared copy of Rilke . . . I see you flitting flower to flower . . . What liquors are you guzzling? . . . What sugars are you snapping at? . . . Buckle up, buckaroo, it won't be long before Zephyr's on his way to join you . . . yes, indeed . . . and won't that be a party."

***

"Let's just say no. Screw them, man. What are they going to do to us anyway?"

"Murder us in our beds."

"Let them try."

"That's what we're trying to avoid, brother."

The main hall was a big dirt-floored barn raised on a spring weekend and painted a delicate fuchsia, just because. They sat in a circle on the hand-hewn benches or on the ground, long tiki torches lighting the assemblage, determined to talk it through. This was the way of the farm, democracy raw, with all its lovely mess—*Robert's Rules of Order* had been ruled out of order long ago—and everyone would get a say on everything for as long as they wanted to say it. In their assemblages, the citizens drank and smoked and cursed and laughed and talked deep into the night until passions were overcome by weariness and they collapsed in each other's arms. And the next day things happened more or less in keeping with any decisions that might have come out of all that talk talk talk. It might not have impressed the Greeks, but no one left the meetings feeling disrespected or big-shouldered, which was different than the politics on the other side of the line and pretty much the point.

"We got guns. We fight to keep them cannibals away. Why do we always got to hide our firearms away when Raden shows up? Why can't we pack like they pack and see how it shakes out?"

"Remember that farm by Old Ottumwa that started shooting it out with Raden? The only thing left was meat for the wolves. How many wildcatter skulls have we seen grinning bald on the side of the road?"

"Does it sound so awful to give him what he wants? If we want to be part of what Raden's becoming, maybe we need to get with his game."

"What about our game?"

"Our game is staying alive, pops. He's rising; let's rise with him."

"Rise to where? What do you want, to start waving around sawed-off shotguns like his crew? Or worse, you want to start wearing ties? Start dealing with banks?"

"Start taking baths?"

"Can we talk about the latrine situation? I've been trying to get the latrine situation under some—"

"Not now, Bones. We got to decide this first. This is existential, man."

"Latrines are pretty damn existential, you get down to it."

"Here's an idea, let's just say no. But with a smile, you know. Everything's better with a smile and a joint. They like you, Martha.

Light them up and then lay it on sweet when you tell them to pound sand."

"But put on the lipstick when you do it."

Laughter.

"You do look tasty in the red."

More laughter, and Martha laughed with them. It was good hearing the back-and-forth, the shouts and the insults. It almost made her forget about Gene for a moment, though the sadness remained lodged like a piece of grit in her heart. She would eventually have to speak, they always seemed to look to her to get the last word, but first she'd let the rest of them have their say.

"What's the big deal, really? So we dig up the berry, so we live in tents for a while. You young'uns are getting soft. Why, I remember before we learned the trick to growing the berry, when we had to hunt it growing wild. We were living in tents before that fancy dormitory was built. Maybe we need to get back to what we were."

"And what was that, old man? Slaves?"

"Farmers, without pretension. It's always hard living off the land. Raden is no different than that tornado that came through, ripping apart the land and our buildings. We lived through it, and we'll live through this. That's the operative word. Live."

"But for how long? With them here no one would be safe. Not the women, not the children, no one. How many would end up like Gene? Who wants to be the next buried in that pasture?"

"You're mighty brave sitting here around the fire, but you weren't so brave when they were roaming about grabbing your girl."

"Hell's bells, what's even the point of being here if he's telling us what to do? We can get that on the other side of the line, and television, too. Maybe we'd be better off with guaranteed jobs."

"I ain't going back. I'm never going back. We'll do what he says or we'll fight him to the death, either way's fine so long as I don't go back."

***

"We have guns, and ammunition, and a burning desire to be left alone, all of us," said Martha, finally, when the debate had quieted just a bit. "But there's a reason we lock our guns away when Raden shows. They're killers and we're not, and I don't regret that one bit. What we know is how to plow and plant and harvest. We know how to can and preserve, how to smoke our meats and prepare our weed and distill our shine. We know how to split the land and pull a good life out of the earth. We're heroes of the crop field, not the battlefield. It's not yet in us to put up the necessary fight. It's also not in us to abandon our land. If we had a champion to teach us to fight and rouse us to victory, I'd think differently, but without such a leader our path is clear. Seasons change, strong men wither, the only way to beat them in the long run is to outlive them. We have a duty to the land and to the future of our children and so I believe we have no choice but to—"

"Someone's coming," called out a voice. "Someone's on the road."

And in that instant, the long arm of Raden grabbed at Martha's throat and squeezed.

They had come back. Not all of them, but enough to ensure that Garth's demands would be followed and to the letter. It wasn't so much a surprise as a sickly disappointment. The farm had decisions to make and now they would be made at the wrong end of a shotgun.

And suddenly she felt a shudder of revulsion at the utter reasonableness that had come spouting out of her mouth just seconds before. Was this any way to live, in constant fear of strength and animus? She had been there once, as a girl, at the mercy of someone else's power, and the defining moment of her life had been her mad escape across the river to freedom. But here she was, in the same situation, and yet, now older and with more to lose, she was all too ready to submit.

She needed to be saved from herself, she needed the arriving party not to be a band of Raden's warriors but her old spunked-out self to slap her on the head and tell her to get with it. She needed a miracle, and maybe that was what she got.

Because when they all left the hall with their torches, like a mob of villagers in a Frankenstein movie, and headed to the mouth of the road to get a look at their visitors, what they saw was not a pack of motorcycle hoodlums with rape in their eyes, but something perfectly strange, as if it had popped right out of one of Zephyr's rainbow monologues.

A single motorcycle, driven by a blond man in white pants, a T-shirt with wide red stripes, and round green goggles, leading:

A multicolored van with boxes and cans strapped to the top, the van itself looking strangely like the badassed brother of the farm's famous box, painted a school-bus yellow with swirls and zags and zigs of all stripe and color, out of which climbed:

A woman in a fringed purple coat whose smile lit the night as she called out, "Zephyr," and the two raced together to hug it out while also from that van came:

A man, tall and handsome, with a rich smile and dark clip-ons over his round glasses despite the darkness of the night, wearing a gilded-up military jacket and a furry blue top hat that he set above his great bush of hair like a ceremonial piece of headgear, looking like a diplomatic emissary from some bizarre off-world land.

"Hello there," he said. "My name is Moonis, Moonis Fell."

"Of course it is," said Martha.

"I hope we're not intruding on your evening, but one of our party is badly hurt. Do you happen to have a doctor on the premises?"

"Not a doctor, but we do have a midwife who's a healer of sorts. She's holistic."

"I don't care how much she drinks," said Moonis Fell with a wink and a smile, "just so long as she gets the job done."

42
Country Mouse

In the star-drenched darkness, Moonis and Clyde dragged Patti from the Every Ship and carried her to the farmhouse and then upstairs to a twin bed next to that of an old lady with gray pigtails who called out for someone named Thaddeus, over and again. Patti was paler than her usual pale, and weak with pain—her neck had been slashed, her blood had been spilled in gouts, and in her delirium she talked way more than usual, a feverish blurt of talk. With the two inhabitants, the room smelled foul and was full of babble.

"Thaddeus."

"This is a bad place, Clyde. We have to get out of this place. Did you see them hyenas what came after me?"

"Thaddeus, you old fool."

"They wanted to eat me, Moonis. They wanted to turn me into sirloin. Krist, their teeth had shark points. We got to get out of here, Moonis. Snatch out Cecily, fast, and then get us all back home."

It was left to Gloria to sit on the edge of Patti's bed, rewrapping the wound and dabbing at Patti's forehead with a wet towel. Moonis and

Clyde stayed until the midwife finally arrived, but when she started fitting thread into a needle by the light of six candles, Moonis fled discreetly and Clyde followed.

They were both outside, on the rear porch, looking at each other with mouths stretched in unease when the screaming started.

***

"She's lucky to be alive," said a woman waiting on the porch, her face cut by the light of lanterns swinging from the porch roof. "The tribe you described generally leaves its victims stripped to the bone."

"Patti shot one of them right through the eye," said Clyde.

"Nice shot," said the woman.

"Army-trained," said Clyde.

"When we got to the man she had shot," said Moonis, "the dogs had already ripped his insides out. They snarled and hissed at us when we got close, their muzzles red with his blood."

"The surviving tribe members will come back and roast what's left. They work together, the dogs and the tribe. It's not clear which group is in charge."

"Nice territory you got here," said Clyde.

"There's something about the land on this side of the river," said the woman. "The wildness, the dark freedom. People revert to their natural states here."

"So what were those cannibals before?" said Moonis. "Bankers?"

The woman's name was Martha, and though Moonis found it hard to figure—the farm was quite loosely run—it was Martha who appeared to be in charge. She was tall and strong, with appealing green eyes and a face marked by beleaguered sincerity, its lines deepened by the angled light of the lanterns. You grew into that kind of face when you cared for too many other people and not enough for yourself. It was a look Moonis found quite attractive, since it was something he hadn't seen much in his life, especially not in the mirror.

"We can put your party up for the night," said the woman. "Are you men hungry?"

"Usually," said Moonis.

"I'll take you to the hall," she said before stepping off the porch and starting to walk with purpose into the darkness. "There's some pig left. I think the old man, the girl, and that friend of Zephyr's are already eating."

Clyde and Moonis hustled from behind to catch up. As he stumbled off the porch, Moonis felt swallowed by the scent of the place, thick and fresh and as familiar as home.

"So when will you be leaving?" said Martha.

"Glad to meet you, here's your hat," said Moonis.

"Maybe you shouldn't have burned Raden's camp to the ground if you wanted to hang around."

"How do you know it was us?" said Clyde.

"Are you saying it wasn't?"

There was a momentary pause before Clyde said, "You had to put on a show."

"No business like show business," said Moonis. "And now Raden's men are scattered across the territory looking for us, which means less of them are swarming like flies around my sister."

"Cecily, right?" said Martha.

Moonis stopped, and the woman herself, after a moment, stopped and turned around to face him. Her eyes caught a gleam of light from lanterns on the porch.

"You met my sister?"

"She was with Raden and his men when they came through. She saw the smoke with the rest of them and sensed it might be you."

"See that, Clyde?" said Moonis. "It wasn't just a warning to Raden, it was a symbol of hope in a cruel and indifferent world."

"And she asked me to tell you," said Martha, "that she was fine and happy and that you should just go home."

"Well, I guess that's that," said Clyde. "Nice to know you, lady. As soon as Patti's stitched up, we'll pack up a load of the berry you supposedly got growing here and hit the road."

"How did she look when she said it?" said Moonis.

Martha peered at him through the darkness, like she was considering things, and then she turned around and continued on toward the dining hall. "She looked miserable and terrified and quite sad."

"Maybe you're not such a good judge of people," said Clyde.

"I've got you pegged," she said to Clyde. "Your sister's not in a good place, Moonis. And because their camp is gone, they're coming back here when they finish their rounds, which means you're not in a good place either."

"Maybe we'll wait for them," said Moonis. "Surprise them when they show."

"With a magic van and a troop of traveling minstrels?"

"I'm no minstrel," said Clyde. "I couldn't get a note from one of them little guitars if you hit me over the head with it."

"We'll put the girl in the children's house," said Martha. "The rest of you can stay in the dormitory. But you have to leave in the morning, that's all there is to it. Even so, when he finds out you were here, we'll end up paying a price. We'd kick you right out now, but it's Stella's farm."

"Stella?" said Moonis.

"The old lady in the room with your injured friend. There isn't much to her now, but her whole life she was the kind of woman who never turned away a troubled soul."

"At least not until the morning," said Moonis.

"I'm not as noble as Stella," said Martha before indicating a barn-like structure suddenly in front of them. An uneven light slipped through large double doors that were barely ajar. "Breakfast is at six. You'll be leaving at eight. Until then, make yourselves at home."

The two men watched as Martha turned brusquely and headed back to the farmhouse, a tall, twitchy figure in the vague light from the hall. "What do you think of her?" said Moonis.

"She's looking for something," said Clyde.

"A little bit of sweet loving?"

"No, not that," said Clyde. "Something else, and she's a little desperate about it, too. If you don't watch your step, Moonis, she's going to get you killed."

***

Moonis was up before the rooster's first call, walking about the farm, breathing in the sweet, manure-tinged air. The sky was clearing, birds were on the wing, the fields spread out around him like a carpet of hope.

Even at that early hour, many of the farmers were up and out, milking the cows, pulling eggs, readying equipment to work the land, performing strange slow motions within the brightening dawn, intricate wavy-arm dances in scattered groups or body-twisting stretches.

Somehow he felt more at ease on a farm than anywhere else in the world, but this wasn't like the prison farms he was familiar with. There was work, sure, plenty of it, too much of it—there always was on a farm—but there were no guards, no shackles, no orders, no subservience. And there were horses, big-shouldered brutes, handsome and frightening all at once. He didn't know much about horses, but he was eager to learn.

After making a long loop around the fields—thick with corn and wheat and tomatoes, peppers, tall green stalks ripening into hay—he stopped by the pasture and leaned on the wooden fence. A rough piece of sod covered a recently dug plot by the fence. Beyond the plot, the horses raced in a pack across the tall grass, their legs flashing, their hooves pounding, their breath snorting out through wide nostrils. They didn't have horses at the LCM, just trucks and machines of all manner and make. But a horse was a link to some other America, a land of wide-open ranges and rugged individualists, of silver spurs and beans in a pot and limitless possibilities.

"Do you know how to ride?"

It was that Martha, who was now leaning beside him on the fence. Her jeans were tight, and the top buttons of her loose white shirt were undone.

"I know enough not to fall off," said Moonis.

"It's not as easy as it looks."

"Nothing is, other than maybe sex."

"Except when you fall off during sex, you don't crack your head open."

"You do if you're doing it right."

"The thing you must never forget, Moonis, is that he's trying to kill you."

"Well, he's tried already, and here I am."

"I'm not talking about Raden, I'm talking about the horse. Raden won't try, he'll succeed."

"It's a beautiful farm."

"It's beautiful all right, until you have to work it."

"I've worked a farm before, believe me. Farms are the only things I ever worked in my life. Not originally by choice, I admit. I had two stints at LCM farms in Illinois. I left the last one when I found out my sister was missing."

"They just let you leave?"

"They don't let you do anything."

"This place must give you bad memories, then."

"You'd think, but no. I loved the work, the air, the expanse. I loved climbing beneath a combine and working on its guts and then taking that same combine into the field and shearing the land."

Martha turned her face toward his, peering into his eyes as if searching for something, before staring out again into the pasture. She let the time drip, drip away from them both before saying, "You know how to fix a combine?"

***

The Massey-Harris self-propelled combine squatted like a dead spider in a shed behind the barn, and was just as likely to up and scuttle forward on its own. Rust had eaten through the flat red paint, oil stained the dirt beneath it, the tines of its reel were spindled and mutilated. It was as lost in the D-Lands as Moonis himself.

"No one can do anything with it," said Martha, giving the rusting hulk of metal a kick. "The problem is, we can't get factory-made parts out here."

"Factory-made parts are for free folk with money," said Moonis. "We made our own at the LCM."

"Think you can do anything with it?"

"I won't know until I get beneath the thing and bang at it with a hammer."

"Perhaps I was a little harsh last night," she said with the slightest of cat smiles. "I believe your friend Patti is going to need another day to recover."

"That's mighty generous of you, Martha. And, conveniently, that would give me time to take a good look at this machine. If I do try to get her operational, I might need some help. Do you have anyone who's good with engines?"

"Zephyr's our tractor boy. He used to work the railroads. He welds."

"He'll do. And Digger will help. But if I do get this heap of rust up and running, you have to do something for me."

"We don't have any money."

"Where would I spend money out here? Besides, Clyde's got a wadful."

"Good old Clyde," she said.

"What I need is for you to show me where Raden went and how best to get there, so I can find my sister."

"You want me to send you into the jaws of hell?"

"Riding atop a combine, if need be."

"You really do want to die, don't you?"

"Clyde says you're the one that's going to get me killed."

"Your friend Clyde might be on to something." She gave the rusted dead thing another kick. "You get this pile of rust running, I'll show you the way. But Clyde doesn't have to worry about my killing you, since this thing is dead as Marley. I'll send Zephyr."

"Along with a jug of shine," said Moonis. "Alcohol is always helpful during a resurrection."

43
CITY MOUSE

Clyde slapped at his neck, drew back his palm to see the dismembered body of a fierce black fly amidst a blot of his own blood.

The place was buzzing with farmwork, the teeth of rabid insects, the smell of crap, a bunch of naked children running around like rabbits. The sooner they got out of this Yokelville, the better, but Martha had informed him they'd be stuck here for another day while Patti recovered and Moonis worked on some stinking machine, and that news hadn't brightened Clyde's morning. The longer they stayed, the easier a target they'd become, and they were easy enough a target already. Their only hope was to move and keep moving, but here they were, stuck atop a pile of manure.

"Isn't it wonderful, Clyde?" said Lydia, walking up to the stump where he sat drinking shine from a tin cup and contemplating his misery. "A real live farm, right out of a book."

"It's wonderful, all right," said Clyde.

"It's like we're living in *Charlotte's Web*—not the web itself, but the little farm, with Fern and Wilbur. Have you walked around it yet? Have you seen it all?"

"I've seen enough." He couldn't help noticing the brightness of Lydia's eyes, the flush of her complexion. And she was barely breathing hard. The sadness that had enveloped her since he had delivered the news about her mother's internment had seemed to recede in this place.

"Come walk with me, Clyde. Ruby and I took a tour earlier this morning and there's something you need to see."

Clyde had wanted to be left alone, maybe to get drunk and fall asleep in the cool shadow of a tree, but he stood, swallowed the rest of the moonshine, and put the cup in a pocket. Lydia grabbed hold of one of his arms and began pulling him toward the fields.

"Did I ever tell you I'm allergic to farms?" said Clyde. "I need walls and streets and crowds of miserable people trudging off to miserable jobs to feel like myself. All this open space makes my skin itch."

"I don't miss the city at all. I miss my mother in every breath, but not the city. It's as if we're on a different planet from home, maybe the planet I was supposed to be born on. I don't know what it is, but I feel like dancing out here."

"Don't worry, whatever it is, I'm sure they have a pill for it back over the line."

"You think my mother would like it here when she gets out?"

"No," said Clyde.

"You see that boy there?"

She was indicating a kid in black pants, suspenders and a straw hat, not much older than Lydia herself, though already tall and gawky. He was in a small field with a hoe, working the soil, chopping out weeds between long lines of leafy sprouts, dark green with curled edges.

"The kid lost in the spinach?"

"It's kale."

"What the blazes is kale?"

"It's like spinach."

"We don't have kale at the Toddle House. Or that other thing they gave us at breakfast, like ground rabbit crap. My view is, if it's not at the Toddle House, it's not worth eating."

She lowered her voice. "His name is Obadiah and he comes from a place in the D-Lands where his father has like forty wives, most of them his own daughters. I was trying to figure it out, and I guess that makes his father his uncle, and his mother his sister. Isn't that crazy?"

"It's something all right, but nothing a shotgun wouldn't fix."

"They send all the boys away on their thirteenth birthday. Just send them walking, roaming about the D-Lands like ghosts. He ended up here. He's very nice, and he has a secret that he told me."

"Other than the fact that his mother is his sister?"

"He can do it, too."

"Do what?"

"You know, the thing that happens with the teacup?"

"I thought we weren't going to talk about that."

"But it happens to him, too. Except he can control it. Clyde, he can kick a ball without kicking it. I've seen it. He can bend forks."

"That comes in handy, I bet. Lot of need for fork-bending on a farm."

"He said he could teach me how."

"We're leaving tomorrow."

"Do we have to, Clyde? Can't we stay for just a little bit longer?"

"We didn't come to stay, or for you to learn tricks from some kid named Obadiah, with all kinds of tricks up his sleeve, I bet. We came to get Moonis's sister and to get a load of berry for you and then to get you to your family in Decatur. You can live a normal life out there. Get married, have a kid, a picket fence."

"What's a picket fence?"

"Something to keep trouble out. You know, with pickets. You can be happy, Lydia."

"Can't I be happy here?"

"No. Just the fact that we're here at all is bad for this place. We have no choice, for their sakes and for our own, but to scram."

"You can figure something out, Clyde. That's what you do, figure things out."

"I figured it out already. Nice town, Decatur."

"Have you ever been there?"

"No."

"Neither has anyone else. Come on, Clyde, follow me. You need to see this."

***

She led Clyde across the open fields toward a rise covered with an orchard of apple and pear trees, chirping all the while as Clyde trudged along. The sun shone down with the weight of iron. When they reached the cool of the orchard, with its sweetly sour scent of lushness, Lydia told him to close his eyes.

"What are you going to do to me?" he said. "I don't want an apple."

"Just close your eyes, silly, and keep them closed until I tell you. Do you promise?"

"I promise, but there better be dancing girls involved."

"This is better than a line of Rockettes."

"What do you know about the Rockettes?"

"There was a Christmas show from New York on the TV last year. I kept on waiting for one of the girls to kick the girl next to her in the face. Come on."

She took his hand in both of her own and pulled. Her hands were small and warm and they tugged him up the hill, weaving him here and there. As he climbed, he began to smell, above the scent of the orchard, something familiar and bright, bitter yet fresh as the sky. When they stopped climbing and stood on a level piece of ground, the scent hit him harder, like a bracing slap, and his lungs seemed to fill with the clean, bitter sky.

"Okay, Clyde," said Lydia. "Go ahead. Take a look."

And he did, and what he saw dropped his jaw with amazement even as it filled his soul with a brutal, righteous rage.

***

It was early evening, just before dinner, and Ruby was singing the blues on a stage set out before the outdoor tables filled with farmers finished with their work for the day. The farmers were of all ages and races, men and women, children, too, a veritable mob. Clyde was drinking shine out of his tin cup, letting the sweet burn of the liquor rip down his throat like a lit fuse. He wasn't drunk enough yet, but he was getting there.

Ruby was fronting a group that included an acoustic guitar in addition to her own, a washboard, a makeshift bass made of two-by-fours and a metal trash can, and a red-haired drummer with crazed eyes banging on a snare drum and a trash-can lid. The gang sounded tight, strong, like they had been playing with one another for years instead of hours. Ruby's singing was a lifeline out of the land of morose.

Patti was still up in the farmhouse convalescing, Moonis and Digger were nowhere to be seen, Lydia was off to the side with that Obadiah, playing with a spinning top. He seemed like a nice kid, that Obadiah—polite and sincere, quiet—and Clyde wanted to rip his face off for some reason, a reason that Clyde surely didn't want to examine too closely. It was only Gloria keeping Clyde company, taking a break from caring for Patti, swaying to the music as she sipped at her shine.

"We've got to get out of here," said Clyde.

"I'm with you on that, Clyde," said Gloria.

"How's Patti?"

"Better."

"Ready to travel?"

"The bleeding's stopped, the wounds look okay. She can sit up."

"Then she can travel."

"If you say so," said Gloria. "Tell me something, Clyde. Does Patricia have a boyfriend?"

"Patti? Nah. Never. She's just Patti. Maybe in the army."

"Any family?"

"Out in Minnesota somewhere. She says she's part Indian."

"I can see it. Why no boyfriend, Clyde? She's pretty enough."

"Really?"

"Sure."

"I don't know. She's Pats, is all. She's like a sister."

"To everyone?"

Gloria was like a different person in her farm dress, wearing her concern for the injured Patti on her features. Clyde maybe preferred her in the long leather gloves and the mesh top that showed off her breasts. Then he'd known what to do with her. He took another swig, hoping that with enough of the shine he wouldn't recognize himself, because right now he recognized himself as the worst kind of dupe.

Lydia had pulled him up that rise and told him to open his eyes and he saw it before him, a great field laid out like an immense carpet rolling on and on toward the horizon, vast and limitless. And without being told, he knew in his bones it was berry growing in near-perfect rows, knew it by the color and the homeopathic bitterness in the air. And it wasn't a carpet of the gray desiccated husks he had been buying from Hooper at a ransom price, or even the less desiccated maroon fruits Ruby had given him. This berry was red as rushing blood, ripe and fresh, bursting with life and power. This was health itself, this was salvation, and not just for Lydia but for a whole city, a state, a nation.

He had been told that berry only grew wild and occasional on the wrong side of the line, that it was so ridiculously expensive because it was so rarely found. Its very scarcity was said to be the reason Balthazar Pharmaceuticals was desperately looking for other answers to the plague. And yet . . .

"Obadiah says they used to have to scavenge for it," said Lydia on top of that rise. "Every time they tried to grow it themselves nothing happened, it just shriveled and died before it bloomed. Until Raden brought in some genius, who taught them a system. And now look at it. Isn't it the prettiest thing you ever saw, Clyde?"

"It's pretty all right."

"I walked through it with Obadiah and felt better right away. I took the deepest breath I had taken in years."

"We'll bring some back with us," said Clyde. "We'll bring a bushel back, and we'll learn to grow it ourselves. We'll find a private little plot in Decatur and grow it for you so you'll have it always."

"There won't be anything to bring back," said Lydia. "Raden ordered them to plow it under, to destroy the crop. He said if they don't, he will. And no one knows why, Clyde. They have to do it, they have no choice, but they don't know why."

But Clyde knew why, sure he did. Those Balthazar boys were something, weren't they? And now it wasn't just Clyde getting duped, it was everyone on both sides of the river.

With a low grunt he pushed himself away from the table, away from Gloria jabbering on about Patti, and stumbled to the shine barrel to fill his tin cup anew. He didn't know if they would end up finding Cecily—there was probably nothing to be done even if they did—but he knew one thing for sure. When he left this stinking farm, finally and gratefully, and hit the other side of the line, he was going to buy himself a brand-new suit and a brand-new life. Because his suit was gone and his life was crap and out there, in those fields, was something with the power to shake worlds. And it was his time to do the shaking.

Rackety tak tak.

He was ladling another dose of shine into his cup when the mechanical hullabaloo rose from just an annoying background noise beneath the music to something that lifted his chin.

Rackety tak tak clump tak tak.

Ruby stopped singing, the band stopped playing, the whole crowd started rising from the tables, all of them moving toward the noise. Clyde took a gulp from his cup, took a step forward, wheeled back and splashed in another swallow from the barrel, and then followed.

All he saw was the back sides of a bunch of torsos and heads. Protecting his drink all the while, he elbowed his way through the crowd until he burst into the open and saw Martha, one hand on her hip and the other shielding her eyes from the sun, staring into the distance. And what she was staring at was a sight for sure.

Rackety tak tak clump tak tak clump tak.

The sound was coming from a contraption, pale and rusty red, with a twisted rotor raised and spinning like the paddle wheel of an old riverboat, the machine belching great clumps of black smoke as it made its way around the pasture, heading right toward the tables. It was being driven by one of the farmers, the friend of Ruby's known as Zephyr, a bare-chested giant who was waving an arm like he was riding a bucking bronco, hooting and hollering all the while, his voice barely registering over the clanking of the engine.

"Yahoo!" Rackety tak tak. "Weehah!"

And behind the machine, like ghosts amidst the black of the smoke, were two figures, wiping their hands as they followed the clatter: Digger, the old man with a hitch in his step, and Moonis Fell, a smile on his face as broad as the pasture itself.

And that smile told Clyde all he needed to know about their immediate future. Somehow, someway, the hunt for Cecily was pressing on.

44
ROUTE 666

The impossibility of their situation was laid out for them on the dining room table of the old farmhouse, the same table where a fried chicken feast had been laid out for Martha her first evening at the Yeager farm. Fifteen years before, surrounded by the bright flowered wallpaper and the plentiful food, she imagined she had stumbled into some mythical land of peace and plenty. Now the wallpaper was shriveling at the seams, the woman who had cooked that meal lay deranged and dying in the bedroom above them, and the only mythical thing on the land was the peace and the plenty she thought she had found.

The scarred wooden surface of the table was set with a trio of lanterns and a series of road maps. "The red X's slashed across the maps mark the old roads and bridges that are now impassable," said Martha to the vagabonds from the freak van. The maps were old, yellowed, mostly ripped at the folds, each imprinted with the name of a filling station that no longer existed. "Sometimes a route not on the map gets clawed out of the earth so that trucks can get through, but not too often, and nothing that lasts."

"Who maintains the rest of the roads?" said Moonis.

"Mostly the Guard," said Martha.

"It ain't the Guard, not no more," said Digger. "There be a crew of ghosts that keep it in repair. I know some who have claimed to have seen them in the sketchy dawn, with shovels in their bony hands and bare yellow skulls 'neath their work caps."

They all looked over to Digger, who nodded a knowing nod, like what he had said made the most perfect sense, and then they all turned back to the maps as if it actually did.

"We travel all over," said Martha, "selling what we can to make enough money to keep Raden off our necks. And every time we hit a barrier, we mark it on one of the maps, giving us the truth about how Raden moves through the D-Lands."

And the maps, with their X's, told the story. Because of the ruined roads and bridges, Raden was forced to make a wide irregular loop around his territory, over a dam that still stood on one part of the loop and then a rickety series of bridges through another. All along the route, according to Gloria, were other group farms, religious settlements, rogue marketplaces, raging tribes of dubious diets, a whole range of insular civilizations created after the Great Disincorporation. And all of them were under Raden's thumb.

"Now right there, right there," said Zephyr in his fast mumble, "where the route there is forced down . . . yes, it is, right down, like a convex lens . . . hard by the river . . . look to the hollow . . . A bunch of fascist neo-Nazi . . . white-power misfits . . . goose-stepping to the cadence of their wacked-out leader . . . Kimmler . . . with blazing red eyes and a fake German accent . . . Heil Kimmler . . . A piece of gristle from the belly of the earth . . . smells bad too . . . like a dead cow I saw once . . . bloated and bursting with flies."

"Kimmler's a neo-Nazi fathead," said Martha. "His men help Raden control the western part of his territory. In return they are given free rein to sell all the speed they can cook while spreading their rancid little creed."

"Raden always camps in the compound for a couple of nights," said Gloria. "His men are anything but racially pure and they hate to be there, but Raden insists and Kimmler tolerates them."

"Hatred always bows to strength," said Martha.

"But the men don't mix," said Gloria. "They'd kill each other if they could."

"So that's it," said Moonis. "Kimmler's compound is the target."

"Did you hear what they said, Moonis?" said Clyde.

"I heard."

"Twice the manpower, twice as deadly."

"What's the route?" said Moonis.

"You could follow the way he went, over the dam, like so," said Martha, sweeping her hand across the map. "Or you could go the other way around the loop. If you left right now, you might be able to get there before Raden leaves, but either way he'll be waiting for you. After the fire you set, he'll have both routes heavily patrolled, with ambushes set every which way."

"I guess that's that, then," said Clyde. "Nothing to be done."

"And if, by some stroke of luck, you do get past the ambushes, what then?" said Martha. "It's a fortified compound, filled with killers. What are you going to do?"

"We'll figure that out when we get there," said Moonis. "Clyde's good at that."

"I'm good at nothing," said Clyde, "except hamburgers and running."

"Oh, Clyde's a trooper, all right," said Moonis. "Isn't he a trooper, Digger?"

"He's something," said Digger.

"I say we run right back over the line," said Clyde.

"Oh, I'm running," said Moonis. "I'm running right to her. And you're running with me."

"I was afraid you'd say that."

Moonis stared at the map for a moment, his face in his long hands. "What about a more direct route?"

"It's not that far as the crow flies, but look at the X's," said Martha. "There are two rivers with steep banks that you need to cross from here to there and the bridges are all gone. One of the bridges was still standing before we blew it ourselves to keep Kimmler out of our faces. Kimmler's compound is on the far bank of still another river. Your van wouldn't make it ten feet."

"Then we need to find another way," said Moonis. "There's always another way."

Martha looked up at Moonis, who was bathed in a confidence as crazy as his mission. And yet Moonis had fixed the combine. He had said he would do it, and next thing she knew the rusted old thing was up and running—running poorly, for sure, but running still. He had made it here out of an LCM, he had burned down Raden's camp, he had sent a message in the sky to his sister that was actually received. You could go broke betting against this guy. There was something about him, some cheerful self-assurance that spoke to her, as if his youthful optimism hadn't yet been burned out of him by this life.

And what it spoke to her was a message of hope.

She had been looking for a champion to teach them how to free themselves from Raden's grip and, as if on cue, he had appeared with his easy smile and his ridiculous van and even more ridiculous hat and coat. She had thought she was seeking a soldier back from the battlefield, a warrior ready to train them in the fighting arts. A samurai. But maybe what the young rebel still inside her was really seeking was someone her older self could never have imagined. Someone that would take them beyond the zero-sum contest of war. And maybe Moonis Fell was it.

"There might be a way," she said finally, going all in without even knowing the game, "if you're willing to endure the pain."

45
ON THE ROAD

The sun rose behind them as they crossed the rolling plain. Six riders with seven horses, they sat with various states of aplomb upon their saddles, in various stages of soreness and distress.

"Is it supposed to hurt this much?" said Clyde.

"Yes," said the old man without an ounce of sympathy. "Yes, it is."

"Use your legs," said Ruby.

"But then I'd be walking," said Clyde.

"Quit your bellyaching, pardner," said Moonis, affecting the tone of a laconic cowboy.

"It's not my belly that's aching."

Decades of disaster, dislocation, and economic dismemberment melted away as they ambled forward. Their saddlebags were packed with fruit and bread and jerked beef, herbal tea, loads of guns and loads of ammunition. Strapped behind Clyde's saddle, rocking with the shifting hind of his horse, was the crate of dynamite they had scavenged from Raden's camp. And along with their provisions, they each of them brought along their determinations and thoughts, as individualized as their postures upon the beasts.

Zephyr, the perfect American athlete—he could throw the touchdown pass or hit the speedball a country mile—was a natural horseman. Because he often rode out to check the surrounding countryside of the farm, he led the party, surveying the landscape with his binoculars, using his compass and a map to make sure they stayed on route.

Ruby had grown up in the saddle in Texas, and volunteered to ride with them and take care of the spare beast that was brought along to carry Cecily home. She sat straight-backed atop her horse, a song of her youth in her heart.

Neither Moonis nor Clyde had ever ridden before and it showed. Clyde bumped and bounced along, letting his bottom do all the work, getting sorer and sorer, while Moonis sat tall on a short horse, reins loose in his hand and his top hat tilted to keep the sun off his face, looking like a multihued Abe Lincoln riding the circuit.

Digger said he had been atop a horse before, but you couldn't tell by the way he sat on the saddle, stiff as starch, bowlegs pressed hard on the animal's flanks, reins gripped tight as gold.

Finally, there was Martha, who had never ridden in her girlhood, but had taken to it quickly once arriving at the farm. It was the horses that kept her rooted those first few years when she had started feeling constrained by the work and the responsibility. She loved them, everything about them, and riding for her was pure joy.

Thus they moved through the landscape, like a troupe of pilgrims on the way to Canterbury, the horses keeping up with the yabbering madman in the lead, as if of their own accord. Forward, always forward they rode, toward Kimmler's camp, hard by the third river they would reach in their journey.

***

They didn't push the horses on the way out; they'd need the animals fit enough to do some running on the way back. Even so, as they made their way with a comfortable pace through the desolate, untouched landscape, the horses' flanks grew shiny with sweat, and foam flew from their mouths as they reared against the bits. Grasses wrapped like whips around the riders' legs. Fields of bush and thorn stretched in all directions. Unseen animals lurched through the thick weeds, occasionally causing a horse to wheel and bolt. It was a hard land leading to a hard place.

When Clyde fell behind, he kicked his horse into a faster walk that sometimes broke into a trot, jarring his knees and chestnuts before he pulled at the reins with a pain-wracked shout.

In the distance they could spy small homesteads carved out of the abandoned landscape, each with a ragged field up against a building of some sort, erected before the disincorporation and roughly maintained. There would be a line of smoke, maybe, or an animal or two, but the inhabitants never came over to say hello, or even appeared, so as to give a wave. They were living off any grid still known and had no desire for companionship. Lack of companionship was maybe the point.

***

The first river was shallow and flat, the water catching beads of sunlight as it trickled across a rocky flat that the horses could cross while keeping their footing.

The second river was not so easy to ford. They first saw stands of wood in the distance, and then the horses, foaming with thirst, smelled the water on the wind and surged forward. But when they reached the river, the waterway was too wide and deep to safely cross. Some of the streams and rivers were more poisoned than others and it was impossible to tell which were only mildly radioactive and which carried death in their swirls and eddies, so as little contact as possible with the water was desired. They traveled at least a mile downriver until they found a wide stretch that appeared slow and shallow enough to cross without swimming. They could see the color of the rocks beneath the white-topped curls on the river's surface.

Once again Zephyr led the way. The water proved swifter and deeper than it had appeared from solid ground, and Zephyr ended up soaked to the waist. The others sat in their saddles and discussed the thing before, one by one, they each of them followed and each of them ended up similarly half-drenched.

On the far side, Clyde, his pants dripping, his thighs and rear raw from the chafing ride, tried to pull his right leg from the stirrup and failed. His knee was too stiff, his leg muscles too clenched, he was stuck in the saddle. He gripped the horn and leaned over until his right boot slipped out of the stirrup and then he tumbled off the horse.

"Krist," he said under his breath while still on the ground, "isn't this a treat." But when he saw Moonis walking toward him with legs so bowed it was like he had a pair of bowling balls between his knees, he couldn't help but laugh.

They unsaddled the horses, brushed their flanks, and after feeding and watering the animals, they hobbled them in a cool grove. They built a fire on the far bank, feeding it collected wood until the blaze rose hot enough to dry the clothes on their bodies and brew tea with the water they had brought, rose hip and hibiscus to aid their digestion, and berry to give some protection from the river poison. They stretched their blankets onto the soil beneath a stand of oak and sat together, eating their fruit and jerky, drinking the tea, listening to Zephyr talk. He smoked some weed and drank some shine and took them on a journey of language into the ninth dimension, and the rest sat back and let the words wash through them like a rinse until their minds were blank and they could see the stars.

Moonis took first watch, setting up so that the river was behind him and the camp before him and the sky clear above him. The crescent moon painted the landscape with its pale-blue touch. Martha sat with him for a bit and they both stared up at the pitch of the heavens pocked with pinpricks of promise.

"I love the night sky," said Moonis. "It makes me feel small."

"And you like feeling small?"

"I find the truth of it bracing. I am a short-lived speck of stardust. I am less than a mote in the eye of a single planet circling a single star, among hundreds of billions scattered across our universe."

"That sounds cold."

"To me it sounds like liberty. I can hardly believe I've never before ridden a horse across an untended prairie. It feels like I'm riding backwards through time into something clean and unalloyed."

"When they chase after you with their motorcycles, riding a horse won't feel so blissful."

"We'll be back to the farm before they catch up to us, and then we'll take the Every Ship right out onto the road. They won't even know you were involved."

"They'll know."

"Whatever we do up there, we'll leave you and Zephyr out of it. There will be no link to the farm."

"No need for such caution, Moonis. We didn't come to sit back and watch. And they have maps, too. Any line they draw leads right back to us, that's just the way it is."

"What will he do to you, then?"

"Burn our buildings, salt our fields, send us scattering. That's if he's in a generous mood. Otherwise it will be his customary murder and mayhem."

"Then what are you doing here?"

"It sounded like an adventure."

"A suicide mission is what you called it before we left. Stupid and foolhardy."

"Stupid and foolhardy used to be my specialty," said Martha. "That's how I ended up on this side of the line. I was sick of being under someone's thumb. I guess I still am, I had only forgotten for a bit. But everything changes, everything dies, that's just the way of life. The farm's over."

"It doesn't have to be, the future's not yet writ."

"I told Enrique what I was doing and what would be the inevitable result. He said he'd pass the word. If by dumb chance we make it back, I expect most of the citizens will already have left for safety."

"What will you do then?"

"Gather my children and head out someplace myself. There's open land west, I hear."

"I always thought I'd be a good farmer," said Moonis. "I like the hours."

"No one likes the hours."

"Up with the sun, ripping open the good earth, pulling out its bounty—that's the life for me."

"Maybe it was, but you won't get to see it. I was right, you know. This is a suicide mission."

"All of life is a suicide mission. But at least on this leg of the journey we have Clyde."

"Clyde? You're depending on Clyde? That's a laugh. All he does is whine and drink and complain. And he rides like a sack of cornmeal."

"Clyde has suffered more than his share. He was badly betrayed in love and life, and hasn't ever really recovered."

"Who betrayed him?"

"Me."

"And he won't betray you back?"

"Sure he will, but only after he saves my sister. Oh, Martha, you should have seen him play football. He tore through the field like a tornado, a brilliant, unspoiled piece of violence. Trust me when I tell you, he's worth ten of them."

"Well, we have Zephyr on our side, too. That's another ten."

"See," said Moonis. "Those sons of bitches are overmatched, they just don't know it yet."

***

Their route beyond the second river took them past a fenced-in piece of pasture with a small huddle of spotted cow beneath a single oak. As they chewed their cuds, the cows looked up at the riders, their eyes blank as fate.

Beyond the pasture was an old farmhouse, and a field with uneven rows of lettuce, peppers, beans of many types, and wild, weedy tomatoes. A woman and three children were picking at the beans as Zephyr stopped at the edge of the field and waited for the rest to catch up. The woman, her back to the riders, kept on working even as the children pulled at her skirt. She ignored the children, just as she was ignoring the snort of the horses and the clop of the hooves, as if the riders were a spate of indigestion she hoped would pass. No such luck.

"You're heading the wrong way," she said as she faced them finally, wiping her hands on the canvas bag tied round her waist. Her face was saggy and swollen, mottled with birthmark and tumor. Her children stared up at them with eyes as big and blank as those of the cows.

"Which way should we be heading?" said Moonis.

"Any way but thataway. You and the old man especially. North is better."

"What's west?"

"Desolation."

"Do they come this way much?" said Clyde.

"Every now and then. I got the scars to prove it, and the children, they daddy's in the ground because of it. If they take someone looks like me, you two ladies will be a treat."

"How do they travel?"

"Like a thunderstorm coming at you from the distance, fast and with no good intent. They got their own horses, if you want to know."

Clyde looked at Moonis, shook his head, leaned over and spit.

"You're not going to heed me, are you?" said the woman.

"No, ma'am," said Moonis.

"What are you after?"

"They have my sister."

"She's dead already, mister, or she wishes she was."

"We could use some feed for the horses, and rainwater if you've got it," said Martha.

"We got some dried-out oats, and plenty of well water, if that's okay."

"Well water's good for the horses, but we'll pass on that ourselves."

"I drink the well water, and I'm still here. I save the rainwater for the children, what with the long futures they got ahead of them. But what difference does the future make to you, going where you're going?"

"Thank you anyway."

"It's been a dry summer, but I suppose I got some rainwater I can spare along with the oats, if you can pay."

"We can pay," said Clyde.

"That's a help."

"And we'll give you enough now for the same on the way back."

"Then you got yourselves a deal. Paying twice for what you only need once will usually leave you good and broke, but going broke is the least of your problems."

"Hang a lantern so we can find you on the way back in the dark," said Martha.

"When would that be, Judgment Day?" She lifted her chin and cackled at that, her open mouth a ruined cemetery. And the children kept on staring, their eyes so flat and open the stares were like stones on the riders' chests.

46
THE BOARD

In the dying embers of the second day they reached the third river, a couple miles upstream from Kimmler's camp. While Ruby stayed with the animals, the rest slipped down the far bank, behind the bushes and through the groves flanking a river that was broad and fast and too deep to cross with the horses. Within the dark woods facing the encampment, they stopped at a berm, behind which they could hunker as they examined the terrain.

Kimmler had taken over a small town abandoned in the disincorporation. The town straddled a road, with most of the weathered buildings on the far side. A large field spreading from the road to the river was haphazardly covered by tents and fire pits and dried mud, except for a large amphitheater cut into the land at the river's edge with a stage abutting the riverbank, where twin lightning slashes built of wood stood ten feet tall at the rear of the platform. A notched bar linked the tops of the two great slashes. To the right of the field was a barn and a corral, where a pack of white horses stood stock-still.

Between the amphitheater and the corral, a wooden bridge led across the span of the surging river.

But the most notable fact of the entire scene was that the field, the road, the far lots, the entire camp was crawling with the soldiers and vehicles of two vile armies bivouacking together. They were coming and going, they were working on bike and truck, they were milling about the fires, drinking from jugs. They were killers, maniacs, racists and rapists, foul-mouthed brigands flashing ragged teeth red with betel juice, and the very numbers of them were absurd, a joke.

With one glance, the truth of things became as painfully clear to Martha as a shard of glass in the eye. The scene itself was the death of hope. It was time to get smart, to grow up, to step back, to ride home, to open her heart to her own utter powerlessness and offer up to Raden what was Raden's.

"Why don't we just go in and say hello?" said Clyde. "They look like a friendly sort. I'm sure we can work something out."

"That's a hoot and a holler," said Zephyr. "Wild-eyed maniacs of the plains . . . flashing rope and saw . . . working our heads off our shoulders."

"I understand you had to come and see for yourself, Moonis," said Martha. "But maybe now you'll listen to your sister and go back home."

"She is my home," said Moonis.

They crouched behind the berm in silence, calculating the odds and finding them growing ever longer with every corner they examined. Just the sight of the two armies pressed the breath from Martha's chest. She fought the urge to run.

"What do you think, Digger?" said Moonis.

"I think we're up against it," said Digger, "which is business as usual as far as I'm concerned. Wouldn't know what to do with myself if the odds was ever in my favor. Let me see them glasses."

Zephyr turned over his binoculars and the old man gazed through them. Moonis shaded the lenses from the setting sun to fend off any reflection.

"Gloria said Raden's men would be camping on the field between the river and the town," said Moonis. "Which means Cecily is in one of the tents."

"There's one of them that's got a man setting out front," said Digger. "That one there, the green one in the center."

"She wasn't being guarded at the farm," said Martha.

"Maybe he's not setting there to keep her in," said Digger. "Maybe he's there to keep Kimmler's men out."

"Let's just assume that's her," said Moonis. "What do we do about it?"

"Why you asking me?" said Digger.

"Who else would I ask?" said Moonis. "See the way the whole camp is laid out? With the square footprints of the tents and the buildings on both sides of the street."

"Why, it almost looks like a chessboard, now that you mention it," said Digger.

"And you were the one teaching me chess."

"I seem to remember you whupped me good."

"Just the first game. You took me down the second, and taught me something, too."

"Maybe I did."

"So what do you see, Digger?"

"Well," he said, staring again through the glasses. "With most of Kimmler's men being on the other side of the road, it's almost like they're trapped behind a row of their own pawns."

"There you go."

"If we work quick enough, we can forget all about them on the other side."

"So speed—speed is the key."

"And we can think of that green tent as the center square over which we're fighting, so the object is to get as many of our pieces focused on that square while sending Raden's pieces dancing away like a bunch of fools. And then we need to protect our flank when we're coming back through."

"So you're thinking of some kind of diversion to send Raden's men scattering. And then some way of protecting the spaces my sister would have to travel through as she makes it to the river. And then we'd need to do something about the bridge, and their horses in the corral, to make sure of our getaway."

"Was I thinking all that?"

"A master tactician like you, Digger, of course you were."

"Maybe I was, too. Maybe I can see it, the whole series of moves."

"Bam, bam, bam," said Moonis. "But something seems to be missing."

"It would really help," said Digger, "if we could have ourselves a knight—you know, a piece that could reach the center square by jumping up and over instead of having to move in a straight line past them guards to the tent."

Martha marveled not just at the way Moonis had led the old man into devising a plan Moonis had evidently already devised, all the while giving the old man ownership, but how the very discussion, the back-and-forth, the revelation of move and countermove, along with the sense that there was always something to be done, eased her own breathing.

"How does one jump over a line of bad guys?" she said.

"I don't know; I'm just talking chess here," said Digger. "Maybe our piece, he could hop it like a kangaroo on a pogo stick. Or hurtle along on vines like Tarzan through the trees. Or maybe become invisible and slip right through them lines."

"Well, that's easy enough," said Clyde. "Maybe we'll just brew up some of that invisibility tea you got in your saddlebag alongside the rose hips."

"Look at the vests," said Zephyr. "Toads by the bridge . . . swastika on the back . . . too greasy for angel wings . . . damn feathers slip right off . . . no angels on that side of the river."

"One of them vests Kimmler's men have on might be good as invisibility tea," said Digger, "depending on who was wearing it."

"We could pull it off one of the bridge guards," said Moonis, "but we'd still need someone to put the thing on. Someone Raden's men on this side of the road have never seen before. Someone who could prance around like a little Kimmler doll and slip in on them unawares."

Martha scanned the deranged little crew: the old man; Clyde, who was apparently worth ten of them; Zephyr, the jabbering madman of the Midwest; herself, a misplaced waif in women's clothing, seeking some way to shatter again her life; and finally the strange Moonis Fell, in orange pants and paisley shirt and furry blue top hat, who seemed to carry within his breast hope itself. The world spins, the universe expands, stars surge and die, life ends as sure as it begins, and yet still Moonis Fell plots the impossible and makes it happen. The only impossibility was not to act. Where wouldn't she follow such a man?

"Hey," said Clyde, with his usual whine, "why the hell is everyone suddenly looking at me?"

***

Night fell hard and black.

The village on the river's far side, the road, the field, the amphitheater were all illuminated by xenon lamps fired by a generator that ran on Raden's gasoline. But beyond the bright borders of Kimmler's camp was the silky dark of a forgotten land, lit only by a sliver of moon and a highway of stars. And within that vague illumination, anxiety crouched atop a ragged band of would-be warriors.

Under cover of night, Ruby brought the horses as close to the camp as she dared, settling them down across from Kimmler's corral so that any stray noises would be attributed to the beasts on the other side of the river. She roped the horses to the trees and kept them saddled and ready.

Under cover of night, Zephyr and Digger slipped over the berm, scrabbled upriver to the mouth of the bridge, and slipped as quietly as the old man could manage beneath its span.

Under cover of night, Martha took a satchel filled with dynamite, a spool of wire, and a detonator, all of it wrapped tight within an oilcloth poncho, and crouched low as she ran downriver.

Under cover of night, Moonis and Clyde huddled together behind the berm and marinated in a silent tension born of a long friendship turned slightly rancid. Out of nowhere, Moonis cuffed Clyde just above the ear.

"What the hell?"

"You're mighty quiet," said Moonis.

"I'm just wondering when was the last time you fired a gun."

"Not too long ago."

"Try never. And you're supposed to be covering me?"

"Don't you worry about my end," said Moonis. "Remember what the freaks called me in the prison?"

"You killed a man with a combine."

"Just think what I can do with a rifle. It had to be you, Clyde."

"I know."

"They'd recognize Zephyr or Martha, and it can't be me or Digger wearing Kimmler's white-power getup."

"I get it. I've been in tougher spots. Remember that time we licked 469—what were they, the Anteaters?—and when the game was over

I was surrounded by a pack of wild-eyed savages with chains in their fists?"

"Cheerleaders, I seem to remember."

"Male cheerleaders."

"Go Anteaters, eat them ants."

"Glory days," said Clyde.

"You nervous about seeing her?"

"Nah."

"Me too. It's sad how badly you can fail someone you love so much. When did you see her last?"

"Right after I came back from the zinc pit. She came into the diner, ordered tea, sat there looking sad."

"You didn't spark up the romance?"

"There was nothing left to spark. She sat on her stool, heart-stoppingly beautiful, and there I stood, behind the counter in my white apron, my white cap. The only thing we still had between us was you. She had dreams for her life and I was a guaranteed joe with a cheap room and no future beyond the grill."

"There's more to you than that. There's worlds in you, man."

"But she was right, that's all they'd ever let me be."

"They should have selected you. I can still see your smile when they called my name instead of yours, as if you meant it."

"I did. I was happy for you, proud. And also, truth be told, relieved it wasn't me. Like I was going to read Shakespeare, study trigonometry? Krist, I would have punked out of that Ventura School quicker than you. And why would I want to play ball for them anyway? I played for us and that was enough. My dreams were never as big as yours or Cecily's."

"We're going to save her, Clyde. And then maybe you two will have another go-round."

"That pipe dream is dead."

"Really?"

"I'm over it."

"Then why did you go off looking for her? Why are you here?"

"Because you asked me."

"That's all it took?"

"That's all it took."

"Damn, Clyde, aren't you the peach."

They shut up fast when they heard something scraping across the ground before them. Scrape, step, scrape.

Clyde pulled a pistol from his belt. Moonis lifted his rifle. Slowly they raised their heads just enough to peer above the rise of the berm, and that's when they saw him, shirtless and huge, muscles rippling, leaves sticking to his flesh as if they had grown there.

Zephyr. Dragging two sacks of something, which turned out to be men. Pulling them along by the collars of their leather vests, their slack bodies gouging tracks in the dirt.

Behind Zephyr, Digger scrambled up the hill with that bowlegged gait of his, carrying the weapons.

"Two?" said Moonis.

"We didn't know the young man's exact size," said Digger. "So we brought a selection. Go ahead there, Clyde, and take your pick."

***

Moonis and Digger, armed to the teeth, belts of ammunition dripping off their shoulders, were now huddled behind a thick tree rising from the sloping bank just above the exit of the bridge. Digger raised his rifle on one side of the trunk while Moonis, with the binoculars, surveyed the scene from the other. Much of the field was blocked by tents, but on the parts of the field to which he had a clear view, Moonis saw no one paying any attention to the unguarded bridge or the delta of land before it.

Moonis tossed a stone toward the berm behind him. A moment later Clyde appeared above the crest, wearing jeans, a black T-shirt, and a leather vest with a skull and swastika on the back. Clyde scratched madly at his neck and chest as he surveyed the scene. A moment later he scrabbled down the bank toward the bridge, pulling a pack behind him.

Moonis kept the binoculars aimed at the field, moving the tight circle of his focus back and forth as Clyde slipped beneath the unguarded bridge. No one Moonis spied was paying any attention.

A moment later, Clyde appeared on the bridge's surface, an unlit cigarette in his lips. He put a bit of the rooster in his walk as he made his way across and, as simple as that, he was in the camp. Moonis followed Clyde's walk up the field, feeling a little giddy at the ease of it all, when an exhale caught in his throat.

One of Raden's men had come out from behind a tent. The man was skinny, tall, with a long unkempt beard. He called to Clyde, and Clyde stopped dead in his tracks.

"Aim at that bastard's head," said Moonis as he kept the two of them in his view.

"Got it," said Digger.

Moonis watched as Clyde patted his vest and pulled out a pack of cigarettes. The man took one and then, with a nod of Clyde's head, took another. The man tugged a lighter from his vest, lit his cig, and then lit Clyde's. The two laughed at something before the bearded man turned away.

"Krist," said Moonis as Clyde moved on, up the line of tents toward where they hoped they'd find Cecily.

***

Martha spied the roadblock from across the river, about half a mile from the camp, two trucks and a pile of logs spread across what was left

365

of the asphalt. Behind the logs, a fire blazed, around which a bunch of Raden's men smoked and laughed and poured shine down their throats.

The vehicles in the roadblock themselves would have sufficed for her purposes. She didn't require much to work with; a ton of metal with a half-full gas tank would have done the trick. All she needed to do was to make enough of a racket to raise the dead.

But in a stroke of luck, there wasn't just the roadblock. There was also a pack of cycles behind the logs and, behind the cycles, glowing dully from the firelight, a silver tanker car with a big red star on the side. Martha knew exactly what was inside that tanker. She had paid enough to drain its contents into the fuel tanks on the farm. In a way it was the symbol of Raden's dominance and her dependence. The farm needed gasoline, Raden controlled the market, and so Raden controlled the farm. Grow this. Burn that. Pay this. Pay that. Dance, woman, dance.

Her younger self would have blown up the thing just for spite and laughed in the face of the inferno.

She examined the river. It was deep enough that she'd have to swim across; hopefully it wasn't too neon. She spied a spot well upriver where she could launch herself and, with the current, emerge about twenty yards behind the tanker. Between the spot where she would climb the bank and the rear of the truck, there'd be only a few yards where she wouldn't be under cover. It wouldn't be so hard to get where she needed to get. Getting away would be a bit harder, even with the long fuse, but she'd recross that river when she got to it. Now it was time to feed the young beast within her.

She shrugged the pack higher on her shoulder and slowly, silently, made her way down the bank. The chess game was about to begin. It was going to be loud, it was going to be violent. Death would play among the horses and kings.

Martha just hoped Moonis's sister was worth the blood.

47
QUEEN'S GAMBIT

Click, snap.

The switchblade glowed like something holy in the candlelight. Long and narrow with a smooth black handle cool to the touch, the knife was a little shard of salvation, long enough to pierce a heart, sharp enough to neatly slice the dark, pulsing veins in a wrist.

She twisted the movable guard, clicked the knife closed, hefted it in her hand, and then pressed the button. The little monster snapped opened with a ferocious assurance. She did it again. Click, snap.

The switchblade had been in the possession of Bear Claw, one of Raden's riders, a mound of a man with a bushy red beard, who had killed one of the men from Yeager's farm. The dead man had supposedly brandished that very knife while Bear Claw was screwing the man's girlfriend before Bear Claw shot him in the chest. Staggeringly drunk the next morning, Bear Claw used the knife to slice off a slab of roasted pig. He stuffed the meat into the maw of his beard and wandered off, leaving the blade in the carcass, the black handle sticking out of the burgundy skin like an invitation. Without a whisper's hesitation,

Cecily sauntered over to the table, pulled off a few fingers of dripping meat, and placed the meat delicately between her teeth.

It wasn't long before Bear Claw stomped back to the tables, searched both the pigs, and raged upon finding nothing but pork and bone. Cecily watched the inevitable accusation and wanton destruction with an air of detached amusement, all while the closed knife was tucked neatly into her soft black boot.

There had been opportunities at Raden's camp for her to grab a weapon, but after the trauma at the cannibal's cabin, she had decided to accept her fate. She was a captive in a brutal system designed to mold her to its will—nothing new there—and so an uneasy acquiescence was easy enough to slip into. Yet as soon as she spoke aloud to Martha her belief that it was Moonis who had set the fire at Raden's camp, the absurdity of the idea hit her full force. Moonis was still imprisoned in the LCM, Moonis couldn't even know that she had been taken. But still, that she could even have imagined that Moonis had come into the D-Lands to save her kicked a spur into the flank of her passivity. Moonis was always fighting his fate, and that his orneriness had ruined every real opportunity that had come into his life only reinforced the beauty of his rebellion. To her brother, acquiescence was anathema, and yet here she was bowing deeply to her fate like a scullery slave. The morning after mentioning Moonis's name to Martha, Cecily had stolen the knife.

And now it sat in her hand, an instrument of escape. She had been shaken by the looks Kimmler's men gave her, hatred for her skin mixed with a boiling desire for her body. And Kimmler himself, that sunken-cheeked madman with the snarl of a cougar, had explicitly shouted out his plans to rape her into a bloody death.

Well, let them come to satisfy their vile urges; they would reap only horror. She would step daintily, hesitantly toward them—she had learned all the stripper moves—and just as their lusts were at a fever's pitch, she would slice her throat and douse their desires with her own happy blood. Let them explain to Raden the great gaping wound in her neck.

Inside the shell of light given off by the flickering candle, she could hear the outside world swirl about her, snatches of conversation, belches and farts and shouts of greeting, orders being given, the roar of engines.

And then footfalls approaching the rear of the tent.

On the taut canvas she could see the slightest blur of a shadow. A figure, tall and broad, was standing before the rear wall of her tent, legs spread like a conquistador ready to subjugate heathen lands. And then the figure stooped low.

Silent and shaking, she stood from her cot—her feet bare, her breasts loose beneath a sheer untucked shirt—and gripped the knife so that the blade jabbed down from her fist. The urge to do violence not only to herself took hold. If she was going, maybe she wouldn't go alone. Even as she stepped forward, she saw the flash of another blade slip through the canvas of her tent and start moving down, ripping down.

She raised her fist as the sliced sides of the tent separated. A head pushed its way through the gap, one of Kimmler's blond-haired minions. She took another step forward and prepared to stick the knife right through the top of the son of a bitch's head, shatter the bone with the blade, carve up his vile little brain, and then take care of her own escape.

But the blade wouldn't make it through a skull so thick and so she waited just a beat, waited until the rapist would lift his chin to get a look at his prize. Oh, and he would see it, every inch of it, he'd get an up-close view as it shot like an arrow through his jaundiced eye.

And then the thug's chin tilted, just as she expected. And the sight of his face, his human face, stilled her hand and stole her breath at the very same time.

"Clyde?" she managed to croak out.

***

Her first thought was so dramatically ungenerous it would shame her only moments later: *what a strange coincidence that of all the people in the world, it would be Clyde Sparrow who had come to rape her.* That her vision of Clyde now contained such a possibility said much about how the years since she had last seen him had bent her thinking.

But then Clyde stood and smiled, that sweet smile of his that had never held an ounce of threat when aimed her way, and she realized the truth. He hadn't come to rape her, the fool had come to save her. When she leaped to hug him, the knife fell from her hands.

"Clyde?"

"Hello, Cecily," he said, softly into her ear, midhug. "Tough spot you're in."

The emotion that flooded through her as she hugged Clyde as tightly as her muscles would allow was as strong as anything she had ever felt in her life—strong enough to swamp her like a pitcher beneath a waterfall. It squeezed out all the suicidal ideations, along with a raft of tears from eyes that hadn't cried in years.

"Clyde," she said, still hugging. "It was you who set the fire."

"Not me. Moonis."

She pushed herself away. "Moonis is here, too?"

"We've both come to take you home."

"But Moonis is in the LCM."

"He heard you were missing and escaped. He came to Chicago to sign me up. And now here we are. Are you ready to go?"

"Go where, Clyde? There are swarms of them and they're maniacs. You don't want to mess with them, and especially not with Raden. I've seen what he can do. Just go. Get away from here and take Moonis with you."

"We're not going without you."

"They're not just going to let us waltz out of here."

"They let me waltz in, didn't they? Who's sitting outside, guarding the tent?"

"Why?"

"Call him in."

"It's just Culbert. He's okay. He's guarding me from Kimmler's men."

"None of them are your friends," said Clyde, taking a pistol out of his belt. "Call him in."

"I don't want you to kill him."

"I'm not going to kill him, I'm going to save his life," said Clyde. "Call him in."

She stared at the gun for an instant and then raised her gaze to Clyde's blue eyes. His face had hardened over the years, lines had been gouged around his eyes, a grip of muscle had grown at the hinge of his jaw. There had always been something dull and easy about Clyde's face, but not anymore.

"How is Moonis?" she said.

"I've never seen him so happy."

"Happy?"

"I can't explain it. It's like he's becoming himself."

"Out here?"

"Why not? He wasn't much of himself back in old Chicago."

"And you?"

"I just want to get us both home."

Cecily nodded for a bit, trying to make sense of it all, and then she felt anew the emotion that had flooded through her as she hugged Clyde. It felt of home and childhood and young love and safety and hope. Moonis and Clyde. Without hesitation now, she stepped to the door of the tent while Clyde scooted to the side.

"Culbert," she said with a soft come-hither voice she had learned at the club. "Can you come in for a moment?"

***

Cecily stood over Culbert's large, lumped body heaped on the ground, without an ounce of pity. There had been something clarifying in Clyde's quick act of violence. Culbert had come into the room upon her beck, eagerness on his pale, bloated face, and before she knew what was happening Clyde smashed Culbert's head with the butt of the gun, once as he stood looking at her and a second time as he fell. It went bam bam, as rhythmic as a pop song. And just as fast, Cecily was on board with everything that was to come. Clyde was right, none of these bastards were her friends; she would have right then killed them all if she had hands and guns enough to do it.

She walked over to the edge of the tent, picked up the knife, clicked it closed. "What do we do now?"

"We wait. Put on some shoes you can run in and some pants that would work for riding a horse."

"A horse?"

"It's going to be a bumpy ride."

"I don't know how to ride a horse."

"The horse knows enough on its own. You just need to know how to scream out in agony. Go on."

Clyde turned his back to her as she dressed, the crumpled body of Culbert between them. Clyde was always so polite when they were together, so gentle, like she was a vase he was afraid of breaking. Somehow she had only remembered him as the rough-and-ready footballer, as the LCM inmate, as the grinning sap in the Toddle House apron from that disastrous visit she had made to the diner, as an almost-embarrassing part of her past. And yet here he was, showing her a respect that had disappeared so fully from her life that she had forgotten it had ever existed.

"How did you and Moonis find me?" she said as she stripped off her shirt and slipped a bra over her shoulders.

"There were crumbs to follow," said Clyde. "Maureen from your school told us about Fosbury's. At Fosbury's we learned about Brad. From Hooper we learned that you and Brad had gone off to Moline. So we went west."

She felt awkward for a moment, vulnerable. Clyde had left out something—noble, gentle Clyde. "Did you learn what I did in Moline?"

"I talked to that Blaze," said Clyde. "She's the one who sent us over the river."

"Funny how things turn out," she said, remembering the way she had gawked at Clyde in his apron, feeling so superior, like the worst V-District asshole. "I'm sorry, Clyde."

"Nothing wrong with dancing for your life," said Clyde. "We all do that. You couldn't breathe. What else were you going to do?"

"That's kind of you to say, but not for that. For the way I behaved with you."

"You kept my picture from the paper."

"Yes, I did."

"It meant something when I found it."

"Is that why you did all this for me, Clyde? Because you found a picture?"

"And because Moonis asked me."

"You always did love Moonis. Even more than you loved me."

"That's not true."

"Yes, it is. It's the thing I always liked best about you. It's funny, if an old boyfriend was going to charge in and save the day, I thought the only one who could actually find me was Bradley."

"That lying twerp? Fat chance that."

She stopped dressing and turned to face Clyde's back. "What do you mean?"

"You don't know?"

"I don't know anything."

"He made a deal. Brad became Raden's new boy in Chicago, taking a piece of all the berry, weed, and horse sold there, while Raden got you. He sold you, Cecily. That's why you're here."

Cecily stood stock-still, taking it all in. It made no sense; it made total sense. It was a complete violation; it was perfectly in keeping with everything they had gone through together. If true, then Bradley was a vile piece of shit; of course it was true, because Bradley had always, in his way, been a vile piece of shit.

"He's a Ventura District slick," said Clyde. "How could you have expected anything else?"

"You're right," she said, anger overtaking her now, anger at herself more than anything else, for all she had wanted, all she had trusted, all the mistakes she had made. She'd never realized before how much she hated money—not just her lack of it, or that others had so much more than her family ever had, or even the way the system doled it out. No, what she hated was the very fact of it. "How could I have expected anything else?"

"You ready?"

"I'm getting there." She quickly buttoned her shirt and grabbed a pair of pants. "What are we waiting for?"

"We'll know it when we hear it. If things work out right, everyone will be charging up to the street while we slip across the bridge over the river. This whole thing will be easy as peach pie."

"There are guards on the bridge."

"There were. Finish dressing and listen closely. Whatever's coming, it might not be that loud."

Wrong.

***

It rolled through the camp like the wrath of God, a thunderous crash that cracked the night and lit the heavens and shook the earth and hurled tin can and motorbike to the ground, along with Cecily, who had been standing on one leg as she slipped into her pants. From the mud floor, Cecily looked up at Clyde, who had turned now to face her, a hand out to keep her calm and quiet.

"Wait," he mouthed.

On the ground, she stayed silent as she finished with the pants, slipped on a pair of socks and then her soft boots. The camp was wild with shouts and shots fired and engines roaring to life. All about were the sounds of men charging away from the tents, toward the explosions. She understood now why Clyde had clocked Culbert. While everyone was running to the fight, Culbert would have been running to her.

"Wait," mouthed Clyde.

She stood and grabbed some stuff she might need—shampoos, shirts, socks—stuffed them in her rucksack and turned to Clyde.

He shook his head. She dropped the bag. "Wait," he mouthed.

She stood now, motionless and ready as the calls and shouts drifted away, as the footsteps receded, as the space around the tent grew quiet while the commotion continued moving into the distance.

"Okay," he said softly.

She came over and grabbed his arm. It felt so solid; he felt so solid. She was less afraid than she should have been, and why not? She had a football hero leading her on.

"Follow," he said.

He stepped to the slit at the rear of the tent, stooped down, pulled out his gun, poked out his head from the tent, looking left and right, and then darted through, without hesitation, disappearing from tent and sight. The speed of it frightened her, and she felt abandoned until his hand poked back through the slit. She stooped down herself, took hold of the hand, and let Clyde Sparrow, of all people, pull her toward her freedom.

***

The space between tents was narrow and empty, a pathway of dirt and cigarette butts and the lingering presence of men suddenly gone. Clyde scurried quickly away from the noise and the burning on the horizon, using the tents to shield them from the great mass of men scrambling toward the explosion.

Cecily stayed close to Clyde, her hand touching his back to let him know she was there, feeling the exhilaration of flight. She remembered her race down the deserted roads of the D-Lands on Kyrk's cycle, the fear and terror that vibrated her bones. She felt calmer now, more assured of the ultimate success of her escape; she could already see herself riding away on a fine brown horse between Clyde and Moonis, galloping toward a new life. She wasn't sure what it would be, but it would be something different, something clean.

She was feeling the bright lift of possibility when, from the slit of a doorway on the last tent on the row, the butt of a rifle shot out and slammed Clyde Sparrow in the jaw, dropping him like a sack of hurt.

Before she could respond, before she could kneel to help or turn to run, before she could do anything other than stare with mouth open and throat silent, she was grabbed from behind by a pincer of steel that dug deeply into her waist. When she fought to get free, her arms were grabbed and she could feel a beard scratch at her neck as a vile waft of rotting breath washed across her face.

"Calm down, girl," she heard in a voice she recognized. Bear Claw. It was useless to resist, she wasn't strong enough to resist, but still she grabbed at Bear Claw's arms and shouted out curses and yelped in bald frustration, until a sight silenced her cold.

She narrowed her eyes and stared out in hate as three men stepped out of the tent. One of them, a slight man in black pants and a leather jacket, stooped down over the fallen body of Clyde Sparrow, and slapped at his face, slapslap, slap. Clyde could barely open his eyes.

"I thought that was you I saw sneaking into the camp in a Kimmler vest," said Bradley Illingworth. "I knew you were stupid, but I just thought you were your basic guaranteed schoolboy stupid, not breathtakingly, epically stupid."

Bradley looked up at Cecily, still struggling against her captor, cursing wildly. "Going somewhere, Cissy?" he said.

"You sold me, you bastard?" said Cecily.

"Yeah, well, welcome to the world. Shut her up," he said to Bear Claw. An instant later a filthy hand covered her face and muffled her curses. She tried to bite the hand, but Bare Claw had it cupped away from her teeth, as if he had done this to many girls many times before.

"Where is Moonis, Clyde?" said Bradley, continuing his interrogation. "Where is that long piece of black stupidity hiding?"

Clyde lifted his head as if to speak, and then he spit a glob of spit and blood into Bradley's face. Something white stuck for a moment on Bradley's cheek before falling to the ground and it took Cecily a moment to realize it was a tooth.

Bradley wiped his face with the back of his hand. "Guaranteed trash."

"You bet I am," said Clyde with a hoarse slur in his voice, "and I'm going to gut you like flounder."

"You know what time it is, Clyde? Time for you to lose more teeth."

Bradley stood, kicked Clyde in the jaw with his boot, and stepped over the writhing figure to get to Cecily.

"I missed you, darling," he said to her. "I missed the taste of you, the softness of your skin, the way you coughed blood on my neck. I don't know why it gave me a charge, but it did. You're looking healthier now, which cuts the charm."

He nodded and Bear Claw took his hand from her mouth.

"How could you?" said Cecily.

"Oh, Cissy, sweetheart, it wasn't much of a stretch. First time I spied you, you were selling yourself at Fosbury's. When I saw the reaction you pulled on the pole, I just followed suit."

"But to turn me over to an animal like Raden?"

"Oh, darling, you sweet thing, didn't he tell you? Raden doesn't need to buy his lovers, he just takes them. I didn't sell you to Raden, I sold you to Garth."

Click, snap.

48
GAMBIT DECLINED

By the time Clyde and Cecily appeared within the scope of Moonis's binoculars, Clyde was on the ground and Cecily was being straitjacketed from behind. Moonis was ready to fire away, make a move, get into the game, do something, do anything, but when he lifted his rifle, Digger put a cautioning hand on the long black barrel.

"Patience, boy," said Digger.

"We need to shoot someone."

"We need to wait. Right now all we'll do is get them killed and usselves discovered. Take a good look at the board with a calm in your heart."

This was the first time Moonis had seen his sister in years and the vision cut into him like a knife. She was so small in the grip of that beast with the red beard, so helpless, again the little girl who looked for Moonis to take care of her when their mother left. The very sight of her jabbed to life something fierce inside of him. And yet here was Digger, telling him to wait, to wait, to be patient and to wait.

Moonis took a deep breath, put down the gun, and lifted the binoculars. With the rifle, he could maybe take out the man holding Cecily, though Cecily might be hit as well. And he could maybe take out one of the men standing over Clyde before the others started firing back. But then Moonis and Digger would be in a gunfight while Clyde and Cecily, if they stayed alive, would still be under Raden's control.

"We got us a 'vantage here to keep," said Digger. "We'll have our moment, but the moment's not now. Patience, son."

It was hard advice to follow, but Digger was undoubtedly right. So Moonis simply watched as a man in black kicked Clyde in the face before stepping over him and talking to Cecily like they were old friends. He simply watched as Cecily lurched to lean over Clyde for a moment before the men dragged the two to the amphitheater. He simply watched as they lashed each of them to the two great lightning slashes rising from the stage like crosses in a revival church.

"When it's time to fight, we're going to do some fighting," said Moonis.

"Oh, yes," said Digger, "and killing, too. There's blood in the air, I can sniff it, and we're going to spill it happy."

***

The switchblade in Clyde's hand felt warm, alive, juiced with possibility and violence. The coaches always said he had plenty of grit. What couldn't you achieve with a blade of hot steel and a dose of grit?

When Cecily had rushed out of the lug's grip and bent over him and put a hand on his swelling cheek as he lay writhing on the ground, he was barely aware of her slipping something into his back pocket. But he was aware enough not to ask her about it as they yanked her away from him, and pulled him to his feet, and dragged them both to the amphitheater in the middle of the camp. They forced his hands behind one of the wooden slashes on the amphitheater's stage and bound them with rope, his arms locked straight and his shoulders screaming with pain.

"I thought over time you would come to accept my love and reciprocate on your own," said some pear-shaped priss in a white shirt, whose name was apparently Garth. This Garth spoke calmly to Cecily, who was bound to the other rising slash of wood. "That was the plan, the purpose of it all. I could have forced myself on you, but I chose the more honorable way."

"Why not just ask for a date?" said Cecily.

"Would you have said yes?"

"No."

"So I bought you, instead. But I decided, somewhat magnanimously, I must say, that our love would have to be reciprocal. I hoped, over time, the two of us would build a bond beneath the umbrella of your fear of Raden. I hoped, over time, you would see my innate quality and fall in love with me as I fell in love with you while you writhed on that pole. And I had good reason to hope. Bradley assured me you had a thing for Ventura boys. Wasn't my breeding up to your standards?"

"No," said Cecily.

"Your high standards are such a pity," said Garth.

"For you," said Cecily.

"Oh, and for you, too," said Garth. "Because I've given up on you, Cecily. You're not my problem anymore."

"Whose problem am I now?"

"Kimmler hasn't been happy about some of our new plans for the territory," said Garth. "I threw you into the bargain to gain his full cooperation."

"I'm not a commodity."

"Says the stripper."

"You make me want to puke."

"I think you'll want to do more than that before Kimmler is through with you."

As they had their back-and-forth, Clyde worked his bound hands until he could slip two fingers into his back pocket. Slowly he extracted the knife and flipped it up until the closed blade rested in his right palm. Now he felt the flat edge of the shank, the sharp edges of the guard, the rivets on the handle, the soft round button that would open the knife's brilliant possibilities.

Martha had done a bang-up job with the diversion, but even so things had gone as badly for Clyde and Cecily as could be imagined. Clyde had been a fool to rely on Moonis and the old man to cover their flight; the old man was as useless as a thrown rod, and when had Moonis ever been reliable? Yet the knife was a way out if he could spring it quietly and use it deftly. Cut the ropes, gut Brad, slice Garth's fat neck, grab Cecily and whisk her to freedom. All he needed was one more frightful sound to cover the snap of the springing blade. In the distance, even as Cecily and Garth had their back-and-forth, there was gunfire, but no explosion big enough or close enough to be of use.

"Could you both please just shut the hell up," he shouted out, finally, the exclamation covering the opening snap. "The last thing I want to hear before I die is your bullshit banter."

Garth turned his face to him slowly, a snake changing targets. "Who are you again?"

"He's Clyde," said Brad.

"Oh, yes, our Cecily mentioned you in one of our talks," said Garth. "You're the one who works in a diner. She said you were dim as a board, if I remember."

"Smart enough to have you pegged," said Clyde.

"And how do you peg me, Clyde?"

"The last kid picked for basketball," said Clyde. "The boy who brought his sister to the prom. A sad-sack loser with bad breath and calluses on his hand from pulling his pud."

Garth looked at Clyde with a blank stare, like he was contemplating Clyde's future, or lack of it. "She was right about you," he said finally. "You are dim. Shut him up."

Brad stepped over and slammed Clyde so hard in the stomach his body jackknifed around his bindings as his breath flew out of his mouth. As Clyde struggled to catch his wind, Bradley backhanded him across his already bludgeoned jaw and Clyde's whole body sagged into the ropes. In a moment where he felt nothing but the pain, thought about nothing but the pain, he caught himself sliding down the bolt and struggled to regain his footing.

The sound of something rattling on the wooden stage beneath him barely registered until he was standing once more and the fog in his head cleared and he realized with a start that he was no longer holding the knife.

"Oh my," said Garth, walking over and picking the open switchblade off the stage. "Now where did that come from?"

***

"Who is that?" said Moonis.

Through the glasses he could see a pack of Kimmler's soldiers walking through the amphitheater, led by a tall man in camouflage pants, gun holster slung low over his hip, bare chest beneath a leather vest, with long black hair and a face scarred by some ravaging attack of adolescent acne.

Digger took the binoculars, peered through them for a bit, handed them back to Moonis. "Kimmler," said Digger. "He breathes toads and spits fire and, saddest of all, he thinks he knows things."

Moonis watched as Kimmler strode onto the stage. He held himself erect, his arms were long, his wrists were hairy. There was about his movements something slow and assured. He spoke for a moment with the man in the white shirt who had picked up the knife that

Clyde dropped. Then he walked over to Clyde and leaned forward and started talking, talking, getting red-faced and angry as he talked. Clyde struggled a bit, but it didn't matter, Kimmler kept talking, talking, talking before he nodded to one of his men.

The man leaped onto the stage with a curled rope in his hand and slipped a noose around Clyde's neck, tightening it with a jerk that brought a scream from Clyde's mouth that could be heard across the river.

Then Kimmler turned to Cecily, still tied to the rising wooden slash. He caressed her face and then put his hand around her throat. With his other hand he lowered her lip, as if a dentist examining her teeth, and then, still holding her jaw, he took a bite of her cheek and pulled.

49
ARABIAN

They didn't have a chance to string Clyde up like they wanted, to prop him on a chair and swing the rope over the notched bar set across the two slashes and pull the noose taut so that he would be forced to grapple for balance on tiptoes.

They didn't have a chance to kick the chair from beneath his dancing, tiptoed feet and to laugh so hard the snot flew from their noses as he hung there, choking, his face reddening, blood pouring out his nose and eyes. (No quick snap of the knot on his neck for these riot hounds, since that was too merciful and quick for a proper belly laugh.)

They didn't have a chance to take Cecily right there on the stage and teach her all about the power and virility that is rightfully part of the white man's legacy. (This last bit Kimmler had shouted at Clyde in his angry singsong, his scarred face reddening with rage before he ordered the noose slung around Clyde's neck for betraying his people.)

They didn't have a chance to chant and sing and drink over Cecily's ruined body and then toss what was left of them both into a pit behind the stage and douse them with kerosene and burn them to ash, like they did with that young black couple they caught that time slipping down from Iowa looking for that Yeager's farm they had heard about and stumbling into the exact wrong place.

No, they didn't have a chance for any of that good clean Kimmler fun before it all went to hell. And it wasn't Moonis making a charge with Digger at his side that short-circuited the party. Instead, roaring down from the road came a pack of Raden's men led by a monster on a motorbike with fists like cudgels and a huge hairless head seemingly scarred by the death grips of the doomed. Clyde had never seen the man before, but he knew right away who it was—who else could it be?—and no matter how bad Clyde's situation at the present, with his hands bound behind him and a noose tight around his neck, he had no doubt it was about to get worse.

***

Raden rode his bike right up the steps and onto the stage, marking the wood and singeing the air with the twining scents of exhaust and burned rubber as he spun to a halt. He climbed off his bike, walked over to Cecily, stood facing her for a long moment. He was so big he had to hunch to look her straight in the eye.

"They came for her," said Kimmler. "That's what the explosion was all about."

Raden didn't respond. Instead he put one of those huge hands on the top of Cecily's head and turned her face this way and that, a doctor in the examining room. He stopped the twisting and held her face still as he stared at the blood leaking from the bite mark on her cheek. He took a buck knife out of his belt, the blade huge and shining, more sword than dagger. With one great swipe he slashed the rope that was binding Cecily's hands.

"They're still out there, trying to free their mongrel princess," said Kimmler. "She's a threat. We can't tolerate her presence here anymore, Raden."

"Tolerate?" said Raden.

"It's our camp, our rules," said Kimmler. "This was all worked out with Garth. We came to an agreement about—"

In the middle of Kimmler's explanation, with a simple movement, as if waving away a fly, Raden smashed Kimmler's face with the back of his fist. Raden's knuckles went through the bone of Kimmler's jaw like an ax through a rotted log. Blood and anguish both left Kimmler's mouth as he hurtled backward, landing with a bounce on the floor of the stage, his head smacking hard against the wooden boards, halting the screaming, though not the blood.

Within the utter, shocked silence that followed, Raden turned to Garth.

Garth started backing away, shaking his head, arms trembling defensively in front of him. "It wasn't like you think," he said, not realizing the switchblade in his hand was now pointing at Raden. "They had come to—"

Raden stepped forward and slashed upward with his knife, a quick, savage hack.

It looked for a moment like it was nothing but a threat, a warning to a subordinate who had gone too far, until Garth's hand, the one holding the blade, quivered in the air before tumbling to the stage, the switchblade still in its grip. Blood sprayed in gouts. Garth reeled away from Raden and fell to his knees, squealing like a dying pig as he clasped his remaining hand over the squirting stump.

"She wasn't yours to give," said Raden before turning toward the rear of the amphitheater, now filled with both his and Kimmler's men. He raised his arms, the red-smeared knife pointed like a warning to the heavens, and he howled ferociously, the bellow of a great alpha lion on the wide African plain.

At first only Raden's men responded, shouting wildly and shooting their guns into the air. Kimmler's men backed away in caution, in fear, in terror. Raden bellowed again, a war cry if ever one was heard in that barren place, and there was a moment where further savagery seemed inevitable, one army devouring another.

Until one of Kimmler's men pulled off his swastika vest and raised it into the air before throwing it onto the dirt of the amphitheater. And then another did the same, and a third, and a fifth, until all the Kimmler vests were on the ground and all the men were hollering responses to Raden's call.

On the stage behind Raden, Kimmler, jaw hanging loose and bloody, raised his torso off the wood and slid the gun from his holster, unsteadily waving it at Raden.

Cecily screamed an instant before Raden, without even turning, pulled a sawed-off shotgun from a sling behind his back and fired into Kimmler's chest.

Kimmler's gore-smeared torso slammed back onto the stage as if on a spring.

There was a moment of silence—a shocked tribute to a fallen leader—and then the wild cheers began, calls to madness, guns firing into the air like fireworks, hyena howls of exaltation. It was an orgy of hatred and bloodlust. It was the triumphant roar of two rampaging armies, now united under the singular brutality of a single man, thundering like a warning all across the D-Lands.

At least until the coming of the horses.

***

Moonis had Raden's head in his gun sight—not that he would have made the shot at that distance, with his whole body shaking in anger and despair—when the horses made their wild charge.

They burst from the corral as if chased by the devil's dog. They ran as if the world was on fire, charging saddleless and wild. Horses, horses, white, shining, silver steeds with their noses in flames. They shot through the camp, through the amphitheater, through the plundering armies of the D-Lands, flanks tight one to the next, bringing chaos and noise and confusion with the thunder of their hooves, leaping, kicking and sprinting, bringing down soldiers like sheaves of hay before a great white scythe. And in the rear of them, pushing the pack ever forward in their crazed sprint, were two riders on the bare backs of white stallions, grabbing fistfuls of mane to serve as reins—a red-haired firecracker with a voice like a banshee and a bare-chested demon with fire in his eyes, shouting to the heavens as he cracked his whip.

Moonis lowered his gun and gawked. It was the most sterling sight he had ever seen. Patti would have loved the anarchy of it.

"Look at that Ruby ride," said Digger. "She rides better than she sings, and she sings like truth. This is it, boy, are you ready?"

"I've been."

"You know what a trigger is, right?"

"Just do your part, old man."

"Count on that."

As the horses rushed through the amphitheater, Raden dashed off the stage to grab at the sprinting herd. Cecily fell upon Garth's severed hand and pried open the fingers to retrieve the blade. She leaped to her feet and began to saw at Clyde's bindings even as she pulled the noose from his neck. As she was cutting the ropes, Ruby and Zephyr ran their horses onto the stage, jumped down from the beasts' tall haunches, and used the animals as shields while Cecily finished her work.

Moonis watched as Ruby, Zephyr, and Cecily bounded together off the back of the stage and headed straight toward the river. They might have made it unnoticed if Clyde hadn't first grabbed the knife from Cecily, hurdled into the crowd, and stuck the blade snap into the chest of the man in the black pants who had punched him in the gut.

IV
THE DISINCORPORATED

50
FROM HELL

They rode as fast as the slivered moonlight allowed, dashing around dark seas of wild bush, picking their way among sparse trees in wide groves, galloping like ghosts through the high grasses of the prairie. Moonis had blown the bridge over the river with the pack of dynamite that Clyde had stuffed beneath the span, Zephyr and Ruby had scattered the horses from the corral and burned the barn with Kimmler's saddles and riding gear—the raiders had done all they could to slow down any overland pursuit, yet still in fear they barreled onward toward the farm.

Six riders with seven horses, they were headed to whatever home would still remain after all the cards were played.

Zephyr was in the lead, pushing his horse ever forward as the rest kicked heel into horse flank to keep up. He was blathering on in a manic rush of words and images, recounting for no one in particular the glorious interdimensional battle between right and evil through which he rode bareback like an ancient Norse god, powered by drugs and righteous purpose, cementing the legend of the wild-eyed man from Colorado.

"Oh, Gene, oh, Gene, you should have been there, boy . . . the way that tanker lit the night sky like an exhale of freedom . . . bang-zoom . . . the way those horses swarmed into the night . . . tearing at the sky . . . avengers of the old ways."

Martha rode just behind him, letting Zephyr's words thrill her heart with their truth and spin. She put herself in charge of the compass, reading their direction by starlight and moonlight. "Just a bit right, Zephyr. That's it, that's the way home."

Ruby followed the two of them, using the sweet rhythm of the horse to power the riotous blues song in her heart, leading the extra mount that might be needed if the punishing pace took any of the others down.

Clyde and Cecily rode side by side, old lovers, older friends, neither having any idea what they were doing atop a horse, just knowing enough to hold on tightly to the reins, to cluck with their tongues and kick with their heels when they started falling behind. Cecily was lost in the exhilarating rush to freedom, so full of gratitude and excitement and the love of her brother and his best friend that she sort of floated atop the charging steed, feeling truly free for the first time in months, years—ever, maybe. Clyde, on the other hand, was so sore of bone and chestnut it was a fight not to call out in agony with each downward jolt. He wouldn't sit for years once he got back to Chicago.

And lapping at the rear was Moonis Fell, sitting tall on his short horse, boots almost scraping the ground, his furry top hat tilted at a rakish angle as he snapped the reins to keep his mount moving, lost in a swirl of love and hope and melancholy. The love was for his sister, and his friend, and his new boon companions from Yeager's farm, and a plot of land on the wrong side of the river from which these last fruits were plucked. The hope was, surprisingly, for the future, where for the longest time he had never sited his hope before. But it was the melancholy that lay most heavily on his heart, bitter and pure it was, and its name was Digger.

***

As soon as Clyde knifed the man in black, with a howl and lunge that seemed more personal than tactical, and then headed for the bridge, the time had come for Moonis and Digger to play their parts in the great and bloody game.

But when Moonis had one of Raden's men in his sights, something rose to choke his breath and still his hand. Lodged in his throat was the sadness he had felt in the Moline prison cell when he confronted his slaying of the guard at the LCM. The sorrow caused him to hesitate on the trigger even as Digger started popping off with that rifle of his.

"Go on, son," Digger said between shots. "It's time to buckle up and get in the game."

Quick as that, with the kind urging of a man who had lost far more than he, and the image of Clyde's heroism still imprinted upon his memory, the hesitation lifted like a shade snapping up and around. He was no longer Moonis Fell, a pacifist soul looking to get along unnoticed beneath the surface of things. Instead he was that notorious freedom fighter He Killed a Man, capable of rising to a cause and fulfilling a purpose. And what cause or purpose was more righteous than his sister's freedom?

Quick as that, he fired, one two three. Quick as that, the chasers fell, one and three (he missed two, the son of a bitch). Quick as that, the battle was joined and the pursuers dived for cover and the tree Moonis and Digger huddled behind shivered and slivered with lead. Moonis was so busy patrolling the scene with his gun, aiming and firing to cover the mad sprint of Ruby and Zephyr and Cecily and Clyde, that he barely registered the "Oof" that came from beside him.

"You okay, old man?" he said.

William Lashner

"Keep shooting," said Digger, sheathed in gun smoke of his own devising. "They're almost through."

"I'll get the bridge," said Moonis.

"You do that."

"Cover me."

"I'm covering them, fool. Let me reload and then get on with it."

When the time was ripe, Moonis dived to his left, away from Digger's firing, and rolled heedlessly down the slope until he was hidden from the other side by the far bank of the river. A moment later Cecily and Ruby and Zephyr charged across.

"Up to the horses," ordered Moonis.

"Moonis," said Cecily. "Moonis."

"Go on up," shouted Moonis over Digger's firing. "Take her, Ruby."

As they scampered up the bank, Cecily fighting to gaze back upon her brother as she was pulled by Ruby up the slope, Moonis took out a lighter, set it aflame, waited for Clyde's footsteps to thunder across the wooden slats of the bridge. When they came, bounding and scampering, Moonis lit the fuse and then followed Clyde up the hill, pushing Clyde forward, up and over, sending Clyde off to the horses himself before he dived back to Digger and the tree.

He lifted his gun and took two shots that scattered dirt at the foot of the bridge. "We'll keep firing until the bridge blows," said Moonis, "and then we'll dash to the horses."

"You go first," said Digger. "I'll keep covering you."

"No need, we'll be gone by the time they swim across the water."

"I'll stay and keep you safe."

"Digger?" Moonis put down his rifle and reached over to the old man, his hand slicked with blood. "Digger."

"I'll just keep shooting while you slip on out."

"I'll help you up. I'll fix you."

Digger shot at one of Raden's soldiers trying to make it over the bridge. The man spun and rolled.

396

"Go on now," said Digger. "I'd rather stay here and cover you than bleed to death on one of them foul horses."

"I can't leave you."

"Oh, yes, you can. And you will. You got things to do, boy." Bam. "Worlds to save." Bam.

"What can I save if I can't save you?"

"You done saved me already." Bam bam. "Go on. Do what you need to do in this world."

"I need to take you with me."

"You have to find your own purpose, son. My purpose is to protect you. How'd I do?"

"Brilliantly."

"That's the truth of it. Now leave me your gun and go. And if you see my boy, Tyrone, tell him I love him."

"He knows."

Moonis would never be certain if Digger heard those last words because just that instant the wooden bridge across the river blew to splintering smithereens. The sound of the explosion rushed into Moonis's ears in a wave of pain, and the world went quiet with just the ringing of a sweet bell to signify everything that was, now or forever, from the birth of it all.

Digger motioned him away. "Go on, go on," his lips said even as all Moonis could hear was the ringing of that bell, before the old man turned back to firing.

And Moonis went. He left his gun by the old man's side and scrabbled like mad away from the covering tree and up the bank, the dirt puffing around him as he climbed. At the rim, before rushing headlong toward the horses, leaping onto his animal and following the others away, away, he took a final look down. Digger sagged against the tree even as he fired—ring ring—keeping the bastards at bay—ring ring—giving the rest of the party time to escape—ring ring—saving the day like he always said he would. And every time the old man pulled the trigger and let off a little explosion and sent a shard of hot lead pouring over the river into the guts of the enemy camp, it was as if he were firing off another piece of himself, and each ounce was filled with love and scornful defiance.

***

It was almost daybreak when they reached the lantern left out for them by the woman with the tumorous face. They had been heading toward it for the last half hour or so. A barrel of water was set out by the lantern, and a sack of oats. They slipped the bits from the horses and let them feed and water before hobbling them and turning them loose to graze and take a blow. With the sun they could make far better progress and they hoped to cross the two rivers and reach the farm by nightfall. Whether that would be soon enough, only time would tell, which, as Zephyr reminded them, was the very nature of the beast.

While the horses rested in the middle of a field of tall grass, Clyde lay on his back. Moonis was reuniting with his sister. Martha and Zephyr and Ruby were off with the horses, clowning and singing, spirits high, not wanting yet to think about the coming deluge. Clyde, as usual, was alone. His legs were bent to keep his sore buttocks from contacting anything but air, his eyes were closed to the rising brightness of the sun, a long blade gone to seed sprouted from his lips as his tongue reflexively rooted around the newfound gap in his teeth.

He was a stranger in the strangest of lands. This wild prairie life of hard saddles and swollen chestnuts and subsistence farming, of dirty water and naked children with dark eyes, this life of violence and fear and cannibals was not for him. He missed the hum of the city, the crackle of traffic, the canned laughter of the television, the rigid rules where everyone knew what was what. He felt outside of things in this desolation and wanted back in.

He even felt outside this group of riders. Cecily was a failed dream, Martha and Zephyr were as foreign to him as Frenchmen, and though he thought he understood Ruby, at heart she was just another freak who seemed to have finally rambled into her place in the world. His only true connection was with Moonis—his oldest friend, Moonis— though Moonis had changed so much, whether in the LCM or in the few days of their chase, as to be almost unrecognizable. There was a sincerity to him now that put an edge to Clyde's teeth.

"It was all you, you know."

Clyde opened one eye and saw Moonis, holding his ridiculous hat, standing over him.

"Everything good we ever did," said Clyde, "we did together."

"Not football."

"Maybe not math class, either, but the rest."

Moonis's laughter was deep and familiar as he sat down beside Clyde. Clyde pushed his torso from the ground so that the old friends were sitting now side by side, Moonis's legs crossed, Clyde's legs bent enough to keep his sore parts aloft. Cecily had gone over to talk with the others. They made a merry crew, the four of them.

"She looks good, doesn't she?" said Moonis.

"She always did."

"She said as soon as she saw you, she felt safe."

"The scar she'll carry on her cheek will be proof of how wrong she was. I'm sorry about the old man."

"So am I."

"He didn't like me much," said Clyde.

"He didn't trust you one inch."

"If I had known the old goat was such a good judge of character, I might have been friendlier. Raden's already on his way."

"I know it."

"As soon as we get back, we've got to load Patti and Lydia and anyone else we can fit into the van and get going. None of what we went through does us any good if he kills us all."

"And so we end up where we started."

"That's the idea," said Clyde. "A guaranteed job, a place to hang our hats, three squares and enough left over for a date and a drink or two at Tunney's."

"And that's the best we can ask for?"

"You ask for more, you end up with a pickax in your hand and a weight around your ankle. That's the way of it, Moonis."

"That's their way."

"Our way, too. It's our country, our land, our city, our way. It beats dying like a poisoned dog out here. And you never know, if I hustle hard, maybe I can save up enough after a couple years to buy my own diner."

"Big dreams."

"Yeah, well, after six years, even in my dreams I dream about cutlery."

"I thought you were sick of flipping burgers."

"A few days in the D-Lands cured the hell out of me."

"I'm staying on this side of the line."

"There are cannibals, Moonis."

"Sure there are, but I like how Martha said people become their natural selves here. That sounds right. That sounds worth staying for."

"And if their natural selves are cannibals?"

"All the better. It's not as if they don't have flesh-eaters on the other side, too. Here at least they're raw and true. I can live with that. And I like the farm."

"With Raden on our asses it's a death trap with kale, is what it is."

"Kale?"

"I don't get it either."

"I think I can find a future on the farm."

"Six feet under, is all." Clyde looked at his friend and for a moment he felt sad for him. If his only hope was a future in some fly-ridden D-Land manure pit with a madman out to kill him, he didn't have much of a future at that. He had been such a promising kid, the most promising of them all, and now Clyde wouldn't trade places with him for all the nickels in the world.

"What's with the hat?" said Clyde.

"You don't like it?"

"It makes you look like a drunken gravedigger who fell into a pot of paint."

"Exactly."

At that moment one of the horses reared its head. Zephyr pulled a rifle from a saddle as the entire party turned anxiously toward the sound of hooves on the prairie.

***

"I never expected you fools to make it back," said the woman with the marks and tumors on her face. She was sitting on a horse with one young child on the saddle in front of her. The two older children sat together on a second horse. The saddlebags were packed full. The children had the same expressionless faces as before, the same flat black eyes.

"We're sorry to disappoint you," said Moonis, standing now.

She surveyed the group of them. "Where's the old man?"

"He didn't make it," said Moonis.

"I'm sorry about that. But I see you got your sister back."

"Yes, ma'am."

"Isn't that something. Isn't that some damn thing. No one's gotten nothing back from them in all the time I been over the line. I suppose you didn't slip in quiet-like."

"No, ma'am."

"Didn't think so. I expect you understand what you've done. They'll be sweeping through after you now, a pack of them, and they won't leave anything standing."

"They know where we're going, they don't need to follow."

"It don't matter," said the woman. "It's not about you. It's about keeping the territory under their fat thumbs. They'll follow your trail like Sherman followed the road to the sea. Only thing I got left to do in this world is keep my children alive. We have no choice but to leave. You headed someplace safe?"

"Hardly," said Moonis.

"Don't matter," said the woman. "If you'll be there, it'll be safer than any other place we might find. You mind if we tag along? We can show you the best route to cross the river."

Moonis tilted his head and gave it a thought. "We'd be honored," he said, his smile suddenly as wide and genuine as the sky.

"So long as you littles can keep up," said Zephyr.

"Oh, we can keep up all right," said one of the children. "You'll be hard-pressed to swallow all our dust."

***

These were not the only refugees to join the group along the route back to the farm. Others came: farmers, trappers, old men and young families, on horseback or in wagons, the scabrous, the unwashed, the natterers and the silent. From neat farms and broken-down homesteads and untended groves deep within the D-Lands they came. With money or foodstuffs or nothing but their hunger they came. The word had been passed the way the word usually is passed, quickly, breathlessly, mixed with spurts of misinformation, word that Raden was coming with guns and torches to spread devastation across the land, and out of a fear that was abject and cold they came.

And Moonis Fell welcomed the new arrivals, one and all. He could promise no safety, he told them, but there would be food at the farm, and from there, all would be free to find their own routes to shelter. It wasn't much he was offering, but he was offering something, and there were others on the journey to give protection and solace, which was also something, and all of it was enough to keep them following. Zephyr was still leading, but he was forced to slow his pace to keep the caravan together. By the time they reached the remaining river before the farm they were forty-three in all.

They all worked together to get the wagons to the far side of that final river. In the path over, they found there was one spot where the wagons got stuck and each had to be lifted, seven on a side, before the horses could pull them the rest of the way across.

Because of the delay at the river, dusk came sooner than they expected and night fell before they reached the farm. Through the darkness they continued, moving forward toward a desperately needed respite.

"Smell that?" said Martha.

"I do," said Moonis, taking a deep breath of the sharp medicinal fragrance of the berry still in the field, its very existence now a symbol of resistance.

"We're home," she said.

The horses of the lead pack gained speed along the road through the berry, racing now for their barn. Up the hill and then down, through the black of the orchards they led the others. Martha stopped every now and then and lit a series of matches so that the rest of the caravan would know the way.

When they left the shelter of the orchard, they expected to see darkness on the other side, a farm quiet, deserted, a farm emptied by fear. What they saw instead chilled their blood.

Laid out before them was a vast array of campfires, the fires of a great army bivouacking through the night, waiting—waiting for them.

51
BIVOUAC

"Miss Martha? Is that you?"

The voice came from among the trees, familiar and soft and rounded, a lifeline out of the despair that had wrapped around Martha's heart at the sight of how late they were, how delusional had been her dreams of escape from the ravages of Raden.

"Enrique?" she said into the blackness, into the nothing.

Enrique suddenly appeared on the road, his face shining in the moonlight. "We've been waiting for you, Miss Martha."

"Please don't call me that."

"I won't, Miss Martha."

She jumped down from her horse and gave him a long-lost hug, tight and desperate. "Enrique, damn, I'm so glad to see you." Then she walked with him away from the others and looked toward the fires spread across the farm like a plague. "When did they arrive?"

"The last couple of days," said Enrique. "At first it was a trickle, but by today it was a flood."

"But we only hit their camp last night."

"Oh, no, you've got the wrong idea. After you left, instead of us leaving, too, I sent out word of our situation on the radio. And then they came."

"Who came, Enrique?"

"Everyone."

"They're not Raden's people?"

"They came from the north, the south, the west. Even from over the line. They're here to help us fight."

"Fight?"

"We're going to make a stand, Miss Martha, like you said. We're going to save the farm."

"We can't fight Raden, we talked about this. He'll kill us all, children included."

"You said all we needed was someone to teach us how. But now we have someone. And the people all came. And they're here to fight with us, to fight Raden and win back the D-Lands. We're making a stand, and the General is showing us how."

"The General?"

"It is going to be something, yes, it is, Miss Martha. It is going to be glorious."

Glorious. The word hit her like a blade in the chest, deflating whatever hope Enrique had poured into her soul. Glorious? Pickett's Charge was glorious. The ride of the Light Brigade was covered with glory. Glorious is what you are when you raise the flag and rush to your doom, a construct devised by old men to convince young men to die.

"We picked up some stragglers on the way home," she said. "Take care of their horses, find them food and a place to sleep. Zephyr and Ruby will help you. The rest of us will take our horses to the barn ourselves."

"I'll get right on it."

"Thank you, Enrique."

"It's something, isn't it, Miss Martha? It's like the whole world is coming to our little farm."

"The whole world is sure coming to something," said Martha.

***

They rode slowly through the fields, Martha, with Moonis and Cecily and Clyde. The air was flush with wood smoke and expectancy. There were scores of blazes, and the light of each of the fires illuminated a different community that had been stirred by Enrique's call over the ham radio, or by a neighbor's urging, to come to the farm and join the fight. The glorious fight. Martha would never understand the sheer enticing beauty of imminent obliteration. The riders detoured to visit each of the groups.

"Anything we can get you folks?" said Moonis to the families, mostly hardscrabble farmers in worn black shoes. The men were thin, wiry, not suited to the martial arts. Kids sat in their parents' laps. "Anything you need?"

"A clear night so we can sleep through to morning," said a man with a long jaw. "You've given us food enough, but it took hours to get here, and then the General had us drilling for hours more. Even the women and children, for as long as they could take it. We could use some rest."

"We appreciate your being here," said Martha.

"We been under Raden's yoke long enough. We figured we're over here for the freedom in the first place. It's time to fight for our liberty and taste its sweetness."

Martha smiled at the man and looked at a young boy sleeping with his head on his father's leg. What would freedom taste like for him?

***

Around another fire Martha could see scores of women with their hair up in knots and bandanas over their mouths. They bustled around a pack of children and a fat old man sitting propped up with pillows in a wheelbarrow, his gray hair sprouting wildly, one leg fitted with wooden braces and resting on an overturned barrel. Martha stopped her horse beside the man.

"Birkenhead," she said, as if chewing a foul piece of gristle from one of his pigs that she had roasted just a few days before. "You look worse for wear."

"You don't look so fresh yourself. You got what you were going for?"

"Yes, we did," she said. "I suppose you're here for the fight like the rest of them."

"Oh, I would love nothing better than to get into the fray, Martha, you know that. But I can't do much with my leg like this. I think Raden sensed something was up and wanted me out of the way. My wives and children, however, will pitch in. The General was showing them how best to be of use. Some of the women had never fired a rifle before—at our place we leave birthing to the women and shooting to the men, like God intended—but I guess when things get like they are, it's all hands on deck. And I can tell you from hard experience, my wives are ornery enough to do some damage."

The women twittered, their bandanas fluttering like chained butterflies.

"Raden has become more than we can bear," continued Birkenhead. "Anything we can do to defeat that beast is worth the trouble. He's what happened to my leg, and he ruined my berry and killed my pigs to boot."

"They were delicious," said Moonis with a wide smile.

"Do I know you?"

"That's Moonis," said Martha.

"Oh, I heard about you," said Birkenhead. "You burned his camp. You started this to get hold of your sister. I suppose that's her. Weren't you at our camp when Raden came through?"

"Yes, I was," said Cecily.

"So you saw it all."

"Yes, I did."

"As far as I can figure, everything happened because of you and your brother. Now answer me this, are you two going to finish it?"

"We'll try," said Moonis.

"God doesn't care about the trying, he cares about the doing. I just wish the General would start listening to my advice. Martha, you tell the General I need to be heeded. The barricade is weak, and the rest of these farmers are not up to snuff. You should put me in charge, Martha. I should be leading this crew into the battle."

"From what I can see," said Martha, "you'll have a hard enough time leading your prick to the outhouse."

***

"It seems like a different place than I remember," said Martha as they continued their slow ride through the fields. "A foreign land populated by strangers."

"I suppose everyone's a stranger at one point," said Moonis.

"And who the hell is this General?" said Clyde. "Some Green Beret who showed up with his little French hat and started barking orders? Why is everyone suddenly listening to the likes of him?"

"Everyone's looking for a hero," said Moonis. "That's why we listen to you, Clyde."

"If you listened to me, we'd be on our way home by now."

"We are," said Moonis.

At one of the fires, a pack of wild dogs milled uneasily around a group of barely dressed folk, themselves nearly feral, tearing into pieces of raw meat with their teeth. The crew of humans looked up with red-tinged eyes, hard to distinguish in the firelight from the eyes of the dogs.

The riders led their horses carefully around.

At another fire, a troop of mimes put on a show, dancing like fools, pretending to laugh in utter silence, while someone played a flute. As the riders made their way past, seeing the faces of the watching children lit by the fire, lit with joy, they could hear in the distance the sound of two acoustic guitars, one playing off the other, while people clapped and sang along. They headed the horses toward the fire with the music. As they grew closer, a voice called out.

"Why, look who it is. He Killed a Man."

"And he's wearing my hat," said another voice.

Moonis let out a bark of laughter before jumping off his horse. A woman with a blanket over her shoulders rushed up to him, grabbing him tightly. Long legs, long blonde hair, wearing a beaded headband beneath the blanket and nothing else.

"Moonis, we missed you," she said before kissing him fully and well. Martha watched with something rising inside her, not jealousy so much as some unwelcome longing—to be that free, that wild, and maybe walking around naked and kissing Moonis like that herself. She shook the emotion from her head as Moonis and the woman separated.

"Nice headband," said Moonis.

"That's the 'Barely' part," the woman said proudly.

Soon Moonis was surrounded by a bunch of refugees in various modes of freaky dress, although all the men were wearing the same red-and-white-striped shirt that Clyde had worn when he'd first arrived at the farm. The sight made her turn and give Clyde an eye.

He shrugged.

"Martha and Cecily," said Moonis, "these are my jailhouse friends. They helped me and Clyde escape the dark clutches of the Moline Police Department. This is Barely Dressed. That there is Occasionally

Committed, and Somewhat Spiritual, and Always Tripping, and Counting Error, and here is my good friend Big Words. Guys, this here is Martha."

"Just Martha?" said Big Words, the slightly balding oldest of the crew, with a knowing smile. "Not Strapping Tall, not Earth Mama, not Horsey Girl, not Big Black Boots, not Whip Me Good?"

"Just Martha," said Martha, "though give me a whip and I would."

"And you guys know Clyde," said Moonis.

"Hey, Clyde," said Barely Dressed.

"Barely," said Clyde, his mouth twisted as if he were swallowing a belch.

"And this here," said Moonis, "is my sister, Cecily."

"You got her back," said Big Words. "Like you said you would. Now that is something to celebrate. We heard all about you, Sister Cecily, but we didn't know you were a nun."

"Thank you for taking care of my brother," said Cecily.

"Did I ever see you dance?"

"Did you?" said Cecily.

"Probably not," said Big Words. "A dancing nun I would have remembered."

"What the hell are you tricksters doing here?" said Moonis.

"We're here for the fight," said Always Tripping, tall with a frizzle of long hair that hid most of his face. "Jarvis passed the word that you needed help."

"Jarvis?" said Moonis. "Is that slime mold here?"

"He got us all over the river," said Big Words. "He commandeered the ferry to do it. He said we had to help our brother Moonis shake up the system."

"I had enough of his help. He almost helped me into a noose."

A woman stepped toward them, lovely as the wind, with long brown hair and a black velvet band tied around her neck. She gave

Moonis a smile full of knowing. "He says he feels bad about that," she said.

"Hello, Trout," said Moonis.

"How do you know Trout?" said Always Tripping, possessively dropping an arm around her neck as he looked at Moonis, then at the girl, then back at Moonis.

"We meditated together," said Trout. "Jarvis brought the whole circus with him, and a film crew, too."

"He's going to make a show of it," said Counting Error, a serious young man with tortoiseshell glasses. "And then sell it in theaters, sell out, make himself rich as balls in Hollywood, smoke high-grade hash and screw starlets."

"He's been looking for the opportunity to sell out all along," said Big Words, "and he thinks this is it."

"If selling out means hash and starlets," said Somewhat Spiritual, tall and splendiferously dressed, with a hat as wild as Moonis's, "count me in."

"You got a new topper," said Moonis.

"That one there fit you too well. I figured I was never getting it back."

"What about my suit?" said Clyde.

"Sorry, man," said Occasionally Committed, with sleepy, unfocused eyes. "I traded it for a hammer."

"Why a hammer?" said Clyde.

"It was a good hammer. I was thinking how much I could do if I only had a hammer."

"Then where's my hammer?" said Clyde.

"I traded it for some ludes. You want one, man?"

"I'd rather have the suit."

"Not after Occasionally wore it," said Big Words. "That thing will smell even after they burn it."

"So Moonis, man, you ready for the fight?" said Always Tripping. "It's going to be a hell of a fight, man. The General says it will be a ball-breaker. They tried to give me a gun, and it harshed my high, so I'm doing artillery instead."

"We have artillery?" said Martha.

"Glass bottles, kerosene, and a rag. Whoosh. A Murgatroyd cocktail."

"Molotov," said Clyde.

"Murgatroyd, man. That's my civilian name. Henry Murgatroyd. The General says I'm going be a thunderclap of righteousness. I like the sound of that."

"We're looking for the General right now," said Martha.

"Go to the barricade, man, at the beginning of the road. The General's always there, building it up higher and higher. It's a work of art, man. Duchamp on speed. The General is something, man.

"Ferocious?" said Moonis.

"Demented."

"That might work."

52
THE BARRICADE

They had raised the barricade with the very bones of the farm: doors torn off their hinges, huge black tractor wheels, rusted metal pipes, bureaus and couches from the big house, hoes with wooden shafts, bed frames from the dormitory, a broken-down piano, shattered window frames, tables, chairs, a rusted red combine (barely working), harvest crates and ladders of various sizes, and the neck of a busted electric guitar reaching to the stars. It was lit by torches and buttressed by great trunks of fallen trees, and it stretched across the road and into the woods on either side with piles of stones to protect the defenders, and loose loops of barbed wire woven through the sturdy trunks to keep the marauders at bay. And smack in the middle of the barricade, serving as its keystone, surrounded and topped by the great heaving mass of stuff that reached ten, twelve, fifteen feet high and higher, was the Every Ship, parked sideways, its swirl of color adding the crowning touch of insanity to the whole manic assembly.

"What the hell," shouted Clyde upon seeing the Every Ship immobilized among the junk. "That van's my route out of this asylum." He had walked from the barn with Moonis, Martha, and Cecily to find the General, and found only this great amalgamation of crap surrounding his ride.

"That little bus was the first piece," said one of a group of farmers milling behind the thing with rifles and tin-pot helmets, a ragged army of Johnny Appleseeds. "The General put it on the road just that way. Everything was built around it."

"It's beautiful," said Martha, her voice wide with awe.

"A snarl of defiance in the very face of fate," said Moonis.

"It makes me want to cheer," said Cecily.

"It makes me want to puke," said Clyde. "How the hell are we supposed to get home now?"

"Horses?" said Moonis.

"Screw that," said Clyde. "My chestnuts are already the size of grapefruits. I'm taking our van. Where the hell is that General asshole?"

"Checking out the other side of the barricade," said the farmer.

"How do you get to the other side?" said Moonis.

"There's only one way," said the man, and just as he said it the front door of the van opened and out scooted a man with a movie camera and another man with a microphone on a boom, and a tape deck hanging from his neck. The men immediately took up positions filming the barricade as two farmers with rifles emerged from the van and then a longhair with tie-dyed pants and a jaw like a rock.

"Moonis," said the bushy-haired freak, rushing over and giving Moonis a great hug, all captured by the camera, even as Moonis moved not a whit to reciprocate. "Brother Moonis, you made it. The whole circus has been waiting for you, and now here you are."

"Screw you, Jarvis," said Moonis.

Jarvis stepped back as if he'd been slugged. "Oh man, we don't have time anymore for timeworn grudges. My jaw's still sore from your elbow, but you don't see me griping, even considering the spot you put me in."

"The spot I put you in?"

"The pressure I was under, oh, Brother Moonis, you wouldn't believe it. It wasn't easy to guide you to the police instead of the Guard. Trust me, you would never have gotten away from the Guard. But enough of the past. The past is demolished by every passing second. We've got a future to pull from the fire, and the only way to do it is to let those old bygones be. It was all for the cause, man."

"Whose cause?"

"This cause. Your cause. Our cause. There's only one cause, man. Li-ber-ty. Everything else is a distraction. Well, everything except sex. Liberty and sex, now that's a platform I can get behind."

"So you're the General?" said Moonis.

"Me? Hell no. I'm a showman, a dancer, a prancing fool out to change the world. I might be a ringmaster under the big top, but I'm no general. Hey there, Cinnamon, you're looking nimble."

"Cecily," said Cecily.

"Good, great. Cecily it is. Must have been a hell of a rescue. If we could have had that on film, man, it would have been a rousing introduction to the epic battle to come. But we'll have enough as it is—the crazed attackers, the brave defenders, the war for the soul of an abandoned land. We're going to create something new here, something that's going to attack the Establishment like a virus. We're going to change the world, Moonis, you and me."

"And Martha," said Moonis.

"I assumed that was Martha," said Jarvis, turning his high beam of a smile right at her. "You're a legend among these people."

"And this," said Moonis, "is Clyde."

"Clyde?"

"No need to worry your freaky ass about me," said Clyde. "I'm good as gone, as soon as I see that damn General and get my van back."

"Your van?"

"Well, maybe Patti's van—she's the one who stole it—but when I get her out of that sickbed, she's leaving with me, along with Cecily and Lydia and Gloria and anyone else who wants to get away from this manure pit."

"We're not going anywhere."

They all looked up, and there, climbing out of the door of the van, was Gloria. Once fully out, she stood with her legs apart, at ease with herself, looking ornery and sharp in army fatigues and a green beret. First, the motorcycle babe stripper outfit, then the farm dress, now the army fatigues. She was like a chameleon, this Gloria, and with each outfit she seemed to be taking possession of a more independent part of her soul. And somehow, against all odds, she looked sexier with each incarnation.

"Who's 'we'?" said Clyde.

"Me," said Gloria.

"And me," said someone else struggling to get through the van. She was wearing black pants, and a man's white shirt over the bandages on her neck, and her long black hair streamed over her shoulders. As soon as Patti appeared, the farmers with their guns all saluted and it became clear to Clyde, after some confused blinking, that the General had arrived.

"I'd been wondering when you lollygaggers would show," said the General. "And you brought Cecily back. Well done."

***

"What do you mean you're staying?" said Clyde.

They stood apart from the rest to sort it out, their faces lit bright by one of the torches, Moonis and Clyde and Cecily and Patti and Gloria, who seemed now to be tethered to Patti by some powerful, invisible cord.

"Of course I'm staying," said Patti. "I'm the General."

"Come on, Pats. To these yokels you may be a general, but to a general you're no general."

"I was in the army."

"You were in the motor pool. How many damn jeeps did you crash?"

"Action is action," said Patti. "In all the time you've known me, have I ever ducked a fight?"

"This isn't our fight."

"It is now. What do you think of the barricade?"

"I think it's magnificent," said Cecily.

"I was going for something that would make you want to stand up and salute," said Patti. "Something Ruby could sing a song about."

"'All Along the Barricade,'" said Moonis.

"And you had to put our van in the middle of it?" said Clyde.

"The van makes it, don't you think?" said Patti.

"It's the cherry on top of the sundae," said Moonis.

"The spit on top of the burger," said Patti.

"Exactly," said Moonis.

"We came out here to rescue Cecily," said Clyde. "Not to get massacred. We've succeeded beyond any reasonable hope. Now let's all get her out of here alive."

"I'm staying, too," said Cecily.

"No, stop," said Clyde.

"I'm not leaving my brother."

"Talk to them, Moonis," said Clyde.

"What do you want me to say?"

"Tell them that maybe you have no choice, with the mess you've made of everything, but that they shouldn't throw their lives away for nothing. Tell them."

"You just did," said Moonis.

"What do I got back there, Clyde?" said Patti. "Tell me how wonderful my life was. Tell me how they won't put a weight on my ankle

417

for boosting that car. Tell me how I won't be in hock to Hooper for the rest of my stinking life. Here I'm somebody, here I get listened to. Back there I was nothing."

"Back there you were Patti. Good old Patti. Always-around-for-a-laugh Patti. Sweet screwed-up Patti."

"To hell with that Patti."

"Raden's going to kill you."

"There's always someone after our blood."

"Cecily, you're smart enough to see it."

Cecily stared for a moment at Clyde and then looked away as her eyes began to glisten in the torchlight. "You came out here, the three of you, to find me. You don't understand what that means to me, how full my heart is." She grabbed hold of Moonis's arm. "My brother came to rescue me. And Clyde . . . Clyde, you saved my life. But going against Raden, rescuing me from his clutches, there were always going to be consequences. These people are paying the price for my redemption. I can't run from them. I know you understand."

"I understand a death wish, is what I understand. Gloria?"

"I'm staying with Patricia."

"Krist, it's a sickness."

"Stay with us, Clyde," said Patti. "Fight with us. We need someone who knows how to box an ear better than he knows how to shuck one."

"We need a hero," said Moonis, "and you're the closest we've got."

"I'm a burger-flipper," said Clyde. "A milk-shaker, a French-fryer."

"It's the D-Lands, man," said Patti. "You can be anything you want out here."

"Except alive," said Clyde, even as he felt the tug of temptation from their entreaties.

So here it was, the chance he maybe had been waiting for, the chance we maybe all wait for. To give ourselves over to a cause greater than ourselves with our best friends and the love of our life. To leave everything in a blaze of violent glory, to reject everything but them, to burn down the whole of the world for them, to die while embraced in their overwhelming love.

And he might have succumbed, too, if at that very moment the distant sound of motorcycles hadn't broken through the night quiet of the barricade. Raden's army drawing close. The sound lifted Patti's chin and spun Cecily around and brought Clyde back to himself. He wasn't a hero, and he sure as hell wasn't a sap for anyone else's cause. He was a man rooted in his limitations like every man, a man with one overriding duty.

"Where's the cycle we picked up at Raden's camp?" said Clyde.

"By the house," said Patti.

"I'm getting the hell out of Dodge and no one's going to stop me."

"No one's going to try," said Moonis.

Clyde looked up at his old friend and saw not judgment or disappointment. Instead his features were clear of everything but love. Clyde lurched forward and grabbed Moonis tightly in a hug that was as surprising to Clyde as the clutch of emotion in his throat.

"I know why you're leaving," said Moonis softly. "You're right to go."

"Enjoy the bonfire," said Clyde.

And then he was walking away, full of anger and sadness and a dose of self-loathing that curved his spine. He stopped suddenly, turned around, pulled a gun from his belt.

"Here," he said, tossing it to Moonis. "You're going to need this more than I will."

***

She was in the children's house, in the front hallway, huddling on the floor with a pack of other kids about her age or younger, including that boy in the suspenders who had been hoeing the kale. The youngsters were fully dressed; like all children, they knew when something big was happening. She was talking in a low voice, a rush of words, her eyes bright, her face shining. And the others were listening, all of them, as if some higher truth were pouring through her pretty lips.

"Clyde," she said when her shifting gaze finally landed on him. She hopped up, ran to him, hugged him around the waist. She smelled like soap and berry. "You made it. And you saved her. Zephyr told us you saved Moonis's sister."

"For the time being."

"You saved the love of your life. How romantic. It's like something Byron would have dreamed of doing if it hadn't been for his lame leg. And I knew you would do it, Clyde. I told everyone you would do it." She turned to the group of kids on the floor. "Everyone, this is Clyde. I told you he could do anything. He's the bravest man in the world."

"I hope not," said Clyde. He took hold of Lydia's arm and pulled her to the side of the room. "Is there any spare berry hanging around?"

"Some, in the kitchen," she said. "Did you see the barricade with the Every Ship right in the middle of it? Have you ever seen anything more marvelous?"

"Yes," he said. "Go grab the berry in the kitchen and then come back, quick. We're getting out of here."

"Everyone's leaving?"

"No, just us. You and me. The cycle's parked out front, full of gas and with an extra gas can lashed to the back. We're getting out of here before the whole thing goes kablooey. I'm taking you over the line, to Decatur, like we said."

"But I don't want to go to Decatur."

"We talked about this already. It's the best thing for you, the only thing."

"Clyde?"

Just then a bell was rung and then another, until a whole series of bells were ringing all across the farm. With the bells came shouts and orders from outside, the roar of engines, a shot into the air. The farm was turning martial.

All the kids jumped up and headed for the door, all but that boy who stood and stared at Clyde and Lydia with his flat black stare.

"Do as I say, Lydia," said Clyde, turning away from the boy's gaze. "And do it now. I've had enough guff and crazy to last me. We're going home."

"That's not my home anymore, Clyde. This is. My mother would want me to stay and wait for her."

"They're going to kill everybody who stays."

"No, they won't. We're going to stop them, Clyde."

"Who?"

"We are. The children. Oh, Clyde, it's going to be glorious."

"The hell with glory." He grabbed her arm, grabbed it tight and lifted it so that her shoulder rose. "We're getting the berry and getting the hell out of here."

"You're hurting me."

"I'm saving you. I got you into this, I'm getting you out, and I don't want any back talk."

"Stop it."

"Let's go," he said, anger jumping over his concern. He was sick of everyone ignoring the truth and telling him to go to hell. Moonis and Cecily and Patti and Gloria and now Lydia. It was enough to burn his ears right off his skull. He started dragging the girl to the kitchen, dragging her to the berry and then to safety, feeling her bones beneath his fingers, pulling her forward even as the blood of the anger pulsing beneath his ears drowned out her cries.

And then suddenly he was no longer holding on to her and pulling her forward. He was instead up against a wall. Even as he thrashed about in his anger to get free and get even, he was held there, fast. Even as he struggled to pull his arms from the rough wood, to gain purchase on the floor with his flailing feet, to get hold of Lydia and carry her to safety, he was pinned to the wall as if with rivets.

And all the while that boy—that Obadiah, with the straw hat and the flat expression of the already dead—was staring, black-eyed, at him. Staring at him as Clyde felt his ribs press into his chest, squeezing the air out of his lungs, squeezing the blood from his heart.

"Oh, Clyde, don't you see?" said Lydia, sounding now as if she were standing far off, in a different world. "Don't you understand?"

***

The light from the motorcycle sliced the darkness, cleaving it to reveal the ragged road along which Clyde raced. The beam was narrow enough to cloak either side of the road in mourning; the engine was loud enough to drown any sound but the cycle's own. They could be waiting in the wings to ambush him, they could be thundering from behind. Screw them. Clyde leaned on the throttle as he peered hard through the motorcycle goggles and remembered the route back as best he could. When undecided on which turn to take, he smelled his way. Whatever smelled pure crazy, he sped in the exact other direction. He couldn't get out of this blasted wasteland fast enough.

Raden's men had already been massing before the barricade when he fled the farm. He was allowed to slip along a passable route on the left flank, past a squadron of tattooed wildcatters from the north who had been defending the position. He pushed the bike silently through the woods and then onto the road and then down the road a bit until the noise from the barricade dimmed enough so that he imagined he wouldn't be heard. He fired the machine to life and hightailed it out of there. Alone.

Even though he was the one running, he felt angry, wronged, abandoned. They were together in their delusion, Moonis and the rest, sparked with the excitement of the coming battle, only too happy to revile and ignore the one man trying to save all their lives. As if Patti were the leader they needed instead of the queen of screwups. As if

Moonis's smile would get them off the hook, when it had found for him nothing but disaster. And the parlor trick by that Obadiah, what would that gain them? Rattling teacups, spinning soccer balls, pinning him up against the wall. Wallyhoo. Let's see him try to stop a load of buckshot heading for his face. The children would lead them, sure, straight into the ground.

He wasn't going to stick around for that. He had buried enough in his time. They thought him a coward—and maybe he thought the same thing of himself—yet wasn't it more cowardly to accept the inevitable rather than to do whatever it took to save your skin, and the skin of those you loved?

Well, the hell with them. The hell with their solidarity and their willingness to die for nothing. The old nation meant more to him than to them. It was his country, his father's country, it had given him a guaranteed job, a guaranteed life. He would do what he had to do to survive in that world. Sometimes he hated being Clyde, but there it was, the truth of his life. He was the bow-tie boy, the Toddle House man, the one who made do.

He wasn't in search of the mystical ferry, he wasn't looking to steal a boat to cross the river, he wasn't looking for a place to hide away while the battle raged. There was one way across that he knew was open and waiting, one way across that gave him his life back and more. The price was high, but the bastards always make you pay. And hadn't he been driven to it?

His anger felt good, felt right and righteous. If he could just stop the blurring in his eyes. It was the wind leaking through the goggles, he told himself as he raced away from the madness, nothing more than the wind.

53
WAR COUNCIL

Raden's army massed on the far side of the barricade, congregating on the edges of the road and deep into the woods as far as the defenders could see. Kegs were tapped, fires were lit, meat was seared, ribs were gnawed, music blasted, women screamed. The sons of bitches were having themselves a prewar blowout. No sign of Raden or Garth, no attack, no communication to the shivering defenders of the farm, just a roiling, riotous party on the other side.

"Why don't we start shooting?" said Martha. "They're like sitting ducks out there."

"A little bloodthirsty, are we, Martha?" said Moonis.

"Maybe I liked being on the right end of a gun for once."

"They're taunting us, which is good," said Patti. "It means they have plans that don't necessarily include everyone dying."

"So what do they want?" said Cecily.

"Submission," said Moonis.

"Probably," said Patti. "But if we wait long enough they'll let us know. Be certain the flanks are defended like we planned; we don't want any of these sons of bitches slipping through."

"Yes, General," said one of the farmer-soldiers before running off.

"We'll just have to wait," said Patti.

"What are we waiting for?" said Ruby.

"A sign," said Patti. And it wasn't long before it came.

A pickup truck drove down the alley of road left by the partying army, ambling forward unhurried with its high beams lit. It stopped about twenty feet from the barricade and sat there for a bit, idling. And then, with a whoosh and a clank, a makeshift trebuchet fitted on its bed sent something flying over the barricade like a huge and ungainly white bird.

As it plummeted from the sky, the defenders scattered, diving from its path, throwing arms over heads. But the white thing landed not with the expected explosion and swarm of metal bits chewing through the air like angry wasps. Instead it landed with a lifeless thud, lying on the road inert as mud.

After a moment's delay, with the camera crew filming from its knees, two of the farmers slid cautiously over and carefully unwrapped a part of the white cover.

"It's a body," said one of the defenders. "An old man."

"I guess they sent their message," said Patti.

Moonis kneeled down by the corpse. The face was cracked and swollen, barely recognizable beneath the mask of dried blood. He placed his hand gently on the old man's cold cheek and felt something transmitted through his touch, something bitter as acid and yet full of love. A final lesson from the old man. And for a moment he felt unmoored from time, unsure anymore to what century he belonged. Was he on the outpost of the old American prairie waiting for the natives to tear him asunder? Was he on an ancient hill before a barbarian attack that would leave his famed city in ruins? It didn't seem to matter just then.

"This is Digger Townes, the chess master," said Moonis as the others circled around in somber tribute. "He died saving my sister. In the distant past he made a life on this side of the river, he had a wife, a son. He cooked, so he said, the best ribs west of Memphis. They took it all away from him in the disincorporation, forced him over the line, but he never stopped being a citizen of the D-Lands. In his way, Digger was the patriarch of everything that has been built on this blighted turf and anything that will be built here in its future. And he remains a father to me. If we survive the night we'll bury him in the morning and let his goodness grace this new land. He would have liked that, and the land sure could use it."

Moonis stayed there, kneeling beside Digger's body, the crowd standing in silence around them both, when a voice was raised from the barricade.

"Someone's coming."

***

The man walked slowly from the pickup truck to the barricade, staggering slightly, one arm raised. His face was drained of color, the raised sleeve of his shirt was red at the cuff. Just above the cuff was a blood-soaked rag wrapped around a stump that ended at the wrist. Lashed to the stump was a long twig with a piece of white cloth tied to its tip. The man stopped a few feet from the barricade and waited, his eyes glazed.

"It's Garth," said Cecily, softly. "Raden's lieutenant."

"He doesn't look so healthy," said Patti.

"His hand was lopped off during the escape," said Moonis.

"By Clyde?"

"By Raden," said Cecily.

"Tough boss," said Patti.

"What can we get you, Garth?" shouted out Martha. "A hook?"

"Just a few moments of your time," said Garth with a dreamy smile as he swayed in place. "Maybe we can avoid you all having to die."

"How's the wrist?"

"Medicated."

"Leave us be, and you might keep your other hand."

"Oh, Martha, Martha, sweet Martha. You helped those fools raid our camp. Now maybe you can spare a few moments to learn the conditions for saving your children and cleaning up your mess. And I do hope you're wearing your lipstick. It is always so charming, the effort you make."

Patti looked at Martha, who looked at Moonis, who gave a shrug.

"We'll unlock the van door," said Martha, "and we won't shoot your face off as you climb through. That's as much as we can promise."

"It's a start," said Garth.

"And don't bleed on the upholstery," said Patti.

***

"We have until seven in the morning to give them an answer," said Martha. "We either accede to Raden's demands or get wiped off the face of the D-Lands. But supposedly, Raden doesn't want to kill us all. What he wants is for us to lay down our weapons. What he wants is for us to go back to our homes and farms and get back to work. What he wants is for us to be part of the future of the D-Lands, all under his benevolent leadership."

"Benevolent?" shouted one of the citizens. "Does Raden even know what that means?"

"Do you?" said another.

"Does it have something to do with Bennies?"

They were hammering out another messy piece of democracy in the farm's fuchsia-sided hall while the music and shouts from Raden's men leaked through the barricade like the ominous banging of drums in the jungle. War was coming, the drums said, desecration, slaughter. And in the face of the dire threat, representatives from each of the communities that had come to defend the land were crowded into the hall.

The delegates were huddled on the floor, jammed into corners, standing on benches. They were a frightened mass of men and women without much faith in talk. Most weren't used to the regular practice at the farm, so they interrupted, they postured, they insulted. It was a little like Congress under the new Constitution, except without the money or the sex.

"What are the terms?" called out Jarvis from the center of the room.

"Blind obedience," shouted someone from the back.

"That leaves me out," said Jarvis.

"Let's hear the details," said Birkenhead, sitting in his wheelbarrow. Two of his elder sons had maneuvered him into the hall, the single wheel squeaking like a dying mouse as they pushed him to the center. "We need to know what Raden is demanding before we decide how to respond."

"We have to burn our berry," said Martha. "We can keep enough to medicate our own people, but nothing to send over the border."

"Is that it?" said Birkenhead.

"We have to give up our guns."

"All of them?"

"We can keep enough to hunt."

"That's almost fair."

"And he wants Cecily back," said Martha. "She's the girl the raiders took from Kimmler's camp."

"They should have let her be anyway," said Birkenhead. "Doing what they did was like shaking a wasp nest."

"Along with Cecily he wants those who rescued her turned over to his justice. The ones he knows about are Moonis Fell, and Zephyr from this farm, and the singer, Ruby, and Clyde Sparrow, who has already fled. Raden doesn't know I was a part, but eventually he'll be wanting me, too."

"You all knew a price would be paid," said Birkenhead. "Seems like the only one with any sense was that Clyde. What else?"

"That's all."

"That's all? And then they'll leave us be?"

"Then it will go back to the way it was before, with Raden selling us his gasoline and other necessities at inflated prices, like at a company store, and expecting to be blindly obeyed."

"Something doesn't add up," said Birkenhead. "It almost seems reasonable."

"There's not much of a territory for him to rule if he kills us all."

"He'll make us pay in the long run anyway."

"We're not handing over Martha," said one of the citizens.

"We don't have to," said Birkenhead. "Just the others and wash our hands of it."

"How can you hand over anyone to that beast?"

"Because we have women here, and children, and God says they must be protected. Because a massacre is a massacre no matter the good intent of the massacred. Because those that went after Raden should have known better than to do what they done."

"Can we talk about the latrines?"

"Not now, Bones."

"With all these people it's become—"

"We're not turning over He Killed a Man," shouted Big Words over the crowd hooting down Bones. "He's why we're here in the first place."

"Who?"

"Moonis, I'm talking about. Moonis Fell. It was his sister they saved."

"Yeah, I met the man," said Birkenhead. "With the hat and the dark glasses. It's a shame about him, but he knew what he was getting into."

"So we should just give him up?"

"We should be smart."

"I'm tired of being smart."

"When did you start?"

Shouts and laughter and a general roar, with one and all hollering out their positions and each taking offense at the curses and insults. A pushing fight started in the corner, a scream of terror sang out, things were rising out of anyone's control, until a gunshot silenced the crowd.

***

"Brothers and sisters, I say stop all this mindless bickering," shouted Jarvis, a pistol in his hand aiming skyward, smoke rising from the barrel. "This gets us nowhere. We've got a war to fight, a world to change, a movie to make. Are you getting this?"

"Every word," said the guy holding the camera aimed now at Jarvis's face.

"You just keep it rolling and keep the boom out of the shot."

The boom rose and Jarvis, lit now with a spotlight, looked around at the quieted crowd.

"The first thing is, man, you got to know the enemy. He's not here, in this barn, or on this farm. Go to the barricade, climb it high, look over at the killers on the other side. While we're bickering with each other they're sharpening their blades. If we do any fighting, they're the ones we fight; just don't ever think it's only about them against us."

"It's not? It sure feels like it is."

"Hell no," said Jarvis. "Those on the other side, they're just Larry and Curly and Moe, man, stooges for something far more deadly. The fighters facing off against us are just as much slaves to the Establishment as you guys are slaves to Raden. This battle is a piece of a bigger war that's been raging since Columbus first landed on these shores. That's why what we're doing is so cool, man, so necessary. We fight them, we're fighting the Man. We take them down and the fat cats in their Ventura District mansions will start shivering as if an ice age is coming to bury them all. We're carrying a virus, man, the virus of real freedom, and it's going to spread, not just across the D-Lands but over the river and through the woods to Grandma's house, and is she ever going to be pissed.

"So we don't give the stooges what they want and crawl back into our caves like so many segmented worms. That's not a revolution, that's not a movie. I say we put on a show they'll be talking about for centuries. We aren't in a fix, my brothers and sisters, they're in the fix. We aren't cursed, we're the lucky ones. We're going to be stars, we're going to be immortals. And the world is shaking in anticipation. All we need, man, is someone to press the action and ignite the fire, someone to stand atop that barricade and wave the flag of freedom and speak for us all."

"Who?" came a shout, not from one but from a score or more. "Who's going to wave that flag? Who's going to speak for us?"

Jarvis stood in the spotlight, a satisfied smile curving his wide mouth. "Let's put it to a vote."

***

"I nominate Martha," shouted one of the citizens. "She's kept us afloat for fifteen years. If anyone's entitled to speak for us, it's Martha."

"Yes, yes, Martha, yes," shouted another, followed by a bunch of whistles and huzzahs that rose into a roar until Martha started waving her arms, quieting the crowd.

"Thank you for the honor," she said, "but I'm not the one to speak for you. I'm done putting on the lipstick and saying things I hate myself for. All my levelheaded practicality has only led us to the edge of annihilation. We need a different kind of speaker to get their attention, with less pragmatism and more wild."

"What about the General?" called out a farmer. "Where's the General?"

"At the front."

"She set up the barricade, set up the defenses, did the training in what time we had. I say the General should be our speaker. Those with the guns always do the speaking."

"That's the problem right there."

"I say Jarvis," shouted the cameraman as he kept filming. "I nominate Jarvis to speak for us all."

A roar went up as the rest of the circus members in the hall danced and sang and sent up cheers, and Jarvis just stood there as the noise elevated around him like he was being blessed with some sort of benediction.

"I am humbled," said Jarvis when the sound died, putting as much humble in his voice as he was capable. "To be at the forefront of such brave souls as you would be the highest honor I could imagine, more than I could ever have asked for."

"You just did ask for it," shouted someone, and laughter filled the hall, until it was overridden by a note, a singular note, rough and ready, jazzy and low, a spiritual note that cut through the noise like an ax. And when it had done its duty, and the crowd was quiet with expectation, Ruby sang a single word, over and again.

"Moonis," she sang. "Moonis, Moonis, Moonis."

And Martha stood up and raised her hands and shouted, "I second that nomination. He's the only one of us who has gone after Raden and won. He saved his sister, he can save us, too. I say we take Moonis as our speaker."

Moonis, Moonis, Moonis.

And Big Words shouted out, "I third it and fourth it and fifth it. He knows what's what, he killed a man."

Moonis, Moonis, Moonis.

"He's got the soul to turn the tide," shouted Somewhat Spiritual. "And the hat to go with it."

And the shouters were joined by the citizens of the farm, who had seen their combine come back from the dead under the ministrations of the stranger with the tall blue hat.

Moonis, Moonis, Moonis.

And by the tricksters, who had been in jail with He Killed a Man and saw the questing of his spirit and felt the sincerity of his word.

Moonis, Moonis, Moonis.

And by all those who had followed the raiders back from Raden's camp to the farm, welcomed and helped along the way by the stranger sitting tall on the short horse.

Moonis, Moonis, Moonis.

And by those who had never met the man but had heard the stirring tale of Moonis Fell's daring raid to pry his innocent sister from Raden's grasp.

Moonis, Moonis, Moonis.

All of them raised their voices in a rhythmic chant that shook the very rafters of the hall.

***

It felt just then to Moonis Fell that he was back to being a schoolboy, back in the auditorium of McGraw-Hill Guaranteed Secondary

School 774, back to watching the mayor read his name for the whole of the city. There are some who want a second chance at their most deeply rooted failures, and Moonis was learning a truth: those people are idiots.

As the chanting continued, he climbed upon one of the benches and then atop a table so that with his height he stood well above the crowd. He took off his tall furry hat, scratched at his scalp through the wild growth of hair, and stood there for a moment, quiet, still, head bowed, until the cheering fell into a rapt silence. He lifted his head and looked out through his dark glasses at the sea of faces that broke his heart with their shining hope.

"You don't want me to speak for you," he said. "I don't even know how to speak for myself. All I ever wanted was to make my own choices and my own mistakes without a system twisting me one way or the other. All I ever wanted was to be left alone to love the world my own way."

"That sounds about right," shouted Zephyr, the cigarette in his lips bobbing crazily. "To be left alone is as American as hard cider . . . peach pie . . . bebop . . . homegrown bud . . . Keep on blowing, Moonis . . . it's coming out sweet . . . like Bird on a wing of cheap red wine."

"I've got no plan," said Moonis. "No agenda to justify your sacrifices. Unlike Jarvis, I have no desire to change the world. I don't give a damn about what happens on the other side of the river. I never fit over there and I'm not sure I'll fit over here either. I've never been anything but a misfit."

"Perfect," shouted Big Words. "We're all misfits here."

"I'm no politician."

"Doubly perfect," shouted Big Words.

"The only thing I can promise is that you can do better than me," said Moonis.

But they didn't hear that, all the shining, hopeful faces. They didn't want to hear that, all they wanted was a champion in which to place their faith, and so before the words could leave his lips they started again their chanting.

Moonis, Moonis, Moonis.

The more he tried to interrupt, the louder they shouted.

Moonis, Moonis, Moonis.

Even Jarvis, taken with the crowd's enthusiasm, was joining in. He had jumped next to the camera and was making sure it was fixed on Moonis's face as Moonis tried unsuccessfully to quiet the crowd.

Moonis, Moonis, Moonis.

Moonis, Moonis, Moonis.

Moonis Fell spun amidst the worshipful calls and felt helpless to alter the state of things. Some fates could not be denied, and this did indeed feel like fate's sure hand. It was as if every step on the road from the LCM to here, every encounter, had prepared him for this moment. Gaston and Handler, Trout and Jarvis and Somewhat Spiritual and Digger, oh, yes, Digger, and Lydia, Ruby, Martha, Zephyr—all of them had been his teachers, guiding him to this spot, atop this table, among these striving people. They needed a hero and so that was what he would have to be. Clyde had taught him that. Somehow, against all expectation, Clyde had taught him more than anyone else.

And he realized that Clyde, in his unwilling heroism, had also answered for him the puzzle of the caterpillar: You were always a caterpillar. There were no solutions, no great tricks of magic, no choices but to forever be subject to the crushing force of gravity. But sometimes, when others invested faith in you, you became a symbol of their own spirits and hopes, and then, maybe, if luck and fate went your way, you could send them soaring high enough to kiss the sky.

54
BISCUITS

By the time Garth appeared before the barricade, this time flanked by squads of armed soldiers, the sky was a powder blue dotted with tufts of cotton, and the citizens had already milked the cows and collected the eggs and fed the pigs. The work of a farm doesn't stop just because everything and everyone inside its bounds might be slaughtered within a scant few hours. Udders fill, pigs get hungry.

"Decision time," called out Garth in a drugged-out voice. "What will it be, Martha? Live or die?"

There was a moment of silence from the defenders, and then the door of the van opened and Martha climbed out. She stood before the van, hands empty and open.

"The Speaker would like to meet with you."

"What is this, a joke?"

"Speaker Fell has asked for a meeting, one-on-one."

"Cecily?"

"Moonis," she said.

"Well, I'll be slayed. We've been looking for that Moonis. Why didn't the so-called Speaker come to meet me himself?"

"He suspected you'd shoot him on sight."

"He suspected right." Garth stopped and sniffed the air. "What's that? Bacon?"

"The Speaker would like you to join him for breakfast," said Martha before stepping aside and gesturing to the open van door.

"Is there enough for my guards?"

"Only for you," said Martha.

"What would stop him from killing me?"

"If he wanted you dead, we could have shot you from the barricade."

"There is that," said Garth. "And the smell of frying bacon does tend to blunt hard reason. Is there coffee?"

"Along with the biscuits and eggs," said Martha.

Garth took another sniff. "Maybe it's time I do meet this Moonis."

***

Garth sat at a table set behind the barricade, not far from the cooking fire on which a coffeepot shook and hissed. Sitting beside his stump atop the table was a plate of biscuits and bacon and fried eggs, the yolks the same orangey yellow as the base coat of the Every Ship. As he snapped a rasher between his teeth, he looked up to see, walking toward him, a tall man with dark lenses clipped onto his glasses, a ridiculous blue-and-gold coat, and a fuzzy top hat. Garth didn't bother putting on a fake smile for Moonis Fell.

Moonis ambled to the fire, picked up the coffeepot with a towel around the handle, and poured himself a cup. He took off his hat, placed it on the table, took a seat across from Garth. They were two former Ventura School boys having a chat.

"How's the breakfast?"

"Hearty as a fat man," said Garth as he dipped a piece of biscuit into the orange yolk and swallowed it greedily.

"We gathered the eggs just this morning," said Moonis. "I never knew eggs could taste so good."

"You're not joining me?"

"Not this morning."

Garth raised his bloodied stump. "I hope this isn't putting you off your feed. It's just a hand. It makes it hard to butter the biscuits, but other than that, it's no big thing."

"It's not the blood. It's just that I hate to die on a full stomach."

"Ahh," said Garth, nodding, not unpleased. "So we're going to war."

"It depends."

"On what?"

"On you. We're not bowing to any of your demands," said Moonis with utter calm. That was the key to this whole gambit, a bland upper-crust calm, like he was asking to be passed the salt. "Thing is, we don't accept your right to demand them."

"Can I finish my breakfast before we begin the battle?"

"Take your time," said Moonis. "We're not in a rush. More coffee?"

"And another biscuit if you have one—buttered, please. I hate to kill on an empty stomach."

Moonis stood from the table and brought back the coffeepot and a pan from the fire. He poured the coffee and popped a biscuit from the pan onto Garth's plate before sitting down again. He took a knife to the pot of butter and slathered the spread atop the biscuit.

"Cecily says that you are the brains of Raden's outfit."

"That's kind of her, but untrue. Raden goes his own way, which my hand could attest to if it hadn't been fed to the dogs at Kimmler's camp."

"We want you and Raden to be part of our community. We can work together to build up the D-Lands, but we will not be slaves."

"You will be what Raden says you will be. That's the meaning of power."

"Power is the ability to get things done. You can't get this done. I understand we have something in common."

"What could you and I possibly have in common, Moonis?"

"We both spent time in a Ventura School but didn't make it to the end."

"Except I left when our money ran out; you left because you couldn't hack it."

"Maybe I didn't want to hack it," said Moonis. "The problem with the Ventura Schools is that their primary subject is not history or physics, but domination. They teach you how to maintain your privilege, how to use your wealth to rule. These are lessons that end up being absorbed into the bone so that the student can't conceive of living any other way."

"If you're on top, why would you want to live any other way?"

"Because there might be better ways," said Moonis.

"I can't imagine them."

"That's the point. Cooperation, collaboration, working together like brothers and sisters toward a common goal. No bosses, no servants, just one helping the other of his own free will."

"Sounds like socialism."

"It's not an ism, it just is."

"Whatever it is, in this world it's a pipe dream."

"Maybe," said Moonis. "But it's also our condition for avoiding a killing war."

"What makes you think we give a damn about your condition?"

"Because if you start a war, you'll have to finish it."

"If you insist." He took a bite of the buttered biscuit and let his eyes flutter with pleasure. "Is that butter freshly churned?"

"Yes, it is," said Moonis.

"Delicious."

"If we survive the night, we'll send you bucketfuls. I'm not a gang leader or a king, I'm just a speaker for the community. The community has decided to fight until we win or you kill us all. And the bands we send to hide out in the hills, they will attack and attack again until you kill them, too. The buildings will burn, the fields will burn, the whole of the land will burn. There will be no one left to buy Raden's gasoline, no one left to provide his food or weed or berry. He'll be forced back into the nation, back under their control, and so will you."

"It's easy to say, but when the hammer comes down, you'll submit."

"It's comforting to think so, I know."

"You're not crazy enough to make everyone, women and children included, die so you can assert your juvenile notion of freedom. There was a story they told at my Ventura School about some selected student who proposed a similar deal to a bully: They could be friends, but if the bully hit him one more time, he would fight the bully every day for the rest of his life, no matter how bloodied he became. And the bully reared back and smacked the selected boy's face and every day thereafter the selected student started a fight and forced the bully to bloody him. Every day. Blood and pain. Until one day—and here's the point, Moonis—the selected student gave up and stopped coming to school. He had guts, you see, but power prevailed. I wonder how happy he is in his guaranteed job, picking up his former classmates' garbage."

"That's not the way the story ended," said Moonis with a slight smile that narrowed Garth's eyes.

"That's the way it was told to us."

"They made it a fable to fit their lesson. But the truth was, the bully got so traumatized by the ferocity of the attacks against him by the selected boy, so sick of the blood he was forced to shed, that he started running away from the boy whenever he saw him. And whenever he ran, the selected boy chased after him, forcing him to fight again and again. Every day. The only tears shed were the bully's. Eventually, it was the bully who couldn't bear it and stopped showing up to school.

Power had failed; the selected boy's determination to live life on his own terms prevailed. At least it prevailed until the bully's father forced the administration to send the selected boy back to his guaranteed school. They could admire his pluck, you see, but not his insolence."

"Cecily never told me why you were sent down from your Ventura School."

Moonis tapped the table gently twice and stood. "You've heard our condition. We want to be friends, we won't be slaves."

"You're not trying to say—?"

"Take your time. Finish your meal. Then take our proposal to Raden. We'll wait for his answer before the killing starts." Moonis began walking away, with his loping, limping walk, and then stopped and turned around. "Oh, and that selected boy?"

"What about him?"

"The greatest gift he ever received was getting kicked out of that school."

55
CECILY'S CHOICE

They were at their battle stations, the defenders of the D-Lands, make-shift soldiers, men and women both, ready to die for some individual-ized idea of liberty. They were huddled behind the barricade, hunkered behind the rocks, in rows guarding the children's house. They had heeded the call and taken up arms and now clenched their rifles with white-knuckled fear while their Speaker stared through the windows of the Every Ship and waited for Raden's response with blossoming doubt. Moonis didn't trust he had been convincing enough. He didn't trust he had swayed the day. He didn't trust his ability to pull off any-thing other than failure.

And then, from down the road, beneath the music and revels on the other side, there came their way a rumble, something deep and terrible, the source of which soon became clear. One of the tankers sliced along the road like a great metal ship, silvery and roaring, with a huge snowplow attached to its bow, scraping up dirt. When the truck reached a spot about fifty yards from the barricade, it shuddered to a stop. The plow was thick enough to bounce bullets like they were melon seeds spit against stone.

"I guess we have our answer," said Moonis, flanked by his sister and Patti, with Ruby and Gloria and a gang of defenders grouped around them. "He wants to take down the barricade with one blow from that plow and then charge through. Can we kill that truck?"

"We'd have to attack it from the side," said Patti. "Heavy calibers and a Molotov could do it, but it would be suicidal."

"Might as well get a start on things," said Moonis. "Put a force together, but only send it on my signal. We need to be sure there's no hope left."

"Don't wait too long," said Patti before heading off to build a team.

The truck revved its engine, a bull pawing the ground of a ring before charging. Raden's army slipped off the road, taking cover within the woods.

Patti gave orders to an assembled group at the far end of the barricade. They were farmers, fathers and mothers both, holding their guns like hoes. With them was a long-haired freak with a bottle in each hand: Always Tripping with his Murgatroyd cocktails. Patti turned to Moonis and waved her arm.

The sun rose over the trees, shooting out beams like flares. Patti stood with her soldiers, her brave kamikazes, her band of the doomed, waiting for a sign. The engine of the truck roared.

Moonis squinted behind the barrier as a crow cawed its defiance into the light.

***

Moonis Fell, full of doubt and fear, with too much responsibility and not enough strength to carry the burden, jerked his head right, left. He was looking for a hero, someone to step into the breach and save them all.

Could Always Tripping be the one, his mind altered and his glass bottles sloshing with gasoline?

Could Lydia and the children be the ones, standing in a pack now within the line of guardians at the children's house? Lydia, with her brilliant imagination and love of stories, had told him not to fear, that the children had a strange and marvelous power seemingly derived from the berry they had ingested since birth. She was a lovely girl, lost in her stories and books and dreams, but could someone so dreamy be the hero they needed?

Could Cecily, empowered by her imprisonment, be the one? Or Ruby, with the voice of a debauched angel and the wild-eyed bravery she showed in the now-legendary charge of the white horses? Or Patti, who had used her bout of army training to convince the poor saps on the farm that they had a chance? Or Zephyr, with his bracing physicality and whoosh of words that beatified everything his eyes beheld?

It could be any of them, or all of them, but the one thing Moonis knew for certain was that it wouldn't be him. He had tried to be the one, to use all his calm and steel to convince Garth to join them instead of kill them, but he had only proved once again that those who looked to him with hope were doomed to disappointment. That was his fate, to disappoint, over and over, until he died. So if it wouldn't, couldn't, be Moonis to save the folk and the farm, who would it be?

The answer came to him in a sound that slowly climbed above the roaring of the truck, above the shouting and cries of two armies preparing for war. A thack-a-wack that rose ever louder, came ever closer.

The snowplowed truck stopped its roaring. Raden's soldiers stepped out of the woods. Patti clambered up the barricade. They were all of them looking to the skies.

Thack-a-wack, thack-a-wack.

And then a call came up from the road, passed forward one throat to the next.

"It's the Guard."

"The damn Guard is coming."

"Back away, it's the Guard."

And Moonis looked up at the great morning sky, basking in the sound of the gunships chopping toward them and the trucks filled with troops making their engine-grinding way across the rutted roads. And he knew with all the certainty in his soul that a hero had emerged, just as he had hoped, though not as he had hoped. And who else could he ever have expected to fill the role?

Moonis could only smile as he said, through teeth gritted at his now-certain fate, "Clyde."

***

"Where are you going?" said Moonis to his sister.

"To Raden," said Cecily.

"What?" said Moonis. "Wait, what?"

Moonis had been leaning against the side of the Every Ship, consulting with Patti and Martha and a group of defenders, urgently discussing the imminent arrival of the Guard and what it meant for all of them. If the Guard showed up in time, the massacre would be averted, yes, but the cost would be undoubtedly high. The farm would most likely be destroyed and Moonis would most likely be executed before he even stepped foot off the land. Clyde sure knew what he was doing as he finally played out his betrayal. The defenders had been trying to find a way to forestall the inevitable when Cecily interrupted their conclave on her way to the van.

"We need Raden to join us in fighting against the Guard," she said.

"He already turned us down," said Moonis.

"Garth turned you down," said Cecily.

"That seems to be all that matters," said Moonis.

"Maybe not."

"She might be right," said Martha. "Garth acts likes he is Raden's servant, but it's never clear how much of his dealings he relays to his boss."

"Everything is changing," said Cecily. "Now we have a common enemy. I think I can convince Raden to fight with us if I can talk directly to him. He'll listen to me."

"But even if you're right, why do you have to go over?" said Moonis. "We can broadcast your offer with a megaphone."

"Do we have a megaphone?" said Patti.

"No," said Martha.

"What about leaflets?" said Moonis. "Maybe we can, I don't know, sail leaflets over the barricades with helium balloons and then shoot them down so that Raden gets one."

"Do we have helium balloons?" said Patti.

"No," said Martha.

"We don't have time for this, Moonis," said Cecily.

"If anyone goes, it will have to be me," said Moonis. "I'm the Speaker."

"They'll shoot you as soon as you show your face," said Patti.

"Then what will they do to my sister?"

"Nothing," said Cecily. "That's the point. Raden's always protected me. That's why he chopped off Garth's hand. None of them will dare to touch me."

"And if they do?"

"The Guard's going to kill you, Moonis," said Cecily.

"But not you," said Moonis, shaking his head. "And not the rest. I can't just give you over to Raden. This whole thing has been about saving you from Raden."

"And you did," said Cecily. "You and Clyde and the rest. But you showed me something, too. My entire life I've been shoved around, by Garth and Bradley and my sickness and our lack of money. But no one's shoving me now. I'm not being sold. I'm not being kidnapped. And you're not giving me over to them. This is my choice."

Moonis stood back a moment, looking around, desperately, like he was seeking some good alternative and coming up empty. "I just keep failing you," he said softly.

Cecily lifted a hand to Moonis's cheek. "You've never failed me, Moonis. Ever."

He leaned his face into her touch, and then, without saying a word, he reached into his jacket and took out a gun.

Grabbing hold of the cold piece of steel flooded Cecily with feelings of peace and purpose and love. How peculiar, how rich, that her brother giving her a weapon should pull out such emotion.

"This is the gun Clyde threw at you," she said. "That seems fitting."

"Here," said Patti as she took the automatic from her grip. Patti checked that it was loaded and then racked the slide to chamber a round. "Get a load of you now," said Patti as she gave back the gun. "Little Cecily Fell, all grown up."

***

Raden's army on the far side of the barricade was looking to the skies when the front door of the Every Ship slammed shut. The men turned their attention to the noise and their breath caught in their throats as she stepped toward them. Her jeans were tight, her shirt was untucked and mostly unbuttoned, her boots were black, her hair was loose. She was as magnificent as ever, with a new gleam in her eye.

Raden's army was hyped on the promise of incipient violence, even more hyped on the meth and cocaine that had been distributed to fuel the war. The men were ready to attack, to kill, to maim, to rape, and they each had the urge to do all at once to the woman walking insolently forward. But instead they backed away, as if she were as dangerous as the glowing water in the Mississippi. They gripped their arms and chewed their cheeks and held in check their instincts, because this wasn't just any piece of woman flesh.

As the men retreated, they revealed Garth in the center of a huddle, a pear-shaped quarterback with a bloody stump calling plays. When he noticed the disturbance, he turned around, staggered at the sight of her, and then sneered.

"It's too late to plead for your life," said Garth, his medicated smile in place. "You had your chance with me and blew it. Now you'll die like the rest of them."

"I didn't come over to speak to you, I've come to speak to Raden."

"Go back to your grave, little girl."

"I'm going to propose a partnership with Raden. We can fight the Guard together."

Garth shook his head slowly, as if awed by her stupidity. "Why in hell would we want to fight the Guard? They protect our interests in the incorporated territories and we are their instrument in the D-Lands. The Guard hasn't come to fight us, Cecily, they've come to help us mop up your blood."

"It doesn't have to be like that."

"Maybe not," said Garth. "But that's the way we want our territory: blood-soaked and cowed."

"I figured you'd say that," she said before pulling Clyde's gun from the belt of her jeans and pointing it at Garth's face.

As soon as she did, scores of Raden's men unholstered their revolvers or lifted their rifles. The sound was like a great malicious engine coming to life, and the whole of it was aimed at her. She didn't back away or turn her head nervously; all she did was smile.

"Don't be a fool," said Garth.

"It's about time I was, don't you think?" she said before bellowing out, "Do any of you men know who I am?"

After a moment of quiet, one of the soldiers stepped forward with a limp, his arm still in a sling. It was Jake, the man who had tried to rape her on the night of her first escape attempt and was beaten bloody for it. "I know," he said.

"And I know also," said another, tall and thin, with a bandage around his head covering one of his eyes. This was Kyrk, the man she had brained with a chair leg and whose bike she had stolen.

"And I know," said Culbert, still weak from the double blow he'd received from the butt of Clyde's pistol, the very pistol she was aiming now at Garth.

"And I know," said another, and another.

"Who am I, then?" she called out.

"You're Raden's girl," said Kyrk, speaking for them all.

"Damn right I am," she said. And then she pulled the trigger.

Even before the resounding of the gunshot had died, or Garth's body, collapsed now in a sprawling heap, had stopped its quivering, she said:

"Now, which one of you mewling little pups is going to take me to my man?"

56
AHAB

They picked up his white shirt and bow tie from a Moline haberdasher, his fedora from the same department store where they bought his brown suit and shiny black shoes. At the base PX they trimmed his hair close to the skull and buffed his nails bright as the sunrise.

"A shave, Mr. Sparrow?"

"You bet, joe."

The speed with which they fulfilled his requests gratified him to no end. It hadn't taken him long to get his head back onto his shoulders. He had let it float free for a bit on the other side of the line, but when the high from Cecily's rescue had worn off, his head had landed where it belonged, back in the real world, where everything had a price and Clyde knew the tolls down to the penny. His hourly wage, his monthly rent, the cost of an Old Style at Tunney's, the cost of a mawk. A world-famous burger? A buck and a half. A future with real possibilities? Twenty thou for a start and the rest on commission. The life of an old friend?

Well now, talk about coincidences.

***

"No shooting until the girl is safe," said Clyde in the front seat of the Homeland Guard ATV, shouting over the growl of the engine and the bouncing of the shocks.

"We'll take care of her," said Captain Edward C. Broome, the hushed rustle of his voice slipping out of his pig face as he steered, turning the wheel crazily left and right while bounding over the rutted D-Land road. "We'll take care of them all, so long as Moonis is there."

"He'll be there," said Clyde. "He's always been a sucker for a false hope."

As they barreled toward the farm, a scrum of armored personnel carriers rumbled behind them and a wing of gunships ripped the sky above. A caravan of empty buses followed. Clyde just hoped that by the time they arrived he wouldn't find a landscape singed black with only corpses to fill the buses.

"Can't you speed it up any?" said Clyde.

"The troop carriers behind us only go so fast."

"Raden will be tough to handle."

"Don't worry about Raden."

"He's a tough nut."

"Yeah, well, so am I. He'll stand down if I tell him to."

"And the Balthazar boys have been notified of the arrangement?"

"Sure they have," said Broome. "Turns out they didn't know there were fields of it out there. They're grateful as hell to have found out."

"That's two of us."

"With your guaranteed cut of the berry's sale, you'll be sitting pretty until hell freezes over. I told you it would work out. You just had to trust me."

"There's always a rub," said Clyde.

***

Clyde's stomach, already made uneasy by the long, jarring ride, turned over in nervous anticipation when they reached the mouth of the road that ran to the farm.

"That's the turn," said Clyde.

"You sure?" said Broome.

"Get a move on. The barricade I told you about is up that way."

"How long would the barricade hold Raden?"

"Realistically?" said Clyde. "A minute and a half."

"That's too bad," said Broome as he made the turn.

Slowly they drove down the road through the woods, leading the procession of carriers and buses, and what they saw as they slowly drove down the road was nothing.

Nothing.

Clyde had expected to see trucks and tankers and the rear guard of Raden's army, but the road and grove were empty except for the discarded cans and kegs and trash left by Raden's raging jackaloons. No soldiers, no vehicles. Nothing. It was as if the army that had been massing when Clyde had fled had been lifted whole cloth into the sky. The road was empty, empty, until in the distance they spotted a single body sprawled on the surface.

Broome ground the ATV to a stop. Beyond the body was the barricade, or what was left of it. The whole right side had been torn apart as if by some great inhuman force, leaving a gap the size of a tanker truck, through which an army could pour without resistance. The rest of the barricade had collapsed in on itself, the whole crazy structure turned back into the rubble of its creation. Even the van that had been its keystone had disappeared in the wreckage.

The two men climbed out of the ATV to get a look. It was the body of a man, facedown, lying in a puddle of blood still slick. Broome slid his boot under the man's chest and kicked him over. There wasn't much of his face left to identify, but there was enough, and the stump helped.

"It couldn't have happened to a nicer guy," said Clyde.

"When you wanted to speak with Raden, you spoke with Garth," said Broome. "Now who the hell will you speak to?"

"Good question."

Clyde looked up at the riven barricade. His fears had been realized; the war had begun before he could stop it. It was just a matter now of counting the casualties. At least that son of a bitch Garth was the first. But something wasn't right.

"Looks like the front door's open," said Broome. "I thought we'd need you to get us through, but that's not an issue anymore. Let's go."

Broome headed back to the truck, and Clyde, sick and lost, looked beyond the barricade for a moment before following. Broome lifted his handset off the dashboard and barked a few orders before putting the ATV in gear. As he drove over the corpse, the truck rocking just slightly, streams of fire swept down from the sky. The woods on either side of them ignited into great balls of flame.

Broome steered between the fires and through the gap in the barricade. The aircraft overhead swept forward with a terrifying roar.

They were all heading into horror, thought Clyde, but something defied explanation. Though there was fire now on either side of them, there was no smoke pouring out of the landscape ahead, no evidence of the pillaging and burning he would have expected if Raden's army had attacked with full savagery. He had assumed the ground would be cinder and the sky filled with the greasy billows of burning flesh, but as they passed through the gap in the barricade, the land before them was calm and green, the sky beyond was clear.

***

Broome pulled up to the sagging old house at the fore of the farm and came to a halt before the front door.

The personnel carriers spun into formation on either side, opening their doors as helmeted Guardsmen spilled out. The Guardsmen wore dark visors beneath their helmets, camouflage vests over their hearts. They gripped rifles the size of small children. They were as inhuman as locusts and there were swarms of them, an army to match Raden's.

"Go on and see if Moonis is inside," said Broome to Clyde. "If he is, tell him I'm here."

Clyde looked at the house, looked at Broome, looked at the Guardsmen lined up like a massive firing squad before the structure, looked at the fire-breathing aircraft hovering overhead.

"Why not one of them?" he said, indicating the Guardsmen.

"Why do you think we brought you?" said Broome. "Go on in. The girl might be inside. You want to save her, right? That's all I been hearing: save the girl, save the girl. Well, we're burning the house down one way or the other. This is your chance to make sure she's not in it when we do."

"What's the point of burning it?"

Broome looked around and spat on the ground. "This farm is an illegal operation on the wrong side of the line."

"They're just farmers."

"They were farmers, now they're going to be refugees. Get going, boy," said Broome. "Ten. Nine. Eight."

Clyde didn't wait for the count to go any lower. He stepped to the door and banged twice before he pushed it open. It was empty inside, lifeless, still as death. He called out for Moonis, and when he heard nothing, he went from room to room just to make sure.

The place had been pulled apart, furniture snatched from every corner to build the barricade. He climbed the stairs to check the second-floor rooms. Empty. Even the room where the old lady had lain, raving to the ceiling, was empty of both bed and bag. He hesitated for a moment, looked out the window facing the farm fields, and what he saw puzzled him.

There was a commotion going on around the pinkish barn that had been the meeting hall, dining hall, dance hall. Personnel carriers where driving toward it, Guardsmen were sprinting behind the vehicles to take up positions, a couple of the aircraft were swooping low.

"Empty," said Clyde outside the farmhouse.

"Get in the truck," said Broome. "They found him. He's holed up in some sort of barn. Cheer up, Clyde, your reward's just a few yards away."

As Broome steered the ATV around the farmhouse and toward the hall to where the personnel carriers had rushed, he bellowed into the truck's radio. One of the sweepers loosed a great tongue of fire and the Yeager house behind them flamed like a matchbox.

***

By the time Clyde arrived at the hall, there was a standoff in place, like a mouse standing off against an alligator.

The defenders in their makeshift battle gear, men and women holding a motley assortment of hunting rifles and axes and hoes, some with tin-pot helmets, all massed arm in arm around the front of the building, standing off against the visored might of the Homeland Guard. Farmer and trickster, freak and cannibal and homesteader, the old lady from the bedroom in a wheelchair ranting away about Thaddeus, Thaddeus. They were a ragged army of the dispossessed, the disincorporated, a bunch of wacked wahoos about to bite the dust.

Ruby was standing beside Zephyr. Gloria in her fatigues was holding hands with Patti, who was standing beside the young Mexican, Enrique, who was standing beside Martha. They glared, one and all, at Clyde as he stood beside the black-uniformed Captain Broome.

Behind the front lines were the children, huddling together in a pack, black-eyed and fierce, their faces set in concentration. Most of the children were staring up into the sky, at the gunships swirling about, except for that Obadiah in his straw hat and suspenders, who was staring now at Clyde. And among the children was Lydia, who smiled at him, the only smile pointed his way, her sweet, calm smile, as if she knew something that would turn the tide. That was the thing about Lydia—she always thought she knew something.

"You burned my house," said Martha, stepping forward, toward Clyde and Broome, her voice barely discernible above the rotors of the gunships circling overhead. "You had no call to burn my house."

Broome lifted a bullhorn he had taken from the ATV. "This is an illegal settlement in the disincorporated territory," he said, his hoarse voice now loud enough to be heard over the thack-a-wack of the aircraft. "For your own protection, the buses are on their way to take all of you to a refugee camp in Tennessee."

"This is our home," said Martha.

"This is nobody's home," said Broome.

Between the two lines were a group of freaks with a camera and a microphone boom, Jarvis standing among them directing the camera's aim. There, he indicated. Now there. Broome pointed to the camera, and one of the Guardsmen directed his aim at the crew. Jarvis stepped between the camera and the rifle, and the filming continued.

"Howdy there, Clyde," said Martha. "You're dressing well."

"It's a new day."

"You're with them now?"

"I'm with the one I've always been with," said Clyde.

"Doesn't it get lonely, darling?" said Ruby.

"How low could you fall, Clyde, siding with Broome," said Patti.

"Not much lower," said Clyde.

"He's the enemy, man," she said. "He's always been the enemy."

"The way I read the picture, Pats," said Clyde, "I didn't have any choice."

"This is poisoned land," shouted Broome through his bullhorn, interrupting the sweet reunion. "At the camp in Tennessee there will be guaranteed housing, guaranteed schooling for the children, guaranteed jobs for the adults. Your children will be safe from the disease there."

"We're safe enough here," said Martha.

"This is not a discussion. The farm will be destroyed. All your crops, including the berry, will be burned."

"What the hell?" said Clyde.

"The orders have come from the highest levels in Washington," said Broome. As he spoke, one of the gunships peeled off toward the distant field of berry. "Everything is to be destroyed."

"We had a deal," said Clyde.

"Shut up, Clyde," said Broome, now without amplification so that only Clyde could hear. "Did you truly expect anything different?" And then, back into the bullhorn, "One way or the other, you all are heading over the line."

"You're going to have to kill us to get us off this land," said Martha.

Broome stared at her for a moment, and then shook his head as if in sadness. "Your problem," he said in his amplified voice, "is that you've been listening to that Moonis Fell. I recognize a strategy born out of his insanity. Moonis Fell has ruined everything he ever touched. Following Moonis Fell is like following a dead man into his grave."

"He saved his sister from Raden," said Martha. "He can save us from you."

"Let me be clear," said Broome. "Moonis Fell is a wanted man, a murderer, a fugitive from justice."

"He's our Speaker," said Martha. "Duly elected."

Just then, Lydia broke through the wall of defenders and walked straight up to Clyde and Broome. In one hand was a pile of mimeographed pages, in the other was a bunch of daisies, picked from the patch around the barn.

"I knew you'd come back, Clyde," she said. "I knew you'd save the day."

"I'm saving you, is what I'm saving. What do you have there?"

"Read it."

She handed a flower and a page to Broome, smiled at Clyde and gave him the same, and then one by one handed flowers and papers to the Guardsmen around them.

"That's the girl," said Clyde to Broome.

"She looks healthy enough."

"Here she does," he said. "We still have our deal?"

"Sure, Clyde."

As Lydia kept handing out the pages, Clyde started to read:

> *My friends, my fellow travelers, know ye that we now proclaim our liberation from their system. Know ye our intent to live our lives according to the dictates of our own intergalactic consciousness. We are deeper than the two-dimensional world into which they intend to stamp us with their money cares and subjugation. We are higher beings. We can fly free to a dimension beyond body and time, beyond the fourth or fifth or sixth—*

"What the hell is this?" said Broome.

"It's a declaration," said Martha.

"Of what? Insanity?"

"You let Zephyr write your declaration," said Clyde, shaking his head. "Moonis really is in charge, isn't he?"

"There is no choice but to accede to our demands," said Broome through the bullhorn. "Your fields are being destroyed as we speak."

In the distance, a brutal line of flame descended from one of the gunships, loosing thick black pillars of smoke from the earth. And with the fire a strange roar began to rise from beneath the thrumming of the gunship rotors, like the guttural scream of the land itself.

"And anyone helping Moonis Fell evade his fate," said Broome, "will be held fully accountable."

"Does that include them?" said Martha, indicating something behind the Guardsmen.

Clyde turned around to see a mob of cycles and trucks sweeping out of the orchard on the far hill, framed by the fire descending from the gunship. The vehicles were driven by an army of soldiers in black leather, the men gritting their teeth and brandishing their weapons. At the fore of the marauding cyclists was a giant with a scarred face: Raden. And on a cycle beside him, her white shirt billowing, her lovely hair pouring behind her in the wind . . .

"Krist," said Clyde.

The line of Guardsmen swung around and backed up uneasily, like a train of spooked horses, as Raden's army charged madly forward, charged madly and then stopped half a football field away.

"Well now, isn't this a party," said Broome, letting the slightest of smiles crease his features as he looked out at the marauders, standing off against the Guard, and beyond the cyclists to the flaming fields. "Go and get him, Clyde," he said. "Earn your money and bring me Moonis before we burn this whole place down around everybody's ears."

57
MOONIS & CLYDE

Later, the occurrence at Yeager's farm would be depicted on a majestic painting of many colors, sited in art history textbooks between Trumbull's *Surrender of Lord Cornwallis* and Goya's *El Tres de Mayo de 1808*. Later, Jarvis's film would be recut into a documentary with erudite narration, backed by a classically scored medley of Ruby's songs performed by armies of violins. Later, in the overwrought, underperforming blockbuster, the characters would be played by movie stars with fake tears rolling down their rosy cheeks. Later, it would all seem as inevitable as the dawn.

But as Clyde, with his hat cocked at a hard-boiled angle, walked through the line of defenders with Martha's permission and pulled open one of the hall's double doors, nothing had yet been determined and fates still hung in the balance. When he closed the door behind him, blotting out the sunlight, the hall was lit only by a single torch burning in the center of the great space, like a single candle set before an altar in a church. And in the halo of the torch's light sat the deranged altarpiece, a work of absurdist art from the heart of Freaktown.

"What are you doing up there?" said Clyde Sparrow to Moonis Fell, who was sitting on the roof of the Every Ship, his long legs crossed, his band jacket around his shoulders, his furry hat set in place.

"Waiting for you."

"Your pal Broome is outside."

"I heard his foul rasp. He likes talking through the bullhorn, it makes him sound like someone. How much are you getting for my scalp?"

"Enough to buy that diner I was talking about, without the wait."

"You always sold yourself cheap."

"It's not me I'm selling. And one diner's just a start. In a few years I'll buy a second, then a fifth, then I'll have a chain. Clyde's Burger World. I'm going to become rich as a mogul, and live fat and happy in some Ventura District."

"And then you'll be able to piss on your own birthday cake."

"And won't that be sweet," said Clyde before spitting into the dirt.

Even with his old friend sitting up high on the van, Clyde could tell there was something different about him. Moonis had developed a certain innate grace in his adulthood, but now that grace seemed somehow inviolable, untouched by the threats of violence crackling about him. It was as if he existed on a different plane than the rest of them, was of a different time. As Zephyr would have put it, Moonis now floated in an intergalactic dimension of his own. And he smiled down with a benevolence that made Clyde's teeth grind.

"You didn't come back to betray me," said Moonis. "You came back to save everyone else. You couldn't help yourself. And you succeeded, though not in the way you might have expected. With the coming of the Guard, suddenly we all had a common enemy to rally against. Cecily was able to bring Raden on board because of you."

"I saw the two of them together and my heart shrunk."

461

"I couldn't stop her. She said this time it was her choice, which made all the difference. And she implied that she was somehow following your example."

"Something else to feel guilty about."

"I had been wondering which one of them would rise to save us—Ruby or Zephyr, Cecily or Patti or Lydia. Funny thing, Clyde, it turned out to be all of them, and they were following your lead. Years from now, schoolchildren all over the D-Lands are going to be asking, 'What would Clyde do?'"

"Tell them Clyde would get to a better school."

"Did you read our proclamation?"

"Just enough to know who wrote it."

"It wasn't only Zephyr, it was Lydia, too."

"Get off."

"She put his rambles into proper sentences, added a 'ye' here or there as in olden times. When I asked her to help, all she could do was talk about you. She loves you like a father. Where does such a love come from, Clyde?"

"You're too busy sitting up on high to find out, you always have been."

Moonis looked around at the top of the van. "You're right." He leaped off the van, reached out his arms. "I love you, man."

Clyde pushed him away. "Shut up with that freak stuff."

Just then, as Broome restarted his staticky amplified bellow outside, a song began to filter through the closed door and shuttered windows of the barn. Clyde could make out Ruby's startling voice singing a paean to the land, straight from the Woody Guthrie songbook, and before long a choir of the disincorporated, fervent and baldly out of tune, joined in. Moonis sat down on a bench, and Clyde sat beside him. The two friends took off their hats and looked into the distance, because it was easier than looking at each other.

"It's been a hell of an adventure," said Moonis over the singing.

"My chestnuts are still aching," said Clyde.

"Mine too, but I loved that horsey part. You and me riding across the plains, like Butch Cassidy and the Sundance Kid."

"How'd it work out for them?"

"Brilliantly I'm sure."

"Krist, Moonis, get the hell out of here while you can. Slip out the back, take one of the horses. Stay alive, start over, start new."

"What about your reward?"

"Screw it. Broome's never going to cough up anyway."

Moonis laughed, the kind of knowing laugh passed between friends that included all the years and all the hurt and all the love of a life together. They were so different—just look at their hats—and yet they were fused by time.

"You need to join us, Clyde."

"This isn't my place or my fight."

"I see our success unspooling like in a dream and you're right there in the middle of it."

"And where have your dreams ever gotten you? Two stints in an LCM and a price on your head. Even with Raden's army joining the farmers, the choppers up above mean you're outgunned."

"Lydia told me how Obadiah put you up against the wall like a butterfly pinned behind a glass."

"That damn Obadiah, sniffing around Lydia like a hound dog."

"I would have loved to have seen you on that wall."

"It was a trick, a stupid trick." Clyde stopped for a moment, cocked an eye, shook his head. "So that's the plan. Krist, you're pathetic."

"Desperate is more like it."

"They're just kids. Maybe they can rattle teacups and spin tops, but they can't bring down a Guard gunship."

"I guess we'll see, won't we?"

"Even if they could, the Guard will just come back with tanks. This isn't only about Broome, there are orders from Washington. They're burning the berry as we speak. Balthazar needs to protect its patent medicines."

"The big boys always need something."

"The adventure is over, Moonis."

Moonis stood. "I remember a football game where you broke through the line and your helmet flew off and there you were, running with those high steps of yours, yellow hair gleaming in the sun. You couldn't be stopped. You wouldn't be stopped."

"I was young."

"You were Clyde, is what you were. We have the right to become as big as it is in us to be."

"They'll kill us first. I thought you learned that already."

"I'm an adjudicated malcontent, Clyde, because I refuse to learn their lessons. You're a giant, be a giant."

"I'm a hash-slinger."

"You're a phone-hacker, a wizard who can make electrons sing. Be the Edison of the D-Lands. Build the future by my side. I don't want to do it without you. Once more I am on my knees."

Clyde looked up at Moonis standing before him.

"Figuratively," said Moonis. "What is it about figurative speech that you don't get?"

"I'm not joining your suicide."

"Clyde?"

"No."

"Clyde?"

"Screw you, Moonis, no."

Moonis put his hat back on and tilted it just a bit. "How do I look?"

"Like a grade-A freak."

"Perfect. I'm going out there right now as the elected Speaker of these people and I'm going to demand freedom for the D-Lands."

"You used to be smarter than this."

"We have right on our side."

"Now you're a jokester."

"I don't know how it will turn out, but I'm guessing that you'll be standing next to me when I find out."

Moonis flicked the brim of his hat before turning and walking with his slight limp toward the hall's wide double doors. He hesitated a moment, his back lit by the flickering torch, his shadow large against the wood, before he leaned forward with the determined hunch of a stevedore and threw open the double doors.

An explosion of color filled the doorway, exposing the whole panorama of madness in dazzling hues of green and orange and red. The farm's defenders, arms linked, singing loudly, heedlessly. The line of the Guard, bunching nervously around Broome, guns pointed every which way. Raden's army, murderous and angry, shouting out insults and catcalls, daring Broome's men to attack. The land itself, rolling into the distance, cultivated yet shaggy, verdant as a farmer's hope. In the sky, the bright-blue sky, a Guard gunship dropping its pillar of flame, the inferno pouring down from the ship, and at the same time flaring back up from the burning fields, filling the heavens with fire as the gunship itself blazed like a second sun, tilting, wheeling.

And in the middle of the doorway, surrounded by the psychedelic swirl of resistance and conflagration, a towering black silhouette, elegant with its top hat, broad-shouldered with the epaulettes of its jacket, looking to its left as if truth itself lived there.

Clyde wondered how everything he loved had ended up on this side of the line.

They would kill Moonis Fell. They would kill him now or they would kill him later, but kill him they would, it was guaranteed. Moonis's sad fate was to be murdered by them, and Clyde's sad fate, it appeared, was to be by Moonis's side when it happened. He stood and fixed his hat just so atop his head. Even when facing fate's cruel hand, the details mattered. A lesson from the Toddle House.

Good as the best.

ACKNOWLEDGMENTS

While this novel started out for me as an adventuring jaunt—two old friends trying to save a kidnapped woman they both love—it found itself changing time and again under the influence of the books and music and art that have become as much a part of me as my blood. In a way, even as this story moves backward through American history, it also revisits some of the American artists I admire most, and so I thought I'd acknowledge a few.

Louis Armstrong—Just as Jimi Hendrix became the greatest instrumentalist of his time, expanding the bounds of music while dressing, talking, and behaving like no one before him, Armstrong did the same forty years earlier. His recordings from 1925 to 1930 contain some of the most perfect pieces of American art ever created.

Edward Hopper—We've all seen reproductions of *Nighthawks*, but to see it in person at the Art Institute of Chicago is always a revelation. The storefronts opposite the diner somehow speak to me most deeply. My grandfather's office in Philadelphia had that same empty, dusty quality. He had an ashtray stand in his waiting room. I'm writing this as I sit on his office chair.

Dashiell Hammett—Is there a novel in the last hundred years as influential as *Red Harvest*? Its echoes can be seen in every detective story, in every western, in samurai movies such as *Yojimbo*, in existential novels such as *The Plague*, in every movie where the lone hero fights against unbelievable odds, simply because it's the thing to do. And more than that, it is still a blast to read.

Jack Kerouac—There is a great split in how to view *On the Road*, but I believe the book is as much an essential part of America as *Rhapsody in Blue*, and *Moby-Dick*, and Emily Dickinson's poetry. To approach *On the Road* with an open heart is to see a portrait of the America of my father's time that is rich and honest and heartbreakingly beautiful. No book has ever touched me as deeply.

And then there is the rock 'n' roll. It started for me with the Beatles, yeah, I admit, and I have a soft spot for Cream and Pulp, both British bands, but it has always seemed to me an American sound, born of Robert Johnson and Chuck Berry and Elvis. There are scores I could list who still slay me, including Springsteen and Ronstadt and Nirvana and the Ramones, but I'll highlight just two, whom I listened to incessantly as I wrote this book (as if you couldn't tell)—two artists linked by great passion, tragic early deaths, and appearances at Monterey and Woodstock:

Janis Joplin—The two greatest rock vocalists of all time are Elvis Presley and Janis Joplin. There is in her voice the pain, the yearning, the love, the passion, the whole damn ball of wax.

Jimi Hendrix—His is the most classic of American stories: A city kid lugging his electric guitar wherever he goes, taking it along as he searches for his voice in the army, in backup bands, and then finally as an expatriate in Britain, where he most fully develops his incomparable style, before coming back home and setting the world on fire—along with his instruments. Any country that can birth a Louis Armstrong and a Jimi Hendrix in the same half century is doing something incredibly right.

Guaranteed Heroes

I'm often asked, *Where do you get your ideas?* The kernel of the idea for this book was contained in a law passed by the Michigan Legislature that gave its governor the power to "disincorporate or dissolve" municipal governments that were facing difficult times. (See MI 2011 PA 4, Section 19(1)(cc).) I also want to acknowledge my use of *Command and Control: Nuclear Weapons, the Damascus Accident, and the Illusion of Safety* by Eric Schlosser, *Visions of Cody* by Jack Kerouac, *The Further Inquiry* by Ken Kesey, *Sleeping Where I Fall* by Peter Coyote, *Magic Trip*, a film by Alex Gibney and Alison Ellwood, and some of the brilliant political speeches by Abbie Hoffman.

During the writing of this novel, when the story took a turn in Moline, I was able to follow along, because I had faith that the folks at Thomas & Mercer would be fearless enough to board the bus with me. Great thanks to my wonderful editors—Alison Dasho, who supported the book from the first and whose insights made it immeasurably better, and Alan Turkus, whose enthusiasm for the project, and for Neal Cassady, kept me pounding on the rewrites. Also many thanks to David Downing and Elizabeth Johnson, who have been with me for book after book and whose astute comments are always welcome; my agent, Wendy Sherman, for her long and avid support; and Daphne Durham, who brought me over to Amazon and turned me loose.

Finally, everything I write is possible only with the support and love of my wife, Pam, and my children, Nora, Jack, and Michael. During the writing of this book, we climbed down the Grand Canyon together. Talk about getting deep into America. I love you guys. Rock on.

ABOUT THE AUTHOR

William Lashner is the *New York Times* bestselling author of *The Barkeep, The Accounting, Blood and Bone,* and the Victor Carl novels, which have been translated into more than a dozen languages and sold across the globe. Writing under the pseudonym Tyler Knox, Lashner is also the author of *Kockroach,* a *New York Times* Sunday Book Review Editors' Choice. Before retiring from law to write full-time, Lashner was a prosecutor with the Department of Justice in Washington, DC. He is a graduate of the New York University School of Law as well as the University of Iowa Writers' Workshop.